MW00479632

Copyright © 2020 by Zack Argyle

All rights reserved.

This is a work of fiction. Any resemblance to reality is coincidental.

No part of this book may be reproduced in any form or by any electronic or mechanical means, including information storage and retrieval systems, without written permission from the author, except for the use of brief quotations in a book review.

www.zackargyle.com

Cover illustration by Ömer Burak Önal

Cover design by Zack Argyle

Interior illustrations by Robert Cristian Robotin

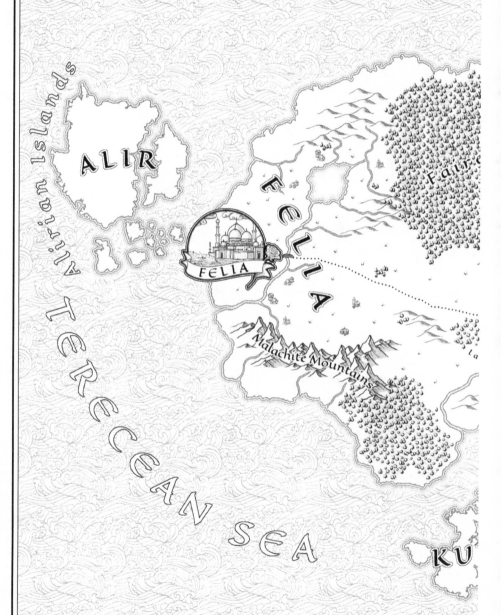

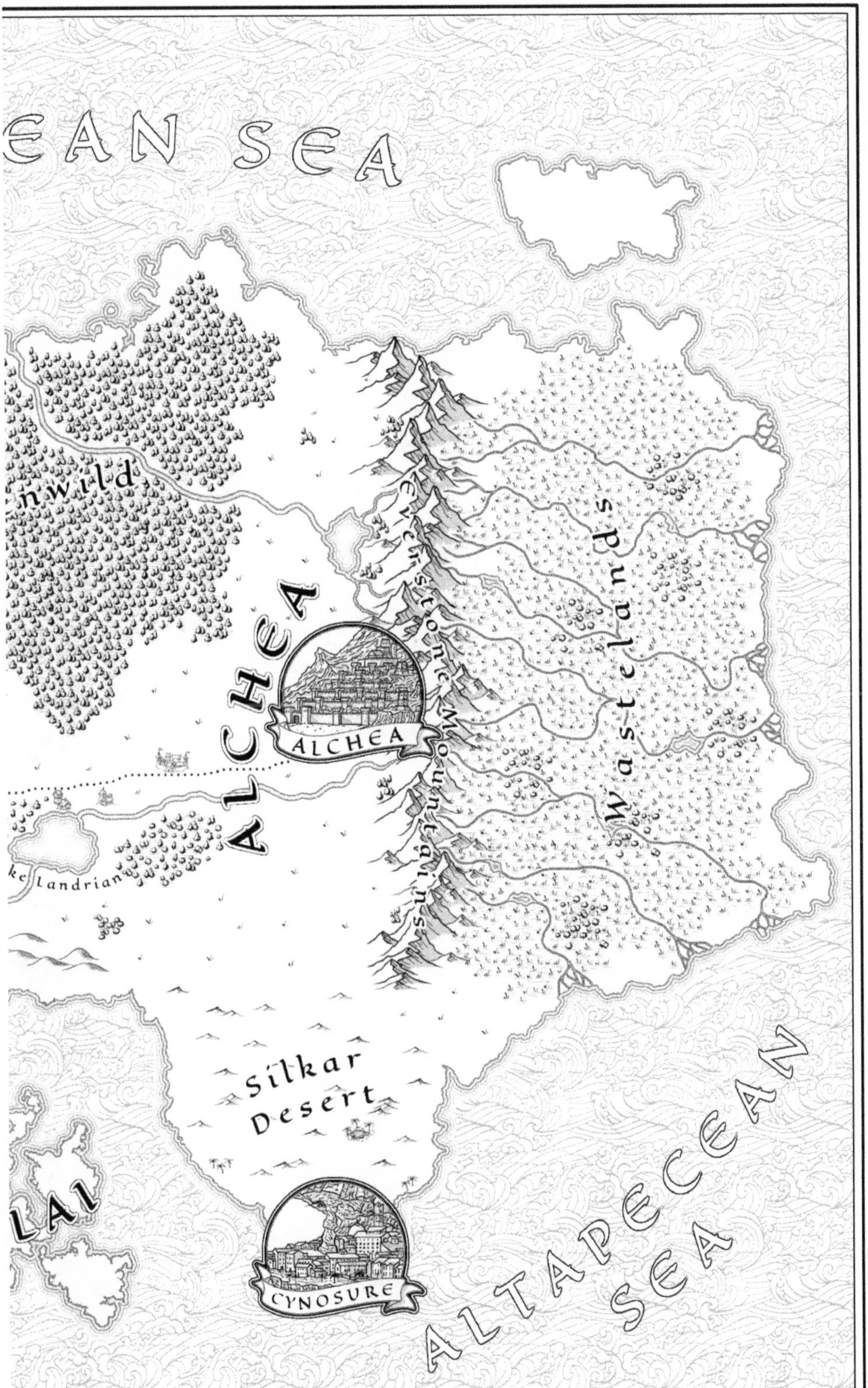
EAN SEA
nwild
ALCHEA
ALCHEA
Seven Stone Mountains
Wastelands
ke Landrian
Silkar Desert
LAI
CYNOSURE
ALTAPECEAN SEA

VOICE OF WAR

ZACK ARGYLE

FOREWORD

This is the first book of the Threadlight series, which follows three characters as their lives weave together to change the world forever. Everything will be answered in time. Enjoy!

— Zack Argyle

CHAPTER 1

A PRIEST, dressed in ritual whites, placed a glove over each of his hands and reached out to the child on the altar. "May the will of the Father be manifest."

Ten feet back, two couples stood staring. Chrys and Iriel were not family but had been given the unusual honor of accompanying Luther and Emory for their son's Rite of Revelation.

An honor Chrys had tried to decline.

Beneath the ritual chamber's domed ceiling, intricate stained-glass windows graced the walls and a hint of lavender lingered in the air. The room spread out in a wide circle. At the center stood a solitary marble altar with a hand-span high lip protruding from its four corners, forming a protective barrier for the squirming infant laying on its padded surface. To the side, a large veil masked a temple worker, set to record the events.

The priest gently felt his way over the curves of the child's face, finding and opening the lids of the child's eyes. He lifted a vial out of his robes and forced a drop of clear liquid into the left eye. The child squirmed but did not cry as the liquid settled over his iris.

Chrys stood with his hands behind him, his back straight and his head tall. His high general uniform was well-pressed and orderly but, beneath his composed exterior, worry whittled away at his core. He'd seen the insides of men displayed on their outsides, he'd seen the life fade from limbless soldiers, but something about a child's discomfort unsettles a man's soul. Not to mention the enormous pressure this moment held for his friend.

He looked to his wife, Iriel, and the mountain inside her dress; their soon-to-be-born child. Her hand was tucked below the mass as if to keep it from falling. His own anxiety must be a drop of rain compared to the storm that raged inside Iriel. She wore her worry in the clench of her jaw.

On the stone floor, an intricate design swirled around a painted gold triangle, the altar centered at its tip. Luther and Emory each stood at separate ends of the triangle. Chrys appreciated the symbolism, but even more so he appreciated the order.

"What is the will of the Father?" the priest asked, his own eyes closed as he held the child's eyes open.

Centuries ago, the Lightfather himself had given his priests a chemical that served as a catalyst to hasten the reconciling of an infant's eye color. In a world where threadweavers defied the natural laws, eye color was everything. Today, it was even more important. Chrys watched Luther and Emory step toward the altar. Iriel squeezed his hand.

The room grew still.

Emory choked on her breath and began to cry. "Brown," she exhaled, trying to hold back her emotions. But that single word

—so colorless, so ordinary—was a herald from which she could not hide.

Achromic.

Chrys squeezed Iriel's hand as they soaked in the word. Having brown eyes wasn't the end of the world. It simply meant that you were not a threadweaver. Most people weren't. But Luther and Emory were, their emerald eyes a sharp contrast to their dark, Felian skin. Their first two children were as well. Emory buried her thick hair into Luther's chest. He gripped her fiercely, his eyes burning resentment. He took her hand and led her away from the altar. What came next would not be something any parent would choose to witness.

Iriel's hand trembled against Chrys'. He glanced over to see a tear falling down her cheek. She was a warrior, not one to cry, but pregnancy had a way of amplifying her emotions, especially in familial matters. He steadied her hand with his own.

As they walked through to the waiting room, he grabbed Luther and embraced him, cursing the law under his breath. In Alchea, families were only allowed to have two children. If, however, a third child was born, it was given to the church to be raised in the priesthood—unless that child was a threadweaver. If the Rite revealed blue or green eyes, the couple could keep their third child. It was a risk Luther and Emory had known beforehand and, still, foresight dampens loss only the slightest.

Chrys held his friend tight. It felt wrong to see a soldier cry. If only he could convince the Stone Council to let them keep the child. Or perhaps he could convince the Great Lord to grant an exception. Doubtful on both accounts. They'd known the risk in having a third child.

As they left the room, the sound of the recorder's pen scratching at parchment from behind the veil reverberated off the vaulted ceilings. It was done.

3

Cursed to darkness. Blessed to serve.

Was that the priest's voice? Chrys glanced back as the door closed behind them. The priest was holding a different vial now.

A solemn echo carried through the hallway and into the waiting room as the door closed behind them.

"What were we thinking?" Luther asked. He ran his hands over the bare skin of his head as he fought back tears.

Chrys shook his head. "You knew, and still you tried. That's damn brave if you ask me."

"I don't know." Luther took a steadying breath. "Thank you...for being here. After everything we've been through."

"You know I'll always be there for you. You've had my back more times than I can remember. Two threads; one bond."

"Two threads; one bond," Luther repeated as they clasped arms. "I should go. Emory's parents are waiting."

Chrys looked him in the eyes. "Get some time. Spend time with your kids. Take care of Emory. She'll need you more than you need her. I'll make sure any of your shifts are covered."

"I know you're right, but the last thing I want to do right now is sit at home all day replaying these moments in my mind. Chrys," Luther's eyes grew serious, "promise me you'll let me know if anything comes up. If we can catch the Bloodthieves—"

A blood-curdling scream thundered out from the ritual chamber. Every person in the waiting room turned to the door, terror-stricken. One by one, they each dropped their head. *Cursed to darkness.* Emory fell to her knees wailing. Luther sank down with her. He squeezed her as they embraced the truth. The child they had known was no longer theirs.

Chrys could picture it in his mind. The priest injecting a few drops of acid in each of the child's eyes. The liquid entangling with tears as they bled down his face. A lifetime of divine blindness. It was cruel. It was horrid. It was commandment. All priests were blind in accordance with the Book of Alchaeus.

"And they shall shed off the light of the world for the light of Alchaeus, for it is greater to see truth than light."

Chrys and Iriel stepped away as Emory's family surrounded the couple. They walked silently, hand in hand. From the top of the temple's stone steps, Chrys could see a broad view of the Alchean landscape. The temple was nestled up against the Everstone Mountains near the top of a large hill. A river flowed down from the mountains through the valley to the south.

Three central buildings loomed to each side, forming an elaborate tapestry of shadows where stone pillars and protrusions battled rays of sunlight. A spiraling dome capped one of the buildings. The top of the dome bloomed like a rose into two figures adorned in floral robes representing the Heralds, a remnant of the old religion.

A pity such lovely buildings were given to the blind.

Iriel winced as they descended the stairs. "We're never having a third."

"Stones, no," Chrys said.

"If anything happened to ours—" she paused, glancing down at her stomach.

"If anything happened to either of you—" Chrys started.

"—It would destroy me."

Once, when he was young, Chrys' mother had found a leafling and let him keep it as a pet. He'd named the small creature Shelly. It had been his first charge, and he'd taken the responsibility seriously. When a neighbor boy had tried to break its shell, Chrys had broken the boy's finger.

A manservant waved to them from atop the carriage. His big brown eyes were flanked by deep wrinkles that shone brightly when he smiled. "Lord Valerian! I always forget how short the

Rite of Revelation is. Any shorter and I'd swear it was an Alirian wedding! Ha! Seems like something that determines the rest of your life ought to be dragged out a little longer. Then again, I suppose it's the kind of thing you don't really want to drag out. Well, come now. I'm stepping on stubble. Was the little one a Sapphire or Emerald?"

"Achromic," Chrys said. From the corner of his eye, he could see the word sink in. The word used for those born with brown eyes. Like it was some kind of disease.

"Well. Well, well, well. Even with two threadweaver parents and two threadweaver siblings?" He shook his head, eyes wide. "I suppose that's why most people don't even try. Like they say, the Lightfather saves whom he will. Still, heartbreaking."

Iriel squeezed Chrys' arm. He knew that with a child inside her, the pain of their friends' loss was a pain to her. They stopped, and he kissed her head. She hunched over with her hands on her knees and puckered her lips as she took in shallow breaths.

"You okay?"

"I don't know." Her eyes squinted shut as she groaned in pain, both hands now clutching at her stomach. She leaned forward and simply breathed, waiting for the pain to subside. She nodded to him and stood up straight once more. She doubled over again as a storm wall of pain crashed into her. She screamed out and nearly tripped down the remaining stairs.

Chrys steadied her, eyes wide with fear. What was happening to her? It wasn't too early for contractions, but they shouldn't be this painful at the start. He'd read as much as he could about the birthing process, enough to know that something wasn't right. He helped her down onto the stone steps. She grabbed his arm and squeezed with a fierce strength as she arched her back and fell back onto the steps. A soiled red patch surfaced far below her stomach.

No. Chrys scrambled around looking for something, anything that could help. He had no idea what to do. He knew how to stitch wounds and care for broken bones, he knew how to *deliver* a child, but this was beyond his knowledge. He checked beneath her dress and found more red spotting. "GEOFFREY!" He screamed out. "Get inside and find a doctor!"

The shocked manservant jumped off the carriage and sprinted up the steps and into the temple while Chrys continued comforting Iriel. "It's going to be okay. We'll find help. Breathe. Breathe." He found himself unable to follow his own advice.

He sat waiting, his blood boiling as anger awoke inside him. His knuckles ground into the stone steps and his jaw clamped tight. There was something he could do. There had to be. He thought hard about everything he'd read, but this wasn't birth. This was something else. He closed his eyes, the skin of his knuckles breaking open as he ground them deeper into the stone.

Mmmm.

No. Chrys closed his eyes and shook his head. *I am in control.*

As he opened them again, a man with a wide-brimmed hat came running from the other side of the carriage. He rushed forward while opening a large leather bag. "Chrys Valerian? I am a doctor and, if you want Iriel to live, you must trust me." He began poking Iriel's torso. With each forceful prod she cried out in pain.

"What are you doing? Get away from her!" Chrys shouted.

He reached out a hand to push him aside, but the man caught his wrist. "I am the only one that can perform such a surgery. Step aside and let me save her."

Chrys saw the man's face for the first time. His skin looked like a man who'd soaked in a pool for too long, thick wrinkles from ear to ear. And yet, his eyes had a healthy air of youth about them. There was something off about it.

He couldn't possibly trust this man with Iriel's life. But what choice did he have? He had no idea what to do, and there was no one else. If he truly did know how to help her, and Chrys didn't let him, he could never live with himself. He looked back for Geoffrey but the servant still had not returned. He hated the helplessness. He hated himself for not making her stay home. He should never have let her come. She was under his protection and, yet, there was nothing he could do. He had no choice but to trust the stranger.

The man must have seen the resolve in Chrys' eyes. "Good. Help me lift her into the carriage. Quickly now!"

Shaking his head clear, Chrys succumbed. Together, they lifted Iriel into the carriage. The man shoved himself between the two of them and pointed back. "Give me space to work and I promise you she will live. There's more at stake here than you know."

Chrys jumped off the carriage and looked back inside. The last thing he saw as the door closed was the shimmer of a long, thin device being extracted from the leather bag. His chest burned with anger and threadlight.

He should be in control.

A minute later, her screams stopped and the carriage went silent. Chrys rose to his feet just as the door to the carriage swung open. The man looked down, took the few steps to the ground, and turned to Chrys, though his eyes stayed low.

"They will be okay," he said.

Again he saw the man's face. Unblemished, yet sickly. Old, yet young. Instinctually, Chrys reached for the knife in his boot.

"The recoil will happen any moment. Chrys, you must listen to me. Your child is the key. They will come for it. You cannot let them have it."

A dark feeling grew in the pit of Chrys' stomach.

"Whatever it takes, you must protect the child."

Chrys felt his pulse quicken. "What the hell are you talking about?"

"You will need this," he said, pulling out a gleaming black dagger from his bag. He tossed it over to Chrys. "Use it to break the threads that bind you. Relek, forgive me."

Chrys caught the knife as it arced through the air toward him. He looked down at the gleaming obsidian and, when he looked up, the man with the wide-brimmed hat was gone. Stones, where had he gone so quickly? He never should have trusted the man. And what had he done to...Iriel.

He ran over to the carriage and looked inside. Eyes closed, her chest rose up and down. Each breath flowing like nothing had happened. Were it not for the red stains spotting her dress and thighs, he could have believed that was the case. A piece of fabric covering her stomach had been slit, revealing a small hole that had been sewn up. What had the man done? Had it worked? He felt the knife in his hand and eyed the shimmering reflection. He'd never seen an obsidian blade before.

"Lord Valerian!" The manservant had returned, sprinting down the steps two-by-two, a crowd of people following close behind. "I found the temple doctor, sir!"

Chrys looked through the open carriage door, his eyes an exhausted shade of red matching the blood on his knuckles. He spoke, more for himself than for the others. "Lightfather, let her be okay."

CHAPTER 2

A BRIGHT SUN crept over the Everstone Mountains, the peaks of Endin Keep casting long shadows over the Alchean city streets. Winding walkways crisscrossed between home and shop with the exception of Beryl Boulevard, a wide, well-groomed street leading from the western borders of Alchea proper directly to the archway of Endin Keep. A straight fixture amidst a city filled with unplanned growth.

The view from the highest tower of Endin Keep was breathtaking, with sweeping panoramic views of the landscape. Yet Chrys sat staring into a book. He'd been there for hours, a melted candle flickering in the dim light of morning. Hundreds of notes written down meticulously onto dozens of parchment papers, stacked in ordered groups, surrounded him. Charts and diagrams and sketches. His eyes were filled with exhausted passion, but he was driven by a profound thirst for knowledge. Never again.

"Good morning, General."

Chrys startled. He hadn't noticed the Great Lord Malachus

Endin entering the briefing room. "Good morning, sir." He gathered his notes, arranging each of them meticulously, and placed them in the sleeve of the leather book.

Malachus approached him. "How long have you been awake?"

"A while, sir." Chrys sat up straight. He adjusted the book so that it was lined up with the edge of the table.

"Is this about Iriel? I hear she is recovering well."

"She is, sir. We were very fortunate." Chrys looked up and met eyes with Malachus. The bichromic gaze of the Great Lord never ceased to unnerve. One deep cerulean blue eye and the other a bright minty green. The colors were accentuated by the long, black hair falling on both sides of his bronze face. Light gray brushed carelessly across a well-trimmed beard. Malachus reveled in eye contact, knowing well how it reminded people of his dual threadweaver nature, and he respected those who were willing to keep his gaze when he spoke.

"I'm glad to hear it." Malachus rounded the other end of the table, looked at the leather book, and laughed to himself. "Chrys, do you know why I chose you to be high general?"

One year had passed since Chrys had accepted the position: one of three high generals to the Great Lord. He had been twenty-nine at the time, young for the prestige of the highest office, but well-respected for his leadership in the War of the Wastelands. Many discounted his achievements and saw him only as the boy that had lived in Endin Keep during his early years. Malachus' wife had taken in Chrys and his mother when they'd first arrived in Alchea from Felia. They'd lived in Endin Keep until Chrys was eight years old, and in those years Malachus had grown fond of the little fighter. Even after two decades, the fondness remained.

"There are many practical reasons, sir. The political..."

11

"No, no, no. Come now. Politically it was an awful choice. Rynan had more years of experience, had spent time in both Felia and Alir, and is possibly the best swordsman in Alchea. Jurius thought I'd gone mad when I chose you instead. It wasn't completely mad, of course. You were a legend after the war. *The Apogee.* For me, that was nothing but a convenient selling point. Even still, some considered it a form of nepotism when I promoted you. But, do you know the real reason?" Malachus gestured to the book and papers. "This. You sitting there with your head in a book is why. When you find a weakness, you wake up with the sun, grab it by the stones, and bring it to submission. Self-betterment is the rarest form of ambition. I admire it greatly."

"I wouldn't call it ambition, sir."

"Sure, it is," Malachus said, his brows furling. "You know, sometimes I look at you and wonder how it's possible. On the one hand, you're this." Maachus gestured to him. "A man completely in control. And on the other hand, we've all heard the stories."

"That part of me is gone, sir."

Malachus huffed. "No, it's not. I know you too well. That fire you get in your eyes. Some fires burn so bright you spend years finding unbridled coals. One of these days, if you're not careful one of them will catch fire."

"I'm managing." The truth was that Chrys had struggled ever since the war. He still had nightmares of his hands dripping red while hundreds of wastelanders lay dead around him. Women and children. Even some of his own men. The Apogee they'd called him. The man who turned the tide.

"Don't shy away from ambition, Chrys. It's a tool as useful as any other. I was once overflowing with it and it won me a nation. These days, I'm afraid I find it in short supply. I like to tell myself that I'm just waiting for the right opportunity but, when decades pass, you start to doubt your own lies. If you'd known Jurius and I thirty years ago, you'd have seen pure ambition personified." He relaxed back in his chair.

In many ways, Chrys looked up to Malachus. His cunning rise to power. His peace treaty with Felia. He had been ruthless in those days, but somewhere along the way he'd grown softer. Chrys had never understood what had brought about the change, but "diminishing ambition" was as good a reason as any.

A knock at the door broke the moment. A man and woman entered and Malachus gave a wide smile. "Speak of the old stone."

High General Jurius, an older man with well-trimmed dark hair and a beard that was dusted with gray, frowned as he entered. Deep bags lay beneath his bright green eyes. "What are we talking about?"

"Ambition," Malachus smiled.

The white-haired Alirian woman, High General Henna, raised her brows. "From Chrys? I've seen more ambition from a fish."

Malachus laughed.

Chrys rose and greeted her with a handshake. "I'll take that as a compliment."

"It's not," she smirked.

High General Jurius took a seat and noted the book in front of Chrys. "What is 'Late-stage Obstetrics'?"

"It's a..." he looked to Malachus.

"The handsome one is a doctor now?" Henna interrupted.

"...weakness." Chrys finished. "I don't like to be caught off guard twice."

Henna ignored him. "That *is* rather serendipitous; I'm due

for my next lady checkup." She smiled. Despite having been born in Alchea, it had been a scandal when she'd been named high general. Angry commoners cursing and calling her a spy. As far as Chrys knew, she'd never even been to the Alirian Islands. "I'll have Geoffrey schedule it."

Malachus pointed at the book. "Knowledge is the foundation of every victory. Rather than mocking Chrys, you both would do well to follow his example."

The room grew quiet. The other high generals hardly tried to hide their disdain. Both were many years his senior, and neither had earned the title so easily. He hoped it would fade sooner rather than later, but a year had passed and the aversion remained.

"Henna," Malachus leaned forward. "Why don't you give me your report."

She nodded. "Of course, sir. The mountain passes have continued to receive pressure from the wastelanders, but only reactively. They appear to have greater numbers than our original estimates, but we've managed to force them completely out of Ripshire Valley and down into the swamps. We've set up an outpost at the choke point and should be able to sustain control of the passes with minimal manpower.

"A small skirmish broke out south of the pass, but we were able to dispatch them easy enough with a small force of threadweavers. We've still yet to see any threadweavers among the wastelanders—probably because they aren't human—so it should be safe to man the outpost with achromats going forward."

Henna was achromic herself, but she was one of the fiercest fighters in all of Alchea and her knowledge of historical battle strategies was second to none. Chrys had started to believe the stories about her. Supposedly, when she'd first joined the Alchean army, a group of sloven soldiers had approached her on her way home. They had surrounded her and tried to convince her that, although she wasn't the prettiest, her Alirian hair and fit frame were enough to find her a special "someone" to take care of her. When one approached with grease in his gaze, she caught him off guard, pinned him to the ground, slipped out a knife and cut his thumb off. Before the others understood what had happened, she held up the finger and told them she'd already found her *special thumb-one* and wouldn't be needing their services. Everyone left her alone after that. A guard had once claimed to Chrys that there was a thumb framed in Henna's living room. Chrys didn't doubt it.

"Proceed to man the outpost as you see fit," Malachus nodded. "And keep me informed of any further advancements. Especially if they become more proactive. At some point, we may want to send scouts deeper into the Wastelands to get a better read on their numbers but, if things have settled for now, do as you wish. Was there anything else?"

She raised a finger. "There is one thing. While scouting the mountain peaks, one of our men discovered a cave. There were etchings found at the mouth of the cave and it appears to go deep into the mountain. He traveled and never found the end, but he did find mining tools and a few weapons along the way. Looked fresher than they would have expected. They are exploring further at my request."

"As long as the wastelanders are kept at bay, you may use your resources as you see fit, though I would not personally spend time exploring caves. Thank you." Malachus turned to his longtime friend, High General Jurius. "And what news from Felia?"

"The roads remain clear of bandits on our side of the border. I've heard reports of trouble on the Felian side but, for now, it's nothing but hearsay. The Empress doesn't care about us so long as we stay east of Shay's Meadow." General Jurius hated his assignment. When Chrys had been tasked with weeding out the Bloodthieves, Jurius had about jumped over the table and strangled him. But for good reason—his son was the first threadweaver that had gone missing.

Malachus nodded. "Good. Any word from the spies?"

"Nothing new," Jurius paused. "There is little to worry about and little to do. I would be happy to help in other areas while my duties are light."

"Jurius," Malachus exhaled. "It's not a matter of qualification or workload. This needs to be handled carefully, and you are too emotionally connected to it."

"It's been more than a month and we have nothing! I don't care how emotionally connected I am. We need results, and we're not getting them!"

Chrys shifted in his chair, his hands clasped atop the book. The words were an attack on his abilities, but Chrys understood. Jurius wanted his son back. As a soon-to-be father, Chrys couldn't even imagine what Jurius must be feeling. While the Bloodthieves were out there, kidnapping threadweavers and selling their blood, none of them were safe. The doctor who'd performed surgery on Iriel the previous day had said something about stopping the Bloodthieves and stopping them from taking his child. He wished he could ask the man why he would say something like that.

"I'm following up on a lead later this morning," Chrys responded. "We're doing everything we can."

"That is well. I want Chrys to focus all of his efforts on rooting them out." Malachus nodded to Chrys then turned back to Jurius. "In the meantime, I would like Jurius to take over the training of the Sapphire threadweavers until the Bloodthieves are dealt with."

"But, sir—" Chrys started.

"It's not up for debate. There is nothing more important than stopping the kidnappings before it gets even more out of hand. Thank you, Jurius. Chrys, what updates do you have?"

Chrys composed himself. He knew Malachus well enough to know when his mind was set in stone. Even more frustrating was the smirk on Henna's lips. He ignored her. "We received a report that the Bloodthieves have a base of operations in the lower westside. The source gave us directions to a warehouse. I plan on taking my team to investigate later this morning."

"What kind of source?" Henna asked skeptically.

"Someone from the area who said they saw a brown-eyed man go into a warehouse and come out with his veins tinted green."

"Someone?" she pressed.

"A boy," Chrys said.

"A boy? How young?" She wouldn't let it go.

"I don't know, Henna. A young boy. Maybe twelve? A source is a source."

Henna frowned. "How much are you paying him for the information?"

"The most recent missing threadweaver was an Emerald. The boy saw green veins. It could have merit. Every source is worth confirming."

Jurius shook his head. "You can't be serious. This is the only lead you have? A deadbeat off the street looking to make a few shines? How could this possibly be the best lead you have after a month?"

"Enough!" Chrys exploded. "We're on the same side. I

understand that you want your son back. I want them *all* back. Malachus trusts me. If you doubt his judgment, then speak up."

Silence.

"And if not, then keep your mouths shut and let me give my report." Chrys felt a familiar anger boiling inside him, a voice in the back of his mind.

Mmmm, the voice spoke to him. *You don't deserve to be disrespected this way. Let me help. I will* make *them respect you.*

Chrys shook his head.

For the last five years, ever since the War of the Wastelands, Chrys had heard the voice. Like a shadow living inside him, a reminder of the day he'd slaughtered hundreds. The world believed that Chrys was the Apogee, that they were one and the same, but Chrys knew better. And he knew how dangerous it would be to lose control once again. No one knew. Not even his wife. Insanity isn't high on anyone's list of leadership qualities. But Chrys had controlled it for years, and he wasn't about to let his guard down now.

He spoke back to the voice. *No, I am in control.*

But you don't have to be.

Malachus scowled. "It appears that matter has been resolved. Chrys, please finish your report."

"Of course, sir." Chrys took a breath. "As I said, I will be taking my team to investigate the warehouse later this morning. Whatever the outcome, I'll report back as soon as possible."

"And what of the missing threadweavers?" Malachus asked. "I assume I would have heard if we'd found any bodies?"

Chrys shook his head and sighed. Four had gone missing, but the body of one had been found the prior week. Bruised and pale, with marks all over his body from cuts they'd used to drain his blood. "Still no sign, sir. This afternoon I am heading to the temple to get a complete list of threadweavers. I am going to see if there is any pattern with those who have been kidnapped in an attempt to predict the next target. It's a long shot. The Bloodthieves have been careful."

"If you find them," Jurius said, scowling, "rip the heart out of every last one of those cowards. They don't deserve a trial. They don't deserve a chance to explain themselves. They deserve a swift death."

"I would prefer to capture them alive."

Henna leaned forward. "I say we drown them in blood. Pour it down their throats and let them choke on the irony of it."

There were rumors that Jurius and Henna had been lovers in the past while Jurius' wife was still alive. Chrys didn't believe it. They respected each other; friends maybe, but certainly not lovers. Jurius was older and reclusive, and Henna had other interests.

"Your creativity is inspiring, Henna." Malachus leaned back in his chair. "I will ponder on a befitting punishment for our transgressors after we find them. Thank you all. You are dismissed."

Chrys gathered his things and left the room, glancing back to see Malachus deep in thought and the two high generals talking as they walked out behind him.

"Chrys." Jurius ran forward and stopped him.

"What do you want, Jurius?"

"I wanted to apologize...for everything. You were placed in a tough situation, and you don't deserve the way I've treated you. I just hate sitting back while my son is in danger."

Chrys looked at Jurius, and the man seemed sincere. "I appreciate that."

"If you ever need help with the investigation," Jurius added,

"I'm here and I'll help in any way that I can. I would do anything for my son."

The words sparked a memory in Chrys. He recalled the odd man who'd saved Iriel, and his words of caution. *Your child is the key. Find the Bloodthieves before it's too late. Stop them. And, above all else, do not let them take your child.*

"Of course," Chrys nodded. "I'm not a father yet, but I know I'd do anything for my child. I promise I'll find them."

Jurius thanked him and walked down the spiral staircase. Chrys was surprised by the unexpected apology. The high general was smart; he must have realized that the only way Chrys would ever let him get involved is by smoothing over the relationship.

Chrys walked forward and made eye contact with two guards posted at the top of the stairway. He stepped forward and fixed the collar on one of the guards. "Soldiers."

"High General," they said in unison.

"Thank you for your vigilance. You are prime examples of professionalism." Chrys turned to the female guard. "How's your uncle?"

"Much better, sir."

She stood a little taller and Chrys was sure that, for a brief moment, he'd caught a smile forming in the corner of the woman's mouth.

A tall, wide window lay just a few strides from the top of the stairs, looking out over the keep's courtyard. Chrys stepped forward, opened the window, and nodded to the guards. His veins began to glow a bright blue as he opened himself to threadlight. Then, as if he'd stepped into a higher plane, brilliant strands of colorful light burst forth into existence all round him, a tapestry of pure energy connecting him to everything around. Below him, a dense, bright thread ran from the ground up into his body. His corethread. His connection to the world itself.

Then, he jumped.

The wind rushed through his dark hair and his cloak flowed high up overhead as he fell to the distant ground. He focused on his corethread and, as he approached the ground, *pushed* energy through it. His veins burned hot, adrenaline mixing with the power of threadweaving. As he *pushed*, it pushed back and his eyes glowed bright blue. He *pushed* harder until gravity no longer had hold of him and, just before he hit the ground, he gave a final *push* on his corethread, stopping his fall completely. He landed with the smallest thud. The veins in his arms radiated a strange, luminescent blue light that seemed to pulse brighter with the beat of his heart.

In a world where Chrys had to be in control, he cherished such moments of ungoverned freefall. He stood up straight, smiled, and clasped his hands behind his back.

His manservant, Geoffrey, bolted upright from his seat on the carriage. "Stones be damned," he let slip. "My apologies, Lord Chrys. My tongue curses quicker than my mind can stop it. Really should keep my eyes up, like the priests are always telling me to do. Again, apologies, my lord."

"No apology needed," Chrys assured him as he walked toward the carriage. "I need you to send out runners to fetch my crew. Have them meet me at The Black Eye. I'll meet them at noon."

"Even Luther, sir?" he asked.

"Yes," Chrys confirmed. He'd thought about what Luther had said about not wanting to be sitting at home with his thoughts, and he was right. If Chrys were in his position, he wouldn't want that either.

Stealing a quick glance up at the high tower window that

was still open, Chrys was sure he heard another "stones be damned" under Geoffrey's breath as he the manservant rode away to notify the others.

CHAPTER 3

THE BLACK EYE was empty save for the scarred-up barkeep and his daughter. Chrys sat in silence for a time thinking about Iriel, hoping that everything was okay with her and the baby. After studying each of the medical books he'd had procured from the keep library, he was fairly certain he understood what had happened to her, but he still wasn't certain what the doctor had done. None of the methods he'd read about required surgery. But whatever the stranger had done seemed to have worked.

Luther walked in the door first, Reina and Lazarus walking in behind him. Chrys greeted each of them as they entered. "Luther, how are you, friend?"

"I've been better. Thanks for letting me come. I needed this." Luther's eyes were sunken and dry. He looked fitting for a man who'd lost his son.

"Let's take it easy if we need to."

Luther nodded.

Chrys turned to Lazarus, a hulking Sapphire threadweaver with bright red hair. Next to Luther's dark complexion, looking at Laz was like looking at the surface of the sun. "Laz, today may be your lucky day."

The big man smiled a toothy grin. "Is bath time?"

"If we're lucky."

The first day Chrys met Laz, the big oaf had made a joke about the city being a child. "Kids are dirty and show no respect," Laz had said. "Sometimes you must take out back, give whack, and give bath." He claimed that when he slid his blade through a criminal, he was simply "giving city a bath." Lovely man.

"We received some intelligence about a warehouse that may be a Bloodthief hideout. No guarantees but, if it's true and we're not careful, it could become a bloody bath indeed. Now, let's see your arms." They were accustomed to this. Chrys always checked their veins to make sure they had not been thread-weaving. Too much in a day was dangerous and, if things went south, they'd need to be ready.

One by one they rolled up their sleeves, extended their arms, and let Chrys examine their veins. Laz was a Sapphire threadweaver, but his veins didn't radiate the bright blue they would if he had been threadweaving recently. Reina was a capable Emerald threadweaver whom they affectionately referred to as The Alirian Spider. Her veins were clean. Professional as always. Luther looked at Chrys and rolled up his sleeves. Chrys could see a slight green discoloration in the veins.

"Stones, Luther," Chrys swore.

"For what it's worth, this *was* kind of last minute," Luther said impassively. "My son was taken from me. Threadlight helps."

Chrys took a deep breath. He was starting to wonder if letting Luther come had been a mistake. "That's a conversation

24

for another time. It's not enough to delay things, but next time I want you clean."

He nodded.

"The plan is to approach the warehouse," Chrys explained, "careful to observe any comings or goings. Be wary of windows and lookouts. We don't want them alerted. If this is real, it could be a huge win for the city. Luther will come with me through the front entrance. The two of you will approach from the rear."

"Won't be the first time Laz approached from the rear," Reina smirked as she clapped the big man on the back.

"Huh? Ah! Ha!" Laz let out a bellowing laugh.

Chrys stared at them, his eyes emotionless. "Thank you, Reina. Are you finished?"

"Wouldn't be the first time Laz finished—" Reina started, unable to hold it in. "Sorry. Please, continue."

Laz and Reina smiled at each other. It was always a sound strategy to pair a Sapphire with an Emerald. Complimentary threadweaving. *Push* and *pull*. Chrys and Luther had been working together since the War. Laz and Reina had started working together since Chrys had become high general. They trusted each other.

"This may be nothing, or it may be more than we can handle. If it's too dangerous we'll pull out on my signal. Any questions?"

"I assume non-lethality is the goal here?" Reina asked, eyeing Laz.

Chrys nodded. "Yes. A nice, soothing bath. Not a blood bath. The more we capture alive, the more we have to question."

The two of them were so different both mentally and physically that it was surprising how well they worked together. Laz was thick. There was no better word to describe it. Huge muscular arms under a trunk of a neck, topped with well-cropped red hair and a stylish beard. Reina was lithe and short, with the white hair of the Alirian island natives. Luther kept his head shaved.

"Bath is bath as long as you scrub few stains."

"Right. I'll take that as a confirmation."

Reina raised her hand, her tattered arm leathers swaying with the movement.

"Yes?" Chrys asked.

"Who was your informant? If someone saw something, then others probably did too. Chances are they've already moved. What if we're walking into a trap? Four threadweavers sauntering into the warehouse of a group that's been kidnapping threadweavers? Could be awfully convenient for them." She folded her arms and her long hair bunched up at the shoulders.

Laz gave them a sadistic smile. "If is trap, I get the soap."

THERE IS nothing like the smell of stale sewage for masking crime. The air permeated with filth as Chrys watched Laz and Reina start down the shadowed alleyway. The lower westside of Alchea was far from the city center and had significantly less foot traffic. Chrys and Luther passed by a man who looked like he was days away from death. He was laying on the corner of an alleyway that smelled like urine. If he'd brought any shines—the tiny gemstones used as currency—Chrys would have tossed the man a few, but instead he walked on.

"Come on," He nodded down toward the opposite road. Luther followed without a word. "Keep your eyes open. We stand out here."

They moved slowly through the streets, peeking around

each corner before rounding it. After a few minutes they reached their destination, a large warehouse squished in between decrepit houses. There were no windows on the ground level, but there were a few on the floor above. From a distance they all looked covered.

They stayed hidden for a few minutes, watching the windows and door. There was no movement, and no passersby. Chrys gestured to Luther and they moved forward.

They approached a large, nondescript wooden door. Upon closer investigation, they noticed specks of blood at the base of the handle. Luther pulled out a whistle and blew into it. The noise was so high pitched that it was hard to hear unless you were listening for it. Laz and Reina would be listening on the other side of the building.

Chrys tested the door; it pushed open with a creak. He signaled to Luther and they prepared for a quick entrance. He thrust his boot into the door, and it splintered near the hinges as it shot open from the force. Dust kicked up in the air, swirling in the misty sunlight shining down through holes in the roof. A partially broken staircase led up to an open second floor that wrapped around the outside of the room. The ceiling was high enough for a third floor, but was left open, exposing beams and a curved, arching roof. Soot and dirt lined the walls and railings.

From the back of the warehouse another loud boom reverberated through the empty air. Laz and Reina came bursting through the doorway, axe and daggers raised, veins lit with threadlight.

Chrys turned to Luther. "It's either a trap or the intel was bad. Either way, proceed with caution."

He signed for the others to do the same. They each made their way through the vast room. Silent, save for the sound of creaking floorboards. There were two rooms along the eastern wall; both were empty. After a few minutes of quiet investigation, they came back together.

Laz lowered his axe and hiked up the bag on his back. His toothy grin broke the silence. "Looks like place needs different kind of cleaning."

Reina laughed. "You've been smiling to yourself for the last minute. I bet you've been waiting this entire time to say that."

"Oh, come on, was good one!"

Chrys leaned against a railing. This was his only lead, and he desperately needed answers. Not to mention how Jurius would react if they came back empty-handed. "Luther and I saw some blood on the door handle out front. Make another sweep and see if you can't find any more. There has to be something in here. Luther, try the roof." He paused. "And Laz. That *was* a good one."

Luther ran toward the north wall, the veins in his arms radiating green threadlight, and he leapt. If an Emerald threadweaver *pulled* hard enough against a wall or ceiling, they could overcome the gravitational pull of their corethread, allowing them to walk up the wall. Luther, a well-trained Emerald, ran up, shifting the base of the thread he was *pulling* as he ascended.

The other three spread out and stared at the ground as they looked for anything suspicious. They spread out from the center into the four corners, Chrys moving toward the southwest wall where the decrepit staircase began. He examined the railing, unsure what he was looking for, still finding nothing out of place.

Luther leapt back toward the ground after checking the roof, *pulling* on the ceiling to slow his descent. It groaned under the weight and Chrys cringed at the idea of the roof collapsing.

Luther's boots hit the ground hard, and he looked down, surprised.

"Aye, Chrys," Luther shouted from across the room.

"What do you have?"

"Nothing," Luther looked confused. "The walls and beams and crates are all covered in dust and dirt, but the floors have nothing. This place isn't abandoned. Lots of people have been walking around here recently. I'd bet they even swept it."

Nothing is better than nothing. Chrys looked down at the ground and was mad that he hadn't seen it earlier. Luther was right; the floors near the wall were dirty, but the rest of the floor was nearly dust-free. He walked around, eyes glued to the floor, searching for anything unusual. He ended up near the west wall and stopped on a dirty, ripped-up rug. The floor beneath his feet creaked.

"Well, looks like we got some bad intel." He emphasized the word as loud and clear as he could, then brought a finger to his lips and signed for the others to join him quietly. He continued his lie. "Stones, Malachus is going to be furious."

As the other three made their way over to Chrys, he pointed to the floor, brushing aside the rug with his boot. Beneath it was a large trap door. He signed for the others to prepare themselves, and hoped that if anyone was listening from below, they would be thrown off by his words. Laz was smiling from ear to ear as they moved into position.

Chrys opened himself to threadlight, the veins in his arms and neck beginning to glow with Sapphire threadlight. Luther's veins glowed with Emerald threadlight just before he *pulled* on the trapdoor. It ripped open, revealing a long ladder leading to a dark basement. Adrenaline pumped through Chrys' veins as he prepared for anything, but nothing happened.

Laz dropped to a knee and opened his bag. He pulled out a

torch, a bottle of alcohol, and a flint kit. Pouring the alcohol on the torch, he struck the flint on the steel of his axe. Sparks flew and the torch blazed to life. He tossed it down the hole into the basement. The echo of the torch hitting the ground reverberated back up through the trapdoor and a small pool of light lit the ground below.

Still nothing.

Laz bent down to get a better view and almost fell in the hole as Reina's foot nudged his side. "Reina! Big men fall hard. Don't be such a hole!"

Reina smiled on the verge of laughter. "Did you just call me a *hole*?"

"Yes. You are a hole." Laz didn't even turn to explain himself further. He continued looking down into the fire-lit basement.

"Looks empty, but we should be careful." They all turned at the sound of Chrys' voice. "Who's first?"

Reina smirked. "Is the Apogee scared of the dark?"

"The Apogee is dead."

She raised a brow.

Luther stood up and shook his arms out. "I'll go first."

The veins in his arms pulsed with bright green threadlight as he prepared to drop down the gap. He stepped forward and dropped down, threadlight blazing in his veins as he *pulled* on the floorboards above him to slow his descent. He landed with a slight thud and took a defensive position as he scouted the room. After a few moments, he gave them a thumbs up.

The other three dropped down the hole one by one into the dark basement. The fall took longer than Chrys had anticipated, the basement ceiling easily reaching two stories high with thick exposed trusses across its surface. Large crates and dusty furniture lined the outer rim of the massive room. A small tunnel barely visible in the dim light led around the far corner. Laz picked up his torch and held it out in front.

A strange sound echoed down the tunnel. Chrys turned to the others and whispered. "There is someone here. Laz, be careful with the torch, it's the only light we..."

A gush of water splashed on Chrys as it poured over Laz. A sound like wind rushed past him before the light went out. Footsteps poured in from all sides. A small amount of light trickled in from the trapdoor in the ceiling, but by the time Chrys' eyes adjusted he had three men tackling him down to the ground. A hard fist cracked into his ribs. He struggled to fight back, but there was no light, and he was pinned.

Three lanterns lit. A dozen men held down Chrys, Laz, and Luther as a gangly man with a tattoo on his neck approached. "High General Chrys Valerian. The Butcher of the Valley. The Apogee. I would have expected you to be taller. And older. I'm underwhelmed."

Chrys stared at the man, scanning the room in his peripherals for anything he could threadweave, but there was nothing useful for him to *push*. "So am I. I want to speak to your boss."

"I'm in charge."

"Maybe so, but you're not the boss."

The man frowned. "I bet we can sell your blood for double, funny man."

"No one on this rock would consider me a funny man," Chrys said, shaking his head. "But I am smart. And you're not. Minimum requirement for being the boss is knowing how to count."

Reina Talfar, the Alirian Spider, dropped down from the ceiling, *pulling* on her corethread as she fell to accelerate the descent. She crashed down onto the confused leader, her boots connecting with his head as he crumbled below the force.

Luther *pulled* on two large crates at the sides of the room and they flung toward the men pinning them down. As they flew through the air, Reina *pulled* against the wall and launched herself toward the nearest enemy. The Bloodthieves dove out of the way of the crates. Chrys and Laz *pushed* on the crates before they smashed into them, and Chrys saw a sadistic smile on Laz's face as the melee began.

He felt the rush of warmth flow through his veins as he let more threadlight flow through him. Dim threads of light swirled throughout the world around him. It was dark, and his ability to see threadlight was connected to his ability to see real light. Threads linked him to the wall, to the crates, to the broken pieces of wood on the far side of the room. Finding the thread of the wall behind him, Chrys *pushed*, launching himself toward the Bloodthieves at an inhuman speed. His eyes blazed blue.

Mmmm. The Apogee awoke. *There are too many of them. Let me out and I can help you. I can protect you.*

Chrys ignored the voice. They needed to capture these men alive. To his left, he saw Luther bury a knife into the chest of an attacker, screaming with a savagery Chrys had never seen from his friend. The rage of losing his son to the priesthood. Stones, he shouldn't have let Luther come. Laz took the kill as a suggestion and brought his axe down into the neck of another. So much for non-lethality. *Keep one or two alive, that's all we need.*

Reina was a blur to his right, and Luther was now somewhere behind him.

Sliding the obsidian knife out of his pocket, Chrys rushed forward. When he'd let the Apogee take over during the War, people said he fought like a god or a demon. But Chrys had been trained his whole life, and he didn't need the Apogee to win. Three men approached him and attacked without hesitation. He sprinted toward the first, sliding down at the last minute and burying his knife deep in thigh tissue, tearing as he slipped past. He ripped it out, spun, and stabbed twice into the back of each of the man's thighs. A knife flew through the air and caught the man in the chest. Chrys looked up and Reina nodded.

A boot connected with Chrys' shoulder as he rolled away. He *pushed* off the ground, blue veins blazing, and brought his knee up into the second Bloodthief's chest. An audible *crack* reverberated from the man's ribs. The last Bloodthief, surprised by the quick defeat of his two comrades, found himself on his heels as Chrys leapt up onto his chest. His knees straddled the man's shoulders as they fell down onto the stone floor. The familiar adrenaline of war coursed through his threadlight-infused veins. It felt good. The anger he'd let simmer inside boiled out, and he twisted the man's neck until it popped.

Stones.

Mmmm.

The man with the broken rib rose to his feet and darted toward Chrys, but before he made it far, Laz's axe buried itself into the man's back from across the room, hitting him like a boulder.

Chrys surveyed the surrounding chaos. Seven dead, two in combat with Luther and Reina, one in the corner. The gangly leader was limping around the corner into the tunnel. Chrys rushed forward, intent to capture him alive. They'd already been careless enough as it was. He rounded the corner and found the man grappling a young girl by the neck with a knife at her back. She was chained to the wall. He met eyes with Chrys and smiled. Next to him lay another man, chained to the wall and pale as a winter moon.

Two *thuds* behind him signaled the fall of the last Blood-thieves.

"Move a muscle and the girl dies." The tattooed man's lip curled into a snarl as his free hand worked the locks on her chains. The heavy steel linking her to the wall fell to the ground leaving only her wrist bindings. The girl was blindfolded and gagged, dressed in dirt-stained clothing with her hands bound behind her back. It didn't look like she'd been here long.

"No one else needs to die," Chrys said with a warm tone.

The man smiled. "For once we agree. You're going to let me walk right—".

Before the man could finish his thought, the girl kicked her heel up into the man's groin. In one smooth motion, she rolled forward, moving her bound hands in front of her and lifting the blindfold off her face. Her veins blazed a bright blue and the knife in the man's hand blasted back into his own shoulder.

The man groaned painfully and ripped the knife out, his left arm limp at his side. He hid the knife behind his back and surveyed the room, but there was no one left to help him. His comrades had fallen. His collateral set free. He was trapped.

Chrys walked forward. "It's over. Come with us, cooperate, and I promise you will not be hurt. Now drop the knife."

The man breathed frantically, deep gulps of sporadic air. Then, as if a storm had passed, he calmed. "My life for yours," the man whispered.

Mmmm.

Before Chrys or the others could think to stop it, the man sliced the blade through his own neck, choking as blood dripped down his chest. He stumbled and fell. The girl turned away, but the others stared on in awful numbness.

Chrys ran to the man, squeezing against the crimson stream. Blood soaked his hands, but it was too late. The man sank down against the basement wall, life gone from his eyes. Chrys found a small towel and used it to wipe his own hands and jacket. He took a moment to fix one of his buttons that had come undone during the fight.

Everyone stared at him, but he turned to the girl. "Are you okay?"

She nodded, eyes examining him with reservation.

"My name is Chrys." He reached out a hand, but she did not return the offer. He looked down at his hands, remembering the bloody stains. "Right. Well you're safe now. We'll take you up to the keep and make sure you're taken care of. I can't imagine what you have gone through. I'll save the rest of my questions for later. Reina. Luther. You two investigate the area. We don't know how many there are, so I want to know if this was all of them. And be careful in case others come. Laz, come with me and the girl.

"Do you have a name?"

She looked him in the eyes but did not respond.

"Fair enough."

They began their ascent up the long ladder to the trapdoor with Laz leading the way. She was young and tall, with long blonde hair running down her thin frame. While climbing he glimpsed what looked like a tattoo on her upper back, hidden mostly by her shifting hair. Tattoos were uncommon in Alchea, but in the western countries they were becoming increasingly more popular. Her veins still radiated a dim blue from her use of threadlight.

When they reached the top, she looked around the room like a predator, sharp eyes scanning as if looking for something.

"It's okay. There is no one here," Chrys thought out loud, knowing she was unlikely to respond. "I have to give it to them, an ambush in the dark was their best chance against four threadweavers. If they'd put blindfolds on us faster, we'd likely still be down there."

Her gaze turned to the ceiling, noting the holes in the roof that let in the afternoon sunlight.

"You can relax now," he said, trying to relieve some of the tension.

She turned to look at him and opened her mouth as if to say something, but paused. Then, she took a deep breath. "Sorry, flower boy, but I can't go with you."

Déjà vu struck him like a storm cloud.

"Little flower, fetch me some turmeric from the garden. Supper will be ready soon." His mother's voice called out to a young Chrys playing outside in the dirt. She always called him her little flower, even if he hated it.

In his moment of confusion, she sprinted and leapt, veins a blistering blue, eyes lit with threadlight, launching herself high up into the warehouse rafters. Chrys shook his head and jumped up after her. Laz ran toward the back door. Before Chrys landed in the rafters, she had already shot out of a hole in the roof and into the sky, flying high above the building.

Chrys ran toward the gaping hole in the roof and *pushed* out into the open air. He looked out and caught a glimpse of her falling below the next building over. He jumped as high as he could, gaining a bird's eye view of the greater westside, but already knew what he would find. Nothing. Streets filled with men and women carrying food and clothing, winding pathways, and shadowed back alleys. But there was no trace of the girl. The first person who knew anything about the Bloodthieves...and he let her get away.

~ Skyflies ~

CHAPTER 4

SHADOWS RIPPLED over Laurel as the afternoon heat burned hot over broken cobblestone. The back alley was far enough away from the warehouse that she felt safe to pause and catch her breath. She pulled her dirt-stained clothing tight to cover her tinted veins. Her body felt far too warm, a collaboration of magic burning her from the inside and sunlight beating down from the outside. It felt amazing.

She moved northwest following the sun, but the streets were a winding labyrinth, and it was hard to maintain her direction. It was also the first time she had set foot inside the city, having been specifically ordered *not* to enter the city during her trips to the temple. The grounder city was far larger and far more confusing than her own home.

As the adrenaline faded to a dull buzz, she felt utter fatigue wash over her. Even without the looming threadsickness, she had been through an experience that would send any sane person to sleep for days. Memories of her capture flooded over her.

Walking from the temple into the city. Adrenaline knowing she shouldn't be there. A fork in the road. A man down one path—weird hat; she took the other. Eyes watching. Danger. Threadlight to look for an ambush. Too late. A bag over her head. Ropes around her legs. Laughing. Whispers. "Young...transfusers...Sapphire." Kicking and screaming. Thud. Darkness.

Then the soldiers had arrived. The one with the dark hair. There was something about his eyes. Not the blue; Laurel was used to people with blue eyes. It was the intensity. Even when he'd tried to calm her down, it frightened her. A sharp blade feigning dullness. Even so, he'd given her the opportunity to escape. She needed to get back home, away from the grounder city. The elders would never forgive her if they found out what had happened.

She paused for a moment and laughed. Had she really done what she remembered doing? Kicked a grounder in the groin? *Pushed* his knife into his shoulder? Escaped from her rescuers?

Bay would never believe it.

Laurel stood up, keenly aware of how much threadlight she'd let burn in her veins and began walking. In the next alley-way, she found a clean shirt hung out to dry and traded it for her own dirt-covered top.

She walked for hours, exiting the city, passing farm-filled countryside, until finally she reached the edge of the Fairenwild.

Home.

The sun was setting, and bulbous multicolored photospores dangled off the ends of long reeds, emitting a phosphorescent spray that glowed in the darkness. The eerie depths of the Fairenwild were illuminated by the dull light radiating from the bulbs. High above, a drove of skyflies drifted in the wind, their long bodies curling under flowery heads.

Then there were the feytrees. Gigantic trunks sprawled out across the grassy floor. Their branches refused to form until high into the sky, then sprouted forth like thick lines of yarn knitting ferociously with the branches of their neighbors. In the afternoon, the interlacing branches were so dense that they blocked out all sunlight to the forest floor, leaving it to be lit only by the light of the photospores. At night, were it not for the glowing fungus, the forest would be dark as the core.

Laurel looked longingly up to the treetops; her eyes dark with fatigue. She wondered why the wonderstone had to be in the middle of the forest, still so many hours away. Awfully inconvenient.

She stepped forward into the trees, careful to give them a wide berth in case a treelurk was nesting there. She reached out and grabbed a handful of photospores, ripping them from their stems. Light emanated out before her, providing a small amount of visibility to areas with fewer naturally occurring spores. The occasional puffing noise nearby accompanied her as she began her journey deeper into the forest.

There was a good reason her people were left alone—the Fairenwild was dangerous. Between the darkness, the eerie ambience from the photospores, treelurks, hugweed, and the howling of chromawolves echoing from afar, outsiders gave it a wide berth. But the Zeda people, Laurel's people, gave it their hearts. To the grounders, her people were a myth, a tall tale, and they were happy to keep it that way.

Laurel trudged forward using the yellow roses to guide her. She was physically tired from walking, mentally tired from being kidnapped, and tired to her core from all of the thread-weaving. How was she going to explain what happened to the elders? Messengers were forbidden from entering the city. She was to skirt the outside, meet her contact at the temple, and then return the same way. It was made very clear from the beginning: do not engage with the grounders. What would they do when they found out that she'd not only entered the city, but been kidnapped by a group that sells threadweaver blood like wine? The winds were not blowing in her favor.

After what seemed like an eternity of walking, she recognized the flora around her. Berries grew on thick vines and moss covered the base of the feytrees. She could hear the chromawolves howling. Always best to be careful. A chromawolf would blend into the forest and tear you apart before you had a chance to breathe. She knew the creatures well enough to avoid them. Not all were like Asher.

Off in the distance was a wide clearing filled with colorful flowers. In its center lay a large circular slab of white stone, glyphs carved across the entirety of its surface. Her people called it the wonderstone. The steppingstone of Zedalum. She was glad to see it not only because it meant she was home, but also because the chromawolves refused to set foot near it.

She relaxed her eyes and let threadlight seep into her vision. The wonderstone burned brilliant as the sun. The bright corethread of each living person was but a dim flame beside the majesty of the wonderstone's threadlight. She stepped up onto it, feeling its pull on her. Not a physical pull, but a mental one, urging her to use her power. Fortunately, in this very moment, that is exactly what she intended to do.

With a rejuvenated spirit, she *pushed* down onto her corethread, the wonderstone amplifying her abilities. It launched her like a catapult up into the air. Wind rushed past her face as she approached the high branches of the feytrees. She passed through a man-made opening and turned, *pushing* on the thin thread of a large wooden plank opposite her. It redirected her momentum toward the other end and out onto a wooden balcony built into the branches. Her boots slid across the wood as she landed. A pinch of vertigo mixed with threadsick dizziness came over her as she looked over the ledge back down.

A Zeda guard sat opposite the landing pad and looked up wearily; brown robes flowed over his seat. There was always someone posted at the entrance to Zedalum, but it was not a coveted position. There had never been an attack on the treetop city, nor had there ever been an unexpected visitor. Their secrecy had paid off.

"Stop! Identify yourself!" The Zeda man blinked, his eyes adjusting to being awake. The moonlight illuminated them both through the wooden stairway leading up to the treetops, but the feytree shadows obscured her face.

"Alder. You know you're a terrible guard, right?"

He stepped forward, getting a better look at her. "Laurel! You're back! Your grandfather's been worried sick. Almost left the city to find you."

"I know. I know."

He gave her a sheepish grin. "Do me a favor and don't tell Rowan about this?"

Laurel laughed. "Of course not."

"I owe you," he said. "May the winds guide you."

"And carry you gently home," she finished. The wooden steps were built securely into the thick mesh of tree branches. She ascended them one by one until she stepped out into the open air. A refreshing breeze fluttered about her, rejuvenating her after a night of musky, spore-filled air.

Alder was a good guy. Not the smartest, but he was always kind to her. At nineteen, just two years Laurel's senior, he'd already married. Again, not the smartest.

Laurel looked out over her home. Zedalum. The city of

wind. Moonlight trickled down like rain over the treetop metropolis, illuminating the carefully plotted walkways that connected homes, centers, and the colossal Zeda stadium. The size of each building was a testament to the strength of the intermingling feytree branches that served as the city's foundation. Towering, heavy threadpoles were scattered throughout the city, many with faces and intricate designs carved into them, providing a quick means for threadweavers to get around. Laurel was tempted to use them, but she was exhausted already. Instead, she let a bit of threadlight seep into her veins and walked along the wooden path toward her home.

The wooden streets were empty as she moved toward her family's house. Before long, she could make out the distinct figure of her elderly grandfather seated in his rocking chair on their porch. When her parents had passed away, he had embraced the "protective parental figure" role wholeheartedly. At this point, he was the second most elderly Zeda in the entire city, having survived two passings of the Gale. The elders had only given him a pass because both Laurel and her brother Bay were still underage at the time. This year there would be another Gale; she worried what would become of him.

As she approached, he stood as if he knew she was coming. Wild, white hair draped over wrinkly, bronzed skin. His mid-length beard danced as he spoke. "You look tired." He smiled wide and opened his arms to embrace her. She fell into them with a smile. "And what is that shirt?"

Gale take me. She'd forgotten about the grounder's shirt she had stolen. She would need to swap it out before going to the Elder's lodge.

"My other one got dirty," she laughed, hoping to ignore the question.

Laurel was old enough to be considered an adult in Zeda

society, and she did her best to act like one, but her grandfather was her refuge. A firm root in the tempest. When the world demanded flawless maturity, he loved her as she was.

"You can tell me if you'd like. Or not. I was worried about you."

"I can tell," she said, laughing. "It's not like you to be awake past sunset."

He smiled but his brows pressed tightly upward. "Now don't make me feel older than I already do, Laurel. I was very worried. You were supposed to be back last night. I spent almost all of today at the lodge trying to convince Rosemary to let me go ground-side looking for you. They act like my heart would give out if I did any kind of threadweaving. I spent the entire evening sitting in this chair convincing myself not to disobey. If I were a few years younger, I'm not sure I could have stayed put, permission or not."

"I know. I—" she paused, realizing that she probably shouldn't tell him everything that had happened. "Sometimes these errands take longer than expected. Your old friend says hi, by the way."

"Pandan, that old fool. Is he coming back yet?"

She laughed. He knew the answer before asking. "He said to tell you that he is still 'waiting for his sun to rise'."

Grandfather Corian shook his head with a look of bemusement. "He's more patient than any man I've ever met. Although, he'd probably have been taken by the Gale years ago were he not so valuable. I suppose he's having the last laugh after all."

The comment brought a solemn tone to the conversation. "I'm the one that should be worried. Maybe I can convince the elders that we need you here. Parenthood is a good reason to pass, and you're the only parent we have."

"Oh, you will be fine without me, and they know that. Bay

on the other hand...that boy has shallow roots. But you're both of age now and, to be honest, I think I'm ready. You're both grown, and there's not much left to me but memories. And even those are fading fast. Odd as it is to say, I think it's about time this old bag of bones lets the wind take him home."

Laurel frowned. "I don't accept that. There has to be something we can do."

"Some winds have no counter," he replied.

Without the threadlight coursing through her veins, she'd be in tears. She hugged him again and looked up. "I should go report to Elder Rowan. I'll see if I can put in a good word. It's not over yet, old man."

They exchanged nods, and she headed to her room to change her shirt, then walked back down the wooden path she'd arrived on. A light breeze rustled the thick floor of leaves to either side of the walkway. Her feet followed a familiar path, but her mind entered a state of hollow serenity. Time passed in a blur.

She arrived at the door to the elder's lodge. There were five of them. Elders, not lodges. Each selected by the others when one passed away, generally young enough to survive at least three Gales. Together, they governed the affairs of all of Zedalum.

Laurel approached the door and gave it a hard knock, the thick wood reverberating out into the quiet night.

An old woman opened the door. Elder Rosemary. Laurel relaxed. The old woman's blue eyes were bright and warm, even in the fading moonlight, and she smiled as she saw who was at the door at such an odd hour. A long pendant hung down from her neck, draped over a green robe and flanked by strands of long gray hair.

"My dear Laurel. It is always a pleasure to see you."

"You as well, Elder."

Elder Rosemary motioned for her to enter. "I'd ask you why you're here, but you've made quite a commotion with your absence. I presume you're here to report to Rowan?"

"Yes, Elder." Laurel stepped into the lodge, the faint smell of incense still lingering in the large entry room.

"Let me give you some opportune advice," she said, bringing her voice down to a whisper. "Rowan is not a morning person. Nor is she a night person. Start with the good news, then sweet talk her a bit, let her wake up a pinch, and then go into the bad parts. And if all else fails, she loves the smell of north Felian oranges."

Elder Rosemary lifted an orange off a side table in the main hall, tossed it to Laurel, and winked. "Trust me."

"Thank you." Laurel remembered her grandfather. "Can I ask you something?"

"Of course."

"My grandfather," she paused. "The Gale is coming soon, and I'm worried about him. I know what you're going to say—I'm an adult now—but I still need him. And Bay needs him even more. Is there anything you can do?"

Elder Rosemary sighed as if recalling a conversation that had happened a hundred times before. "The Gale takes whom it will in the time that is right. It is not the decision of any one person. It is what's best for us all."

Laurel wanted to say something to convince her, but from the look on Elder Rosemary's face she knew it would serve no purpose. "I understand."

"Can I ask you something in return?" Elder Rosemary's eyes pinched in at the ends.

Laurel raised a brow.

"Do you ever let go of the threadlight?"

Laurel looked down at her arms and noticed that her veins were glowing just the slightest. She immediately stopped the flow of threadlight in her veins and it hit her like a windstorm. A deep thirst awoke inside her that could only be quenched by the taste of the magic.

Elder Rosemary looked at her, concerned. "One can never be too careful. Powerful feelings demand powerful fealty. You wouldn't be the first to become dependent."

"I'm not," Laurel scoffed. "I'm just tired."

They ended their walk in silence, stopping at a large door around the corner with the sign of the elders stenciled into the wood—a large circle divided into five segments with unique designs in each. Elder Rosemary gave her a gesture of good luck and walked slowly back down the hall. Laurel took a deep breath and knocked three times.

The lodge was so quiet that Laurel could hear the bed creaking as the Elder stood up, followed by the light pitter-patter of footsteps. Her heart started beating faster. She fought her instinct to embrace threadlight, knowing well how Elder Rowan would respond. Something about the old woman made her nervous, despite them having worked together for the better part of a year.

The door opened. Elder Rowan was wearing a brown robe and a scowl. Her typical leather headband graced her forehead, partially covered by a mess of wavy gray locks. Laurel remembered what it was that made her nervous. The crescent shape of Elder Rowan's mouth was an eternal grimace, and she wielded it like the sharpest of blades. Her green eyes were creased with a lifetime of disappointment and sharpened to a terrifying point.

Without a hint of emotion, the old woman spoke. "You look rotten, but you smell wonderful. You can leave the orange on the nightstand. Come in." She turned and walked over toward a rocking chair without turning to see if Laurel had followed.

Laurel smiled as she closed the door, the fragrant Felian orange still in her hand. She took the second chair opposite Elder Rowan and placed the fruit on the table.

"It's an ungodly hour. Please do not waste my time. Give me your report and tell me why you're a day late in returning to us."

So much for small talk. Laurel remembered Elder Rosemary's advice. Good news. Sweet talk. Bad news.

"Yes, Elder. I made it from the Fairenwild to the temple with no problems and approached the temple cautiously." The events replayed in her mind. She had a sharp memory which was one of the reasons she'd been chosen as messenger. It also helped that she was a Sapphire. *Drifting* made the trip go faster. "I waited for sunset and found Pandan on the bench he always sits on. We talked a little, he told me a story about my dad, and then I asked him if he had anything to report.

"He told me about some concerning developments within the grounder city." If she lied, there wouldn't have to be any sweet talk or bad news, but if they ever found out what happened she'd never be able to leave the Fairenwild again. "There is a group of people that the grounders are calling the Bloodthieves. They are kidnapping threadweavers and selling their blood. Apparently, if someone who is not a threadweaver drinks threadweaver blood, they can see threadlight temporarily. They can't *push* or *pull*, but people will pay a lot for the feeling. Pandan doesn't think we need to act, only that we should be aware in case things get worse. The grounders have men out trying to stop them."

"Despicable," Elder Rowan remarked. "Barbaric, the things the grounders do. Heretics *and* imbeciles. Next time you return, we'll ask Pandan to dig deeper. Any group that defiles the honor of threadweaving must be watched carefully."

Laurel nodded. "Of course."

Elder Rowan sat staring at the wall for far longer than Laurel was comfortable. "Well, and what of the delay? Looks like you have a brand-new shirt on, old one get dirty?"

The old treelurk was smarter than Laurel gave her credit for. More than anything, she should have planned out the lie ahead of time. Laurel racked her brain for something believable. An idea popped into her head. "I know I shouldn't have, but I went out looking for the pack." She hung her head in shame, only partially an act. She hated that she was using her dead parents as an alibi, but Laurel was sure the elders had lied to her anyway. Her parents hadn't died from a pack of chromawolves, but no one would tell her the truth.

"You did what?" Elder Rowan choked out a horrid sounding cough. "You think to get revenge? Fool child. It's been years. The pack has moved on, and so should you. You think to kill a pack of chromawolves all by yourself? You're as self-aggrandizing as your father was." She paused, thinking through the story. "So, you slept in the woods? Explains the dirt. Surprised you're not dead. For your own sake, I hope it was grim and uncomfortable. That's what you deserve for such senselessness."

"I'm sorry, Elder." Laurel kept looking at the floor in defeat. She always found self-deprecation to be the key to a good lie. If others feel sorry for you, they're less likely to scrutinize your story.

"This is your one warning. If you ever do something so stupid again, I'll find myself another messenger. I've a mind to do it right now. Can't have such poor judgment roaming the ground. Do you understand?"

Laurel nodded fervently, sniffling as if her emotions were rising. "Yes, Elder."

Elder Rowan kicked Laurel's chair. "Well. Get out. I've at least an hour of sleep left before sunrise."

Without lifting her eyes from the floor, Laurel turned and left. The adrenaline of deceit raged through her shaking body. She couldn't believe that she had lied to Elder Rowan. And more so, she couldn't believe that the Elder had believed it!

She passed through the main hall and saw no sign of Elder Rosemary. Next time she saw her, she'd have to thank her. Laurel opened the door and burst out into the open night. She looked back into the candlelit lodge and smiled. No one needed to know what had happened to her in the city. She'd learned her lesson on her own.

Like Rowan said, it's better to move on.

~Chromawolf~

CHAPTER 5

LAUGHTER FILLED LAUREL'S HOME, spreading forth like an obnoxious weed from the family kitchen. She'd tossed and turned all night despite her overwhelming fatigue. A nightmare had taken her back to the Bloodthieves' basement, and then her mind refused to relax in fear that she might return yet again. She looked down and noticed that the veins in her arms were tinted blue; she must have been threadweaving unconsciously while sleeping. At least she'd been able to get some rest.

She slipped on day clothes and stepped out of her room, quietly treading down the hall toward the kitchen. Her brother, Bay, and her grandfather, Corian, were smiling and talking about the latest Threadweaver Games. Corian loved taking Bay to the stadium to watch the Sapphire Long Jump tournaments. While many Zedas idolized the competitors, Laurel had always found it monotonous.

"No way!" Bay coughed as he laughed. "Euca is for sure going to take the Long Jump this season. She's so reed-thin that the wind basically does the work for her."

Corian smiled. "We'll see. Dogwood has the best form. On a good day, I think he could win it all."

"Don't get him started on Dogwood again," Laurel said, smiling and picking up a strawberry off the counter. "You've been waiting for him to have a 'good day' for three years. There's no chance he steals it from Euca."

"Oh, what do you know?" Corian took his spoon and scooped out a bite from his ripe, blue fyrfruit.

Bay's eyes lit up. "You're awake! I knew you were okay. What took you so long to get back?"

Laurel nervously glanced at her grandfather. "Just took a little longer than expected."

"Oh, come on. Is it secret? For the elders' ears only? I bet it is." Bay leaned back in his chair triumphantly.

"Something like that."

Her grandfather stood up and threw his finished fyrfruit out the window and into the feytrees below. "Before I forget, Cara was looking for you yesterday. You should head down and pay her a visit if you have time this morning."

"Will do." Laurel took a bite of strawberry.

Corian stepped out of the kitchen and walked down the hall to his room. He had left a bowl of feyrice pudding on the table for her; it was her favorite. The feyrice they grew in Zedalum required less water than normal rice, but it was also not as soft. She still loved a bowl of it with strawberries and a pinch of white clover mixed in.

She settled into her chair and scooted in closer to Bay. "Want to know the truth? The part I didn't tell the elders?"

She grimaced looking at the bruise on his chin. Bay had a blood disease—he'd had it since he was young. Some days were better than others, but usually it meant that he tired easily, bruised easily, and sickened easily. His skin was pale even when he felt well, and his muscles were atrophied from a lifetime of careful living. Even his long Zeda hair, shaved to the scalp on the right side, was thinner than most. And to pluck the last fruit from the tree, he was the only one in the family that wasn't a threadweaver.

He pulled his hair up into a low ponytail in the back. "Tell me everything."

"Elder Rowan sent me to the grounder temple again to check in with Pandan. It was fine. I've run the route half a dozen times before. But I was bored, so I took a detour into the city."

His eyes widened. The grounders were off limits. Which is exactly what made the city so hard to resist.

"I know. I *know*. You can't even imagine what it's like. Huge roads of stone twice as wide as our streets. Hundreds and thousands of houses, and people. *So many* people. I kept to the edges so I wouldn't get too far off course, but even still it was overwhelming. But then..." The flashback replayed in her mind.

"Then what?"

"I was kidnapped." Her heart beat faster remembering it. "Blindfolded. By this group of grounders that steal threadweaver blood. They sell it and others drink it. They were going to drain me and sell my blood."

Bay's eyes were wide as plates. "Gale take me. You can't be serious."

"Dead serious."

"Father of all," he swore. "But the elders would never let anything happen to you."

"What could they have done? They didn't even know I had gone off course. I was *underground* in some broken-down building. No one could have found me. I froze. I just sat there in the dark waiting for them to steal my blood. I didn't do anything."

"Of course, you didn't! It would have been stupid to try and escape." Bay paused. "What did the elders say? I bet they were furious!"

"I may have told them a different story."

Bay almost fell out of his chair. "You *lied* to the elders?"

"They would have stripped me of my assignment! What was I supposed to do?"

"I don't know." He slouched back, shaking his head. "Wait, if you didn't fight back, then how did you get away?"

"Some other grounders showed up and killed them all. One minute I was blindfolded and bound, the next the sounds of fighting and screaming. Then there was a knife to my back. You should have seen it. I kicked him, rolled away, and *pushed* the knife in his shoulder. Then I got away and ran. *Drifted* as fast as I could 'til my veins were burning, but I got away.

"I know it sounds crazy, but it was the most fun I've had in years! Bay, you have to promise me you won't tell anyone."

After a few moments of silence, Bay took a deep breath and closed his eyes. "I won't tell anyone. But lies are dangerous, Elle. Things like this can't be tucked away and forgotten. They fester. You're my sister, and I'm here for you always, but I'll judge you if you make stupid choices, and this was top-of-the-tree stupid.

"But I'll always love you no matter what. You know I live my adventures through you, and I don't want you getting killed over it. So, if you promise me that you won't go back to the grounder city, I promise you I won't tell the elders."

Laurel hugged him tightly. "I don't deserve you, little caterpillar."

"No, you don't, little wolf." Bay stood up slowly.

"That reminds me," Laurel said. "I need to get down to Cara. Thanks for understanding."

He smiled and shook his head as she stepped out of the house.

Zedalum was much different during the day. People crowded the wooden walkways, young threadweavers leapt between threadpoles floating through the air like dancers. Laurel preferred *drifting* down the runner lanes.

She *pushed* a small amount of energy down through her corethread and shifted the thread to be slightly behind her. It gave gravity less of a hold on her and helped propel her forward as she started to run. Her speed picked up quickly. It was a trick all Sapphire threadweavers learned early on. With it they could jump higher and run faster. There were tradeoffs of course. Try turning a tight corner without the added friction of gravity to lean into. Many new Sapphires could be seen tripping over themselves as they learned to rely less on that most basic force of nature.

The designated drifter path was open, and she took off like a wolf. She passed by the marketplace, with dozens of stands selling all manner of food collected from the farmlands that were built on the treetops outside of Zedalum. Beans, carrots, tomatoes, spinach; any vegetables with shallow roots did well in the Zeda farms. She rushed past a group of people standing in line for use of one of the dozens of wells built to pump water up from the streams and ponds below the city. Each well ran down the base of a feytree toward the nearest water source. Some people had begun building water basins outside their own homes to catch the rainfall. She understood the concept, but thought they looked absurd. Far in the other direction she could see the elders' lodge and the towering stadium. But she was headed back to the ground.

As she approached the entrance to Zedalum, she was

greeted by an older Zeda guard. Alder must have gone home to rest. The woman wrote down her name in a log and let her through. They kept detailed records of each Zeda that descended to the surface. Of course, anyone could drop down between the branches if they wanted, but the only sure way back up was using the wonderstone, especially for a Sapphire. Some of the more rebellious Emeralds were known to drop down between the trees, and then run back up the feytrees to return.

She descended the steps and approached the ledge of the landing pad. Without a second thought, she leapt. The ten second freefall ended as she used the wonderstone to slow her descent. She landed with the faintest thud.

Light trickled in from the gap in the canopy, providing more useful light than the glowing photospores. Whenever she stood here on the wonderstone she'd always get the distinct urge to *push* off the ground and fly, as if the curious amplification that it provided could not only boost her higher but could give her wings. There were stories about the windwalkers who could stay airborne indefinitely. Of course, there were also stories about people who could breathe underwater, kill you with a glare, and topple mountains.

Because the fauna stayed far away from the wonderstone, the flora thrived. Especially the roses. Blue, green, yellow, and white. The roses of the Fairenwild were unique, each variety useful in their own right, opening and closing their petals in their own time. The green dayroses and the brilliant, white threadroses were all fully bloomed around her as she stood atop the wonderstone. Further away, she spotted some wild green laurel, her mother's favorite.

As she drifted farther away from the wonderstone she heard

the sound of birds chirping overhead. She couldn't see the birds, but high above her she saw a drove of skyflies darting back and forth, their wispy green tails floating in the spore-illu-minated canopy.

A few minutes later she arrived at the large wooden enclo-sure to the nursery. Reaching over and moving the latch, she entered. The nursery was a training ground for young chroma-wolves, and the only settlement below the treetops. The Zeda people had learned early of the dangers of these Fairenwild natives and looked for ways to tame them. What they learned was that young wolves, when exposed to humans early on, would be less likely to attack later in life, and the individual bonds made during those formative years would stay forever. The couple that currently served as their caretakers, Cara and Mace, had bonded dozens of wolves over the years. Of course, the chromawolves weren't the only danger in the Fairenwild.

After three years of life within the nursery, when Cara deemed the time was right, the young chromawolves were brought back to their packs. The reintroduction had a high success rate, but there were times when the packs no longer accepted them, or the chromawolves did not want to return. Mace had an elderly chromawolf, named Leadpaw, that never returned to its pack and still lived with him.

The chromawolves here were young, but still strong. Best to be careful. Laurel entered through the gate and saw Cara's house right next to the entrance, a single-story log cabin built with thick wood that had dozens of deep scratches along the exterior. A few pups wrestled on the ground nearby, snarling and biting playfully. On the front porch, Leadpaw lethargically watched the younger wolves. The old wolf reminded Laurel of her grandfather.

Off in the distance she saw Asher coming—he always knew

when she was nearby. The young chromawolf dashed toward her at an incredible speed, howling all the way. His dark green fur was dusted with curling white strands, like roots running down his back, that shimmered in the light of the photospores. Laurel took off toward him at a run, two astral bodies bound for an earth-shattering collision.

As they closed the distance, Asher leapt high up into the air front paws extended, and Laurel followed suit. They collided hard. Asher tackled her to the ground and they rolled. He jumped back up playfully and danced around her with his twin tails whipping back and forth, snarling and growling with the fierce energy she'd come to love. She laughed and snarled back.

A year after Laurel's parents had died, her grandfather had asked Mace to let Laurel raise one of the new pups. It had seemed cruel at the time, forcing her to confront the beasts that took her parents. But as she came to be with the chromawolves, she no longer believed that that was how her parents had died. She was sure the elders were keeping the truth from her.

Laurel and Asher had bonded quickly, two high-energy creatures cut from the same branch. She spent too much time with him—she knew that—but it felt good to spend time with someone that didn't lie or judge or expect anything from her.

Cara walked out of the cabin. Nearly the size of her behemoth husband, broad shouldered and fit, she managed to maintain an air of femininity through the rough outer layer. Like many Zeda, she kept the side of her head cut close, but the rest of her light brown hair she kept braided and pulled back. Cara was the closest thing that Laurel had to a mother now.

She spotted Laurel wrestling with Asher. "Laurel! Tempest take you, girl. You gave me a right fright not showing up yesterday. You know them grounders are dangerous."

"I'm wrestling with a chromawolf and you're worried about

the grounders?" Laurel laughed as she swiped down at Asher. "You should know I can take care of myself."

"Spendin' too much time with them wolves, girl. And that's coming from me! One of these days you're gonna bite off more than you can chew." She was only half joking. "So, what's the story? Find yourself a grounder boy and plannin' an elopement?"

Laurel gave her a look of pure ice, but then she realized the horrible truth: she couldn't use the same lie she'd told Elder Rowan. Cara would know it was a lie. But she also couldn't tell her the truth. Yes, she was like family, but she was more like the family that tells on you for your own good. She couldn't risk it. It had been a single day and she'd already trapped herself in her own web. She tried to think quickly.

"Want to know what I told Elder Rowan? Or do you want to know the truth?" Her mind raced, still unsure what she was going to say. Maybe a partial truth?

Cara raised a brow. "I'd like to know both, but you can start with the truth."

Laurel took a deep breath. "I was walking down the big hill at the grounder temple, and it started to rain. Not a lot, just a light sprinkle, but I didn't want my clothes to get soaked to the core, so I left the path and ran toward a little house not far off. It smelled terrible and there were all kinds of strange animals inside."

"You went into a grounder's house? Tempest take you, girl. You're walking a narrow path."

Laurel cut her off. "It was a house for their animals. It wasn't a big deal."

Cara turned away covering her ears. "Don't tell me another word. I don't want to know. The grounders find you out and you'll be tortured. The elders find you out and you'll be exiled. Nothing good will come of this. I don't need this kind of weight on my shoulders, girl. You were smart not to tell them what happened. But wait, that couldn't have taken a whole day? Nope. Don't want to know. If you don't tell me, I can't tell them. Whatever you did, promise me you won't do it again?"

Laurel nodded.

"Good enough for me." Cara walked toward the gate shaking her head. "Come along now. We gotta go take Asher back to his family."

"Wait, what?" Laurel's heart was beating rapidly from the lies, but then it stopped. The words buried deep into her chest. She practically whispered the next. "Take him *back*?"

"Why did you think I wanted you to come down here? This wasn't a social visit, girl. The pup's too big to stay any longer. He's fully grown. Could probably jump the fence now if he tried. Too dangerous to keep around."

Cara was already walking, her whistle beckoning Asher to follow. Laurel watched in shock as the two exited out the gateway. Her feet trailed without thought, the forest blurring in her vision as the world spun around her. She was going to lose her grandfather to the Gale. She was going to lose Asher. And she was going to lose her position. Everything she held dear swirled around in a dark cloud, slowly dissipating into the darkness of the Fairenwild. It felt as if the Father of All was punishing her for disobeying the elders. But it was only one mistake. What were the chances she'd be kidnapped the one time she went into the city? Deep down she knew what she was doing when she stepped onto those stone streets.

She let threadlight run through her veins and calmness washed over her.

They walked for what seemed like an eternity, her sense of direction lost in the endless glow of the Fairenwild. A duskdeer ran past on her right, jet black legs hopping over a small creek running across their path. Asher moved to chase, but Cara commanded him to stop. And he did.

After a short time longer, Asher roused. Recognition kicked in, and he bolted forward. Cara had always said the chromawolf pups had an uncanny memory for their old homes, but Laurel had never seen it until now. Cara ran after him, Laurel still following silently behind. A minute later they came to a clearing with a small pond. Dozens of photospore reeds grew out of the water, their bulbs emitting their luminescent spray. A rock formation was built up along the far side of the water with a pack of chromawolves standing atop at attention, staring fiercely at Asher. He watched boldly in return.

Laurel had only ever seen the docile pups; these creatures standing in front of her were something different. Their eyes seemed to growl along with their mouths. The alpha wolf leapt off the rocks with its chest puffed up and walked toward Asher. It had the characteristic green fur of the chromawolves with chunks of white hair weaving throughout its coat like vines over moss, but its paws were far wider and larger than Asher's. The fur split apart at the rear into two distinct tails, each a brilliant white where they weren't covered in dirt. She thought Asher was large, but this alpha stood even taller. The lithe muscles in its legs rippled as it approached, its paws poised to pounce.

Despite the time away, Asher knew what to do. He stepped forward, keeping his posture low and unassuming, then approached. He stopped within an arm's length and dropped his head as if bowing to a more formidable elder. The alpha stepped forward and sniffed him, weighing and measuring who he had become. He paused, considering his verdict, then roared. A powerful swipe of his paw crashed down onto Asher's head. The young chromawolf was thrown down to the ground, whimpering in pain.

Something broke in Laurel. Threadlight exploded in her veins, and she ran at the alpha with blood in her vision. Anger rose like a swelling wind and drove her forward. She refused to sit idly and watch her friend be hurt.

Cara saw it too late. "Laurel, no!"

The alpha saw her coming and snarled a deep, nasty growl. The other chromawolves stayed put on the rocks watching their leader. It compressed its legs and pounced.

Hot, burning rage rose to a boil, bubbling out of her. She screamed a feral battle cry and *pushed* with all the energy inside of her against the nearest feytree. The thread between her and the tree seemed to expand with force, and then exploded out both ends. She crashed into the alpha like a cyclone crashing into a mountain and drove her elbow into its stomach. They both fell to the ground.

A thick vine snaked its way around Laurel's leg and started to squeeze. Hugweed.

The alpha howled and it started to rise, but its left hind-leg was injured from the collision. Still, it pushed forward with surprising speed toward Laurel who lay trapped on the floor with her foot constricted by the vines. The alpha lunged toward her, clawed paws extended, teeth quivering with hunger. She tried to *push* against the hugweed, but nothing happened. She was trapped and the alpha's thick teeth flashed in front of her.

Just before it reached her, Asher sprang forward, blindsiding the alpha and knocking it off course. The alpha was stunned and confused. Asher was family, and he would protect her. He bore down on the alpha with a savagery she'd never seen from him, teeth clamping down on green fur, paws digging deep into flesh.

The alpha kicked Asher off. Bloody and furious, it stood on all fours and growled. It sprang forward. Its back leg buckled from the effort, but Asher was still recovering. The alpha swiped a second time at Asher's face, gnarled claws connecting with tender nerves that ripped out hair and skin. Blood jutted out from the open wounds.

Asher howled out in pain and launched himself forward, headbutting the wounded alpha between the eyes. An audible crack reverberated through the air. Asher wasted no time. He dove back on top of the larger beast, swinging uncontrollably. A wild claw swiped through the alpha's neck, and blood sprayed out onto a bright photospore. Red-stained light projected out over the Fairenwild floor and washed over the motionless corpse of the alpha.

It was dead.

Laurel shook her pounding head, the blood in her veins burning hot, her chest ready to burst. Threadlight still danced brightly in her vision; she couldn't make it go away. It was too much. Bright threads of light danced in every direction, exciting her already overstimulated senses. She couldn't focus the light.

The young chromawolf nuzzled her gently. His blood-matted fur brushed her cheek, leaving a smeared stain. He moved to her leg and tore into the hugweed, releasing her from its grasp, then lifted up his head and howled. The other chromawolves, still watching from the rock formation near the pond, howled in return, then jumped down and wandered over to Asher. He stood tall to match their stature. One by one each of the chromawolves bowed their heads to their new alpha. He brought a gentle paw to each of their noses, recognizing the gesture of submission. He was family now.

Laurel's eyes glazed over with tears as she watched Asher embraced by his pack. She was happy, but still she cried. Would she ever see him again? Part of her wished they wouldn't have accepted him. Everyone else seemed to find their place in the world, but she was yet to find hers.

CHAPTER 6

"LUTHER, we should talk about what happened," Chrys said as he walked through the dark basement.

"What are you talking about?" Luther's eyes were cold.

"I said we wanted to capture them alive."

Luther turned away and walked toward one of the crates. "It's not like I'm the only one who killed somebody."

"Yeah, but you were the first. The feel of a fight changes when men start dying. Every death spurs the likelihood of the next."

"You're right, okay?" Luther raised his hands in defeat. "Is that what you want to hear? You're right. I shouldn't have come. I should have stayed home and drank myself to sleep thinking about my damn son. Thinking about those damn priests that took him. I should have sat there and yelled at my wife because I'm no good at dealing with emotion."

"Luther—" Chrys started.

"No. You're right, Chrys. I'm a damn fool."

Chrys knew that Luther was in a sensitive place. He would

spiral if Chrys let him. "Stop it. This situation, it's on all of us. It's not all on you. I killed a man today. We all did. Two threads; one bond. Do I like it? No. But it is what it is. Now clear the rocks out of your head and let's see what we can do to fix it."

Silence floated through the air of the warehouse like a storm cloud. They each knew they'd bungled the mission in their own way. Not a single Bloodthief alive. The captive escaped. The pale threadweaver they'd found chained up was Harlon Brandock—one of the missing threadweavers—and he was dead too.

They wandered the basement scouring the crates and tables for clues. A small fire had presumably been used to burn evidence. On the tables, boxes of equipment were ready to be moved. One crate held a collection of extraction equipment, bloodied bowls, and binding kits. If they'd had any doubts that these were Bloodthieves before, those doubts were gone.

Chrys picked over the bodies. It was everyone's least favorite job, so he felt like it was his responsibility. Besides, his hands were already red with blood. There was little to be found save for a few weapons and some shines. There should have been more equipment, more something. This wasn't everything.

He kept replaying the phrase the Bloodthief had said before he killed himself: "My life for yours." He'd heard it before. It was an old Felian religious phrase, spoken to the Heralds. Were the Bloodthieves from Felia?

What frustrated him more was the feeling that they had been prepared. How had they known? Was it a coincidence that they'd packed up already? The two prisoners were still there, so if they'd had a warning, they hadn't had much of one. It nagged at the back of his mind, wrestling with the thought that maybe he was making excuses for his failure.

Reina was on her hands and knees poking at the embers

with a stick. She spoke up as she pulled a partially ripped paper out from under a charred piece of kindling. "Hey, I might have something here."

The others all stopped what they were doing and approached her. Laz was still clutching his arm from an arrow that had struck him, and Luther was quietly staring at the aftermath of the brawl, his chest moving with long, deep breaths. Chrys watched intently as Reina squinted, trying to read what was left of the note.

"...cular mineral craft?" She looked up to Chrys. "It's a little smudged but pretty sure. Anyone know what the stones that means?"

They all shook their heads.

Laz snorted. "We're fighting necklace-making old women!"

"Take it seriously, Laz," Chrys snapped. "This raid is a disaster enough as it is. If we have nothing to bring back to Malachus, he's going to lose his mind. Let me see the paper."

Reina handed it to him. It did look like it said *cular mineral craft*. Stones. But it was a little smudged at the start of the last word. "Could this be a *d* or a *g*? Mineral craft. Mineral draft. Mineral graft? Any of those ring a bell?"

"It might not be anything. My old teacher used to say the obvious answer is usually the right one." Reina shrugged her shoulders.

Chrys stared down at the paper. Crafting. Drafting. Grafting. This was the only clue they had; it had to mean something. "Maybe. I'll bring it to the Great Lord and get his opinion. Maybe he knows something we don't. How are the rest of you doing with the sweep?"

"There's nothing here," Luther mumbled.

"Agreed," said Reina.

Laz smiled, big teeth showing through his red beard. "The

city has taken warm, soothing bath this day. I think it is our turn. We all stink."

Even when they were standing in the bloody basement of a decrepit warehouse, Laz was always able to think optimistically. Dead bodies scattered around them? Crack a joke. Chrys wasn't sure if it was a gift or a sign of insanity but, knowing Laz, it was probably a bit of both.

"I'm going to head up to the keep to report to Malachus. He'll want a full recounting of what happened. I'll send back a crew to clean this up, but we need at least one person to stick around and wait for them to come."

They all looked at him blank-faced.

"What? Do you want to carry the bodies up to the keep yourselves?"

They all looked at each other, waiting for another to speak up. No one wanted to spend their afternoon standing in a warehouse full of dead Bloodthieves. After a few moments of uncomfortable eye contact, Laz raised his hand. "I will do this thing. But only if Luther and Reina buy drinks tonight!"

Reina jumped on the offer, "Deal!"

"Bring deep pockets, friend. Staring at dead bodies all day will give me great thirst!"

A look of disgust crossed Reina's face. "That is incredibly disturbing, Laz. Even for you."

"What?" Things clicked in Laz's mind. "Oh, stones, no! Real thirst, not sexy thirst! Gross, Reina! I will not have thirst because of the bodies. I will have thirst from long time of waiting in dusty warehouse!"

Reina laughed. "They did just take a bath after all. Always want your lovers to bathe beforehand."

Laz slapped her on the shoulder. "You are terrible person, but I love you."

"Alright, Laz. Stay up in the rafters just in case, but it looks like they were done with this place. I'd be very surprised if any Bloodthieves came back." Chrys turned to Luther and Reina. "The two of you are off duty. And Luther, get some rest.

"Here's to hoping Malachus is in a better mood than I am."

It was nearing sunset by the time Chrys reached Endin Keep. The warmth of the sun faded below the western horizon. He was starving, but he was also parched, which made him smile as he thought of Laz.

As he approached the keep, he passed a pair of guards, waved to each of them, and greeted them by name. They were well-poised and alert, even though their shift was almost over. Standing guard in a low-traffic area was mentally exhausting, and Chrys liked to reward men who stayed vigilant. He tossed them each a few spare shines for their diligence.

It wasn't the first time he'd done this, and word had gotten around that High General Chrys would give shines to guards on occasion. At the start, it had been purely out of good will, but then he realized that it both improved his standing with the guards and made them better at their jobs.

He gazed up at the keep. It was nestled up into the base of the Everstone Mountains, a vast mountain range that spanned from the northern sea all the way to the deserts of Silkar. The positioning gave it away as a wartime fortification. Great Lord Amastal had built it two hundred years before, during the Binding War. He'd started the work the same year the wastelanders had first been defeated. Chrys could still picture their beady eyes and small frames attacking with a brutal savagery.

People called them cannibals, but Chrys had never seen any proof to the claim.

A short way south of the keep's outer wall was the only real pathway through to the other side of the mountains. It was brutal, snow-covered at times, and rife with dangerous wildlife. The map in Malachus' study had a big blank space for the Wasteland; Chrys had always dreamt of exploring the region and completing the sketch.

As he took his first steps up the winding staircase of the north tower, a familiar face greeted him. Eleandra Orion-Endin, the gem of Alchea. The Great Lord's wife. But, unlike him, the people loved her. She had pale blonde hair wrapped up in a perfect chignon atop her head, her elegant neck covered by the high collar of her dress. The color of her hair came from mixed descent. Her mother was a white-haired Alirian and her father was from Felia. She was the perfect compromise—though her skin tone was far more Alirian. If she'd been born with colored eyes, she'd be empress of the entire Arasin continent, but instead she subtly guided the most powerful man in Alchea, the nation's first bichromic Great Lord.

She lifted a hand in greeting, beautifully manicured furs resting over narrow shoulders. "Chrystopher!" She smiled knowingly.

"Lady Eleandra," he replied, smiling and giving a slight bow. Many years ago, she'd asked if Chrys was short for Chrystopher; he'd told her it was not. She found it so peculiar that she'd been calling him the incorrect name impishly ever since.

Half the city-state was in love with her, and it wasn't hard to see why. Her light brown eyes were shaped like almonds, and the sweetness with which she looked at each person she met was intoxicating. To Chrys, she had always felt more like a mother.

Iriel, on the other hand, was the spell that bound him wholly.

"What brings you to the keep today? Should you not be taking care of your lovely wife? She is due any day now, isn't she?"

The conversation was a timely distraction. His shoulders relaxed as he stopped thinking about the warehouse. "She is. But you know Iriel, she's a mind not to be coddled. I'm here to talk to your husband. He asked me to oversee important work, and I am not one to forgo my promises."

"Indeed, you are not. An attribute more would do well to adopt. And are your families planning to help after the birth? I'd be happy to help or have someone sent if you need anything at all."

Chrys smiled. "That is a very generous offer. My mother will be around to help, and Iriel's will as well. We should be well cared for."

Eleandra lit up. "Oh, I just adore your mother so much. She must be ecstatic to have her first grandchild. And, tell me, what is the count up to now?"

Chrys' mother, Willow—despite being a threadweaver and quite fetching—had turned down dozens of marriage proposals. Willow and Chrys had arrived in Alchea when he was a toddler, two foreign threadweavers escaping a broken life. They had been the talk of the whole city for months. Every eligible bachelor in town had tried his best to woo and pursue her, but she'd systematically turned them all down. Over the years, the efforts had decreased, but never ceased. Eleandra had always looked at Willow's independence as a badge of feminine honor.

Chrys scratched the back of his head. "Sixty-seven? Unless another delusional man has tried his hand at the Valerian gambling table in the last few days."

"I reckon the odds at that table are not so good."

"Hard to win when the dealer won't play the game!"

"Yet, hard not to play when the prize is so lovely." She cocked her head to the side and winked. "When you see her, tell her I miss her dearly and that she needs to come visit."

Chrys gave her a small bow. "Of course, my lady."

With that, Eleandra wished him well and headed off. Feeling renewed, Chrys began the ascent up the winding staircase. His footsteps were muffled by a black rug that ran the entire length of the stairs like a stripe down its center.

After climbing multiple stories in the tall tower, he finally arrived at Lord Malachus' study. Two fit guards flanked the large mahogany door, each nodding to Chrys as he approached.

"Gentlemen."

They both stood at attention and spoke in unison. "High General."

"How's the shift?"

"Boring, sir," the taller guard said.

"Boring is good."

"Boring is good," they repeated.

Chrys gave them a nod of approval before moving forward to open the door. It opened with a loud groan, like the seal of a crypt. Inside was the definition of Alchean finery. The north wall was a two-story library of ancient and modern works. The south wall was an enormous map of Arasin, with three dimensional representations of the Everstone Mountains east of Alchea and the Malachite Mountains south of Felia.

A dark mound of green representing the Fairenwild covered a section of land between Alchea and Felia. The Alirian archipelago floated in the sea west of Felia, and the islands of Kulai could be seen south of the Alchea-Felia border. A rough, rust-colored material covered a huge swath of desert south of the Everstone Mountains. Silkar. East of the Everstone Mountains the map faded to black with a single calligraphed word written in a murky green: Wastelands.

Scholars claimed that it was the most to-scale representation of Arasin ever made. But such hyperboles are typical of scholarship and impossible to verify. Whether or not it was true, the massive depiction of continental landscape was beautiful in its own right.

Toward the west wall, past a sprawling silk rug, the Great Lord Malachus Endin sat behind a walnut desk, back turned, looking out over the city far below with a book in his hand. A small lamp burned brightly on a side table. The sun had dropped below the western skyline, casting a scenic orange glow into the sky. He glanced over his shoulder and motioned for Chrys to come over.

"Have you ever been in this room during sunset?" His eyes still focused out over the streets of Alchea.

Chrys stepped forward, getting a better view of the scene. "I'm not sure, sir. I've been in the briefing room below, but the view from this altitude is far more impressive."

"It's the shadows. The mountains cast sweeping shadows over the city in the morning. But at night, there is nothing but flatlands to the west."

This odd beginning nearly caused Chrys to forget the bad news he'd come to report. "Sir, I have news from the raid this afternoon."

Malachus brought a finger to his lips. "Shhhh. It's beginning." He extended that same finger out toward the city, pointing toward the residential district.

Small lights flickered into existence. Lamps, candles, torches. One small light would pop, and, like a rippling pond, dozens of others nearby would follow suit. After a few minutes of silence, tens of thousands of lights were burning down below them.

"A flame is a fickle fortune," Malachus said as he held up the book he was holding. "Thoralan. One of my favorite scholars. I always think of that quote this time of night. Have you heard it?"

"I have not."

"Oh, come now, Chrys. You really do need to read more philosophy. You're too grounded in the hard sciences. It would be good for your soul, although I'm not sure either of our souls have much chance at redemption."

"Redemption isn't something that can be obtained or withheld," Chrys replied. "It's a commitment you make."

"Perhaps for you, Chrys, but I'm not interested in the warmth of redemption." Malachus turned back to the window. "Life itself is a flame. Fickle as any. Some burn brightly and die swiftly. Some burn dimly and live far past their need. In the end, all flames die. Look out there; in a few hours, all of those lights will die and the city will be lost to darkness. But in the morning, it will be reborn. More flames will burn, and they too will be forgotten the next day.

"I've spent a lifetime looking down at those lights and it seems that the only flames that are remembered are the ones that burn the world. Do you want to burn the world, Chrys?"

Chrys shuddered thinking of the War of the Wastelands. His memories of the war were a blur, but he preferred it that way. Leave the past in the past.

"Do you want to do something so drastic the world will remember you forever?" He didn't wait for a response. "Thoralan called it a *Legacy Complex*, people who become overly fixated on leaving a lasting impression on the world. I find it hard not to feel that way when the only social ladder left to climb is that of historical relevance."

Chrys often felt kinship with Malachus, a paternal bond from his time spent living in the keep, but in this thing they were opposite. He wanted nothing more than for the stubborn flame of the Apogee to be forgotten. "Five years ago, maybe, but I was a different man then."

Malachus smiled. "I'm not so sure. I think that man is still there, hidden under a brittle layer of self-control. Every once in a while, a crack breaks through the armor and that man comes out. It's a bit refreshing to be honest. As a leader, I like the new you, but I must say that as a man there are times when I wish the Apogee lived on. That kind of man has his uses too."

It was true. It *was* a brittle layer, but it was growing stronger over time. Chrys had never told anyone that he heard a voice in his mind. It started during the war, the day he'd butchered hundreds in Ripshire Valley. Now the Apogee spoke to him daily, begging for Chrys to let him out. But the one time he had, death had flowed like a landslide and Chrys couldn't recall any of the events. "I fear that, no matter how hard I try to change, the world will always see me as the Apogee."

"It's fascinating to me that your greatest fear seems to be yourself." Malachus breathed out sharply through his nose with a smile pricking the corner of his lips. "What's even more fascinating is that I actually believe you. It's refreshing to be honest. I have always appreciated that about you. Fearless candor. Unlike the leeches I spend most of my time with. Now, enough of an old fool's ramblings. You came here to brief me on the warehouse raid."

"Yes," Chrys squirmed. "The good news is that the reports were true. It was a Bloodthief hideout."

"That's wonderful news. So, why does your tone make it sound like bad news?"

Chrys went on to explain how the four of them had carefully walked the streets and saw nothing suspicious. When they'd entered the warehouse it was empty, bare. They were ready to call it when Luther had noticed the peculiarity in the floor's dust patterns which led them to the trapdoor. An ambush, Reina's sly trick, and a brutal fight. He hesitated as he described the prisoner.

"She was young, tall, blonde hair. Blindfolded and gagged, hands bound behind her, with a knife to her back. She got away from him, I told him it was over, and he slit his own throat before I could stop him. Which means that despite the intel being good, all we have is ten dead Bloodthieves and no more information."

"Unbelievable. Almost like they knew you were coming."

Chrys nodded. "Exactly what I thought. But we have no proof of such a claim."

Malachus leaned back in his chair, deep in thought. "There are many who knew of the operation, but little time for them to warn someone all the way on the westside. And what of the girl. Who is she? Has she told us anything helpful?"

"I've never seen her before, sir. A young Sapphire. She played like she was coming with us and then...she escaped. I tried to follow her but lost her in the lower westside alleys. It's my fault she got away. I never should have trusted her so quickly. But, stones, I did not expect someone so young to have such skill." Chrys straightened up. "Of course, that is no excuse. I take full responsibility."

Malachus slammed his fist down onto the table. The force of the pounding shook the wood with such force that it displaced the clean organization. "She just...got away? From a team of my most skilled threadweavers? Stones, Chrys, you're not making this easy on me."

One of the guards burst into the room to check on the noise.

"Leave," Malachus dismissed him, and the guard left.

Here it came. Chrys braced himself for impact. The moment he'd been preparing himself for all afternoon. Every step down the cobblestone streets felt like the countdown to a concussive blast, the heat of it already tangible across his nervous skin. Malachus was likely to give Henna or Jurius control over the investigation, or if Malachus was really furious, he might dismiss Chrys from his duties altogether.

"Unbelievable." Malachus rubbed his temples, all sense of joviality wiped clean from his face. "The closest we've come to uncovering their operation and we come up with nothing. If Jurius finds out about this, you're done. He'll revolt unless I give him control of the investigation, but there's no way that ends well. Chrys, I trust you. Probably more than I should. If you say you did everything you could, but she got away, I believe you. Jurius won't. You know he came to me after I gave you charge over the Bloodthief investigation? Told me all the reasons it should be him instead of you. He was absolutely furious.

"He can never know about this failure. In fact, no one can. There *was* no girl. Understand? There was a group Blood-thieves that you efficiently dispatched, one that killed himself rather than be questioned. Can you make that happen? More importantly, can we trust your team to keep the secret?"

Chrys was in shock. Rather than demoting him, Malachus was going to lie for him. "Yeah...yes. Yes. We can trust them. Luther would do anything for me, and we should be able to trust Reina and Laz."

"*Should* isn't good enough. Make sure they're on board," Malachus demanded. "We need to find out who the girl is."

Chrys had been so busy worrying about telling Malachus the bad news, that he hadn't even thought about trying to find the girl. "Absolutely. I can pull records from the temple and look for any Sapphire girls between the ages of fourteen and twenty-two. The list should be small, and that bright blonde hair is uncommon enough that we should be able to filter it down even more."

"Perfect. Do it discreetly." Malachus grabbed a quill and jotted a name onto a small slip of paper. "If anyone bothers you, find Father Jasper and tell him you're on assignment from me. He's on the Stone Council and I've known him for decades; he'll be discreet."

This was not how Chrys had expected this conversation to go. Malachus had every reason to be furious. Stones, he'd killed men over smaller mistakes. But here and now, he was putting his own credibility on the line to protect him. If the others ever found out, they would not only depose Chrys, but the integrity of the Great Lord himself would be damaged in their eyes. Perhaps he could find new high generals, but it was less work for Malachus to keep the ones he had happy.

As if on cue, a knock on the door revealed the white-haired high general peeking into the room. The twinkle in Henna's eye made Chrys uneasy.

Malachus raised up a finger, and she retreated back into the hallway with the guards. "My brain is telling me that this is a poor decision, Chrys, but my gut says to trust you, and it's never led me astray. Tell me you can handle this."

"I can handle it." Doubts flooded his mind as soon as he'd said the words. So many uncertain variables: Luther, Laz, Reina, the Sapphire girl, the temple workers, or even any passerby who saw the girl's escape. This was a dangerous lie, but at least he had Malachus on his side. "You can trust me, sir. This will be the last time you hear anything about it."

"Good. You're dismissed. Send Henna in after you. And Chrys," Malachus said with a voice of warning, "don't let me down."

Chrys walked away from the desk feeling both lighter and heavier at the same time. The entire encounter had taken a different turn than he'd expected, and mostly for the better...at least for the moment.

He reached the door and opened it.

High General Henna was outside, still with big, excited eyes. As soon as she spotted him, she smiled and greeted him. "Chrys. What was that about? He looked pretty serious."

"Nothing important."

"Good, because you won't want to miss this." She slid past him beckoning him to follow. A small bag swung below her hand, weighed down by its contents.

Well now he *was* curious.

Malachus stood up, still not having shaken off the irritation from his face. "General. What is this about?"

"My Lord..."

Malachus interjected. "What is *this*? Why do you look like *that*?" He waved his hand out gesturing to her face.

"Sir?"

"Like a bad card player with a good hand."

She laughed. "I've never been good at hiding a winning hand, my Lord. And I'm not positive yet, but I think that's exactly what we have here." She raised up the small bag and bounced it around a few times.

"Go on," Malachus leaned forward.

Henna dropped it on the desk, drawstrings still closed tight. "Remember that cave my men were exploring? They found something. At first it looked like it was just the remains of an old miner settlement, some rusty century-old equipment, a few broken down wagons, some cracked support beams. But then we found one of these."

She untied the bag and pulled out a small shard of black mineral. "Some of the engineers think the mine has obsidian deposits."

Malachus raised a brow. "This is your winning hand? A deposit of a low-demand mineral buried deep in a mine in the mountains?" The look of irritation chiseled deep into the wrinkles of his eyes.

She grabbed the piece and stepped a few paces back, still smiling like she knew something they did not. Without explaining, and before anyone had a chance to ask, she threw the rock right at Chrys' torso. His eyes and veins flared blue as he *pushed* it away.

But it didn't work.

The obsidian struck him hard in the chest—the force nearly knocked him off of his chair—and it fell down onto his lap.

"Stones, Henna!" Chrys rubbed at his ribs.

"Henna!" Malachus roared, stepping forward. "What is the meaning of this? Petty revenge? This kind of behavior is unacceptable!"

She waited, saying nothing, the same obnoxious, knowing smile pasted on her face.

Chrys broke the silence, an earth-shattering realization forming in his mind. "Stones."

Malachus turned to him.

Henna smiled something wicked.

"That's not possible," Chrys said.

"Quit with the theatrics."

"Malachus, look. In threadlight." Chrys held up the chunk of obsidian in his left hand.

Malachus' veins swirled with green and blue energy as he glanced into the realm of threadlight, his left eye glowing green and his right eye glowing blue. "That's impossible." He walked over and pulled it out of Chrys' hand.

Henna finally spoke. "Exactly what I said, sir. I had two different threadweavers verify it. For some reason, this obsidian is different. It's thread-dead." The crass slur was common among threadweavers when referring to those who could not threadweave. The more acceptable name was *achromat*. Despite the word coming from Henna, an achromat, in this moment the word seemed appropriate.

"Henna. Do you realize what this could mean?" Instantly, Malachus' eyes took on the same excited look as hers. "If we could mass produce weapons that threadweavers could not influence...Imagine a threadweaver assassin with one of these weapons. They'd be unstoppable; not even other threadweavers could stop them. A threadweaver with a blade against an unarmed threadweaver. Gah! Tell me everything, Henna."

Chrys didn't like it. The world had rules. As a Sapphire threadweaver, he had the power to *push* on anything around him. An arrow coming toward him? Send it away. The idea of something with no thread was frightening. A volley of thread-dead arrows raining down toward him? He would be helpless. If they found more of this, and mass-produced weapons, the safety that threadweavers had come to expect would be gone.

Henna went on to explain that she'd sworn the few who knew to secrecy, and then had sent the expedition further into the cave to look for more obsidian under the guise that Lord Malachus wanted an entire table built of the mineral. They were exploring even as they spoke.

"Well done, General. This could change everything. I have much to think about. Do not share this information with anyone else and keep me up-to-date with any further findings in the cave." Malachus sat back down, smiling to himself, and stared back out the window down at the candlelit city. He turned to Chrys and smiled. "Looks like I may have found the kindling for that wayward ambition."

CHAPTER 7

CHRYS TOSSED AND TURNED. Sleep taunted him within sight but never within grasp. As Iriel returned to bed after her fourth trip to the toilet, he kept his eyes closed so she wouldn't think she'd awakened him. The truth was that the whole situation didn't sit right with him. He'd been ready to receive his punishment—he deserved it. He'd failed. And yet, Malachus had let him off the hook. He'd realized while lying awake that his own failure could be seen as a failure in Malachus' judgment for entrusting him with the task in the first place. If Chrys could make the failure disappear, it would be better for Malachus as well.

The morning passed quickly and, now, he stood in front of the great temple of Alchaeus, eager to find information on who the mysterious threadweaver girl was. If he could tie up that loose end, he was sure things would be easier with Laz, Luther, and Reina. At some point he'd need to send for them, and he was hoping to have more information before asking them to lie for him. They didn't need an explanation—they were loyal enough—but it would put Chrys' mind at ease.

The dual spires of the temple's eastern building loomed over him, eclipsing the rising sun over the mountains. The vast library was the only part of the temple he regularly visited. Over the years he'd read hundreds of books, most relating to medicine, biology, or history, though Malachus' influence had caused him to pick up a few philosophical works as well. The books by Gauxin about threadweaver physics were some of his favorites. In them, Gauxin attempted to apply mathematics to explain the effects of *weaving* threads. There was, of course, a religious aspect to the text that covered some of the more esoteric aspects but, overall, he found the text to be quite enlightening.

Chrys wasn't particularly devout himself, but he did believe in the Lightfather, Alchaeus. Chance and luck were poor explanations for too many of life's questions.

Being back at the temple reminded Chrys of the terrifying incident with his wife only days before. He could almost hear her screams as he looked out toward the steps leading up to the temple. The mysterious doctor that had saved her. *Your child is the key.*

He reached down and pulled the black blade out of the latch on his leg. Looking down at its surface, he thought of Henna and her thread-dead obsidian. What if...he relaxed his eyes and let threadlight wash over his vision. Dozens of brilliant, pulsing threads flowed between him and the world around him, but there was no thread connecting him to the knife. *Stones.* He muted the rest of the threads and focused harder on the obsidian knife, searching the other realm, but he found nothing. This knife too was thread-dead.

How had he not realized it before? He was carrying one of the most valuable weapons in all of Arasin, given to him by a stranger. The final words of the man sprang back into his memory. *Use it to break the threads that bind you.* The man knew exactly what he'd given him. A weapon with a broken thread. The priests told stories about the Lightfather walking the earth in the form of a man...what if they were right? He shoved the knife back into his boot sheath. If it had been the Lightfather, then he had all the more reason to find the girl and stop the Bloodthieves.

He walked up the steps into the library, greeting several temple workers, a priest, and a group of priestesses. They all knew who he was—something he was still getting used to after a year as high general—and let him through. He exchanged pleasantries but was happy to evade more in-depth conversation.

The library itself was enormous, built centuries before and maintained with the utmost care. Even during decades of brutal warfare, the temple was left alone—a prize for the victor. There were two levels of shelving, four rows of books on each, with stairs leading up to a walkway that bordered the entirety of the library. The ceilings arched high overhead with large windows letting in bounties of morning sunlight. Dozens of aisles spread out across each room like silken rows of a great web. Each aisle was labeled meticulously by the temple workers and organized by the priestesses.

The blind priests were the religious leaders of the temple, but the seeing priestesses were the operational leaders. The priests performed the ceremonies and served as liaisons with the congregations, but the priestesses organized it all.

Chrys turned a corner looking for one of the private sections that contained records of the populace. Information about each family: number of children, homes, debts, alliances, education, etc.

The priestess on duty led him into the records room. Chrys

had never entered the room before and found himself over-whelmed by the size. There must be a hundred thousand records, all in alphabetical order.

Seeing the letter "v", he walked forward and thought how interesting it would be to see what his own family record looked like. There would be a page dedicated to the Apogee, and the family section would be small. It was just him and his mother, Willow. He had no aunts or uncles in Alchea, and no father. His mother refused to talk about him, calling him a coward. As a kid, Chrys had always wanted to meet his relatives.

A priest wandered into the room, walking slowly with a white cane tapping gently out in front of him, probing for colli-sions. He heard Chrys' footsteps and lifted his head. "Ryana? Is that you?" His voice was low and tired.

"Good morning, Father. Just looking through some records, maybe you could help me."

The old man scrunched his brow and pursed his wrinkled lips. "Perhaps I can, my child. Perhaps not. Tell me who you are, and what you need, and I will do my best to assist you."

Chrys felt distinctly absurd asking a blind man for help searching written records. "My name is Chrys Valerian, I'm looking for some records."

"Chrys," he repeated, smiling. "Valerian is a unique name. Did you know the valerian plant has asymmetric flowers? Something the blind do not fancy so much. We much prefer symmetry and predictability over uniqueness, as you can imag-ine. And if I'm not mistaken, the plant also has medicinal usages?"

"It does. It is supposed to help you sleep." Chrys had learned that from his mother.

"Indeed." The priest smiled as if he knew it were untrue. "Your mother has taught you well. To be truthful, I have wanted to meet you for quite some time. Perhaps not in this way. I wish I had known you were coming. You have made quite the name for yourself."

Of course, everyone knew about the Apogee. The bloody butcher of the valley. He couldn't even hide from the blind.

"They call me Father Xalan."

"It is very nice to meet you," Chrys lied. He gestured over to the wall of records with his left hand. "Not to be curt, but I'm on assignment from Lord Malachus. I need to find some records. Do you know if the threadweaver records are kept separately? Or here amongst the rest?"

Some blind men kept their eyes open, which Chrys found quite unnerving. But Father Xalan kept his closed. Chrys looked at him and felt grateful for that small detail. "I believe that, in general, they are kept here with the rest of the records. However, my dear friend Father Jasper had a collection of threadweaver records pulled just a few moments ago. I can only assume he was more prepared for your arrival than I. The records were taken to his personal study. You can find it in the west wing, first floor, third door on the left."

Of course, they'd known he was coming. They must have spies in the keep. Well, perhaps not spies. Malachus technically headed the church's Stone Council, though his participation was more for show than anything. If the church had spies—if he could even call them that—inside the keep, it would have to be with Malachus' blessing.

"Thank you, Father. I'll head there right away."

"I believe we will be meeting again soon. Your wife is with child."

"She is."

Father Xalan grinned again. "Will your mother be attending? She is your only family, I believe?"

"She is, and she would tear down this temple before letting us come without her. For the ceremony itself, though, it will just be Iriel and I."

"That is..." The priest smiled and shook his head. "I look forward to seeing you again. A word of advice. The most sacred moments in one's life are also the most vulnerable. Childbirth most of all. Be kind and patient and loving. Iriel will need you. May the Lightfather bless you and your child. I pray we both find what we seek."

Something about his tone struck a chord in Chrys' mind. That's why he looked so familiar. Father Xalan was the same priest that performed the Rite of Revelation for Luther's child. Which meant that he was also the priest that took their child away from them. A flash of anger toward the priest passed over him as the thought entered his mind, but he knew it was irrational. It wasn't the priest's fault. The rite and its laws were predetermined. He was just doing his duty. Chrys could respect that.

"Lightfather bless you as well, Father."

They parted ways and Chrys headed toward the west wing. Getting there was the most difficult part. The campus seemed to be a winding labyrinth of unplanned expansions. Even with directions, it took him some time to find the west wing.

The entire corridor was lined with private study rooms, each door marked with inset carvings to set them apart. He found the third on the left and gave it a hard knock. A door down the hallway opened up and a woman looked out toward Chrys. She was dressed in the temple robes of a priestess. She started to walk toward him but then the door in front of him opened. She stopped and returned to her room.

In front of him stood an unnaturally old man. The most surprising thing about him was that despite the deep wrinkles of his face, and the sagging bags under his eyes, his long, gray hair was quite luscious.

"Good morning," he said. The wrinkles near his eyes shifted as he turned his neck.

"Good morning, Father."

"Ah, a voice I do not know. Humor me." He smiled and extended his neck a bit, as if trying to see through his blindness. "You've a knock of authority yet waited for me to speak first. Nobility but not by birth. Male voice, deep but not profound. I'd venture mid-thirties. I hear no one else with you, which means you've been given permission to wander the temple or have a face recognizable to most. Tell me, child. Are you clean-shaven?"

Something about the question made Chrys smile. "I am not. I have a short beard, well-trimmed."

The old man stepped forward and extended his hand. "In that case, High General Chrys Valerian, it is my honor to finally meet you. I am Father Jasper."

Chrys smiled as he reached out and shook the priest's hand. "The pleasure is mine, Father. For a man that has almost certainly been waiting for my arrival, you really struggled to come up with my name."

"It seems my wit has aged less gracefully than the rest of me."

"I had an advantage, of course, knowing that you had pulled the records. If I hadn't known, I'm sure the trick would have amazed and astounded. Which reminds me. I wanted to thank you for gathering the records. The Great Lord said you'd be helpful; I can see why he holds you in such high regard."

"Oh, come now. I'm too old for flattery. I know very well that I am but an arrow in the quiver to that man. He's less religious than the last Great Lord. I imagine he'd get rid of the Stone

Council altogether if he could. After all, arrows in a quiver can still be a thorn in your side.

"But that is beside the point. You came for the records of the threadweavers, possibly to find a connection between the kidnappings. More likely it is for another, more covert, purpose conveniently disguised behind the other." He paused, waiting to see how Chrys would react. "We have eyes everywhere but in front of ourselves." He left the explanation at that.

"Nothing nefarious, I assure you," Chrys said. "It's true that we're looking for connections between those abducted by the Bloodthieves."

"Good, good. I hope you find them."

"I hope so too. But if it's as difficult as it was to find your study, don't hold your breath. And that was *with* the help of Father Xalan's kindness."

"*Kind* is too bland a word to describe him. That man is a warm fire in the winter woods." Father Jasper smiled, thinking of his friend. "Now that you're here, what can I do to help?"

Chrys thought for a moment. It would be nice to have someone help look over the records with him. Unfortunately, a blind priest was not the best resource for that sort of aid. "Do you know how the records are organized? Birth year, gender, threadweaver classification?"

"Ah yes. That would be useful. They are sorted simply by birth year. Sapphires and Emeralds are not partitioned separately, and neither is gender."

"And this is all of them? No records have been omitted?"

"None that I am aware of."

"Good," Chrys said. "I think that is all the help I need. I can handle the rest on my own if you need to be somewhere."

Father Jasper coughed a light laugh. "This is my study, child. The only time I leave is to eat and sleep. And when my bones are too tired to make the trip, sometimes I sleep in here as well." He pointed over his shoulder with his thumb and Chrys saw a small cot tucked into the far corner of the room. "I'll be doing my own studies. Don't worry about being quiet, my hearing is poor enough that, unless I'm talking to you, I'll probably forget you're here."

The next hour was spent pulling records for every female blue-eyed threadweaver between the ages of fourteen and twenty-two. There were only a dozen, but it took significant time to continue filtering. There were, of course, no portrait drawings associated with the files, but by using familial nationality he was able to filter the list down to who he thought might have blonde hair. He also knew most of the names from his time running training for young Sapphires over the years and could cross many off of the list. By the end he had one unknown name that he thought might be a blonde threadweaver, and one other unknown name that was more likely brunette based on her northern Alchea ancestry.

He turned to the blind priest. "Father Jasper?"

"Yes? What is it?"

"Do you happen to know anything about either of these names?"

Father Jasper sat up and turned, raising his brows.

"Anna Coramine and Jessa Saltar?"

"Hmm." Father Jasper brought his hand to his forehead and rubbed as he thought. "If I am not mistaken, Jessa Saltar is a pseudo threadweaver. She does have blue eyes, but they are a murky mix of brown as well. I believe she can see threadlight but does not have enough power to effect change on those threads."

Chrys had heard of that happening, but it was extremely uncommon. Generally, the world thought of people as threadweavers or achromats; in reality, there was a spectrum of power. On rare occasions some could only *see* threadlight, and others had blue or green eyes but could not. It was hypothesized that these people could affect change on the threads were they able to see them—the complement of Jessa's condition.

"Interesting. Would that information be..." He looked through Jessa's file and saw the note. *Unable to threadweave.* "Ah, yes. Thank you. I see that now."

The records were incredibly detailed. They had information about when and where they were born, relatives, education, jobs, likes and dislikes, and myriad other seemingly mundane notes about their life. Chrys assumed that such detailed reckoning was saved for the threadweavers. There was no way the temple had this much information about every person in the city.

How detailed were his own? Was it possible, through some mistake of his own, that they knew the truth about the Apogee?

Father Jasper grunted. "And Anna Coramine, you said?"

"Yes."

"If she is who you are searching for, you may have some troubles. Anna passed away last year of a blood illness." He nodded his head with a look of sadness. It was not uncommon for threadweavers to have issues of blood. A lifetime of threadlight coursing through your veins took its toll. Some died young of a blood disease, often from overusing threadlight, and others lived into their fifties and died of a heart attack. No threadweavers lived much longer than that. Some threadweavers, like Chrys' mother Willow, abstained from all threadweaving in order to prolong their life, but it only ever gained them a few years in the end.

The worst part of Anna's death was that it left him back at

square one. He was pretty confident he knew the rest of the Sapphire threadweavers in the list. So, who was she?

"That is unfortunate to hear. Do you know if there are any other records missing from this list? I'm looking for the record of someone I met recently, but I'm not sure who she was. Maybe you'd have an idea." Chrys was wary to share more information with Father Jasper, not knowing who he'd share it with, but Malachus had said he was trustworthy. "Young girl, somewhere between fourteen and twenty-two, I'd guess. Blonde Sapphire. Fairly tall and thin."

Father Jasper thought for a moment, rummaging through the vast library of knowledge he'd gained over his long lifetime. "Anna would have fit that description. Jessa is a brunette amongst the other classification issue. Do you know the Tarata girl?"

Chrys sighed. "I do. It wasn't her."

"Unfortunately, I cannot think of anyone else that fits that very specific description. But, as you can imagine, a blind priest might not be your best resource here. Perhaps many years ago when my mind still held its edge. It is possible that she's not Alchean. I'm told that, so close to Alir, the light-skinned population in Felia is almost all blonde haired. Visitor, perhaps?"

That was exactly what Chrys feared. There had been something exotic about her. He remembered a small detail. "Are tattoos popular in Felia?"

The priest looked surprised and excited by the question. "I do not know. I'm told the people of Kulai are of tattoos, but I do not believe that blonde hair is common on those islands."

Chrys thought hard, picturing her hair waving back and forth as she climbed up the ladder out of the dimly lit warehouse basement. He was pretty sure it was a tattoo. Large. Maybe multiple. "Perhaps. Anyway, I should be on my way.

Father Jasper, you have been a wonderful help today. I can't thank you enough for having all of these records gathered for me beforehand. I'm sure it saved me half a day's work. Still not sure how you did it, but thank you. May the Lightfather illuminate the threads before you."

"And may they never grow dim, General Valerian. It has been my pleasure to meet you. You are, as I've been told, an honorable man of great respect, and I pray the Lightfather bless you for that." Father Jasper gave a small bow to Chrys, his long hair shimmering in the daylight. "Maybe you'll humor an old man and pay me a visit when you come for the Rite of Revelation for your new child."

"Of course, Father."

Chrys left the room, pleasantly surprised by the easy conversation with the priest, but displeased with the lack of information he'd gained. Who was she?

The tattoo was the only thing he had left. It reminded him of the stories he'd heard when he was young. Stories meant to scare children. Stories of when gods walked the earth, and the corespawn fed on the minds of men. He'd loved the stories as a kid, each night asking his mother to tell a variant about corespawn attacking and a hero protecting the people. She'd made all kinds of variations. They ate minds. They ate hearts. They ate souls. The heroes could fly. They could turn to stone. They could disappear. In the end, the heroes always won, and they tattooed themselves, so they'd never forget the dark history.

Telling bedtime stories was one of the things he looked forward to doing with his own child. Unfortunately, he worked late most nights with his new position. He would have to figure out how to better balance that once his child was born. Though if he didn't find the Bloodthieves soon, he might not be a high general much longer. There had to be something he could do.

95

He was starting to believe that Jurius was right. Maybe Malachus had chosen the wrong person to lead the investigation.

Chrys needed help.

He didn't want to admit it but, with no leads and no plan, he only had one choice. Jurius. He was well-connected and cared deeply about stopping the Bloodthieves. As long as his son was missing, Jurius wouldn't be sitting idly by. Chances were high that he'd been running his own covert investigation, which meant that he might have information that Chrys could use.

Before he realized it, Chrys was out of the temple and well on his way to Jurius' home. He spent the long walk rehearsing the conversation—he would start by telling Jurius what happened in the Bloodthief warehouse—and trying to predict how Jurius would respond to the request for help.

The sky dimmed as the sun began to set for the day. Chrys was only a few streets away from Jurius' home when he saw the high general walking down the street. Chrys ran to where Jurius had been walking, but he'd already disappeared down another road. Chrys jogged up the road and caught another glimpse of him as he darted down a side alley. Odd. He was heading west.

Chrys knew he shouldn't—if Jurius found out there would be hell to pay—but he followed him anyway.

CHAPTER 8

AT FIRST, Chrys thought Jurius was headed to the lower west-side, but then he turned south. He had almost left the city proper by the time he slipped into a building, farmland visible just past the next street and horizon as far as the eye could see. Chrys had never been to this part of the city before.

What was Jurius doing?

He moved with caution around the side of the building, observing bricks, windows, and possible blind spots. Each window was locked tight and boarded up with no way to see inside. The building was small enough that, if he entered, Jurius would know. He doubled back over each of the windows, checking for any gaps he could see through, periodically looking over his shoulder to make sure no one was watching. But then he noticed a bit of smoke rising up from the top of the building.

Chrys opened himself to threadlight and leapt, *pushing* hard on the thread that bound him to the earth. His meager jump turned into soaring flight as he shot up to the rooftop.

It was late, and the dark red brick glowed softly with the falling sun. The building was shaped like a huge box, each side equal in width to the others. On the roof, a large chimney released smoke from a fire, and two small windows lined the rooftop floor to let in sunlight below. A bright fire blazed in the hearth below him, and candle light flickered in the increasingly dark ambience left over from the setting sun.

There were three people in the room. A woman, Jurius, and...his son.

Chrys backed away from the window. Jurius' son was alive. But he'd been kidnapped by the Bloodthieves. What did that mean? Was this woman a Bloodthief? Was Jurius bargaining with her to get his son back? Or worse, was Jurius working with the Bloodthieves? Had he been working with them all along? No, Jurius' emotions had been real. He hated the Bloodthieves. Chrys peeked back over the window and into the building.

The woman was in her late thirties, with dark hair slicked back behind her ears. Black pants and a tight-fitting tunic of curious design, like raven feathers, partially covered her collarbone. The shadows accentuated a strong jawline and high cheekbones.

Jurius and the woman spoke to each other, their mumbled words reverberating through the window. They were unintelligible by the time they reached Chrys' ears. Jurius walked over to his son and embraced him with a sense of desperation.

He needed to hear what they were saying.

Chrys moved to the latch on the window. He laid on his stomach and slowly twisted the handle. When it started to groan, he paused, looking down at the three below him. None of them shifted their attention upward. He twisted the handle even more slowly, pushing down slightly to release the pressure. It stopped as he reached the end. But then, the pressure he'd been applying popped the window's seal and it flung wide open below him.

Chrys reflexively opened himself to threadlight.

All three of them looked up.

Threads, like hungry tentacles, burst forth from the ground toward the ceiling. Chrys had never seen anything like it before. He dove out of the way, but they were too fast. The threads latched onto his body and *pulled* on him, multiplying the force of gravity. He tumbled down through the window toward the ground. Mid-flight, he gained his bearings and *pushed* down hard on his corethread, counteracting the wild threads, launching himself back up toward the ceiling. But then he stalled, suspended in the air like a drifting cloud. He *pushed* harder, but the opposing force grew stronger. When he looked down, he saw the woman staring up at him, dozens of tentacles of threadlight fastened onto his body, each one pulsing with profane energy. He *pushed* harder, but the sheer number of threads increased until he crashed to the floor, pinned down like a nail in wood.

It was impossible. What she was doing defied the primary law of thread physics: thread permanence. Somehow, this woman was *creating* threads.

His hands were bound near his feet, his legs trapped in a deep crouch. He couldn't move, but he could still threadweave. As she approached, he *pushed* a chair at her, but a single thread appeared and fastened the chair to the floor.

"What have we here?" the woman asked. She walked around him, observing him with a wicked smile.

"Jurius! What the hell is going on?" It took all of Chrys' strength not to collapse to the earth beneath the weight of the threads.

Mmmm. A foul voice rose in his mind. *She should not be. Let me out! You cannot fight her. But I can.*

He tried to ignore the voice, but it was right. There was no way to fight back.

Jurius clenched his jaw. "You shouldn't have followed me."

"You know him?" the woman asked.

Jurius nodded. "High General Chrys Valerian."

The weight of gravity applied through the threads faded. Not completely, but the pressure was lessening over time. Chrys took a deep breath and turned to see Jurius' son. He stood tall, a strong Emerald threadweaver like his father, but his eyes were so deeply set they were hard to see in the twilight. Jaymin. That was his name. He should be dead, or close to it.

"He's strong. Good blood," she mumbled as she finished a circuit around Chrys. He finally got a good look at her. Her eyes were yellow, like bright amber dancing near a subtle flame. They radiated, along with her veins, as if she were a thread-weaver, but threadweavers were either Sapphire or Emerald, blue or green. There were no other kinds of threadweavers. *Push* and *pull.* The two halves of the Lightfather.

"Don't get too close to him," Jurius advised. "He is not one to be underestimated."

"The boy is yoked. Until the threads fade there is nothing he can do."

"If Chrys goes missing," Jurius thought out loud, "Malachus will blame the Bloodthieves. He'll send the entire damn army into the city searching for him. But, more importantly, he will almost certainly give me charge of the investigation. That would simplify things for you."

She smiled, full lips parting like honey. "Pity to kill him. His blood would sell for a high price."

Stones. Jurius *was* working with the Bloodthieves. But why?

It explained how the Bloodthieves had been tipped off at the warehouse. It also explained why Jurius wanted to be in charge of the investigation. But, stones, his anger and worry had seemed so real.

Chrys fought against the threads holding him down, but they held him fast. His blood boiled as he strained against them, anger rising like a tide.

Mmmm. Don't be a fool! Let me out!

For a moment, he considered it. It was foolish to leave a tool unused. He was outclassed. Overpowered. Like a thread-dead soldier fighting a threadweaver.

The spark of a memory lit in his mind. *Thread-dead.* He didn't need the Apogee. He had another tool. The obsidian blade. If she couldn't threadweave the knife, maybe he could surprise her with it. It was in his boot pocket, right next to his bound hand. If he could kill her, the threads might release him. He felt confident he could handle Jurius if it came down to it.

"You know, general, you ruined a perfectly joyous moment just now." She stared down at Chrys. He continued reaching down toward his boot. "Jurius made two important realizations today. First, he realized that I am not the enemy. It was a long road, but the truth is that we all do what we must for a better future. And second, he realized that your Great Lord is unfit to rule."

In that moment, the truth dawned on Chrys. Despite Jurius being one of the most powerful men in all of Alchea, this woman was in charge. After seeing what she could do, Chrys understood. What hope did Jurius have against someone with her power?

Chrys waited patiently. He could feel the force of the artificial threads continuing to ease, his arms and legs almost free. He tested the threads, pressing against them.

"How heroic of you," the woman said with a smile. The yellow glow in her veins pulsed brighter, her eyes glowing like the sun. Chrys could see the jungle of threads morphing into each other, forming five thick threads attached to each of his limbs, and his head. "There, that ought to make you a little less bold."

LET ME OUT! the Apogee screamed in his mind. SHE MUST PAY!

The strength of the fused threads was unreal, like his body was being sucked into the earth, each of his muscles straining to stop it from taking him under. The thread attached to his head pulled him back into an unnatural arch that he worried would break his neck if he didn't resist. There was no escape. There was no hope.

But then he realized that, although his arm was bound, his hand was free.

He slipped the knife out of his boot and kept it hidden behind his wrist. With the blade in hand, his mind flashed to the steps outside the temple, the voice of the man in the wide-brim hat echoing in his mind. He remembered the words.

Use it to break the threads that bind you.

He thought of General Henna and her discovery, the thread-dead obsidian. Thread permanence dictated that no thread could be created or destroyed. Each thread was a permanent entity indicating the celestial bond between two terrestrial constructs. But this woman had just proven that it was a lie. She had *created* threads from nothing.

What if?

Chrys opened himself to threadlight and slid the knife toward the root of the thread latched onto his arm. Out of the corner of his eye, he watched as the blade slid weightlessly through the pulsing line of light. The thread popped out of existence just as the knife passed through its end. Then, like a chain reaction, each of the sibling threads burst apart in an explosion of threadlight.

The woman inhaled sharply, as if she could feel the destruction of her creations. She turned to Chrys and saw him freed from her yoke. "Heralds be—"

Moving before she could react, Chrys *pushed* with all his strength onto his corethread, launching him back up into the air toward the open window on the roof. Tentacles of light flung up toward him again, attempting to latch back onto his body, but he sliced through them with the obsidian blade. Her threads burst apart and disappeared in a mist of light. The woman hissed from below and Jurius came running up the wall after him, his veins surging with green threadlight.

Chrys landed on the roof's edge and immediately *pushed* back off toward the inner city, leaping from roof to roof, his heart and veins burning. He turned back to see Jurius standing on the roof watching him, fists clenched.

After a dozen rooftops, Chrys dropped down into an empty street and ran, *drifting* with a light *push* on his corethread. He ran and he ran, his heart beating like a thunderstorm. Finally, he collapsed into an alley, vomiting forcefully. His head was pounding in concert with his chest, and the entirety of his skin sizzled with a deep heat.

He stood back up and forced himself to move. He had to get back to Iriel. A reckoning was coming. They were no longer safe.

CHAPTER 9

You should have let me out! the Apogee thundered in his skull. *She is too dangerous to keep alive. She will come for you, and there is nothing you can do to stop her!*

After an hour of running, vomiting, and vain attempts at muting the Apogee, Chrys finally arrived at his home. It looked so peaceful in the moonlight, but all he could see was red. The small garden blossomed against the cottage-style architecture, and candlelight flickered in the windows. He stumbled forward, still looking over his shoulder, sure that the woman, or Jurius, would appear at any moment. He had to get Iriel out. Somewhere safe. He had no idea where they would go. His mother's? No. It had to be somewhere Jurius wouldn't look.

"Chrys, is that you out there?" Iriel's voice sang out from the kitchen window, her pregnant silhouette standing in the lamplight.

Chrys pushed the door open, the bright lights inside burning his threadsick eyes.

Iriel caught sight of him and hurried over. "Chrys, are you

okay? You look terrible. And your eyes! How much have you been threadweaving?" Her hands moved across his cheeks and his forehead, feeling for temperature and signs of sickness. She used her fingers to look deep into his eyes, blue veins breaking out of a Sapphire iris.

He practically collapsed into her as they moved into the living room. Everything was spinning. The room. His thoughts. Their entire life was spinning out of control and Chrys couldn't stop it. "We have to leave, Iriel. It's not safe here."

"Chrys, you're scaring me. Tell me what's going on."

"They're coming for me." He couldn't think straight. How could he possibly explain what he saw—what he experienced. It was impossible. And the more she knew the more danger she was in. That was the last thing he wanted. "The Bloodthieves. I know who they are, and they know that I know. They'll come tonight and I don't think I have it in me to fight."

"How much time do we have? I can help fight. Stones, no I can't. You're sure they're coming now? Can we send for help?" she asked, rambling until she broke down into tears. "I can't deal with this right now. Not with the baby so close."

Chrys had no idea what to do. Iriel was always his balance. When he was upset, she was calm. When she faltered, he was her firm foundation. Pregnancy had taken that away right when he needed it most. "Gather your things, we need to leave now. We'll get you somewhere safe and then I'll figure out what to do."

This answer did not satisfy Iriel. She buried her head in her hands as she fought back tears. He hated doing this to her, but there was no other way. Her face paled. She choked on her breath, gasping as she tried to contain her emotions. She shivered, then went still. Her mouth dropped in shock as she looked down between her legs. A large puddle of water sank down to the floor, pooling up on the beige rug. She brought her hands to her mouth, terrified at what had happened.

"Chrys."

"Stones," he said knowingly.

"I'm having the baby."

Stones. Now? Of all times. They needed to leave. They had to get somewhere safer. Anywhere but here.

"Can you hold it until we get somewhere safe?"

Her eyes were cold fire. "Can I hold it?"

"Sorry. You're right. Stay here. I'll figure something out."

He sprinted out of the house, adrenaline fueling his movement despite the profound exhaustion that permeated throughout his body. He ran to his neighbor's house and told them to go fetch their midwife, Mistress Amarra. It was all part of their birth plan, so the neighbors knew exactly what to do.

Chrys stood staring down the road, time passing like a dream. Every well-laid plan crashing down around him. Every bit of his perfect life crumbling to dust, suffocating him as he held tightly onto any semblance of order that remained. But there was none. It was over. His perfect life, their perfect plans, nothing but smoke in the night.

Then he saw the first shadow.

He counted four stalking down the dark road. He lifted his chin high and stood with his hands behind his back. He was tired and threadsick, but he knew the power of appearance. There is no greater motivator than to see your enemy's lack of confidence. On the other hand, it is a sobering experience to approach an enemy that has been waiting for you.

The Bloodthieves walked forward in lockstep, trained predators in the night. They looked behind and scattered off of the road and into the trees. Two other figures followed behind, running up the road toward Chrys' home. As they approached, he recognized them as his neighbor's son and Mistress Amarra, the midwife.

The older woman was always serious, and no more so than she was now. "Chrys! The baby is coming?"

Chrys nodded his head and surveyed the tree line behind her. "Her water broke. I don't know how long it's been, but she is inside."

A scream of pain echoed from within the house. Mistress Amarra rushed toward the door and opened it. "These things usually take time, but if her water broke, it's possible the child could come quicker. That didn't sound like a woman with time to spare. What are you waiting for? You need to be inside comforting her."

"I..." Stones. He couldn't. Could he? Was he going to miss the birth of his child? Iriel needed him. But what choice did he have? Go inside and risk their whole family being slaughtered by the Bloodthieves, or stay outside and miss what was supposed to be the most joyous moment in a man's life? His jaw clenched tight. Iriel needed him, but he would have to serve her in a different way. "I need to speak to the neighbors first. You go in. I'll be right there."

He watched as Mistress Amarra hurried inside with a scowl. Chrys could hear Iriel's deep breathing until the door swung shut. Then silence. He turned, eyes probing the tree line for any sign of the Bloodthieves. He slipped out the obsidian blade from the side of his boot and spun it in his hands. This wasn't supposed to happen. He was supposed to be settling down with a family.

Deep within himself he could feel the familiar rage that had engulfed him so many times as the Apogee.

Mmmm, it said. *She is in danger, and you are weak. Let me out. I can protect you. I can save you both!*

107

Chrys couldn't let it take over him. He couldn't lose control. The Apogee was friend to none. Would it kill the shadows? Almost certainly, but, in the war, the Apogee had killed friend and foe alike. He couldn't risk it.

But...he was so tired.

No. I am in control, he replied.

Threadlight ran through his veins, bright blue radiating across the skin of his arms and neck. He relaxed his eyes, waiting for signs of movement. There. To his right, he caught sight of a figure prowling in the shadows. He knew better than to let them get in position. Never let an enemy choose the grounds. Chrys took off toward the shadow.

An arrow flashed in his vision just in time for him to flare his threadlight and *push* it out of the way. He continued running toward the shadow. They must have known he was a Sapphire but, even still, an unexpected arrow always had a chance at landing.

The shadowed man walked forward. Chrys paused, surprised to find glowing veins peeking out from beneath the dark mask. The other three Bloodthieves stepped out into view, surrounding Chrys from all sides. All four were threadweavers, and each had their face obscured by a strange mask.

"Our mistress is merciful and offers you your life if you'll come with us. We bind your hands and eyes, and you live. If you haven't noticed, you are outnumbered."

"If you haven't noticed," Chrys spat, "you're outclassed."

The Bloodthief smiled beneath his partially veiled face. "Can't say we didn't try. Kill him. Then we kill the wife."

Iriel's voice screamed out from inside the house. Chrys' lip quivered. He knew what he was missing. And he knew the stakes. They would never have his family.

The four Bloodthieves settled into the stance of well-trained

Felian combatants. Chrys had trained enough to know what to expect but, more importantly, he had an advantage they couldn't possibly expect. He kept the black knife concealed behind the joint of his wrist as he shifted onto his toes and watched the Bloodthieves' movement. Two Sapphires and two Emeralds.

As if on cue, all four rushed him in unison. Adrenaline burned alongside threadlight as Chrys wasted no time. He leapt forward toward the Bloodthief he'd seen in the trees and crashed hard into him. But the man didn't move. It was like charging into a stone pillar. The Bloodthief's veins were lit with green threadlight as he *pulled* against his corethread, increasing his weight ten-fold. *Stones.* A thread-*pulled* elbow came crashing down on Chrys' shoulder from behind, knocking him to the ground. Chrys *pushed* hard on his corethread, launching himself back up into the air. He slipped the knife out as he rose, and let it slice through the first Bloodthief's chest. Blood sprayed out across Chrys' face as the Bloodthief dropped to the ground.

Mmmm.

The other three were on him before they could see what happened. The Emerald came barreling down onto him with an unnatural descent, threadlight burning in his veins. Chrys turned and threw him off to the side as he thrust the blade forward at one of the Sapphires. The Bloodthief instinctually *pushed* at the blade, but instead of diverting it, he watched as it buried deep into his chest. Chrys jabbed twice more through the gap in the man's rib cage before the Bloodthief fell.

Let me out. I can finish it!

Chrys turned and hurled the knife into the second Sapphire's stomach, then rushed him, pulling the knife out, and slit his throat. The last Bloodthief—the second Emerald—

rolled to his feet and stared at Chrys holding the thread-dead blade with his three companions motionless at his feet. He cursed under his breath before he sprinted for the trees. Chrys ran and *pushed* off the ground, sending himself in a high arc toward the Bloodthief. While in the air, he threw the black blade at the man's back, but it hit hilt-first. It did little damage, but it did knock him off balance, sending him tumbling into the dirt. Chrys was on him like a wolf, rage boiling inside him. His fists rained down like hellfire onto the Bloodthief's face. Fist after fist, fueling the hot fury inside.

The stranger's words filled his bloody mind. *Find the Blood-thieves before it's too late. Stop them. And, above all else, do not let them take your child.*

He'd stopped them, but he was losing control.

Inside, he could feel the Apogee squeezing through his defenses. He caught himself. He shook his head and looked down at the disfigured face below him and lost his breath as he understood how close he'd come to releasing that *thing*. He collapsed onto his back, the moon staring back at him as if it were the judgmental eye of the Lightfather.

I am in control, he lied.

He breathed on his back, bloody and broken, and remembered Iriel. A foreign sound rang out in the night. The sound of a child. *Stones.* He forced himself back up, lifted the Blood-thief's body over his shoulder, and dragged it back behind his house. Then did the same with the other three. By the end, his face was covered with dirt, blood, and sweat. He washed his face and hands in the water basin behind his house. Iriel and Amarra didn't need to know what had happened.

Chrys ran back to the front door, stripped off his outer shirt, and opened it. His red eyes filled with emotion as he saw Iriel holding the newborn child. Not because of love—no, he felt

that too—but at this very moment, he felt a profound emptiness where a beautiful memory should have lived. He'd missed
the birth of his child. This was a night he would never forget,
for reasons that should not be. The tainted frame of a perfect
moment.

At least they were safe...for now.

"I'm so sorry I missed it. I—" Chrys closed his eyes. "I'm so
sorry, Iriel."

She looked up at him, lips quivering with emotion. But it
wasn't anger in her eyes. It was resolve. "Did you kill them?"

"I—"

"Are we safe, Chrys? Tell me we're safe."

Chrys broke. A stream of heavy tears poured down his face.
He covered his eyes and shook his head up and down. He didn't
deserve her. He didn't deserve to be a father. He was nothing
but a broken man with rage in his heart. He'd already broken
the first promise he'd made when he found out Iriel was pregnant. He had promised to be to his child what his father had
never been: present. He'd failed on day one.

The midwife came back in and gave Chrys a disapproving
scowl as she helped him lift the towel-wrapped infant. "I need
to run back to my home to pick up a few more things. If the
baby gets fussy, he's probably just hungry."

He. It was a boy. The realization struck Chrys like freezing
rain, rattling his bones, and sending a shiver down his spine.
The clouds of death and danger clashed with joy and possibility. He'd wanted a boy.

But not like this.

After Mistress Amarra had stepped out, Chrys turned to
Iriel. Her breathing was calm. Even now she was more beautiful
than anything he had ever seen. Her pale complexion was
blushed and shimmering with sweat from the effort of delivery.

Her brown hair draped down, accenting her bright green eyes. He would do anything to protect her. "Thank you for not being angry."

"I *am* angry!" she said. "But not with you. We're parents now, sacrifice is part of the job."

Chrys looked at his son. She was right. Sacrifice is the core of parenthood. But while others were sacrificing time or wealth, Chrys had sacrificed a memory. An irreconcilable sacrifice. And, somehow, Chrys knew deep in his heart that it was nothing compared to the sacrifices he would have to make in the future. Tonight, they were safe, but as long as Jurius and the woman were out there, it wasn't over.

~ Flame-tailed ~
Halken

CHAPTER 10

THE NEXT MORNING, Chrys awoke to the sound of a crying child. When had he fallen asleep? He'd stayed up most of the night staring out the kitchen window, watching for the next wave of attacks. Every hour or so he'd go outside and take a loop around their home to check for Bloodthieves. The bodies of the four threadweavers lay motionless not far from the well. No one had come. He knew he should eat, but the threadsick nausea and fatigue took away any semblance of hunger he should have had.

As Mistress Amarra finished cleaning Aydin, Chrys walked over and picked him up. He felt clumsy with the child in his arms. Undeserving. He felt like an almost-hero that held the fate of the world in his hands yet knew that someday he would fail. If he could make Aydin a better man than himself, he would consider it a success. Stones, if he could keep their family alive through the week, he would consider it a success.

Mistress Amarra moved quietly to the other side of their bedroom and picked up a piece of paper. She read it over, and then pulled out a quill and stopper of ink. Her brush strokes were quick and precise, a professional in all of her midwife duties.

"Have you chosen a name for the child?" Mistress Amarra asked. "If not, you'll need to make sure you have one by tomorrow."

"His name is Aydin." Iriel turned to Chrys after saying the words, and there was a moment of mutual agreement. Chrys nodded, looking down at his son, a worthy memory of Iriel's grandfather whom Chrys had only met once before he'd passed.

"Aydin. A beautiful name." She wrote it down in her records. "I'll have this sent to the temple to have it recorded. Though there may be some leftover disarray with the passing of Father Jasper."

"Wait, what?" Chrys asked, shocked. "Father Jasper passed away? I just talked to him yesterday."

She seemed discomforted by his words. "He had a heart attack last night. He's been in the temple for so long that it's hard to imagine the place without him. And they'll have to find a replacement on the Stone Council."

Chrys didn't know how to respond. The old priest had been so lively and happy when they'd met. Unfortunately, everyone is lively until they're not.

Mistress Amarra put the birth record into her satchel. "In the spirit of being healthy, Iriel, you should stay in that bed as much as you can for the next week. I know how you thread-weavers think that you can heal faster than you actually can, so take it easy. Chrys," she turned to him, "you don't look so well yourself but, whatever you're feeling, it's nothing compared to what your wife is feeling. Take care of her. Food, pillows, anything and everything she needs for the next week. She will be fragile and in need of a little patience and tenderness. There are some notes by the bedside. I trust you can handle the task?"

Chrys nodded.

"Well in that case, I'm going to go rest up a bit myself. Make sure to keep the child well nursed. I'll be back later this afternoon to check on you." A twitch in the corner of her eye said she would rather not return prematurely.

"Thank you," Chrys responded. "We are forever in your debt."

She grunted. "If every family was in debt that I helped midwife, I could amass an army to rival the Great Lord himself. Just doing my job, General. Take care now. And don't forget, tomorrow is Andia. They will be expecting you at the temple."

As she left, Chrys saw the worry on Iriel's face. "Iriel. It'll be okay. If someone like Girtha Dimwater can have eight children, and none of them ended up deformed or dead, an intelligent, careful person like yourself will be able to figure it out."

"Girtha. Ugh. She's the worst."

He moved over to sit by Iriel on the bed. Her jaw moved up and down as she chewed on an herbal root Mistress Amarra had given her to quench the pain and exhaustion. Chrys held out Aydin in front of them so they could take a good look at their child. He touched Aydin's closed eyes. "Blue or green?"

"Green if he's lucky. The less he takes after his hideous father the better."

Chrys almost laughed. "Misshaped head, discolored skin. I'd say he's taking after *you*."

A knock came at the door.

For a brief second, Chrys panicked. He should have been watching the window. Stones. He looked down at Aydin, bundled up and sleeping quietly in his arms, and handed him over to Iriel. He went over cautiously to the door and opened it.

At the door stood a woman. Blue eyes under brown hair that ran just past her shoulder blades. Part of her looked young and beautiful, but a closer look revealed a weariness only gained by age and bitter experience.

"Mother," Chrys sighed. He fell into her embrace. He needed her there to help with the baby, but the last thing he wanted was to put her in danger as well. It took all his willpower not to unload his burdens on her. He would tell her everything, but not yet. Instead, he turned to her and introduced her to the littlest Valerian. "Say hello to Aydin. Healthy and happy."

Willow Valerian was an odd woman. Harder than most, but soft as a feather when it came to Chrys. And despite her being a threadweaver, Chrys had never seen her use her abilities, claiming the health benefits of a life free of threadweaving. She was immovable when it came to her resolve. Every opinion she held was carefully thought out and firmly held. In her roots, she was a protector, and had passed that along to her son.

"He's beautiful." She reached out to take the child, smiling as his weight shifted to her hands. "So small. I remember when you were this small, my little flower."

The phrase triggered a memory of the blonde Sapphire calling him *flower boy*. He still needed to find her, but that need was drowned out in the cacophony of bitter reality that surrounded him. Not to mention how tired he was. The physical drain of heavy threadweaving mixed with a sleepless night and emotional turmoil all weighed on him like an anchor in the Terecean Sea.

"Everything okay? You look worse than Iriel, and she just gave birth!" Willow laughed, unaware.

"I…" Chrys wavered. He wanted so badly to tell her everything, but was it safe? The last thing he needed was for his mother to be in danger as well. Unfortunately, the truth was that if she was here with them, she was already in danger. "I killed four Bloodthieves last night. Their bodies are behind the house. It's not safe for us to be here, but I don't know what else to do."

Willow's eyes grew wide. She opened her mouth to speak, but stopped, turning toward the back of the house as if she could see through its walls. "Tell me everything."

He did. He told her about Jurius' missing son. The Blood-thief warehouse. The woman with the amber eyes. The obsidian blade. About the four Bloodthieves come to slaughter their family. And through it all, Willow sat emotionless, same as Iriel had the night before. They were blank slates, absorbing each mark as Chrys penned his story. The two women were similar in many ways.

Willow stood at the end, clenching her jaw. "You were right. It is not safe for us to be here. Give me an hour and I'll come up with a plan."

"There's nowhere to go. What Jurius doesn't already know is most likely available in our records at the temple."

"They don't know everything about us."

A creaking sound rang out from the street, followed by the pitter-patter of hooves. Chrys ran over to the kitchen and gazed out the window into the street beyond. A familiar carriage trudged up the street toward his house. Stones. Two stallions led forward at a steady pace.

He turned back to the others. "Malachus is here."

Chrys hid himself as he kept an eye on the carriage through the window. Black boots exited the carriage door. Stones, no. General Jurius, face ripe with bitterness, stepped out onto the street. He bolted back out of sight, scrambling, terrified at the realization of his greatest nightmare. He had hoped to talk to

Malachus in private, but now that wouldn't happen. He reached down and grabbed the obsidian knife from his boot pocket and hurried over to Iriel and Willow.

"Both of you, take Aydin and go to the back. Lock the door. Keep the back window unlocked in case you need to go. Jurius is with him."

A minute later, a loud knock came at the door. This was it. The two women had gone to the back of the house, and Chrys prepared himself for battle. As he opened himself to thread-light, his stomach churned with discomfort. He fingered the black stone dagger in his hand. If anything was going to give him an advantage against Jurius, it was the knife.

He walked over to the door and opened it.

The Great Lord Malachus Endin and Lady Eleandra Orion-Endin stood in front of him, dressed in full regalia and flanked by both High General Jurius and High General Henna.

Malachus was grinning like a fool until he saw the knife in Chrys' hand. After a second of confusion he laughed. "'Welcome! Now I'm going to assassinate you! Stones, Chrys. Put the knife away and let us in. The breeze is chilly out here. Eleandra thought it would be nice if all of us came together to support you and Iriel."

Chrys backed up, hand still clenched onto the knife. His eyes fixed on Jurius' every movement. What had he told Malachus? The snake must have whispered something nasty before they'd come. Some smooth lie to convince Malachus that Chrys was the enemy, maybe even switching their roles and persuading him that Chrys was one of the Bloodthieves. He wanted to drive the knife into Jurius' chest and be over with it. Rage boiled in his core.

Mmmm. He will lead you to her. Let me out and I will kill them all.

Chrys shook the voice away. *No. I am in control.*

Malachus grimaced as he looked at Chrys. "You look like you spent a week starving in a Kulaian monastery studying the ancient art of insomnia. Is that what childbirth does to a man?"

Eleandra slapped his arm then glided through the waiting room. "Is Iriel sleeping? We were hoping to meet the child this morning."

He wasn't sure how to respond. Eleandra was a good woman and, if she was there, it most likely meant that they weren't there to kill or imprison him. Perhaps Jurius had said nothing. If the Bloodthieves were smart, they wouldn't want Jurius connected to Chrys' disappearance.

Chrys turned to the Great Lord. "You and Eleandra are welcome to come say hello. They should be awake, but I don't want to overwhelm her." He turned to Henna. "I hope you don't mind staying out here. I really do appreciate your visit."

Henna nodded and Jurius clenched his jaw.

Malachus and Eleandra followed Chrys back toward the bedroom, leaving the other two in the main room. They reached the door and Chrys knocked. "Mother? Lord Malachus and Lady Eleandra are here. Just the two of them. Can we come in?"

"You didn't tell me Willow was here!" Eleandra whispered excitedly; she had always been enchanted with his mother.

The door opened and Eleandra practically burst through the gap pulling Willow into a tight embrace. "Oh Willow, it has been far too long. We have so missed you around the keep."

"And I to you, my lady." She eyed Chrys out of the corner of her eye, unsure how she was supposed to react to the situation based on his previous comments.

Chrys added, "Jurius and Henna are in the waiting room. I told them we want to keep the visits small for now."

Willow nodded, making room for the Lord and Lady to enter. Smiles were in surplus as the bedroom filled with people. Eleandra found her way to the bedside to see the child, like a root to a water source. She had always wanted children but was unable. Rather than succumbing to jealousy, she had appointed herself the Mother of Alchea and taken great pride in the stark contrast of her compassionate care to Malachus' cold rule. None who had met her questioned the self-prescribed title.

"He is absolutely beautiful," Eleandra said with tender eyes.

Iriel looked up to her. "Thank you. Would you like to hold him?" She lifted Aydin toward Eleandra and gave a nod of encouragement.

"I would love to." The Lady took off her gloves and reached over with gentle hands. She lifted the child, bringing him to her chest as if she had been a mother many times before. "I am glad you trust me enough to hold him while he is still so frail. I washed my hands carefully before coming just in case."

"If anyone deserves our trust, it's you." Iriel knew she had spoken well when the corners of Eleandra's mouth curved up.

Malachus stepped over to Eleandra to look at the child who slept soundly in her careful swaying cadence. He moved to feel the child's cheeks with the back of his hand. After a single stroke he seemed satisfied with the softness and his index finger moved toward Aydin's eyelid.

Eleandra slapped his hand like a mosquito. "And what do you think you are doing?"

"Just one little peek," he said. "With Chrys and Iriel as parents, Aydin will surely be the greatest threadweaver of his generation!"

"I don't care if he is the next Drayco the Fearless, his eyes will be revealed in the temple. Even you cannot circumvent the commandments of Alchaeus. And anyhow, the color has likely yet to settle. Even if you managed a glimpse, you'd likely know as much as you do now." Her voice was passionate. Somehow, despite the innate nobility that Malachus exuded, Eleandra could still put him in his place. Some wives are trophies, some are burdens, but others are the very heartbeat of a man, so beautifully harmonized that without her the man would fade to naught.

Malachus withdrew his hand, feeling sufficiently chastised. A mischievous grin crossed his face, warning of the deep temptation to disobey. In his younger, more brash, years, he likely would have done it to spite her. The recklessness had faded, but the boldness remained. Eleandra turned from him and handed the child back to Iriel before he had a chance to reconsider. They exchanged a glance that seemed to say, *husbands, a necessary evil.*

Knowing he'd lost the battle, Malachus reached into his suit jacket and pulled out a small box. "As diverting as is your company, we have come here to present the child with a gift."

"Oh, you really don't have to," Chrys said.

Malachus gave him a bright, wide smile. "Friends do things they don't have to all the time. It is the gulf that divides acquaintance and friendship. A gift from all of Alchea, to your son." He handed Chrys the box.

Friends? It was the first time Malachus had said it. Chrys had always seen him as a master, a mentor, but friends? Chrys wasn't sure if he agreed. He hadn't even known it was an option.

The box was small but heavy. Should he open it now, or wait until they left? He hated receiving gifts. He would much rather choose something out for himself. What if he hated it? He was a terrible liar. Fortunately, it was for Aydin, not him, and newborns tend to be less judgmental.

"Go ahead and open it," Malachus said. "It's more for you than it is for the child."

Great. Chrys untied the ribbon that held the lid fast to the box. He lifted the top and set it on the nightstand. Inside was a...what was it?

The confused look on Chrys' face seemed to be the cue Malachus was waiting for. "They call it a pocket watch! The lines along the perimeter of the face represent the times of the day, and the thick line that starts from the center moves at the same speed as the sun. You don't have to go outside to tell the time of day!"

"That's incredible," Chrys whispered, turning over the device. "I've heard of the grand clock in Felia's city center, but this is so small. How does it work?"

"It's from that famous Alirian craftsman. He just invented it, and there are only a few that have been made because he refuses to teach people. He's charging a kingdom for a single watch, but they made a deal when I said I wanted a second one." A hint of pride pricked in his voice. "Anyway, congratulations on the child. I hope you like it."

"Of course," Chrys said. "It's incredible. Malachus, thank you for everything. You have been so good to us." He turned to Iriel and the child and held out the gift. "Aydin, what do you think of the pocket watch?"

"It's beautiful," Iriel responded for the sleeping child.

Malachus looked to Eleandra, who motioned to the door. "Enjoy the rest of your day and, if you need anything, you know where to find us."

Chrys' face grew serious. "Actually, there is one thing."

. . .

"Henna!" Lord Malachus came bursting out of the room followed by Chrys. "The Bloodthieves attacked Chrys and his family at their home last night. How have I heard nothing about this?"

The high general choked on her words. "I...it is the first I've heard of it, sir."

"You are supposed to be my eyes in the city. I should not discover things before you. While Chrys is here, I want a dozen guards posted out front for protection. At least two of them should be threadweavers. And Chrys says there are bodies out back behind the house. Get it cleaned up and let's see if we can identify any of them. Can't have my high general's getting murdered in their homes now, can we?"

Jurius' jaw clenched tight. "The Bloodthieves attacked him at his home? That seems very unlike them, sir. Are we sure it wasn't something else?"

"Chrys says it is Bloodthieves, and he would know better than anyone else. He says all four attackers were threadweavers as well."

"Threadweavers? We've seen no evidence that the Bloodthieves have threadweavers on their side. I'm not convinced. Is there any proof? I don't understand why you are so quick to trust his word."

"Because Chrys is a good man."

"Tell that to the children of the Wastelands."

Lord Malachus slapped Jurius across the face. "Watch your tongue, Jurius. Good men do what must be done, even if it is dark. Enough with your petty jealousy. Henna, send for the guards. Jurius, take over the Bloodthief investigation while Chrys is home with Iriel. Don't make me regret the decision."

Jurius suppressed a victorious smirk alongside his injured pride. "Of course. I apologize, Malachus. I was out of line."

As Henna and Jurius moved toward the doorway to leave, Chrys stepped forward and grabbed Henna's hand. "Thank you for coming. It was exactly what I needed. I know I may not show it often, but I have always respected your judgment."

She gave him a strange look as she glanced down at their clasped hands. He'd slipped a folded-up piece of paper into her hand. She nodded, acknowledging the secrecy. "Glad we came all the way here and were able to enjoy your living room."

Henna and Jurius made their way to the carriage as Malachus and Lady Eleandra prepared to leave. Eleandra nodded to Chrys. "If there's anything else we can do, let me know."

"Protection is more than enough. Thank you."

"Stones," Malachus laughed shaking his head. "You killed four threadweavers last night—the night your son was born. If that isn't fitting for the Apogee then I don't know what is."

"Malachus!" Eleandra shoved him out the door. "Apologies for my husband. You two get some rest when the guards get here. Congratulations again. I'm sorry it was clouded by such gloomy circumstance."

Chrys stood in the doorway and watched the four visitors climb into the carriage. Jurius was last, holding the door open for the others. A pure image of traitorous chivalry. He looked back to the house and saw Chrys standing in the doorway. He didn't smile. He didn't scowl. He stared. Chrys might be safe for the moment, but a storm was coming.

CHAPTER 11

DURING HIGH HEAT, the children of Zedalum were hired to sprinkle dirt across the main walkways. The hot, wooden pathways, encouraged by the light dusting, cooled to a dull warmth for the Zeda people traveling barefoot. At sunset, the same children would sweep the dirt into buckets to use again the following day.

Laurel walked across the soot-sprinkled path leading back to the Elder's lodge, a place she had spent far too much time at in recent days. Her thick, leather boots—a requirement for all messengers with groundside assignments—left curious lines in the dirt with each step. It was midday and the streets were filled with foot traffic. Congestion was a real issue, especially near the markets where people would carefully step off the wooden paths and onto the tree branches to avoid others. This, of course, was highly discouraged, and a few particularly congested intersections had added standing pads. They were meant to get conversations off the main road so that foot traffic would not stall. In reality, they were more often used as a quick shortcut around corners.

Laurel chose the quickest option: the threadpoles. She opened her eyes to threadlight and *pushed* on her corethread, launching herself high into the air toward a wooden beam a short distance to the side of the road. A large spherical chunk of wood hooked onto the top and a dozen support beams branched out from the center like a wooden mushroom with multiple stems. She landed atop the top sphere, wood groaning under the pressure, and immediately *pushed* back off toward the next threadpole. She smiled as she rode the wind, a bird in the sky above the busy streets.

The threadpoles were designed to be used in emergencies but, in reality, people used them whenever they wanted. Since she was headed to the Elder's lodge, she didn't expect anyone to question her. It also felt good to threadweave again. Her grandfather, Corian, had told her not to, but it relieved some of her stress to let the energy flow through her veins. The headache she'd had since waking up promptly disappeared.

She reached the lodge and found Elder Rosemary sitting on the porch with a warm cup of tea in hand. Her old teeth shined bright as she smiled at the sight of her young friend. "Well hello, my dear. Once again, I find myself painfully aware of why you are here. It's becoming quite the pattern, I do believe."

"I hope not," Laurel mumbled.

"Oh? Us old people are such a toil to be around, are we now?" Elder Rosemary peaked a brow.

"That's not what I...I'm sorry, Elder. I..."

"Come now. I was playing. We're not all bones and blood here. Some of us even have a, dare I say it, youthful spirit. Now, go get inside before you catch a case of old age."

Laurel rushed away from the awkward encounter, leaving

the elder on the front porch. She was sure that old people liked to joke about their age as a defense mechanism. Her grandfather did it all the time too. Or maybe they did it to remind her how young she was? Laurel planned on dying in some dramatic fashion long before she was as old as Elder Rosemary.

She started to threadweave, *drifting* as she walked through the halls of the Elder's lodge. She felt lighter, stronger, faster. She felt ready to take on whatever Elder Rowan could throw at her.

Down the hall, she found the lodge's council room and knocked on the door. Muted voices mumbled from the other side. Elder Rowan was generally nicer when she was giving assignments, which is what Laurel presumed this meeting was about, but part of her wanted to go find a Felian orange and try Rosemary's trick again. Just then, Elder Rosemary walked down the hall back behind her, catching up just as the door to the council room opened.

Elder Rowan, living up to high expectations, wore a frown. Unexpectedly, each of the other elders were there too. Elder Ashwa, pretty and rotund, sat to the right of Elder Rowan's empty seat. Next to her was the eldest member of the Council, Elder Violet. She should have been taken by the previous Gale, her mind already showing signs of wear; over the last five years it had continued to decline. This year's Gale would surely take her. Last, in the seat next to Elder Violet, across the circular table from Elder Rowan, was the youngest member of the Council. Elder Ivy was in her early forties, and her fair skin was a constant reminder to the other elders of their age.

But why were they all there? Laurel's mind raced with possibility. Maybe it had to do with the Bloodthieves. Some kind of super-secret mission with the future of Zedalum at stake. Or maybe she was finally going to get to travel to Felia in the west.

The port city sounded fascinating. An endless sea of water as far as the eye could see. That was the kind of adventure she wanted.

Elder Rowan made no attempt at a greeting. "Have you been weaving, girl?"

Laurel looked down, realizing that her veins were pulsing with a light blue aura. "I took the threadpoles. I didn't want to keep you waiting."

"I'm sure." Elder Rowan motioned Laurel and Elder Rosemary to enter and close the door behind them. The two elders took their seats at the table and they all stared quietly. "Laurel, we heard about what happened with the chromawolves. First, we are glad that you're still alive. You did a very stupid thing and are lucky they didn't tear you apart. Though Cara commended you for your bravery, our position on the matter is quite different. We don't need to be losing any more of our people to those blasted creatures."

Elder Violet, skin sagging and wobbling with every motion, nodded her head as she spoke. "You of all people should know how dangerous those beasts can be. This is Corian's fault for letting you spend so much time at the wolf nursery. Gives you a false sense of reality."

Laurel wanted to defend herself, to defend her grandfather. All she had done was protect Asher. When someone was in danger, you helped them. It was simple. Why were they being so harsh about it? Was she supposed to just watch as Asher got mauled and killed by the alpha? That's not the kind of person she wanted to be. Asher was her friend—one of her only friends— and she wasn't going to lose him.

You of all people. The words infuriated her. They claimed her parents had been killed by chromawolves, but Laurel knew it wasn't true. They'd covered up the truth and refused to tell her what really happened. She wasn't as naïve as they believed.

Elder Rowan continued the lecture. "Secondly, there is the matter of why you were a day late in returning home from your last assignment. It was completely inappropriate behavior for someone with such a vital role in our community. And lastly, Laurel, we believe that you've become addicted to threadlight and are no longer in a good state of health. We've discussed it at length and, effective immediately, you are relieved of all duties pertaining to serving as a messenger to the council."

The wind flew from her lungs as the words seared into her soul. She felt like she was falling. Her worst nightmare realized in the flicker of a moment. It couldn't be happening. Everything she'd worked for. Everything she'd cared about. She wanted to scream. Run. Fight. Everything about it seemed unfair. With all her heart she wanted to weave a thread so hard it shattered in an explosion of pure force. She couldn't breathe.

No longer in a good state of health? Addicted to threadlight? These women were fabricating problems to fit their narrative. They were conspiring against her. She didn't deserve to be treated this way.

Elder Rosemary leaned forward. "We like you, girl. We really do. But until you learn to rein in whatever it is that's driving you to such brashness, we can't trust you with matters of such import."

Part of her wanted to spit the whole truth about the kidnapping at them—in pure spite—just to prove some point that she knew didn't need proven. But she also knew that, if she did, the chances of ever becoming a messenger again would be gone. Did she even want that? Did she want to be beholden to the whims of these *blasted creatures* seated in front of her? They clearly didn't understand her, or respect her, or even care about her.

No. She realized in that moment that she didn't want to be a messenger. Gale take them and their rules. If she wanted to visit the grounder city, she was going to visit the grounder city. If she wanted to visit Asher, she was going to visit Asher. If she wanted to go ride on a boat at the ports of Felia, what could they do about it?

"Well?" Elder Rowan piped. "Do you have anything to say?"

Laurel looked at all five of the elders and smiled, though her eyes said otherwise. "It is what it is." She started to walk out, then turned around before rounding the doorway. "And I hope the Gale takes you all."

She could hear the shocked gasps of each and every one of the old hags as she walked away feeling invincible. It was horribly rude—a nasty Zeda curse—but they deserved a moment of real honesty from her. After all the lying she had done recently, it was the least she could do. She felt strong. She felt purpose. She was going to go back to the grounder city. She was going to explore and discover and learn. She was going to stand up for herself.

As she exited the lodge, she prepared to *drift* until she made it to the threadpoles, but realized she had already been weaving. She wondered if she could increase the threshold for her threadsickness like a muscle. Slowly stretch it to its limits, or even reset her body's expectations of what was normal. What if she could change her natural state to one that was open to threadlight?

Laurel knew exactly what her grandfather would say. "Life is more valuable than threadlight." Was she going to tell him her new plan? Probably not. He only had a week left to live anyway; no point in ruining those last few days. But she would tell Bay. He would understand. He'd be jealous because he didn't have the health to join, but he would understand.

She took off down the wooden walkway, kicking up dirt as she *drifted* along, then launched herself up toward the first of many threadpoles on the path home. People looked up at her with disapproving frowns—which was stupid. For all they knew she was rushing toward an emergency. She was starting to realize how judgmental her people were. Surely the grounders were more open-minded. The thought made her even more excited to learn about their culture and customs.

She reached her home in no time, sweat dripping down her temples from the exertion and the heat. But it felt good. She felt alert and alive.

Her brother, Bay, was in his room reading. He was always reading. It was his way of experiencing the world. For someone who'd never left the treetops, let alone the Fairenwild, he knew more about the grounders than anyone.

She couldn't help but smile as she approached the room, giving a small knock on the door and peeking her head in. "Hey, little caterpillar. Whatcha reading?"

Bay smiled as he set his book down. "I know that look. You've either done something mischievous or have a mind to. Go ahead. Spill it."

"You know me too well." She sauntered over to the bed and hopped up next to him. "There is bad news, and there is good news. What do you want to hear first?"

"Bad. Best to get it out of the way."

"Bad news is that I am no longer employed as a messenger by that pack of old, shriveled beans."

Bay shook his head rapidly like he was trying to shake something off it. "Wait, what? Are you serious? Laurel! I'm so sorry! I can't imagine...wait, why did they do it? Is it temporary?

Is this about Asher? I can't believe it. Wait, why are you smiling? What is the good news?"

"I'm going to the grounder city." She said it proudly, as if it were a divine mission from the Father of All himself.

"You're what?"

The voice did not belong to Bay.

Behind her stood her grandfather, Corian, concern plastered over his wrinkled face. He walked forward faster than she would have thought possible and loomed over her. She forgot how tall he was when he stood up straight.

"Did I hear you say you're going to the grounder city? The week before the Gale?" Corian could light a candle with the fire in his eyes. His usual level-headedness gave way to a rage that frightened her. "I can't have you going off and getting yourself killed by a bunch of miserable grounders. Who is it, Laurel? Who gave you the assignment? Rowan? I've a few words to say to her."

This is exactly what Laurel was hoping to avoid. She looked to Bay, who looked more confused than Corian. Her first instinct was to spin some elaborate story about a secret mission, but she knew Corian would find out the truth. She wished that the Gale was farther out; it would make the situation much less complicated.

She took a deep breath and stood a little taller. "No one. I'm going because I want to go."

"Out of the question! You know the laws. They'll have you killed, Laurel. This is not some game. There's a reason why we stay away from the grounders. The Elder's take containment very seriously."

Something about the way he said it made her blood boil. What gave the elders the right to control them all? She had no plans to divulge the location of the Zeda people. Laurel could feel the energy burning hotter in her veins, a hint of blue radiating across her arms. "So, we're slaves? To a few grumpy, old women? I don't think so. They can't stop me any more than you can. The winds take us where they will."

"You're as stubborn as your mother. I told her not to go out on the hunt that killed her, but she wouldn't listen to me. And look what happened! I won't sit idly by and let that happen again. You're not leaving this house. I forbid it."

She choked out of amusement. "You think you can keep me here?"

"I do." The way he looked at her, she knew he believed it.

Laurel accepted the challenge. She reached deep into her core and *pushed* against the wall next to her. The weave launched her to the side in a blur. Corian turned and his arms lit up with green. He staggered against the wall.

"Stop it!" Bay screamed. "You're going to kill him!"

Corian fell to his knees. His hand clutched at his chest. His breathing grew sporadic and irregular. Bay moved to his side. The two of them coughed in concert, a pair of weak, sick men that wanted to control her.

"I'm done being told what I can or can't do."

Laurel walked away from her family out onto the hot wooden streets of Zedalum and *drifted* toward the exit. A warm, dry breeze brushed past her as she ran. Adrenaline coalesced with the hot energy burning in her veins. Each jump from threadpole to threadpole heated her on the inside as the sun heated her from the outside.

Sweaty and angry, she reached the exit. The guard waved to her as she dropped down through the man-made hole in the feytree branches. She *pushed* down on the wonderstone and floated down to the ground like a leaf in the wind.

The call of the wonderstone was strong. It spoke to her

raging soul, urging her to release the energy inside of her in one wild *push*. But even in her adrenaline-fueled rage, she knew better than to succumb.

One of the first things Zeda messengers learned when they visited the ground was that the wonderstone was dangerous. Every once in a while, someone would return from the ground threadsick, or worse, because they'd succumbed to its seduction. It felt physical, like the wonderstone had its own gravitational pull, drawing her in toward it.

Legend was that the stone could not be broken, but Laurel figured that, if she could *push* with enough force, it would almost certainly crack. Everything breaks if you push hard enough.

She'd asked her teachers how it was built, or even why it was built, but none of them seemed to know. They gave vague answers like "the Father of All helped them." But when she asked why, they would say "he loves us" and "to protect us." Nothing about their answers felt satisfying, or even intelligible. Maybe the grounders knew the truth.

She turned away from the wonderstone, clearing her head of its cloudy enticements. Before heading to the grounder city, she needed to make a quick stop to visit a friend.

A drove of skyflies floated overhead, translucent wings fluttering in the dim light of the photospores. The green, insect-like creatures never surfaced above the treetops, but some people would capture them, bring them up, and sell them as pets. Their thin, coiling bodies were fascinating to watch as they moved through the air.

She took the path she'd taken the previous day and, after a time, found herself at the pond with rocks built up around its edge. There was no sign of the chromawolf pack. Scuff marks painted the ground where the alpha had died. Blood still littered the forest floor where they'd fought. The alpha's body was no longer there, but there were bloody drag marks to the east. She hoped Asher was still okay. Memory of the alpha swiping down at Asher's face still gave her anxiety. She was glad the alpha was dead.

The drag marks ended not far to the east near a rock formation. Fascinating. It was a boneyard. Laurel had never heard of such a thing, but surely Cara knew something about it with all the years she'd spent among them. The chromawolves gathered their dead. It seemed such an odd thing for a beast to do. It gave her more respect for them and proved that they were far smarter than most gave them credit for. She'd always sensed it with Asher, the feeling that he understood her when she spoke.

As she walked the chromawolf boneyard, she noticed a collection of fresh prints headed farther east, which she followed for quite some time before finding the pack lounging near a small stream. She set down the photospores she'd been carrying like a lantern and stalked forward, looking for Asher. He was flanked by two females. She pictured the other chromawolves bowing to him after he'd killed the previous alpha, accepting him as their new pack leader.

Among the Zeda people, women were the leaders. It seemed wild to have your leader chosen by physical strength alone when there were other attributes so much more important. The grounder nation to the east was ruled by a man, but that solidified the Zeda perception that they were fools. To the west, a woman ruled. Another reason to visit. Her grandmother used to say that true leadership is not taken by brutish means, but is earned by exemplary service to others. Men have a hard time with the latter. The idea that her culture was different than the chromawolf culture made her feel good about the matriarchy. Sure, life at Zedalum had its issues, but at least they weren't living like animals.

The trick now was getting Asher's attention without calling down a pack of chromawolves on herself, some of which were even bigger than her friend. She wondered if some day one of the larger wolves would try to dethrone him, but qualification and aspiration are often at odds, especially in leadership. Maybe she *had* spent too much time in the chromawolf nursery; she was starting to analyze their political motivations.

She snuck around the perimeter until she was closer to Asher's position. Then, she nudged him by subtly *weaving* a rock on the ground in front of him. He looked at it, confused, and then perked his head up excitedly. Without a second thought, she stepped out from the big feytree she was hiding behind and snarled.

Asher seemed like he'd already grown in the time they'd been apart. He ran forward and they leapt at each other, colliding in an explosion of laughter. It felt good to wrestle. Fortunately, the other wolves did not make a movement, and as her eyes met theirs, she could tell that they recognized her. Did they consider her part of their pack?

They tumbled on the ground for a few minutes before they were both panting of exhaustion. "I have to go away for a few days, but I'll be back. Stay safe. Maybe I'll bring you back a leg to gnaw on."

In the far distance to the east, the clear howl of a chromawolf echoed in the twilight. Then another, and another. Asher jumped to his feet and let out his own raucous howl. He looked to Laurel and gestured with his head, as if beckoning her to follow.

Together, they raced toward the sound.

CHAPTER 12

IT WAS JUST after high noon and the sun was drifting from its peak, scattered by clouds that danced over the curves of the Everstone Mountains. The white marble of the temple reflected a brilliant light that acted like a beacon for the rest of the city.

Every noise in the night had awoken Chrys, including the constant crying of their newborn when he grew hungry. Even still, he felt refreshed. His family was alive. They might just live through the week. The bad news was twofold. First, they'd had to leave their house for Aydin's Rite of Revelation day. Second, the Alchean soldiers accompanying them couldn't watch over them forever. Time was not on his side.

Part of him wanted to storm into Malachus' office and tell him everything but, without proof, what would Malachus do? Jurius was his most trusted friend for more than thirty years. Would Malachus believe that Jurius was capable of betraying him? Jurius could spin the details to make it look like Chrys was the traitor and, when Jurius had tried to stop him, Chrys had killed four men and manipulated Malachus into providing protection. It would even explain why Chrys had failed to capture any Bloodthieves in the warehouse.

He needed proof, and he needed it fast.

Chrys, Iriel, and Willow traveled up the road toward the temple accompanied by a dozen Alchean soldiers. It was a quiet journey despite the distance. The gentle rumble of the carriage put Aydin to sleep early on. Chrys walked beside the carriage; he needed the walk to distract his mind. Iriel had joined him for a very short time, wanting to stretch her legs without putting undue strain on her body. Threadweavers recovered faster from injury—the threadlight in their blood provided a small amount of healing—but not so much as to nullify childbirth after a day.

They traveled alongside the Jupyter River that ran from the ravine at the base of the Everstone Mountains all the way to Lake Landrian south of the Fairenwild. The trade route followed the river all the way from Alchea to the lake, where it split west toward Felia. It was the best way to get between the countries and, near the border, a favorite spot for bandits.

The grass was bright green against the backdrop of the wide cerulean river water, and it had Chrys wondering about the eye color of his newborn. The Rite of Revelation was such an important event for a parent, but would a parent really love their child less based on the color of their eyes? Love is not a calculated result of features and faults. Love is the unseen thread binding two souls together no matter the externalities.

He found himself at ease knowing that he would love Aydin regardless. While the rest of his life burst into raucous flames, at least he knew that. It sickened him that they were in danger because of him. He would fight the Lightfather himself if it meant they would be safe.

After another mile of walking, they reached the front steps

of the temple. Iriel paused halfway up, taking in the architectural masterpiece and catching her breath. Huge columns lined the steps up into the waiting room, where white chairs sat next to old-world mosaics lining the wall. High above the entrance arch was a pale blue stained-glass window that added to the already ethereal ambience. It was also where she'd almost lost the baby.

Chrys looked around to make sure there was nothing suspicious but saw only hills and a few temple workers. He turned to the soldiers. "You may wait out here. We'll be safe inside. And thank you."

They hadn't invited any friends or additional family. Chrys knew that at least one of Iriel's sisters would be offended, but it was better than adding more risk into the mix.

Iriel's head propped back in awe at the statuettes lining the high domed ceilings. Some things inspire wonder no matter how frequently they are experienced. A young priest sat at the front desk, eyes closed, yet keenly aware of the visitors. His hair was cut short, and he had the characteristic black robes of a priest of the Order. Beside him sat an older woman.

"Welcome, friends," the boy said. "How may I help serve you this special day?" With so many people in the city, dozens of children were brought in each week on the first day, Andia. There were three smaller temples in the city for those unable to travel up to the great temple, each with rooms set apart for performing the Rite of Revelation.

"We are here to present our child to the Lightfather," Iriel said.

"May Alchaeus bless your child." The young priest tucked his chair back and stood. "If you follow this hallway to my left, you will find a room with a few other couples waiting. Please take a seat and join them. The servant will instruct you when it is your turn." He smiled and motioned to the left. "Alchaeus bless you both."

They nodded before realizing that nodding to the blind is as effective as yelling at the deaf.

"Thank you," Chrys muttered.

The boy ironically nodded in return.

They walked through the hallway, feeling the warmth of the candles that lit the walkway. Before long they walked into a large waiting room that could have easily held twenty-five couples. Fortunately, there were only three others waiting. Some periods of the year tend to have more births. This season must have been the trough in the wave.

The other couples looked nervous and stressed. All six of them were achromats from what Chrys could tell, and he could almost hear their silent prayers begging the Lightfather to bless their child. The chance for a privileged life.

Iriel sat first, giving a courteous nod and smile to the other couples as she sat straight backed and confident. She understood that there was more to life than the color of your eyes. Of course, there was an unavoidable pride that came with giving birth to a threadweaver, much like a baker pulling a perfectly formed pastry out of the kiln. We sit and wait, hoping that our creation will come out lovely.

Time passed and the temple worker standing at the door ushered in the first couple, and then the second, and then the third. Half a dozen other couples entered the queue, keeping a steady flow. With each new couple, Chrys' unease grew. He watched them carefully, looking for any sign of duplicity. It was eerily quiet. Seven infants in a strange room should have been disastrous. The world was funny that way. Silence can calm and silence can unnerve, but it's never the one you're expecting.

The temple worker glanced behind for a moment as if he

had heard something. "Brother Valerian. Sister Valerian. The priest is ready to see you now. May Alchaeus bless your path." He opened the door and gestured for them to pass through. As Willow rose to follow, he added, "Parents and guests may wait in the room to your left."

Chrys could have requested her company like Luther had, but it was more common for the couple to go alone. Willow exited left and handed Aydin over to Iriel, but not before giving the temple worker a dirty look. As they passed through the doorway, they found themselves in the enormous ritual room. A beautiful mural covered the domed ceiling, and huge mosaics, stained glass, and ornate tapestries covered the walls. Chrys couldn't help but remember the Rite for Luther's third child and the horrible outcome. If nothing else, at least the church couldn't take his son.

To the right there was a man dressed in white seated behind a wooden desk. He smiled at them as they entered. Directly in front of the desk was a large white veil blocking his view of the rest of the room. The recorder had a pen in hand and began scribbling down notes onto the thick book in front of him. Chrys thought of the detailed records of each of the nation's threadweavers. Today they would begin Aydin's.

Directly in front of them stood a waist-high stone altar. It was covered with a white brocade fabric and curved in a manner to hold firmly whatever was placed atop. Standing at the side of the altar was a priest, dressed in an immaculate white robe in contrast to the stark black of their daily garb.

It's Father Xalan from the library, Chrys thought.

The priest beckoned them to bring the child forward and place him on the altar. Iriel moved slowly, placing Aydin down atop the soft temple linens. She had bags under her eyes, but she was indomitable.

"Welcome, and congratulations. It is just the two of you, I'm told. Willow is in the waiting room?"

"She is."

"That is well." The priest's lips curled into a smile. "I should very much like to meet her. I try to meet the families of all who come through."

"Of course, Father." Chrys realized that the statement wasn't completely true. He hadn't met with Luther's family. But it would be quite uncomfortable to meet the relations of a child you'd just blinded and taken away.

Father Xalan lifted his hands, palms up. "Again, congratulations. There is great beauty and knowledge that can be learned from the Rite of Revelation. I pray you are humble enough to see the hand of the Lightfather this day. Chrys, it is wonderful to be with you again. As patriarch you may take your place at the left point of the triangle. And Iriel, as matriarch you will take your place at the right point." His hands spread out, motioning to the ground.

They took their places. There was a knock on the floor, and they turned to see the recorder poking his head from behind the veil with a metal staff in his hand. It was the sign given to let the priest know when the parents had taken their places.

Father Xalan dropped to his knees at the altar and raised his hands high above his head. "Father of light. We come before you this holy day to present this child. Open our hearts as we open these eyes. Glory and power are yours, let us be but small conduits of your supremacy. As you will, let it be, and let our will be a thread bound only to you."

There was a reverent air of silence after the prayer as Father Xalan rose to his feet using the altar to lift himself.

"The will of the Father be manifest in this child."

He placed white gloves over each of his hands, then reached

toward the child's face, seeking through touch the insets marking Aydin's eyes. Slowly, the lids were lifted, and he placed a few drops of the clear liquid he held in a small vial. The priest opened his mouth to speak but said nothing.

His hand dropped to the side and his face washed over with stern solemnity, brows furling in thought. After a moment of silence, he turned away from the altar and walked toward the veil, reaching out a hand to motion Chrys and Iriel to wait, anticipating their confusion. He made his way across the room and disappeared behind the veil.

Glancing toward the altar to make sure that Aydin was safe lying there alone, Chrys turned to see if Iriel had any idea what was happening. There was no similar interlude during the Rite for Luther and Emory's child. But then again, that was their third child and a whole different situation.

There were whispers from behind the veil, and then the room echoed with the sound of something heavy hitting the floor. Chrys and Iriel turned to each other confused.

Father Xalan walked back around the edge of the veil into view. But something had changed. His posture was stronger. His head was higher. His eyes were open.

Eyes that were not blind.

Eyes that were not murky from acid exposure.

No. They were bright eyes that shined like Sapphires in the daylight.

"We need to talk," the priest said.

CHAPTER 13

A CHILL SHOT THROUGH CHRYS. Father Xalan wasn't blind. Which meant that he wasn't really a priest. And that almost certainly meant...Bloodthief.

They were in danger.

Chrys reached instinctively for a weapon. Finding the obsidian dagger at his side, he left his corner of the triangle and jumped into position between the priest and his family even as Iriel jumped forward to grab their son. Rage boiled inside him.

Mmmm. Let me out! I can protect you!

Chrys focused. *No, I am in control.*

He balanced himself, feet wide, ready to intercept the priest. He let threadlight pour over his vision and waited only a moment before his anger sent him charging toward the false priest. Xalan was not as fast as Chrys and took a blow to the chest after dodging the hilt of the blade.

"Chrys!" The priest leapt back out of range. "You must listen to me. I am not here to hurt you."

"You cannot have my family!"

Chrys leapt forward again slashing with his dagger. The priest extended his hand, expecting the dagger to redirect as he tried to *push* the thread that was not there. The knife sliced across his palm, bright red blood staining the sleeve of his white robes. The priest stumbled back, clutching his cut hand to his chest.

"Open his eyes!" the priest shouted, backing up and placing his hands up in the air. "Open your son's eyes and tell me what you see. I am not your enemy! The farthest from it. The truth is ...just look at the boy's eyes."

It took all of Chrys' control not to heave the knife into Xalan's chest then and there, but it was clear that the man was too old to escape.

"You move, you die," Chrys commanded.

It could be a trick. He backed up, walking toward the altar where Iriel held Aydin, then turned, reached down and opened Aydin's eyes.

Staring back at him was...impossible. They were not blue like Sapphire. They were not green like Emerald. They were not brown like an achromat. They were a piercingly bright yellow. The same color as the woman, like the pollen of a daisy had been suffused over the iris.

Chrys' eyes widened, and he took a step back. A thousand questions flashed through his mind as he took in the information. He looked back to Xalan. "What did you do to him!"

The priest shook his head. "I could not do this if I tried. There are stories of people with such eyes. Let me bring you to those who can answer your questions. We can keep the child safe, and they will have answers for you."

The stranger who'd saved Iriel once again came to mind. He'd said, *"Do not let them take your child."*

Chrys snarled. "If you think I'm so easily deceived, you've

misjudged your standing. Do you work for Jurius or the woman? You'll find that killing me is a much more difficult task than you're prepared for."

"I'm fifty-two years old, child. Not a prime choice for an assassin."

Chrys' lip twitched. "The veil worker disagrees."

"He's not dead. And it doesn't matter; we need to get your son out of the city. I had far different plans for today, believe me. But if we don't leave now your child will be taken from you. They will kill him, imprison him, or worse. The way I see it, you have two choices. You can come with me, or you can burn the color out of his eyes."

"Or I can leave with my family and figure it out on our own."

Just then, the recorder limped out from behind the veil holding his head. He looked to Chrys and the priest and his eyes grew wide. Father Xalan wasted no time, slipping a pen out from under his robes and sending it surging through the air with a strong *push*. It ripped into the recorders neck and buried itself deep into his artery.

Chrys wasted no time, lunging forward and holding Father Xalan with the black knife to his neck. "I should kill you."

Mmmm.

"The world will think it was you," Father Xalan said stoically. "You gave me no choice."

Thoughts raced through Chrys' mind. Was he right? No. Chrys was reputable enough that people would believe him. Except for one problem: Jurius. This would be the perfect opportunity to paint Chrys as a murderous traitor. He'd be the Apogee once again. And if Jurius ever found out about Aydin's eyes...

"Tell me the truth. Who are you?"

"That is more complicated than you know."

"Simplify," said Chrys.

"It is easier if I show you. May I?" Father Xalan pinched at his robes. "I promise there are no weapons—or things that could be used as weapons—beneath my robes."

Chrys released him but kept the knife at the ready.

Father Xalan peeled off his ceremonial garb, down to his blacks. "My name is Pandan. I am from Zedalum in the Fairenwild. I came here many decades ago as a spy in hopes of finding...that is not important. It is my duty to send reports to the elders of Zedalum about the happenings in Alchea. I was not here for your son, but I think the Father of All may have had this in his plans all along. I promise you on the wind that I will do everything in my power to protect him."

The room spun. Chrys had heard of the Zeda people. They were supposed to be deformed, dark creatures that lived in the Fairenwild, feasting on the raw flesh of animals. The Wasteland savages of the west. A scary story to discourage youth from going into the forest. No one actually lived in the Fairenwild. The dank darkness was less inviting than a sewer. Not to mention the chromawolves. This liar claimed to be a Zeda. But what if he was telling the truth? If there was truly a city in the Fairenwild, what safer place could there be for his family?

"Prove it."

Pandan hesitated. "Our people mark ourselves when we come of age." He pulled the black robes off his shoulders, exposing his bare back as he turned. A feytree was tattooed between his shoulder blades, roots growing over a large circle. The branches...the girl.

A vision swam before his eyes, a girl climbing a ladder, her hair swaying to reveal a tattoo on her back. The tattoo he'd seen; this was it. She too was a Zeda.

"Are there others of your people here in Alchea?"

"No. Just me."

"Was there a young, blonde Sapphire here last week?" Chrys hoped to have at least one answer to the thousand questions piling up.

"Laurel?" Pandan looked concerned. "How?"

That was it. "She and I had a brief encounter. I saw the same tattoo on her back. We'll need more answers when there is more time but, if you'll lead us to Zedalum, we'll go with you."

"What?" Iriel exploded, her eyes smoking fury. "Are you insane? Stones, Chrys. We can't go with him. He just killed an innocent man!"

Chrys turned to her. "Jurius will pin the murder of the recorder on me. If he's telling the truth—and I have reason to believe he is—then we found our safe house while we figure things out with the Bloodthieves. I understand how it sounds, but do you trust me?"

Iriel's jaw clenched tight. "Yes."

Pandan started walking toward a door on the far end of the room. "I promise more answers will come, but now is not the time. The temple workers will be checking on us soon. We need to leave."

"I still think this is a bad idea," Iriel reiterated.

"You'd be crazy not to, but Aydin's eyes are the same as the woman I told you about. Whether what he says is true or not, we're in even more danger than we were before." Chrys moved closer and whispered to her so that Pandan couldn't hear. "I believe him, but I don't trust him. Keep an eye out."

They ran through a sunlit corridor that curved to the right, taking them further into the vast temple interior. Pandan moved swiftly without looking back, assuming that their decision to follow him still held true. The way he moved was slightly off, like a warrior returning to the battlefield after a time away.

They came to a door and Pandan stopped. "Follow my lead. If anyone asks, I am giving you a tour. Only priests are allowed in this part of the temple, but your status and name should grant some leniency. They can punish my disobedience tomorrow."

No one smiled at his joke.

He closed his eyes and pushed open the door. "This building is often referred to as the Dreams," Pandan announced loudly. "Home to many of history's greatest prophecies and dormitory for the vicars of the Lightfather."

There were upward of twenty people in the room, three of which were priests, a handful of temple workers tending to their needs, and a dozen priestesses. It looked to Chrys like some kind of common room, with large circular tables, bookshelves, and storage containers filled with tools.

An older priest rose from his chair and stepped toward them.

"Father Xalan?" the elderly priest asked. "I thought you were leading the Rite of Revelation today. I presume there to be a good reason that you bring a tour through our sacred halls?"

"Of course, Father Andrum," Xalan said humbly. "The Great Lord has asked me to show High General Chrys Valerian, and his lovely wife Iriel, the inner sanctuary of the temple. For anyone else I would have denied the request. I'm aware it is quite unusual. If it displeases you, I will end the tour early and send word to the Great Lord of the misunderstanding."

Father Andrum stood thoughtfully with his lips pursed. "It is our solemn duty to observe the commands of our blessed ruler. Please, continue, but next time be sure to warn the brethren, so as to avoid interjections. Apologies for the disruption, Lord, Lady. May Alchaeus bless you all."

"Thank you, Father."

Chrys sat back and watched Xalan, or Pandan. Stones. How long had he lived here among the priests, the only one able to see? The only one able to read facial expressions and body movements.

There was something morally wrong about manipulating the blind, blasphemous even. Pandan was a professional counterfeit. How long had they lived with a traitor in their midst? Unaware.

Apparently, they were blind in more ways than they knew.

A loud bell rang out from across the campus. They moved across the room and Pandan opened a door, ushering them through, eager to be away from the other priests. Chrys saw two guards burst through the other door and into the common room just as their door closed.

"They must have found the body." Pandan continued walking. "There is an exit close by, and it should be guarded by no more than three men. That shouldn't be a problem."

"We are not killing more people," Iriel said. "One is more than enough. We still don't trust you, and a flippant suggestion of murder isn't helping your case."

"I agree. The guards are good men and shouldn't be harmed," Chrys said. "Can we not just walk past?"

"I was not suggesting...it does not matter. The bells are a complete lockdown of the temple. I was hoping to reach the exit before it sounded. We should obviously try to get past them without violence if possible," Pandan hesitated, "but if they refuse, then we may need to try an alternative approach."

They all understood his implication and nodded. Pandan led the way through a long corridor. A servant ran past them going the opposite direction and stopped in his tracks as he realized that Pandan was running with his eyes opened. They slowed to a walk and turned a corner, out of sight of the servant, Pandan closing his eyes as they rounded the bend.

At the end of the hallway were two guards in front of a large wooden door. They stood strong with their hands on the hilts of their swords, alert and ready for action. *Stones*, Chrys thought, *any other day and I'd give them a few shines for their vigilance.*

"Father," the left guard spoke as they approached. "The doors are sealed until the bell chimes again. I apologize for the inconvenience."

"There is a time for obligation, and there is a time to set it aside. We are the reason the bell rang." Pandan spoke with authority, as if his word was law. "You may recognize High General Chrys Valerian. This is his wife and son. They are in danger. A guard was murdered during their Rite of Revelation, and I am leading them away to safety. Your duty is not to protect a door. It is to protect the people inside. Let us pass or raise your blades. I am taking this family through that doorway."

The guards looked to each other, unsure how to respond to the imposing priest. They both waited for the other to make the call, scared of the repercussions. Chrys wasn't sure what he would have done in their position. When promise and purpose differ, which do you choose?

"We probably report to the High General anyway," the left guard said. "Father, keep them safe."

Chrys let out the breath he'd been holding.

"Thank you, brother," Pandan said. The comment was more than a simple thank you. Most priests, when speaking to others, referred to them as son or daughter. In calling the guard *brother*, Xalan had given him an acknowledgement of respect. The guards parted, and they passed through the doorway.

Iriel paused. "If we turn back now, Chrys, we can tell the guards what happened. We can take Aydin and go home. If we go with him, we're complicit. *He* killed the recorder. *He* lied about who he was. *He* made a mockery of our religion." Her skin grew redder as she continued. "You saw how easily he lied to those guards. Who's to say he hasn't done the same to us?"

"I assure..." Pandan started.

"Quiet!" Chrys snapped. He felt the fire burning within him. His mind raced back and forth, weighing the realities of their situation. If they left with him, there was no doubt he'd be tied to the murder of the recorder, never able to return to Alchea safely. If they did not leave with him, he might still be tied to the murder and his son's eyes would put his family in even greater danger than it had been. Either way they needed to leave Alchea.

Jurius and the Bloodthieves were a guaranteed danger. There was still a chance that Pandan was not.

Iriel stood staring at him, trying to discern his expressions while waiting to hear his thoughts. It was a gamble, but following Pandan was the best move. "I trust you, Chrys. If there were another way, you would have thought of it. Say the word, and I'll stop questioning."

Chrys nodded, turning to Pandan. "It is the best choice we have. Lead the way."

CHAPTER 14

OFF IN THE DISTANCE, Chrys could see a few of the Alchean soldiers still surrounding their carriage near the entrance to the central building. The rest must have rushed inside when the bell rang. Soon, Chrys would be the enemy.

Pandan stole three horses from the front steps and brought them around the corner to where they were hiding. They helped Iriel up and gave her Aydin to hold. He saw a hint of green in her veins as she promised Chrys that she could handle the ride. It was common practice not to threadweave while your child still nursed—some claimed that it caused the milk to go rancid—but it was just a superstition.

Pandan and Chrys jumped up onto their own horses and they headed toward the city.

The journey was long, but they made good time. Not long before sunset, they reached their home. Pandan took point watching outside the house while they gathered their things.

"Take only necessities, we need to move quickly. We have to get to the Fairenwild before we're followed."

They all jumped at a rustling in the bushes not far off, but nothing appeared.

Chrys gathered a large bag of clothing and other supplies, then paused. This was the only home they had ever known. This could be their last chance to see it. Years of memories were being put to rest out of fear. Fear for their son. Fear of the unknown. Was he making the right decision?

When he got to the doorway, Chrys saw his elderly neighbor, Emmett, waddling over toward their house. He was the oldest man Chrys knew, far older than he had any right to be. His eldest son looked after him and was the one who'd run to fetch their midwife.

He was intercepted by Pandan.

"Good evening, brother."

"Huh?" Emmett squinted at him. "Oh yes, you must be the estranged half-brother my father told me about all those years ago. Pity you lost your manhood in that fight with a frisky Felian."

Pandan's jaw dropped and a strained smirk crossed Chrys' lips.

"Unless of course you're the half-brother from my wife's side. The one with three nipples and a mole larger than the lot. Or perhaps you're just in my way. Do move, young man. Chrys and I have a matter to discuss."

"Young man? Chrys is...he's helping with the baby. Can you come back another time?"

The old man scowled at him. "I can see him standing in the doorway. Are you blind? Now, this is important, and won't take long. So why don't you roll your stones out of the way before I test their resolve."

Without giving Pandan a chance to respond, Emmett

ambled down the path and up the porch to the front door. "Chrys."

The old man was one of the nicest people Chrys had ever met. Quirky as a crystal, but soft as silver. They had become genuine friends over the last few years. "What can I do for you, Emmett? We're in a bit of a hurry."

"Your mom asked me to keep an eye on the house. Said some strange folk been showing up and to let you know if I saw anyone. Well, when you were gone, I saw someone sneaking around your house. You tell your mom I let you know. She's a fine woman she is."

Ignoring the disturbing conclusion, Chrys thanked him and rushed back to the bedroom.

"Iriel, we need to go."

She was at the bedside table, nursing Aydin in one hand and holding the pocket watch Malachus had gifted them in the other. "If we can get to Felia, all we have to do is sell this and we'll be okay."

Chrys watched as she packed it away and tightened the drawstring on her sack. For a moment he stood quietly in the bedroom doorway staring at the bed, eyes glazed over as he stored away the precious image for what might be the last time. He was leaving behind a piece of himself.

He walked out of the house. Pandan still waited with the horses. Chrys helped Iriel back up into the saddle and lowered his voice. "Someone was here earlier, and they very well could be watching us right now. No more stops. We go straight to the Fairenwild. Stones, but I wish we could have grabbed my mother. She'll be in danger because of her connection to us."

"Your mother can take care of herself," Iriel said, looking down at him from the horse.

"I too would love nothing more than to wait for Willow,"

said Pandan, "but the first place the guards will look is where we are. The elders will let us come back for her at a better time."

As much as Chrys hated it, Pandan was right. They took off back down the road, galloping and moving as fast as they could. The journey through the fields west of Alchea passed in a blur, the group only stopping for a few minutes to give Iriel time to reposition herself so she could nurse the child while they rode. The perpetual movement of the galloping horse helped lull Aydin into a deep sleep.

Finally, the top of the Fairenwild came into view.

Chrys had only been there a few times, and only when he was younger. Some youth found it entertaining to see how deep they could go before turning back. An appalling brand of childish machismo. No one made it far. Between the eerie darkness, hugweed, treelurks, chromawolves, and tales of the Zeda, no one dared venture far.

The trees looked like they were made for the gods. Huge lumbering structures taller than most buildings in Alchea, without a single branch growing until their highest peaks. Limbs sprouted forth every which way, fighting and clashing with their myriad neighbors, creating a curtain of darkness overhead that draped the ground in shadow. The branches, so dense in their mesh, formed a single structure, like a roof held up by thick support columns.

It was wonderfully quiet, which was exactly what they needed. With all of the commotion and intensity at the temple mixed with the hovering cloud of danger, the silence was refreshing. They slowed to a walk, the tree line only minutes away, and Chrys looked up at Iriel and their new son. No other woman could have endured so much so near childbirth, but Iriel was a fighter. If he lost his home, his position, and his friends, he knew that it would be okay so long as he had her.

Chrys wondered how they would navigate the Fairenwild. If Pandan wanted to spring a trap, it would be the perfect place. Chrys still didn't trust Pandan, and there were surely dangers in the Fairenwild waiting for them, but at least Jurius was behind them.

"Run!" Pandan shouted, snapping Chrys out of his reverie.

Chrys looked back over his shoulder and was terrified to find a troop of twenty soldiers riding warhorses toward them. The Fairenwild was close enough that they might be able to reach it before the soldiers overtook them. He slapped the horse to move and they all galloped as fast as they could.

The wind grew stronger as they drew closer to the trees, the pounding of horse feet growing louder and louder behind them. The angry flame in the pit of Chrys' stomach grew stronger, but this time he didn't want to suppress it. Twenty soldiers? Not impossible.

Just then Pandan stopped. "Keep going! I'll hold them off. You have to get to Zedalum. Head toward the center of the Fairenwild. Follow the yellow roses."

Chrys scowled. The soldiers *would* catch up to them; it was only a matter of when. In the dark of the Fairenwild they could hide, or fight. On the green fields, the warhorses would put them at a much greater disadvantage. Pandan might be able to slow them down long enough for his family to hide, but finding a secret city in the middle of the Fairenwild without a guide was highly unlikely.

"Not an option!" Chrys kicked Pandan's horse in the rear and it took off running.

The beating of hoof on dirt grew to a roar, like a wave crashing overhead. Chrys' heart beat fast, burning hot with adrenaline and threadlight. They were almost there. He turned around just in time to see an arrow falling down toward him. He *pushed* its thread, sending it off in another direction, then realized that Pandan had stopped once again. Arrows streaked down toward the Zeda spy, but he swatted them out of the sky like flies, his veins glowing Sapphire blue.

There was no time to go back for him, so Chrys made a decision. He ran. The old man was going to die for them. It was in that moment that Chrys understood. Pandan had been telling the truth. Somewhere in the Fairenwild were the Zeda people, and they had answers.

———

PANDAN HADN'T FELT this way in decades. His blood sang with threadlight as his horse charged toward the oncoming soldiers. He jumped off as soon as he grew near and danced between the enemy's horses. He *pushed* spears out of the way, spun around rearing hoofs, and dodged incoming arrows. His body wasn't as sluggish as he would have expected, but threadlight had a way of making up for lost years.

A thick boot thrust toward his head, but he dropped low, moved in close, and *pushed* hard on the ground. He launched up in a monstrous uppercut that knocked the soldier off his horse, dropping his spear to the ground. Pandan picked it up and used it to stab into the thigh of a second horse. It crashed forward causing two others to collide.

He'd been a guard once upon a time—before he'd convinced the elders to let him go—but nearly thirty years had passed since those days in the Fairenwild. His breath was heavy and his muscles sore after only a few moments of combat. At least half of the soldiers had stopped to deal with him; the rest were led by a copper-colored stallion that chased off toward Chrys and his family. Hopefully it would be enough. He smiled because he knew that this very moment was the reason he had been at the grounder temple all those years. It wasn't for her—she was just who the Father of All had used to keep him there. It was for Chrys. For the child. The Gale should have taken him long ago but today, with the wind in his face, he would die knowing that he'd served a greater purpose.

He prepared himself for the soldiers that charged him, but then his left arm went numb. His heart was too old for so much threadlight. It was giving out. He fell to the ground, clutching at his chest just as a soldier tackled him from behind. Dust rose from the ground as his knees hit. He could feel the threadlight in his chest, it was too much for his aged heart.

Just before the world faded away, Pandan caught one final glimpse of Chrys at the edge of the Fairenwild.

And smiled.

As CHRYS and Iriel reached the edge of the Fairenwild, their horses reared back, neighing wildly, refusing to enter even a step. Iriel was almost thrown from the beast before Chrys helped her dismount. They left the horses hastily and dashed into the forest. Strange, bulbous spheres swayed back and forth glowing from the end of long reeds. Photospores.

Chrys glanced back. A familiar man rode a familiar stallion. Jurius. Less than a dozen soldiers followed close behind. Chrys ran deeper into the forest. From behind, he heard the whinnying of the warhorses as they reached the edge of the Fairenwild, refusing to step foot inside.

They rounded a small hill and Chrys whispered to Iriel. "We can't outrun them. We need to hide."

"But Aydin."

Stones. "Feed him. Pat him. Rock him. Whatever you have to do to keep him quiet."

From the small hill, he could see a group of large bushes with relatively few photospores nearby. He pointed to them and started moving forward. Iriel followed close behind. Pulling out his dagger, he cut his way into the shrubs, creating a small pocket for them to burrow into. It was uncomfortable, tight, and hardly provided enough cover to hide but, in the dark forest, it would have to do.

They sat in silence, Aydin cuddled up to Iriel, and Iriel cuddled up to Chrys. Sharp, jagged branches pricked from every angle. Jurius and the guards rounded the hilltop. It took all of his willpower not to break out of the bushes and charge forward in fury. Chrys' stomach churned with hate.

Mmmm, the Apogee whispered. *Let me out! I can protect you! I can protect them!*

Chrys closed his eyes and shook his head back and forth. *No. I don't need you. I am in control.*

For a split second his mind lingered on the idea. The Apogee had killed far more men by himself during the War. Was it more dangerous to let him out, or to keep him in? No. He couldn't become that man. Never again.

Far in the distance, a deep howl echoed beneath the vaulted canopy.

Stones.

Eight soldiers prowled like predators, each footstep a muffled echo on the mossy dirt. Chrys held Iriel tight. Jurius yelled something, pointing every which way. The guards fanned out to search. One of them veered right and set his trajectory directly toward their hiding spot. His eyes peered into the darkness, searching, but the lack of spore luminescence made it difficult to see.

He moved, now only ten feet away from the bushes. His attention diverted as he looked back toward his companions. They were widespread and the quiet intensity told that none had yet found their quarry.

He moved, now only five feet away from the bushes. They could hear his breath as they inhaled and exhaled through their hands to mute the sound of their own.

He moved, now only two feet away from the bushes. Dangerously close. His boot brushed up against the twigs at the base of the shrubs. His eyes brushed over the bushes but then looked away.

They held their breath.

Another howl echoed in the distance, drawing the attention of the soldier.

He moved, now five feet away from the bushes. They exhaled. He kept walking forward, oblivious to their location.

Little Aydin, understanding only the cold and his hunger, let out a small screech. The guard turned around. It was loud enough that several of the others turned to face the source of the noise, including Jurius, who came sprinting.

Iriel clapped her hand over the infant's mouth, aware that such a dangerous action was the only choice. It successfully muted the noise, but the closest guard could still hear the faint whining. He approached, squinting to see better.

Chrys' chest seethed with fury. This is not how they were going to die. He wouldn't die hiding in some brush like a coward. He would die fighting.

Mmmm. Let me help!

"I don't need you!"

Chrys screamed as he kicked his foot out of the brush into the guard's stomach. He ripped himself out of the hiding place, twigs and leaves cutting deep into his skin as he exited. He got low and tackled the guard to the ground, yanking the dagger out of its sheath. By the time they hit the ground, he'd already thrust it deep into the guard's breast.

Yes! Let me out! Let me finish it! You cannot protect your family alone!

The other guards saw him and sprinted forward.

As Chrys rose to his feet ready to make a stand, veins burning blue and soul filled with anger, death flashed before his eyes. He imagined Iriel, run-through, bleeding out. Pandan, trampled, rain falling on broken corpses. And Aydin, dead, lying on a table. He knew what would happen if he failed. He couldn't fail. He was going to kill them all.

Mmmm. I will kill them all.

"Get out of my head!"

An arrow flew through the darkness and slammed into Chrys' shoulder. He stumbled back, shouting as he ripped it out of his arm.

Mmmm. You will fail!

"No, I will not!"

Jurius appeared, leaping forward while Chrys wrestled his demon. His fists blurred in the dim light, cutting low, swinging wide, testing boundaries. Chrys reacted in turn, blocking and swatting aside each attempt. Jurius kicked hard and Chrys caught a foot in mid-flight, rotating and throwing Jurius down to the ground. The high general launched himself back, *pulling* recklessly against the base of a feytree. He blasted forward into Chrys' body. The black knife broke free of Chrys' grip and tumbled to the ground.

Chrys looked to the knife, but Jurius was on top of him

before he could move, pummeling his face and chest with ruthless savagery. Years of aggression released in moments of unadulterated brutality. The forest grew darker and darker with each primal punch. Slam. *Iriel*. Slam. *Aydin*. Crack. *Pandan*.

As Chrys' consciousness fled from his broken body, he had a sick realization.

He *did* need the Apogee.

Mmmm.

"No!" Iriel screamed out from the bushes.

A massive shadow burst out of the darkness and crashed into Jurius. Enormous canine teeth clamped down onto his shoulder. Jurius flared the threadlight in his veins and *pulled* hard against the nearest feytree, tearing his body away from the chromawolf's jaws.

More chromawolves crept out of obscurity and pounced on the Alchean soldiers. Tendons and ligaments ripped away from their mortal frames.

Chrys lay panting on the ground, watching the photospores bobbing back and forth, shadows dancing on dying men.

Jurius scuttled away, rebuffing another advancing chromawolf. He took off to the east, leaving his men behind, desperate to escape.

Chrys was barely conscious—his sight blurred in and out—but he could hear everything. He lifted himself to his feet, groaning as his broken rib jutted into tender flesh. He walked in circles trying to make sense of the chaos, but all he could hear were screams, and all he could see was a family of dancing shadows and shades of red.

Iriel. Where was Iriel?

A low growl drew near. Chrys' blurry eyes sharpened, and he turned to see a massive creature standing in front of him. Thick green fur mixed with cords of white running down its back. Two tails, like a scorpion's barb, danced high above it as it bore its monstrous fangs.

He'd failed.

They were all going to die.

He fell to his knees and closed his eyes. If only he'd let the Apogee take control.

"Asher! Stop!"

He tried to open his eyes, but they'd gone black. A blurry figure stepped forward. A girl's voice. She spoke to the beast. It bowed its head to her. His mind spun along with the world around him.

"Gale take me, it's you!"

~ Sandhog ~

CHAPTER 15

Alverax lifted a hand to shade his eyes from the beating desert sun. He groaned. A deep soreness throbbed in the muscles throughout his shoulders and neck. As he tried to sit up, a searing pain ripped through the flesh of his chest, drawing his eyes to a complex weave of fresh markings and a large scar over his heart. He fought through the pain and stumbled to his feet before realizing that the unstable footing below wasn't sand. It was bones. His head swung on tender hinges as he took in his surroundings.

Heralds save me.

He was knee deep in decayed human remains. The smell hit him like a scorpion, inserting its stinger down his nostrils and tickling his throat. He heaved but managed to keep himself from vomiting. Most of the corpses had finished their course, but a few scattered throughout the crater still clung to their hollow shells. The freshest of them had festering wounds across its chest. The sight of it terrified him; he had never seen a dead body before. His heart pounded in his chest and his head pounded in his skull as he tried to recall how in the hell he'd got there. He was alive, wasn't he?

Pain answered the question quite regrettably.

He looked down at the source and remembered the marks on his chest. His finger traced a single line of raised flesh that arced under his collarbone and circled over his heart. It was tender, but the wound was sealed. He was no stranger to scars after a careless life, but this was no simple scar. It reminded him of the large line of scarred flesh on his upper back. At least now he was symmetrical.

His eyes darted back and forth over the dozens of skeletons baking in the pit around him. What was he doing there? He had no recollection of dying, but then again most people don't.

Breathing was difficult as he took careful steps toward the edge of the crater. He tried his best to use femurs as stepping stones, their wide surface area lending well to the task.

It is a curious thing to experience horror. The mind has a way of dulling such moments to preserve its own sanity.

Bones crunched under foot as he traversed the pit. A rib jutted upward from the force of his step and cut into his heel, leaving a red stain on the ivory landscape. It's not good to be naked in the desert. The thought brought a smile to his lips. He knew he shouldn't laugh, but the sun was blistering and his mind was swimming with pain and confusion.

The first step was to get out of the crater. He laughed as his foot crunched down on bone. *Technically, the first step was a pelvis.*

He climbed up over the rim of the pit, awkwardly maneuvering to avoid pressure against his chest. When he got out, he counted like his grandfather had taught him. *One. Two. Three. Four. Heralds calm a troubled core.* But it didn't work. As he looked out into the desert beyond, he knew where he was, and he was starting to remember what had happened to him.

"*SUBJECT THIRTY-ONE. With a focus on insertion strategy four—pertaining to specific placement within the left ventricle—and incision process six.*"

Alverax lay next to the surgeon, eyes closed, counting over and over again as his toes shivered on the cold bed. His arms and legs were double strapped to the table with another band across his forehead. He was shirtless, his chest covered with ink marks that the doctor had applied. Four others watched over him, one of them taking note. Amongst them was a woman with jet black hair and eyes the color of the sun.

She stepped forward to get a better view. "Proceed with caution. We're getting low on material."

He felt sick. Of course, it was either this or be fed to the necrolytes, and he'd watched that happen before. Herald's knew he wasn't going to die that way. The tingling of his toes had spread to the rest of his body, each limb now numb. Whatever they'd given him was working. They'd told him that he had to be alive, and he had to be awake.

It hadn't gone well.

Alverax's body shook like an earthquake, vicious spasms sending his chest and limbs flailing as his body rejected whatever they'd done to him. His veins turned black, then pulsated a dark, radiant energy as he let forth a blood-curdling howl. His eyes opened wide, irises black as night, twin voids of pure darkness.

The woman cursed the response, and Alverax succumbed to the pull of death.

So, he *had* died.

That meant he was free! No one comes looking for a dead man. Debts? Gone. Justice served. He laughed out loud, a naked mad man in the middle of the desert. Better to be naked and mad than dead.

Alverax stumbled toward the entrance to Cynosure, the desert hideout for a growing group of anti-establishment rebels. It had been around for nearly one hundred years. Everyone knew about its existence, but no one cared. It was far enough south into the deserts of Silkar for its reality not to matter. Alverax had lived there his whole life, like many others. As he walked closer to the entrance, he hoped his friend was on duty, otherwise he'd have to make up some elaborate lie about how he got there. It was the only useful thing he'd ever gotten from his father: the gift of guile.

A small leafling scuttled past his feet. Stepping on its jagged, leaf-shaped shell would tear his foot apart, but otherwise they were harmless little lizards. Some people ate them, but Alverax preferred fish.

He rounded a shaded rock overpass and found himself face-to-face with the entrance, a tall, wide gap in a massive sandstone mountain. At first glance it looked like a deep cave, but he'd been there once before and knew it for what it was. One of the three entrances to Cynosure.

Two guards were posted inside, and neither of them were his friend. They looked at his nakedness with cautious curiosity.

"Gentleman!" Alverax laid on the charm.

The guards put their hands to hilts. The taller of the two spoke first. "Who the hell are you?"

"Alexander Grant. But let's cut to the part where you ask why I'm naked. As much as I'd love to chalk it up to some form of skin therapy I learned in Kulai, the truth is that I lost a bet with Jelium. You know how he is. Not the type of man to let you keep the clothes on your back." He lifted his hands to the side, palms up.

Everyone was terrified of Jelium. His fat face, his fat hands, and his fat head. The man was a big pile of lard that controlled everything. Commerce. Women. Gambling. But neither his prestige nor his girth was what was most terrifying about Jelium.

The taller guard raised a skeptical brow. "What the hell happened to your chest?"

"Torture is a psychopath's favorite pastime."

The other guard who had been silent up until then, slapped the other on the shoulder. "Heralds. Just let him in. He looks like death."

"Alexander Grant, you said?"

"From head to toe, and every bit between."

The guard shivered, still standing face-to-face with Alverax' dangling indecency. He wrote something down on a ledger and let Alverax through the wide passageway. They all but turned away completely as he entered. He was so happy to be out of the sun that he almost forgot. "Either of you have a towel I can borrow? Err...that I can have?"

They shook their heads, still facing forward, neither wanting any further exposure to his exposure.

Alverax had been out the front gate once before with his father and had a good memory for directions. If he took the first fork to the right, it should take him directly to the city. Then he needed to find Jayla so she knew he wasn't dead. She'd always been fascinated with the scar on his back, her hands tracing it over and over as they kissed. She was going to love the new additions. And that meant...his feet moved a little bit faster.

The pain in his chest throbbed with each step, but he was used to it now. They had done something to him, but it had failed and killed him. Almost. His grandfather was right. *Us Blightwoods don't die easy.* Of course, his father had also said the same thing the night before he was executed. Thieves were always optimistic until they were dead.

He wondered what they would do if they found out he was alive. The whole situation was infuriating. He'd been framed, and because of who his father had been everyone believed it. They'd never told him where their "intel" came from that indicted him, but it was almost certainly Jelium, the man who looked like the human version of a sandhog. Someday he'd pay.

Alverax rounded a corner to a panoramic view of Cynosure. The city was a sprawling metropolis, tucked away under a sand-stone mountain in the southern deserts of Silkar overlooking the Altapecean Sea. Thick, portable tents and sprawling pavil-ions lined the lower division's marketplace. Towering stone buildings were spread across the upper division, their styles stolen from modern Felian and Alchean architecture. Alverax needed to get to the lower division but, first, he needed some clothes.

He slipped past what looked like a small caravan preparing to leave. A few empty wagons were watched over by a few tired men lounging on small cushions. One of them leaned over and vomited. Oddly, it reminded Alverax how hungry he was.

Light crested over the city, finally casting off the morning's shadows. The northern quarter of the city, where Alverax stood, was always covered in shadows. A massive sandstone lip protruded out over the city like a half-built roof. The rest was open air out to Mercy's Bluff overlooking water as far as the eye could see. He'd always loved the sea, the water, the freedom. He was yet to find someone who could hold their breath longer than him, and that victory—however small it was—had always felt significant.

He ran from building to building, surprised with how stealthy one could be while nude. The next building over was a clothing shop, but he had no money and no way to walk through the front door without being seen. He walked around the back and found an open window. It was small. The sill rubbed against his scarred chest as he squeezed his way in, and it took everything in his power to not curse out loud. As he flopped over the ledge, the sill scraped him in even worse ways. That time he did curse.

He looked around for some clothing and found a black shirt and tan pants that he slipped on as fast as possible. A large wooden box in the corner held a collection of leather sandals; he borrowed a pair, then exited through the same window, but this time it was less painful with the help of a crate to give him a bit of a lift.

After another thirty minutes of walking, he found his way back to Jayla's house. It was just outside of Jelium's fortress where he kept all of his children. Close, but not within his own walls, a reminder that they were of him but not with him. Father of the year.

He rushed to the back door and let himself in like he had done a hundred times before. This time, he was careful that no neighbors saw him as he entered. If he wanted to be free from Jelium, he needed everyone to think he was dead.

Inside, the house was free of the sand that riddled the city roads. It was a tremendous effort to keep a house clean in Cynosure, but Jayla had cleaners that would come each week and painstakingly purge the floors. Alverax took his sandals off out of habit, not wanting to muck up the floor, and walked in. He stopped himself before calling out to her, knowing that others could be in the house. With his luck, Jelium would be there visiting daughter number sixty-three.

There were whispers coming from down the hallway. He started to turn around but wanted to see who it was. There were a few others he wouldn't mind knowing he was alive, like his best friend Truffles. Inching forward, he tiptoed barefoot across the rug that ran the length of the hallway until he came to the bedroom.

What the hell?

Jayla lay beneath silk sheets, entangled in the arms of his best friend, Lariathoralan, whom everyone called Truffles. They'd been friends for almost a decade, and here he was, the snake, making love to *his* woman. The sounds and movement coming from the bed didn't stop as he stared in horror. It appeared that his friendships had died alongside him.

Alverax was not an angry person. His father had taught him that it was better to wit than hit, so he'd grown up outthinking bullies rather than sparring with them. Even so, his broken heart pounded in his chest, rage bubbling up in his arteries. He tried to count—*One. Two. Three. Four. Heralds calm a troubled core*—but the pain of a beating heart against his bruised ribs made him even more angry. He closed his eyes. His body felt like it was on fire. The veins in his arms and neck itched under his skin. The darkness behind his closed eyelids filled with a bright white light. When he finally opened his eyes again, the world had changed.

Hundreds of thin strands of multicolored light pulsated around him, overwhelming his senses. Tears streaked down his cheeks as his eyes darted back and forth taking in the ethereal vision in front of him. The world was the same, but different. It was like some kind of spiritual realm was overlaid on top of the physical one but, unlike in the physical world, each thread he could see called to him, whispers in the chaos.

He looked down and saw a thick, bright thread below him. It seemed to give off a ghostly mist as energy darted back and forth across its surface. Like the others, its connection points moved erratically, the base swaying across the ground as if it were trying to find something. He reached down to touch it, but his hand passed through unimpeded. Still he felt it calling. His mind ordered an unspoken command to it, an attempt to connect with it.

But then, it popped.

It burst apart like a knife to a bubble.

Weight lifted off of his shoulders. Every care, every pain, floated away from him. He coughed out a laugh as the sensation overwhelmed him.

Jayla looked up at the noise and saw him standing in the doorway, no, floating in the doorway. Alverax was suspended in the air, veins dark as night, eyes black as the abyss. An angel of death come to reap his reward. She screamed, squeezing tightly against the sheets away from Truffles, as if realizing for the first time the injustice of what she'd done. Truffles cursed and reached for a knife in his belt on the floor.

Alverax didn't care anymore. They were nothing to him. They were worms, and he was a bird in flight. The silence demanded him speak, but he just stared. His black-eyed gaze bearing down in deific judgment.

Tears bubbled up in Jayla's eyes. She coughed out a babble of desperate words. "You're dead! They told me! This isn't possible. They told me you were dead!" She buried her face in her hands sobbing.

Alverax looked down at them. "Us Blightwoods don't die easy."

He floated back down to the ground and walked away.

Every vein in his body pulsed with blackness. He looked down at his arms as he walked away from Jayla's home. He had been reborn. He was a threadweaver. He'd heard descriptions of threadlight enough times to recognize it, especially from rich acquaintances who'd taken transfusers. But he was different. He'd *broken* that thread. Not a *push* or a *pull*. He was something different.

He'd spent his whole life trying to be more than his father was, but everywhere he went he was "the thief's son". Never quite able to escape the stain. This was his chance. With this new power he could become someone. He could be anything.

But first, a little payback.

~ Treelurk ~

CHAPTER 16

LAUREL WATCHED as a woman climbed out of the brush, dozens of tiny lines of blood scattered across her forearms.

Gale, take me, Laurel thought. *She's holding a baby.*

Tears flooded down the woman's cheeks as she gestured to the grounder man. "Please, help him."

Laurel didn't know what to do. She recognized the man from the Bloodthief basement. He'd saved her life once; the least she could do was return the favor. But how? Take them to Alchea? If there were any more soldiers, that would not go well. There was only one other option and, if she took it, the elders would be furious. She smirked. That she could deal with.

She turned to the chromawolf. "You're not going to like this, buddy, but I need you to carry that man."

Asher huffed, but bent low so Laurel could lift the grounder onto his back. He was heavy, so Laurel *pushed* against the ground to ease the process. Her veins were alive with thread-light by the time he was safely draped over Asher's back. She tried to remember the man's name. It was a common name. Fenn? Cardam? Chrys? That was the one.

"Thanks, buddy," Laurel said, scratching behind Asher's ear. She turned to the woman. "Can you walk?"

"How far?"

"A ways. You're an Emerald, yeah? You can use the canopy to *drift* if it helps."

The woman looked to the dark awning above and nodded. "Thank you for helping us. My name is Iriel, and that's Chrys."

Laurel smiled. "I know."

Iriel raised a brow.

"We need to get moving. I'll explain while we walk."

They walked silently for hours. Laurel kept her hand raised high carrying a bouquet of photospores to provide additional light as they walked through the Fairenwild. Fortunately, with Asher as their guide, they wouldn't be in any danger traveling through. Chrys was in more danger than the rest of them, and not only because of his injuries. Iriel's eyes were daggers.

The uncomfortable silence was broken only by the sounds of creatures skittering through the brush, birds chirping high overhead, or the occasional puff of photospore luminescence. Laurel wasn't sure what to say, so she didn't speak. After she'd explained how she knew Chrys, Iriel had grown gravely quiet.

Chrys was in bad shape. His face was battered and bruised, his eyes swollen shut, and dirt smeared together with blood covering his left cheek. Asher had complained less than she had expected, which made her wonder if he'd ever let her ride him like the grounders rode horses. Cara said a chromawolf would never allow it but, watching him carry the wounded grounder, Laurel had her doubts.

She still couldn't believe it was the same man that had rescued her. Climbing up the ladder out of the Bloodthief basement. Reassuring her that everything was okay. Even now, there was something different about him. It was anything but reassuring. Iriel looked like she hadn't slept in days, her arms speckled with blood, and yet she walked without complaint while carrying their sleeping child.

Laurel wasn't sure she ever wanted kids. They seemed like more trouble than they were worth. One messenger she knew had retired after having children because she didn't want to be away from her family. That kind of familial chain was not something Laurel was interested in. She wanted to be out in the world exploring, adventuring, discovering. Her people siloed themselves off so much that they were missing out on an entire world that was ripe for exploring. Of course, there were some bad grounders—she would need to be careful—but there had to be good ones, too.

Iriel flinched as shadows flitted back and forth across their path.

Laurel smiled. "It's just shadows. When the spores move, sometimes the shadows move too. You get used to it. It's the treelurks you have to watch out for."

"What is a...treelurk?"

Laurel pointed to one of the feytrees. "There's one right there."

"Where?" Iriel asked. "I don't see anything."

"They change their color to blend into the feytree bark. It's dark, so the shift in color is really effective. Once you know what to look for, it's pretty obvious."

"I see something toward the base. Is that it?" Iriel took a step toward the feytree. "Stones! It's a spider!"

Laurel laughed out loud. "Pretty much. A really big, color-shifting spider. If you get too close, they jump out and sink their fangs into your arm. It's venomous, but treatable with the right salve."

Iriel frowned, "I hate spiders."

"Same, but they hate light, so if you have some photospores with you, you'll probably be okay."

"Lovely," Iriel said. "I hate to ask, but how much longer? I'm surprised Aydin has gone this long without crying, and I don't want him giving us undue attention."

"Not much longer. If you get bored, I like to count the skyflies." She pointed up high overhead. A drove of green and white colored insects floated about near the high canopy.

Iriel eyed Asher as they walked, still unsure of the creature. Finally, she let it out. "I have to ask? I watched some of those ripping people apart, but this one seems to defer to you. Why? Am I missing something?"

Laurel laughed, her blonde hair shaking as she looked to Asher. "We're family. I helped raise him. Chromawolves are much smarter than you grounders give them credit for."

"I swear I saw him nodding to you earlier. Not the blood-thirsty monster I grew up hearing about. And what's a grounder?"

"Oh, that's just what we call your people. Because...well, it'll make more sense when you see it for yourself."

"So, you really live in the Fairenwild?"

Laurel looked for a yellow rose to follow. "We don't really live *in* the Fairenwild. Just trust me, it'll make a lot more sense when we get there."

"How can you even tell we're going the right way? It all looks the exact same. You can't even see the sun to reorient yourself."

"That," Laurel said, "is a great question. The roses in the Fairenwild are not the same as yours. There are four types:

dayrose, stormrose, threadrose, and the Zedarose. The last one we named after ourselves, but it's really more like a Trailrose. Our people planted them a long time ago to remember the way, and they've grown naturally ever since. I've been following them the whole time."

Iriel was drifting off into her own thoughts, but Laurel was ready to get her own question answered. "So, what happened back there? Who were those soldiers?"

Her distant eyes grew cold. "It's complicated."

"What's so complicated about someone trying to kill you?"

Iriel stopped walking. "Is there anything more complicated than someone trying to kill you?"

"I guess not. I just thought we should talk about it before we get to the elders. You're going to have to tell them anyway."

"Fine," Iriel snapped. She held out the baby toward Laurel. "You want to know why they were trying to kill us? Look for yourself."

Laurel cocked her head, confused, but walked over to Iriel. The young mother was probably a decade older than her, but a few inches shorter. "What? The baby? Is it someone else's or something?"

"Look." Iriel took her fingers and opened Aydin's eye. The bright amber in his iris glowed in the darkness.

Laurel jumped back, startled. "What's wrong with his eye? Is he sick? Am I going to be sick now?" She looked back up to Iriel. "Sorry. I'm not so good at this. Why are his eyes yellow?"

"We were hoping you could tell us."

"Why would I know anything about that?"

Iriel sighed. "Not you, your people. The priest said that your elders could tell us more. We're hoping that's true."

"Wait, what priest?"

Iriel frowned. "The one that was from Zedalum. Father

Xalan, I think. He killed a man in the temple and basically forced us to follow him. Said that the Zeda elders could give us protection and answers. He's the reason we came this way."

Excitement pulsed inside of her. "Did he head back to the temple? Why didn't he come with you? Seems like a bad decision to send you both into the Fairenwild by yourselves. Especially with an army after you. I thought he was smarter than..." Then it dawned on her. He *wouldn't* send them on alone. Especially if he thought that their son was important enough to break Zeda law and take a grounder to Zedalum. "Is he dead?"

A small bunch of photospores moved back and forth in the breeze, causing the shadows of a small fern to vacillate over their path. Iriel looked to Laurel and nodded. "He saved our lives. When the soldiers were arriving, he stayed behind to stall them. I never trusted him. Not until that moment at least. Anyone willing to sacrifice themselves for a stranger is either completely mad or perfectly trustworthy. Did you know him?"

Laurel nodded.

"I'm sorry. We owe him our lives. And you as well. If not for you, the chromawolves would have eaten us. So, thank you. We owe you a life debt, Laurel."

Laurel was silent the rest of the journey, mind captivated with the idea of coincidence. Was there such a thing? The only two Zedas in Alchea, both in the right place at the right time to protect these people. Her arriving at the very moment the one wolf that would heed her voice was about to attack the man that had saved her life. It was as if coincidence was a unique point in time that had been pulling each of their lives toward it, like an immense force of gravity, until finally they came to a brilliant intersection.

Asher whimpered as they approached the clearing where the wonderstone lay. He was afraid. It seemed to speak to the wolves differently than it spoke to her. It drew her in and begged her to threadweave, to amplify her own power through the power that churned beneath its surface. It repelled the wildlife.

She ran her hand across Asher's green fur and nodded. Only problem was that Chrys was still passed out. There was no way she was going to carry him the rest of the way. She turned to Iriel. "Can you help me wake him?"

His eyes were bloated masses of skin and dry blood. Laurel noted the look of sadness that knit together across Iriel's lips. Whatever grief Laurel felt for the man was nothing compared to Iriel. She put her right hand on his cheek, left hand still clutching tightly to Aydin. She whispered something into Chrys' ear and his face contorted in pain as he awoke.

"Take your time," Iriel said. "You're hurt."

After a minute of struggling to slide off of Asher's back, and realizing he could only see well out of one eye, Chrys finally stood on his feet ready to walk. He looked up and saw Laurel for the first time. "You."

"Me," Laurel responded playfully. Asher nuzzled Laurel and licked her cheek before he dashed off back in the direction they came. His fur quickly blended into the dimly lit greenery in the background. "I already explained how we met."

"You did?"

"She did," Iriel repeated, her eyes a storm of judgment. "And I don't appreciate hearing about dangerous events from a third party."

Chrys winced as much from pain as from the jibe. "Where are we?"

Laurel gestured forward. "Almost to Zedalum. Asher doesn't like this place, but neither do the treelurks. We'll be safe. Do you think you can walk?"

He nodded.

They moved slowly along the grass until they arrived at the clearing where the wonderstone lay. Bright flowers dotted the floor surrounding it. As they approached, Chrys and Iriel both stared at the white, circular stone slab in front of them. It was thick, almost up to Iriel's knees in height, and wide as a room.

"Stones." Iriel's eyes grew wide. "Chrys, look at it in threadlight."

They walked forward in reverence. The wonderstone shone like a multicolored sun, but its light did not illuminate the physical world around it. Threadlight did not increase the light in the world but overlaid a higher form of light that transcended the physical realm.

Small gaps in the feytree branches overhead let in tenacious rays of sunlight. They approached together, and Laurel watched as Chrys stepped up onto the raised platform, his eyes fixed to the bright threadlight of the stone. He bent his legs as if preparing to jump, and Laurel rushed up to him, grabbing his arm.

"Chrys!" she said, clapping. "I should have warned you. I'm sorry. I've never shown someone the wonderstone before. It has a way of making threadweavers want to threadweave so much they die. Seriously, it's happened before. You'll get your chance though. Not to die—gale, take me—to threadweave. For now, just try to ignore it."

As Iriel approached the wonderstone, Aydin grew increasingly fussy. She rocked him back and forth and hummed a song in vain attempts to keep him from crying. Unfortunately, music can't fill an empty belly.

Laurel looked up above the wonderstone, high up into the gap in the feytree branches. As her eyes adjusted, the wooden landing pad came into view. From the distance, and backlit by sunlight, it was hard to see what it was unless you already knew.

"I'll show you how to do it, then I'll come back down, and we'll send you up. Iriel, you're an Emerald, so you can't get up by yourself. I'll take the baby up to Chrys once he gets up, and then I'll come back and we'll make the jump together." She made her way to the center of the stone, glyphs chiseled into white stone beneath her feet. "Careful not to get off center, otherwise you won't make it to the platform."

Chrys sneered at her words. "You're telling me you are going to jump all the way up there? That's impossible."

"Scared, flower boy?"

He gave her a strange look, but she didn't wait for him to respond.

"Impossible is my specialty." She exploded off the wonder-stone like a streak of lightning rising up toward the break in the branches. Her speed slowed as she rose higher into the air, up, up into the vaulting branches of the feytrees. After a few moments, she came soaring back down through the air, her blonde hair flailing in the wind, her feet landing with hardly a sound.

"What, you can't do that?" The look on his face was worth the whole experience. "All Zeda Sapphires can do it. Maybe you grounders just aren't as powerful."

Chrys stood silently staring into the canopy.

"Okay, okay. I'm just fanning your chimes. It's the wonder-stone. It amplifies your ability to threadweave without making you threadsick. It lets you use its energy to fuel your own *push*. I promise you can do it too. Zedalum is up there."

"It's up there?" Chrys stepped into the center. "Stones, I can feel the stone's power in my veins. Feels like I could fly. So, I just jump and *push*? That's all? And I'll soar as high as you did?"

"There's a threadpole on the left side when you get to the top. Push on it to position yourself onto the platform on the other side."

Chrys focused, bending his knees and looking up into the break in the branches. His veins lit with threadlight and then he *pushed*. Laurel watched as his eyes blazed blue just before he launched up off of the wonderstone. She was sure she saw a smile on his face. As he reached the top, his body took a sudden horizontal shift, and he was out of Laurel's sight.

Iriel stared at Laurel. "There's no way I'm handing you my son to do that."

"It's perfectly safe," Laurel said. "I've done it a thousand times. There's nothing to be worried about."

"Sorry," Iriel repeated, "but I just met you, and that's not a risk I'm willing to take. Tell Chrys to come back down. He can do it."

"I didn't say anything before but, in his condition, I wasn't even sure he'd be able to get up once himself. You make him do it again and who knows if he makes it." Laurel looked up to the opening high above. "I promise you it's more of a risk to make him do it than me."

Iriel thought for a moment, then begrudgingly handed the baby to Laurel. "I swear if anything happens to Aydin..."

It took all of Laurel's self-control not to reply with something snarky. Of course, she would be careful. Laurel held fast and *pushed* off the wonderstone, sending her and the child soaring up into the air. The shock of it actually stopped the screaming for a moment. It was glorious.

She rose higher and higher, leaving behind the darkness below, rising up toward the gap in the branches. She *pushed* off the threadpole opposite the platform and sent herself off to the side, landing gracefully on the platform.

Laurel handed Chrys his son—who was still quiet—then remembered that they weren't alone on the platform. A Zeda guard looked at the two of them with confusion. He had his ledger in hand but didn't need it to see that Chrys wasn't a Zeda; his high general uniform made that very clear. Laurel lifted a finger to the guard, smiled, and jumped back off the platform, leaving Chrys and Aydin.

Somehow, she'd forgotten about the guard at the entrance. How was she going to convince him to let them through when his sole purpose was to disallow just that? If she was lucky, he wouldn't know that she was no longer Elder Rowan's messenger to Alchea. She could work with that.

Laurel landed back on the wonderstone and gestured to Iriel. "Ready? Hold on tight."

When threadweavers use threadlight to *push* themselves into the air, it is not like a regular jump. *Pushing* against their corethread diminishes the force holding them to the surface. If they *push* hard enough, the force becomes like a magnet repelling them from the surface. The threadweaver becomes weightless. The person they are carrying? Not so much.

Laurel's veins burned with threadlight as she *pushed* harder than she'd ever *pushed* to offset Iriel's weight. Luckily for her, the wonderstone made that much less painful. They reached the top—though the landing was a bit less graceful than her own—and made their way back over to Chrys and Aydin.

"Laurel, what is this?" the guard asked. "These are grounders! It is forbidden!"

"It's not forbidden. It's highly discouraged. And the elders asked me to bring this family to them. Elder Rowan specifically. And you know how she gets. Obviously, this isn't a normal situation. I'm taking them directly to the Elder's lodge." She held up her hand. "Swear it on the wind."

The guard looked nervous. "Why don't you go get the elders and I'll watch over the grounders here."

"There's not a chance the elders are coming all the way out here."

He bit the inside of his lip. "If they won't come here, then I'm coming with you. And we go straight to the lodge. No stops."

"Fine by me. Let's go."

She nodded to Chrys and Iriel and they followed her up the wooden steps built into the thick branches until finally they stepped out onto the windy treetop haven.

Laurel watched as awe spread over Chrys' face. She'd never had a good look at him in the sunlight. His jaw was strong, though hidden behind a short beard. His hair was pushed to the side, but long enough to cover his eyes. He stood with his hands behind his back, straight-backed and strong, despite the myriad bruises.

She looked out over her home. The sunrise cast a warm glow. She had a pretty good idea of what Chrys and Iriel were feeling. It was the same thing she'd felt the first time she traveled to Alchea. The contrast. The otherness. His was a city of stone, hers was the city of wind.

"My grandfather has a saying: Wonder is the passing wind. In other words, you'll get used to it." Laurel wasn't sure they'd heard her. Their eyes were still glazed over, staring. "I'm taking you to see the elders. If anyone knows about the yellow eye thing, it'll be Elder Rosemary."

Chrys' eyes grew wide. "It's amazing. My whole life, I've seen the Fairenwild peeking out over the western horizon. And all the while this was here? Unbelievable. I have so many logistical questions. Do you know why they did it?"

"Did what?"

"Why did they build a city here, on top of the Fairenwild?"

Laurel kept walking. "Well, I never really thought about it. I guess because they want to be left alone. Don't get many visitors here. And it wasn't safe to build a city down there. Up here, it's just us and the wind."

They walked down idle streets, crowds walking farther along on an adjacent street near the marketplace. The guard trailed close behind, watching intently as they moved toward the elder's lodge. When they arrived, the sweet smell of incense wafted out through an open window near the entrance.

Laurel opened the door and walked in. There were several people in the large entry room, all lounging around and talking. All but two had one side of their hair shaved close to the skin. They stopped as Laurel entered, then stood when they saw her guests. Iriel's face was speckled with dirt and her hair was a ratty mess, but Chrys looked worse. One of the Zedas rushed away down the hallway.

"Is Elder Rosemary in?" Laurel didn't address it to anyone in particular but asked the group in the entry room.

One of those standing in the room was a curly blonde Sapphire named Meg who was currently serving as Elder Ashwa's messenger assigned to Felia. It was the most coveted messenger position of all. The exotic port-city was a melting pot of culture and information, everything a girl from a reclusive treetop city could want.

Meg walked over to Laurel and pulled her to the side whispering. "Are those who I think they are? I heard what happened to you yesterday, and now this? You're going to get yourself exiled!"

"Don't be so dramatic. I'll be fine. It wasn't my decision anyway. Sometimes you have to break the rules for the greater good."

"Laurel, this isn't breaking the rules, this is burning them to the ground! There has *never* been a grounder in our city. And you brought three!"

"More like two and a half." If Meg was looking, she would have seen a slight tint of blue in Laurel's veins. "Why does it matter if we bring grounders to our city? Do you just blindly follow everything the elders say, or do you think for yourself on rare occasions?"

It was harsh—Laurel knew it—but she was tired of everyone treating her like she wasn't thinking through her actions. Meg had no context into the situation or who these people were. She had not even asked her why she'd brought them, and still she felt entitled to tell her it was wrong.

A moment later the man who'd run off down the hall returned and summoned Laurel, Chrys, and Iriel, gesturing for them to follow him back farther into the lodge. Laurel held onto the threadlight coursing through her veins. It felt like a warm embrace.

They were led back to a familiar door. The man knocked and opened it. Laurel shifted from one foot to the other. She had been so sure they would understand—especially since Pandan had been bringing them—that she discounted the power of tradition. What if they did banish her? Did she even care?

Inside sat five women, scowls at the ready, fire burning in each of their colored eyes. She could see it in that moment— they were tired of seeing her. They had already preconceived her guilt. She should have thought beforehand how she was going to explain it all. Should she start with an apology? Or by talking about Pandan? She was no good at these types of political maneuverings.

Chrys stepped forward, beaten and weary, and addressed

the elders. He must have read the room because he spoke humbly and reverently. "We are honored to be here. My name is Chrys Valerian. The girl, Laurel, has warned us that this is quite unusual, but this was not our decision, nor hers. It was the decision of an Alchean priest whom we knew as Father Xalan, but I believe you know him as Pandan."

As soon as he spoke Pandan's name, the air in the room changed. The elders sat taller and listened more intently. Laurel felt grateful that Chrys had spoken first. Rowan and Rosemary whispered to each other, eyes darting back and forth between each of the Valerians. The question now was whether Pandan had been compromised voluntarily or not.

Elder Rowan, eyes sharp as knives, leaned forward. "If that is true, why would he want you to come here? Every Zeda knows well the law restricting such actions." She eyed Laurel at the end.

"He said you had answers. That if we wanted to keep our son safe, you could help us. Stones, he killed an innocent man because he believed it."

"He killed someone? We will need a full recounting of this." Elder Rowan glanced down to the child. "Tell me, what kind of danger threatens your child?"

Chrys looked to Iriel, who nodded her approval. "It is easier to show than to explain." He walked forward and set Aydin on the table in front of them with his hand cupping Aydin's head. Laurel had no idea how the elders were going to respond. She had thought the baby was sick. Would they think the same thing? Or was Pandan right that they knew more? The baby fussed and wiggled as Chrys opened its eyelid to reveal the bright yellow iris.

Every elder gasped in turn, hands springing up to cover their mouths, shock pasted across their faces as if they'd seen a ghost. The oldest of them, Elder Violet, whispered loud enough for them all to hear. "It cannot be."

Elder Rosemary, kind and gentle as ever, looked to Laurel and said, "Our apologies for presuming your guilt. You have done well, Laurel. Chrys, you said? The three of you are welcome to stay as long as you like. Our home is yours, and our protection will forever be open to you. Fenn, take them to the empty room at the end of the hallway. Laurel, you will give us a full report of what happened. I imagine your son needs food and a good cleaning. I will send someone to help with the child and to provide ointments for your wounds. You both would do well to get some rest. The five of us have much to discuss."

CHAPTER 17

WILLOW VALERIAN—MOTHER to the most wanted criminal in all of Alchea—sat in a quiet room with High General Henna Tyran. The general was as cold as the room; Willow rubbed her arms to keep warm. When she'd set out that morning, she hadn't expected to be detained and questioned by the Alchean guard.

They had shown her the evidence, but Willow knew Chrys too well to believe that he was guilty. At his core, he was a good man. Of course, she'd never fully accepted the stories of the Apogee's murderous rampage during the War of the Wastelands either. The man she raised would fight to protect, but never with glee.

General Henna sat across the table, her white Alirian hair messily covering the side of her face. Her eyes were red with fatigue, but she continued the questioning. "Willow, you have to give us something. You were there with them at the temple and spent the previous night in their home. There's nothing I can do for you if you won't help."

"Maybe you should ask Jurius," Willow said.

"And what is that supposed to mean?"

"Chrys is innocent." Willow was steel.

The truth was that it looked really bad. A dead temple worker and two guards that testified that Chrys left with the priest willingly? If she didn't know Jurius' secret, she might have been convinced. But she did know, and she knew that she couldn't trust anyone. Chrys was worried for his family's safety and for Willow's in turn. And now here she sat, being interrogated by one of the Great Lord's high generals under suspicion of aiding a criminal. There was a connection, but she couldn't figure it out.

A knock came at the door.

General Henna walked over to answer. There were whispers and confusing hand gestures as the man on the other side explained something to the high general. She turned around, closing the door again as she walked back to the table. "They found Chrys. He's dead."

Willow flinched.

"Tell me who Father Xalan really is and why they were going to the Fairenwild."

Willow stared, unable to process the words. "He's not dead."

Henna sighed. "Jurius caught up with him at the border. There was a fight. They captured the priest, but Chromawolves came out of the trees and started ripping men apart. We have ten men unaccounted for. Chrys, Iriel, and the baby were right next to those men."

"LIAR!" Willow screamed, slamming her fists down on the table.

"Sit down." Henna rubbed her eyes. "I'm not here to feed you lies. I just want to know why. Why did he kill the temple worker? Who is the priest? Where were they going? You've been a respected woman for many years, but you have to understand that your life is on the line for collusion. Malachus wants answers. He liked your son. Trusted him more than the rest of us. A betrayal like this is as deep as they come. So, whether you tell us the truth or not, the priest will. His questioning will be far less diplomatic."

Willow gathered herself. Fury bubbled wildly below the surface. If Chrys was truly dead, she would slit Jurius' throat herself. She didn't know how, but this was his fault. Father of All knows she had reason enough.

"Well?"

Willow clenched her jaw. "I have nothing to tell. Clearly if I had known what was going to happen, I would be with them right now. Chrys is too smart to leave such an obvious loose end. So, unless you're going to place me in a cell, I think we're done here."

Henna took a deep breath and stared at her for a moment. "We're not going to lock you in a cell, but you should know that all of the keep guards have been ordered to keep you within the walls. I'm sure you understand. A security precaution. There is a room prepared for you on the third floor. I believe you've been there before."

It was the same room she'd stayed at when she came to Alchea thirty years ago. It felt like another life. Just her and little Chrys walking into Alchea. If it weren't for the fact that they were both threadweavers, they would have been living on the streets. Instead, a young Lady Eleandra had taken a liking to them, and offered to put them up in the keep to protect them in case her husband came looking.

By the time Willow reached the room on the third floor, her wrists had finally stopped hurting, and the rage in her blood had faded to a dull ire. She would never sleep tonight. The truth was that they couldn't really make her stay; she was a Sapphire threadweaver after all. But she hadn't done any threadweaving since she'd moved to Alchea. It was part of a renunciation of her former life. It had all been lies, of course. Threadweaving draws far too much attention and that was the last thing she wanted when she'd arrived in Alchea. Better to be a woman running away from an abusive marriage, in need of help to hide. Lady Eleandra had been all too eager to save the damsel in distress. In all her years in Alchea, she'd never let anyone get close enough to discover the truth.

What she needed now was to talk to the priest. Henna said they'd caught him, which meant he was down in the dungeons below the keep. Even if she wasn't allowed to leave, she was still a threadweaver with political influence. The dungeon guards might let her speak with him. On the other hand, it would make her look even more guilty if the high generals found out. She didn't care. If Chrys was dead, it didn't matter; if he was alive, she had to go to him. The priest was the only one with answers.

Later that night Willow made her way down to the kitchen, passing a few guards that eyed her warily. A friend from her time living at the keep was still the night chef. Most nights the woman would sit reading while everyone else slept, waiting for someone to order something. Willow embraced her and they talked for a few minutes. She then grabbed a loaf of bread and headed down the eastern staircase toward the dungeons. The elegance of the keep faded to a dreary ambience as she reached the entrance to the dungeon. A guard stood at attention on her side of the gate and placed a hand on his sword as she approached.

"No one is allowed past here, my lady. General's orders." He did his best to avoid eye contact with her as he spoke.

Willow continued her approach until she was right next to him, uncomfortably close. "Lady Eleandra asked me to bring the prisoner some food. But I'm also a threadweaver, which means that you can either believe me and let me in like a gentleman, which I highly recommend, or I can let myself in. The latter would surely tarnish people's opinions of us both."

His hand rested on the hilt of his blade, but a sense of understanding seemed to wash over him as he finally looked up into her blue eyes. "The Great Lord's wife, you say? I suppose her orders would take precedence over a general's. Be quick about it. And be careful. He's blindfolded, so he can't thread-weave, but they say he's still dangerous."

"You are wise for your age." She walked forward as he unlocked the gate.

As soon as she was through, he locked it behind her. "Nothing personal, my lady."

Willow nodded. "No offense taken."

As she looked out into the dark dungeon, she couldn't help but smile. She was finally going to get some answers. What would she do if it was true? What if Chrys was dead? No, not possible. But who was the false priest, and why were they traveling near the Fairenwild? She had an unlikely suspicion, but she had to be careful in case she was wrong.

A dank musk filled the dungeon, filling her nose with the stench of sweat and worse. She grabbed a torch off the wall and used it for light as she traveled deeper. There must have been two dozen empty cells she passed before finding the priest bound, gagged, and blindfolded. Dry blood stained the rag in his mouth, and his shirtless chest was marked with bruises and pain. He looked dead. So still. So calm. She was worried she wouldn't be able to wake him.

"Hello," she whispered. "Hello!"

He didn't respond.

She tore off a piece from the loaf of bread and threw it at his face. He winced as it struck and started mumbling through his gag. It was working. She tossed in three more chunks of bread. One missed, but the other two struck him across his bruised face. Each time he grumbled louder until his head was up and he mumbled something through his gag. She looked around for something she could use, like a broom, to reach in and dislodge the bloody rag from his mouth, but there was nothing. The dungeon hallways were bare stone, flickering shadows, and torchlight.

"Can you hear me?"

He nodded.

"Good. Do you know Chrys Valerian?"

Nothing.

"I'm his mother, and I need to find him."

He started shouting through his gag and shaking wildly against the chains that bound him. If only she could understand him. After a few moments he settled down. His chest rose up and down with each painful breath.

When he finally calmed down, Willow spoke. "I'm going to ask you a series of questions. There is no one else here but me. Please, I need your help to find my son."

He nodded.

"Do you know where he is?"

Yes.

She smiled. "Is he alive?"

No answer.

"Was he alive when they caught you?"

Yes.

It was difficult; she needed to ask *why* questions. Why had they gone to the Fairenwild? Why had they killed the temple worker? Why had they left her behind? But he wouldn't be able to respond. How could she obtain useful information with a simple yes or no?

"Did Chrys kill the temple worker?"

No.

She nodded and smiled. It felt good to know that she had been right about his innocence. If he hadn't though, that meant...

"Did *you* kill the temple worker?"

Yes.

"Why were you at the Fairenwild?" Stones, she needed to ask something else. "Was the Fairenwild your destination?"

Yes.

"And you know there are chromawolves and other dangerous beasts inside?"

Yes.

"Is there something else in the forest?"

Hesitation. Yes.

"Were you headed to Felia on the other side?"

No.

It must be. The implications were troubling, but the possibility that she had been correct also invigorated her. How could she ask without asking? If she was right, then she knew exactly where they were headed. "There are four types of flowers in the Fairenwild. Yellow. Blue. Green. And white. Do you know them?"

Yes.

"Which of the four should I follow?"

She thought she saw a smile through his gag.

"Green?"

No.

"Blue?"

No.

"Yellow?"

A vigorous yes.

Her heart was racing. She had to be sure. He was still shaking his head excitedly when she finally asked him. "Are you from Zedalum?"

His body relaxed. *Yes.*

She wished she could run in and hug him, blood stains and all.

He lifted his head and smiled through the gag.

Memories of her old life flooded over her. The wind rushing through her hair as she ran along the wooden streets of Zedalum. Aqueducts. Threadpoles. The wonderstone. The Gale. The elders refusing to listen. Her husband refusing to believe. A young mother giving up everything for what she believed. That girl was gone. She'd taken her son and left, then she'd spent the last thirty years trying to forget, as if accepting its existence proved her fallibility. But here it was, bloody and broken, kneeling in front of her in a dark dungeon, beckoning her to return home. And she had no choice but to succumb.

"Thank you. I wish I could help you, but I have to go to him. I'll make sure your family knows you were brave. May the winds guide you and carry you gently home."

The priest dropped his head and Willow thought she saw tears running down his swollen cheeks. She considered trying to help him escape, but it was too dangerous. So, she turned and left. As soon as the guard opened the door, she sprinted up the stairs, around the corner and up several more staircases. As she slowed to catch her breath, her chest ached and her mind raced. She didn't care that it was the middle of the night, what better time to slip away. Her legs moved faster than they had in years, but it felt right.

As she rounded the stairs to the third floor, her path was blocked by a familiar face.

Lady Eleandra Orion-Endin.

Not now. Father of All, please not now.

"Willow?"

She didn't have time for this. When Jurius and Henna found out that she'd spoken to the prisoner, she knew what they would do. And now she had a place to be, even if it was many hours away. She had no time to talk to her old friend.

"Eleandra. As much as I would love to stay and chat, I'm afraid today has not been the best of days. I could really use some rest."

Eleandra kept her head held high as she looked at Willow who was only slightly her senior. "We've been friends for a long time, Willow. I know you better than anyone, and I feel like I hardly know you at all. You've always been a guarded woman. Chrys is the same, but he has always been honest. He never offers more than requested, but his motives are clear as quartz. What do you know about this business with the priest? There is something off about it."

Willow gave no response.

"I don't know what I expected, coming up here to speak with you. Even if you knew where Chrys was, you would never divulge it." Eleandra cocked her head and looked deep into Willow's eyes, reading her expression. "So, I was right. You do know where he is. Don't tell me. I don't want to know. I want you to bring him back. Malachus needs someone like him by his side. Henna and Jurius are bad influences, but Chrys sparked a paternal side of my husband that I cannot let go. Please, Willow, bring Chrys back."

Tears formed in Willow's eyes. She stepped forward and hugged Eleandra. "Thank you."

She truly was the *Gem of Alchea*.

Willow headed down a long, dark hallway until she arrived back in her room. She slipped out of her dress and into a pair of light gray pants and a long-cut blue jacket.

Purpose fueled her every movement. There was nothing to bring where she was going but stale memories and regret. She stepped over to the high window near her bed and opened it. A vicious night wind blew over her, tossing her black hair out behind her. She threw her hood up and stared out into the sky. The moon shone high overhead, illuminating the keep's fields.

The blue in her eyes, like a sleeping dragon, awoke in brilliant fury. Threadlight washed over her vision, overwhelming her like it had so many years ago. It took her breath away. Her feet swayed with the wind, and she grabbed the windowsill for support. Hundreds of threads of vivid, prismatic light pulsed around her, each competing for the attention of her aging mind. It felt so natural. So familiar, like friends reunited. She focused, relaxed, and let the many threads fade away, all but the thick corethread pulsing beneath her.

It felt amazing. It was invigorating, intoxicating. Her heart pounded harder than it had in years. The blood rushing through her veins warmed to a dull heat, but she could feel it flowing out from her chest to the edges of her hands and feet. She'd forgotten the feeling, the craving. She would be happy letting threadlight keep her warm for the rest of her life. And that terrified her. She almost shut it out, but she needed to do this.

For Chrys.

She leapt. Gravity grabbed hold of her corethread and pulled, sending her falling toward the field below her window, but she *pushed* back with the power running through her veins, altering the force pulling her down. But not enough. She hit the ground hard and rolled into a somersault as she landed.

There were no guards nearby; they would be staggered across the keep's wall. She found her way toward the northwest wall where she expected there to be less of a guard detail. In the distance, she saw two pairs of guards staggered, walking along the field below the wall. Maybe twenty years ago she could have fought her way through them, but her bones were frail now, and her anger kindled only for one man.

There was no good way to get to the wall without being seen, so she took her hood off and walked over, trying to do so in an unthreatening way.

One of the guards saw her. He stepped forward and yelled, "Hey! Who goes there?"

Acting a fool is the wisest way to fool the wise. Willow herself was in her late fifties, far older than the guards in front of her. She hunched over and gave her voice a scratch. "Oh boys, please help me. I've lost my cat! I saw her run this way. I swear it on the Lightfather, she did. She's an inside cat. Cute as can be. She'll die if I don't find her. Please, boys. Please help me find my precious little Luker!"

She was able to close the distance with the guards, now only a short walk from the outer wall. One of the guards spoke. "Ma'am, you can't be out here. The fields around the wall are off limits, especially at night time. If we see your cat, I promise we'll bring it back inside. What's your name? We can send for you if we find it."

"Her. Luker is a her, not an it. And she does so love playing with her yarn. You should see it, her cute little paws swatting the ball back and forth. I need to find her. Wait! Was that her?" She waddled closer to the wall, leaning over as if she were going to catch something. "Luker, is that you Luker?" When she was close enough, she released an explosion of energy into her corethread, sending her blasting up into the night sky. She landed on the top of the wall chest first. She'd be bruised in the morning, but it was good enough.

"Sound the alarm!" The guards pulled out their bows but were too late. Neither of them were threadweavers. There was nothing they could do.

She ran and jumped off the other side, feeling the familiar burn in her veins. Far off to the west somewhere was the Fairenwild. She threw her hood back over her head and walked. She had a long way to go if she was going to make it to Zedalum before sunrise.

CHAPTER 18

A LOUD CRACK reverberated off the walls of the Great Lord's study. High General Jurius spat blood into his hand and wiped it across the thigh of his pants. He didn't deserve this kind of treatment. All that he'd done for Malachus over the years, and the only reward was a bloody lip.

The entire keep had awoken an hour earlier to the sound of bell tower alarms, only to find that it was not some enemy threat entering their walls, but Willow Valerian escaping. Henna was questioning the guards to figure out what had happened. It was easy to forget that Willow was a Sapphire; she had always refused to use her abilities. Apparently, that was no longer true. On the bright side, it made Chrys look even more guilty.

"This is unacceptable. I am done with failure, Jurius. First Chrys, and now his mother? I gave you the benefit of the doubt the first time—Chrys is resourceful—but now I'm starting to believe that you may have lost your touch."

Jurius stood tall, his mouth still bleeding from the discipline. "Henna's the one who questioned Willow, not me. I was busy at the time not getting eaten by chromawolves."

Malachus rolled his eyes. "I admired you, you know. All those years ago when we first took down Great Lord Larimar. I thought to myself, 'That is a useful man.' Lately, it seems all you have are pretexts. And it is quite unbecoming."

"Respectfully, I have done more for you than any single person in this damn country. If it wasn't for me, you wouldn't have taken the throne and the wastelanders would be pouring down the passes."

Malachus' eyes fumed. "Without *you*? You think I couldn't have achieved all this without you? *You* are nothing without *me*, Jurius. Not the other way around. You are nothing but pride and pretexts. Don't forget your place."

Jurius was trying hard not to lose his temper, but the Great Lord was making it damned hard. Through clenched teeth, he feigned humility. "You're right, of course. I apologize for over-stepping. We do still have the priest. He will tell us everything we need to know to find Chrys. No one stays tight-lipped forever."

"I hope you're right." Malachus sat back down in the large chair behind his desk. "We don't have time for pleasantry. Whatever it is they're planning, we can't give them more time to prepare. Go down, and don't leave until you have answers."

Jurius nodded. His tongue licked at the blood in his gums as he walked away. It was the middle of the damn night and Jurius had other orders. He should have rammed a knife into Malachus then and there, but Alabella had made him promise not to do anything rash. A chill ran down his spine thinking of her.

Their first meeting would be forever seared into his memory.

. . .

"Ah. My dear general, I have been very much looking forward to meeting you."

Jurius was bound to the ground, eyes covered with some kind of fabric. The woman's voice was smooth and warm, but sharp in its pronunciation. He thought he heard a pinch of the Kulaian islands in her accent. Despite not knowing where he was, he was painfully aware of how he'd gotten there. He'd been walking to his son's house when a group of men had jumped him in a dark alley. It happened so fast. They'd pounced on him and he'd fought back, snapping the neck of one of his assailants; that had earned him a nice pair of bruises on his chest later.

The woman removed his blindfold and looked deep into his eyes. A trick of the light made them look a sickly, pale yellow color. "What do you want?" he snapped.

She smiled, cocking her head to the side as she studied him. "I've a feeling you haven't yet grasped the gravity of the situation." Her eyes gestured to his hands.

When he looked down his eyes grew wide. Where he expected to see rope, his hands were bound together by nothingness. He pulled his hands apart, but they wouldn't budge. He looked down to his waist and feet, finding both bound by some invisible force. But there was only one invisible force he knew of. He opened his eyes to threadlight.

A dozen strands of light bound him in impossible ways. A short, thin thread ran from one wrist to the other, with another linking that thread to the floor, somehow feeding it with gravitational energy. Half a dozen ran from his torso down into the ground like inverse supports. Two at his feet. Two at his knees. He looked back up to the woman, her full lips curling into a devious grin.

"Perhaps now you understand."

Jurius felt a drop in his gut but did his best to keep his resolve. She wanted him to feel helpless, but he wouldn't give it to her. "What do you want?"

The woman had jet-black hair, slicked back and running down her neck like a pitch waterfall. "The first thing you must understand is that I will never lie to you. As you can see, I have the power to create threads. In short, it means that at any moment I could crush you with the weight of the world. But, my dear General, that's not why I've brought you here. You see, you are not the only one here with us."

She gestured behind him. His son was chained and blindfolded against the far wall with guards on either side of him. After his wife had passed away, Jurius' son was the only thing he still loved in the world.

"Please, not him."

She smiled. "Cooperation is the key to abdication."

AT FIRST THERE wasn't much of a choice: obey or watch them drain his son's blood before they drained his own. He'd betrayed the Great Lord, his old friend, in the name of survival, but somewhere along the way—perhaps to justify it to himself —he'd begun to see the lack of appreciation, the coldness, and the outright disrespect that Malachus offered him. Disrespect deserves no loyalty.

He descended a flight of stairs and reached the dungeon gate, finding a guard with his hand on his hilt looking at him. The guard relaxed his hand but tightened his stance as he saluted Jurius. "High General."

"Your shift is over. Leave."

The guard furled his brow, confused. "But, General, my shift doesn't end for another hour. And if you go in, protocol is for me to lock the gate behind you."

"Damn the protocol! Who do you think created it? Give me the keys and get out."

The guard grabbed the chain around his neck, hands shaking, and handed it over to Jurius, keeping his eyes fixed to the floor. Jurius opened the gate and walked into the dungeon, blood on his lips, and fire in his eyes.

The table outside the false priest's cell held all of Jurius' tools. Torture was a dirty business—he loathed the process—but he'd seen its effectiveness. At the base was an empty bucket that he filled with water. He picked it up and walked over to the prisoner. With one hand he grabbed the back of the man's neck and, with the other, he poured the bucket of water over his head.

The prisoner inhaled a gasp of air, choking as water trickled in past his gag. It ran down his face, a sick intercourse of blood and water where one of Jurius' captains had taken a blade to split his nostril earlier.

Jurius threw down the empty water pitcher and released his grip on the man's neck. He stepped back toward the table and picked up a thin blade with dry blood speckled across the hilt. Up above the table, the word *fortune* had been carved and painted into the wall.

The prisoner looked pathetic. Blindfolded, bound at the ankles and wrists, drenched in water and blood, and deathly pale across his naked chest. But he'd fought bravely at the border of the Fairenwild and had not revealed any secrets when the captain had questioned him. Impressive, when you looked at the slice marks down his upper arms, the swollen clamp marks on his fingers, and the torn flesh of his nose. But time is the master negotiator. The most stubborn of men yield to her words.

Everyone breaks.

He stepped forward and pulled the gag out of the man's mouth. "Wake up."

The first step to breaking a man is breaking his hope. Jurius knew this well. He stood in front of the shivering prisoner. "No one is coming for you. That is a reality that you cannot change. Not Chrys. Not Willow. You are alone. Well, you do have me."

Jurius took his knife and traced it over the man's cheek. "I know you're a Zeda—the tattoos give it away. I need to know how to get to Zedalum, and I need to know why you were taking Chrys there."

"I will not betray them." His head bowed humbly.

"Yes, you will!" Jurius shouted. He calmed himself and spoke to the false priest in a way that he would understand. "No man can stand against the wind forever."

Jurius shoved his knife through the man's cheek, ripping through skin and tissue. The old man sobbed. His eyes squeezed shut as he tried hard not to move his head. Jurius spun it in a circle, grimacing as the sharp edge stretched raw flesh. The false priest's hands were bound; the blood, spit, and dripping water drooled down into his beard. Jurius took a deep breath. He was getting too old for this.

He wiped the blood off his knife on the man's other cheek. "Let me ask again. Why were you taking Chrys to Zedalum?"

The old man laughed, once, and then again, his cheek still running with his blood. "The breeze is pleasant down here."

Footsteps echoed from the distant stairwell, stopped, and then continued.

"The winds have only begun to stir, Father." Jurius' eyes grew colder. "Have you heard the metaphor of the sticks? Grab a stick at both ends, you bend it, and it breaks. Gather a bundle of sticks together, grab it at the ends, and you cannot break them. The problem is that sometimes there are stubborn sticks that refuse to break, even on their own. No matter how hard you twist and bend, they refuse to snap. I have an eye for identifying those sticks. When I find one, I don't waste my time on it. I grab another from the same tree and make the stubborn stick watch as I break its brother."

The footsteps grew louder as a guard came into view. A second hooded figure walked slowly beside him. He understood the false priest's resilience, respected it even, but Jurius had two masters that both wanted answers, and he had no time for games.

"Why don't you say hello to Dalia, priestess to the ever-absent Lightfather."

The guard lifted the hood off the figure revealing a terrified woman with long dark hair and skin pale as a pearl. Tears streaked her face, and garbled sounds sat masked behind a thick rag in her mouth. The man's eyes grew wide.

"To be honest, she doesn't deserve this—I take no joy in the process—but I don't mind breaking a few dishes for a good meal. So, why don't you tell me why you were taking Chrys to the hidden Zeda city?"

The old man shook his head, face filled with resolve. "I'm sorry, sister. Some truths are greater than any one of us."

"How unfortunate."

Jurius drove his blade through the woman's stomach.

"No!" The false priest fought against the chains that held him, screaming at the top of his lungs.

Jurius stepped forward and met eyes with the prisoner. He then leaned in and whispered to him. "If you have a bundle of sticks, breaking them all at once is pure foolishness. One at a time is far more satisfying. It makes it easier to save the stubborn stick for last. Turns out, the temple is full of sticks."

The man said nothing.

The guard nodded to Jurius and walked out of the dungeon. After a few minutes, the woman finally stopped moving. Her lifeless eyes stared forward into the darkness. Tears stained the old man's cheeks.

Jurius shivered. He wished he could have made someone else do the torturing, but the answers he needed were for Alabella, not Malachus.

"If my information is accurate, then you know our next guest very well. Perhaps too well."

The guard returned with another hooded figure, moving more slowly than the first. He pulled the hood off to reveal a shriveled old man with a long beard. He looked malnourished and frail, but the lines of his face still held some semblance of grace.

"Impossible," he said as panic washed over his bloodied face. "Jasper?"

When Alabella had discovered that the church's Stone Council had begun to investigate the Bloodthieves, she'd ordered a false death for the old man. They'd kept Jasper alive for days now, collateral in case of some catastrophic failure in their plan. Today, Jurius was glad they hadn't killed him. Supposedly, the two priests had had a particularly intimate relationship.

The guard led Father Jasper over to Jurius, who placed him in the cell directly in front of the false priest. As he put the chains on him and cranked the gear to lift him up, Xalan begged him to stop.

"Please, don't."

"Oh, trust me. He will last much longer than the first. She

was the appetizer, but Father Jasper here is the main course. I'll make sure—for old time's sake—that you savor every morsel."

Xalan slumped in his chains, bloody and defeated.

"I'm afraid you'll be needing to watch this next part." He turned to the guard. "Watch over him. If he turns away or closes his eyes, we'll clamp his head and pin his eyelids. Understood?"

The guard's eyes darted from Jurius to the prisoners. He nodded, but Jurius saw a hint of fear in his eyes. Not all men are made for dark places.

"Please, don't do this," Father Xalan begged.

"You had your chance to plead for mercy. We've moved on to a harsher reality." He brought his knife to Father Jasper's feeble arm and let the tip scrape against skin as he dragged it lightly from wrist to shoulder.

"Please, I beg you. Not him."

Jurius walked over toward his table, and perused the instruments laid out across it. "Now typically, I would start with removing a finger, but I just can't help picturing a blind man with no arms." He lifted up a hack saw and nodded.

Jurius walked over to Jasper and placed the saw on the crook of the old man's arm. "Shall we count? Three."

"No, please."

"Two."

"Stop it!"

"One."

"I'll tell you how to find it!"

Jurius paused. "So, the rumors are true. You and old Jasper here were closer than friends? I must say I didn't believe it at first. I suppose gender matters less to the blind. It's a pity really. He'd have made a fine-looking amputee. Now to start, tell me why you are protecting Chrys?"

Xalan lay forward, his arms held up by the shackles that

bound them. Tears dripped down into the hole in his cheek. "It's not about Chrys. It's his son."

"The child? What about the child?" Jurius leaned forward.

"It shouldn't be possible."

"What?"

The old liar shook his head. "They aren't born."

"Enough! Tell me what it is about the child!"

The prisoner, defeated and broken, looked from Jasper to Jurius. "The child has Amber eyes."

Jurius opened his mouth, then closed it. He stared down at Xalan. Was it possible? Could there be another like Alabella? Did he mean for Chrys' son to be a weapon for the Zeda people? "What else?"

"That is all. I performed the Rite of Revelation. When I saw the Amber eyes, I knew I had to take him somewhere safe."

"What are you not telling me?"

"Nothing! I was taking him to Zedalum to protect his son. I swear it on the Lightfather."

"On the Lightfather? Seems you've spent too long in another man's skin." Jurius walked over to Father Jasper, the hacksaw still swinging in his hand. "I actually believe you're telling the truth."

Jurius was tired, but at least he had what he needed. Both Malachus and Alabella would be pleased. He stepped back toward the table and traced his fingers on the wall where the word was carved. "You haven't asked why it says 'fortune' here. It's to remind you that the power is in your hands. With two strokes of a pen, any man can change *torture* into *fortune*."

The man's eyes were closed.

"We share a lot in common, believe it or not. We're both willing to sacrifice others to protect those we love." He turned to the guard who was frozen in the corner of the room. "Go get something to clean up this mess."

The guard wasted no time in retreating.

"Now all that's left is for you is to tell me how to get to Zedalum."

Jurius walked away from the dungeon annoyed at the stains on his hands but pleased that he'd learned all he needed to know. Malachus would neither understand nor appreciate the implications of an Amber-eyed child—Jurius would have to feed him some other lie—but more importantly, he needed to play his cards in proper order.

Both of his masters were waiting.

But the lady was much more dangerous.

~ Pilliwick ~

CHAPTER 19

LIGHT AFTERNOON CLOUDS diffused the sunlight as it beat down high overhead. More and more, Jurius hated the sun. After such a long morning, the clouds seemed a more appropriate compliment. The general ruckus of the previous evening had settled and the grounds of Endin Keep had quieted, though the guards remained on high alert.

A large marble gazebo covered in budding flowers lay surrounded by a team of threadweaver guards as the Great Lord ate lunch with his friends. The structure was large and white with a myriad of pink and red flowers blooming across its surface. Beautifully trimmed greenery surrounded its borders, and inside there was a light, oak table with an elegant white runner down its center. Flowers and a smorgasbord of food were laid out with care.

At the table sat a variety of people close to Malachus. The luncheon was a weekly scheduled occurrence, but the invitees changed for each event. Today, as always, to his left sat Lady

Eleandra Orion-Endin. Her blonde hair curled and ran down across the neckline of a flowery white dress. She laughed with joy as her nephew, Fain, along with her brother and his wife, Kent and Brooke Orion, told a story about a pilliwick and a lonely widow.

On the other side of the Great Lord sat Henna followed by Jurius. It was a slight to his recent failures; he knew that. Next to him sat a beautiful, dark-skinned, black-haired woman. Some would call her nothing but the companion of a lonely man, but Alabella was much more dangerous.

There were eight other guests in attendance including the illustrious Tyberius and Mirimar Di'Fier, and a popular artist who went by the name Alexandrite. Jurius never liked the woman. She was too prideful for the quality of her work.

Servants brought out platters of desserts. Sunlight reflected feverishly off the silver. Mirimar—a purveyor of privacies—turned to Eleandra, a mischievous smile on her lips. "Now that dessert is here, how about some conversation that is a little bit... tastier. Tell me, dear. What is this I hear about Willow Valerian being a fugitive?"

"Mirimar, come now."

She ignored her husband. "Was she involved in the death of the temple worker? I've so many questions but, quite honestly, I always found her to be a particularly curious woman. You know, some say that her and Chrys are scheming to take the throne. The scandal! Can you even imagine that woman in charge? A disaster, surely."

Eleandra sighed. "Nothing so dire, I assure you. She simply wanted to go out searching for her son, and my husband wanted her to remain in the keep."

"So, she did sneak away," Mirimar smirked. "The mother of

the most wanted man in Alchea slips out from under your nose? You know, the people are quite distraught that General Chrys hasn't been found. He is the Apogee after all. We worry for our own safety. Surely you all are getting closer?"

She directed the last question to General Henna who nodded in response. "He's most likely lying face down in the Fairenwild."

Alexandrite, wearing a layered dress that shifted from red to green depending on the light, gave a slight puff of disregard. She spoke with an unnatural air. "That man is as hard as his name. I would not put him off so lightly."

They all looked to her, but Tyberius nodded his head as if he understood.

"Chrys. As in chrysoberyl? The way he spells it, I presumed he was named after the precious mineral. It is known for being quite difficult to break, you know. Of course, the name could very well be in reference to chrysocolla or chrysoprase, but I find those two minerals far less interesting. Alexandrite is a variety of chrysoberyl. I must admit the connection may give me a bit of a bias. Yet still, I make it a point never to trust a man who's handsome as he is hard." She blushed, dawning the insinuation. "Unwavering that is."

Jurius scoffed. He looked down at his hands, bits of blood still crusted under his nails. "The boy is nothing. A murderous traitor and a mistake."

He knew he'd misspoken when Malachus shifted in his seat. No one insinuated the Great Lord's fallibility.

"That's not what I heard," Fain said. The boy, Lady Eleandra's nephew, paled as soon as he spoke.

"Oh? And what is that?" Henna asked.

Mirimar perked up. "Yes, do tell."

His father gestured for him to go on. "Down at the shopping

district, I heard people saying he was the rebel leader, and that this whole time he was undercover, planning to bring down the entire Alchean government!"

"That's absurd," Jurius spat.

Malachus laughed out loud. "Rebels? It is nothing but a dozen angry farmers. The last thing Chrys wants is to lead a nation. Henna once said he had the ambition of a fish. It was hard enough to convince him to become a high general. No. There is another reason. It's not power."

"Hmm. A small taste of power *can* intoxicate the soul." Alabella's lips curled up at the ends.

Stones. The damned woman had promised she would stay quiet if he brought her with him. Introductions only. Play coy. Meet Malachus. It wasn't like he had much of a choice in the matter, she'd wanted to see the nobility of Alchea, and Jurius was one of the few invited to the table.

Malachus looked at her. They were the first words she'd spoken since Jurius' introduction. Her jet-black hair was slicked back behind her ears, falling across her collarbone, and brushing against small black feathers adorning her light summer dress. Jurius had introduced her as Lady Sia, an old friend from Felia. She wore lightshades over her eyes, quite popular among the Felian people, and convenient for hiding her secret.

"Is that so?" Malachus cocked his head to the side. "I suppose a Felian would know a little of intoxication."

Forced laughter broke out across the table, led by Tyberius, who's jowls tossed back and forth like a ship at sea.

Alabella looked back at Malachus, an uncomfortable look of hunger in her posture. "Intoxication, not so much. Power, now there is a taste my tongue has savored."

"But have you tasted these poached pears? The ginger and

cinnamon with the red wine and mulberry. Stones. This is the most wonderful thing I've tasted in years!" Tyberius shoved another bite of dessert into his mouth. His wife looked at him cheerily and slapped his shoulder with a smile.

From the other side, Lady Eleandra glared at Alabella.

Malachus stared at her. "A story for another time, perhaps. Tell me, Lady Sia of Felia, as an outsider, what do you think of our country? What do you think of Alchea?"

She smiled, white teeth contrasting with her mahogany skin. "Felia is beautiful and diverse, white spires and ocean blues. But Alchea is a rarity. You can feel it in the air. Look around this table. Almost every one of you is a threadweaver. That may seem normal to you, but not to most of the world. I've traveled far, and never have I seen so many threadweavers in one place. So, what do I think of your country? I think it is lucky. Or blessed. Or both. It is certainly memorable. But if I had to boil it down to one single statement, I would say that Alchea is the future."

"Well said, my lady. To the future!" Malachus held up his goblet, looking at her with profound interest.

"To the future." They all pitched back their goblets and drank to the toast.

"To the pears!" Tyberius raised his glass again, drinking before anyone had the chance to ignore him.

Lighter conversation ensued, and Malachus continued to steal glances at Alabella. Damn her but she knew how to leave an impression.

Jurius eavesdropped as Lady Eleandra started up a conversation to distract Malachus. "Have you thought about what these rebels are saying? I know they are few, but I think they accurately express real concerns that the people have."

"Fanatics do not speak for the masses. We cannot let those

who speak loudest do so for those who do not. Besides, what is it they want? They want me out of the throne, but they would want the same for any other."

"They just want to know that you think of them, of their well-being. People yearn for acknowledgement, even if it is artificial. Surely there is something you can do to appease them."

Malachus rubbed his temple, closing his eyes as he thought. "Do you have a suggestion? You always end these conversations with a suggestion. So, let's have it."

"What about the Festival of Light?" She smiled. "What if we opened the keep to the commoners, invite everyone in. It would mean a lot to the people if they felt like you were letting them be a part of your life. It would make you more relatable and accessible. We wouldn't let them into the main tower, of course, but we could put a big event together at the central fountain. Just imagine how beautiful it would be to have the fountain surrounded by all those people."

He turned to her. Her light brown eyes stared back into his bichromatic gaze. He let out a sigh of defeat. "General Henna, work with Eleandra and see if you can make it work. Security will be a nightmare. I'm not going to risk my life for it, but I am open to the idea."

She leaned forward and kissed his cheek, whispering something into his ear. He smiled something devious, then stood up and patted himself down. "Thank you all for coming. As always, the pleasure is ours. Fain, keep practicing your threadweaving. Tyberius, leave some pears for the rest of us. And Lady Sia, it has been an immeasurable pleasure. Please tell us you'll be staying in our city a little while longer?"

"Oh, I do think so. I'm quite taken with your city, and I mean to return the favor."

He nodded and turned to the others. "Friends. Stay. Drink. May the Lightfather bless you all."

Alabella leaned into Jurius and smiled as she whispered in his ear. "To the future."

CHAPTER 20

"YOU CANNOT RECOVER if you do not try." Staunch-faced Elder Rowan hardly glanced up as Chrys stepped out of his room. She had a leather strap across her forehead and green eyes that pierced in the early morning light.

Chrys had not rested much. He'd found it hard to sleep with the sporadic pains across his face and a headache that seemed to rise with the sun. One eye was black, and his nose was a little more crooked than it had been, but he was a threadweaver. His body would recover quickly. What kept him up the most was knowing how he'd failed to protect his own family.

He feigned a smile for the old woman. "I'm well enough."

She shook her head. "I've known men like you. Stronger than most. Rugged. Handsome. Those tricks don't matter to an old woman like me. Sit your arse down and don't get out of that bed until you're better."

Chrys wasn't sure if he should be offended or grateful but, either way, he was too exhausted to fight. He slipped back into his room without responding and imagined the old woman smiling to herself in the hallway. The other elder had been much nicer; he hoped the rest were more like her.

A light breeze brushed against the walls outside, causing the occasional creak as he went back into his room. Iriel lay asleep in a rocking chair in the corner of the room. She'd been up feeding Aydin on and off throughout the night.

He walked over to a window and pushed back the wooden slats so he could look out over the city. It felt impossible, an entire city built atop the feytrees, and yet the ground was sturdy as stone. The branches of the feytrees were so thick and twisted together that it created an immovable foundation. From the forest floor you couldn't see the sky or the city overhead. The audacity to build such a monument was commendable.

He had so many questions. What was the genesis of the city? And the matriarchal government? The curious relationship with the chromawolves. The hair. Why did they all shave one side? He found his eyes wandering back to the basket of vegetables on the side table. Stones, where did they get their food?

The rocking chair groaned as Iriel stretched out atop it. She reached her hand over her shoulder and arched her back. Little Aydin was swaddled tightly and nestled up in the crease of her other arm. Her lips arched upward as she caught Chrys' eye.

"Good morning my winter rose."

She coughed into her hand and laughed. "Your winter rose? That's a new one. A little mushy for my taste, but not your worst."

Chrys smiled just the slightest as he walked over to her. "Something my mother used to call me whenever I came out the other end of something hard. She said any rose that could live through winter was something special. And stones, Iriel, if we haven't lived through winter these last few days, I don't know what we've done."

"When you explain it that way, I kind of like it." She smiled through a bit of pain. "I changed while you were sleeping. I'm still bleeding a lot from the birth. As much as I want to go explore, I need to relax. I'm worried my body won't heal properly if I don't. Frankly, I'm worried even if I do."

It was incredible how much she'd managed to do the day after giving birth. Sure, threadweavers healed faster than others, but no one healed that fast. The pair of them were a mess. Both so beaten and broken that they were hardly recognizable from the man and woman they'd been only days before. Yesterday, they were nobility. Today, they were nothing.

Chrys took a seat on the bed. "The elders offered to help with Aydin. I wasn't sure what to tell them, but it sounds like it might be a good idea. Give you more time to rest."

She looked down at their child, sleeping peacefully in her arms. "If they have silksap milk, a night nurse would help so I could get some uninterrupted sleep."

"I'll ask around, but we're in the middle of the Fairenwild. I'm not sure they have many food options."

"It is quite strange."

Chrys nodded, looking around the room. "It's even more strange to think that this is home now."

Iriel stared at him, silent for a moment before she spoke. "No, it's not."

"It's not as bad as it seems, and we're safe here."

"Not that bad? We're living in a forest like a bunch of savages."

"Come now, Iriel. There's nothing savage about these people."

Her voice rose. "Have you forgotten that I just had a child? I don't want to raise a baby in the forest!"

"You think *I* want to?" he asked. "Of course, I'd love to be back home! But the reality is that our child is different. We don't have the luxury of choice."

"There's always a choice," she replied.

"And where would you have us go?"

"A small town outside of Felia? A quiet island in Kulai where no one knows us? Anywhere else! I don't understand why you're acting like the Bloodthieves won. We got away. We can do whatever we want."

Chrys took a breath, kneading his temples in a vain attempt to rub away the headache. "And how would that work out for Aydin? You think in Felia or Kulai they'll treat an Amber-eyed kid any better than the people back home? At best, he'd be bullied his whole life."

"And you honestly think that it will be better here? Aydin will be different no matter where we live. We might as well live somewhere we're happy."

"We could be happy here."

"That's where you're wrong. Maybe you don't care because you don't have to take care of a baby but let me make this very clear: I will never call this place home."

She was infuriating. Unreasonable. Stubborn as stone. They were safe in Zedalum. Aydin would be accepted. She wasn't thinking through the consequences of leaving. He wanted to scream that she was being foolish. And, stones, his head was pounding. The pressure near his temples had been rising ever since he woke up. He wanted to take a pin, jam it in, and let it all out.

Mmmm. I can be quite convincing. Let me speak to her.

The pressure intensified with each word. He leaned forward, grabbing his head. *Leave me alone! Not now!*

"This is on you, Chrys. Figure it out, because I'm not staying here."

Mmmm. I can help.

"Are you even listening to me, Chrys?"

Mmmm.

"Get out!" Chrys yelled, his hands still clutching the sides of his head. His fingertips were white with pressure as he squeezed tight against his skull.

"Are you serious? I'm your wife, not a damn soldier you can send away because they displease you. You need to figure this out," Iriel exhaled in disbelief, anger flashing in her eyes. She opened her mouth to speak again but, when she looked at him, she knew something was wrong. "Chrys, what's happening right now? Are you okay?"

He was a dam on the verge of collapse, and the voice of the Apogee was the last tap. He broke. Tears poured like a river down his bruised face. It was too much. After everything they had been through, after everything they had lost, he couldn't deal with the Apogee anymore. He couldn't keep the secret to himself. He couldn't do it alone.

Chrys looked up, his eyes red with agony. "Iriel, something is wrong with me."

She placed Aydin on the bed and grabbed hold of Chrys as he cried onto her shoulder. "Talk to me, Chrys. What is wrong?"

He wanted to tell her—he'd wanted to tell her for years—but the fear of letting her see the darkest parts of his soul was too much.

"You'll think I'm crazy."

"Never."

He knew it wasn't true, but he wanted to believe it. He wanted to believe that if anyone could see past his problems and still accept him, broken as he may be, it was her. But the world is cruel, and people act rash when expectations misalign with reality. What if she didn't accept him? What if she thought he'd gone mad?

But, then again, what if she didn't?

"It started during the war. I don't know when, maybe after the first battle. A voice. I started to hear a voice." He let the words sink in, expecting a deluge of questions, but instead she sat quietly, listening. His voice shook as he continued. "It's the Apogee, Iriel. *I'm* not the Apogee. There is something inside me, or someone, that begs me to hand over control. But when I do, it kills everything. I don't even remember the slaughters they say I committed in the war. The battles I'm said to have won are cloudy at best. By the time I understood what was happening, I'd killed some of our own men. I swore to never let him out again, but his voice is there. Every time I get angry, I hear him. 'Let me out. Let me out. I can help if you let me out.' I thought I could control it, but I've lost control of everything else in our life. I just don't know if I can do it anymore."

"Oh, Chrys."

He shouldn't have told her. It was foolish. If ever she needed him to be strong, it was now. He could see it coming. The pity. The shame. She would never look at him the same. Every piece of insecurity and fear that had built up over the past five years came rolling through him like a ghostly tremor. There was no turning back now that she knew the truth. Her husband was broken. Unstable. A clay pot turned dry, cracked to the core, fit to be cast out.

But her eyes, soft as silk, met his own. "You've fought this alone for all these years? I can't imagine how exhausting that must have been. You should have told me."

"I couldn't. I..." He trailed off.

They both sat, neither speaking. Chrys stared at the floor, feeling the weight of the silence as each moment passed. His chest was a boulder dragging him into the ground. Pressure continued to build up in his head. What did he expect? That she would be happy? That she would smile and tell him "It's okay"? It wasn't. He wasn't. None of it was okay.

"I had a neighbor when I was a child." Iriel finally broke the silence. She nodded her head as she recalled the memory. "His garden was beautiful, full of bright colors and exotic flowers. People from all over the city would come to see it, but they were careless. They stepped on his grass, picked the flowers, and muddied the walkways, so, he closed it off with a wall. But people still came. He added decorative stonework and ivy that bloomed in the springtime. It took all his time to care for the wall, but everyone admired him greatly for it. One winter, the people stopped hearing from him, and when my father went to his home to check on him, he saw the garden for the first time in years. It was dead. All of it. He walked on cracked stone, over thriving weeds and dead flowers. The neighbor had been neglecting the garden to care for the wall. My father walked into the house, and you know what he found? The man had taken his own life.

"Chrys, it doesn't matter how beautiful the wall is if the garden inside is dying. No one can live like that forever."

He struggled to breathe. She'd seen his withered garden and she accepted him, nonetheless. In that moment, his load lightened. The weight remained, but a weight held by two is easier to bear.

Her hand rubbed away his tears. "It's you and me, Chrys. You don't have to fight this alone."

CHAPTER 21

IRIEL LAY asleep on the bed as Chrys snuck out of the room. She'd spent the last hour holding him as he'd let out five years of bottled up emotion. The relief was tangible. Oddly enough, if none of this had happened—if they were still back in Alchea in their quiet home—he wasn't sure he ever would have told her. At least one good thing had come of it all.

As he peeked out of the room, he looked for any sign of the grouchy, elderly woman. She was gone, so he meandered down the hallway. He passed a young Zeda boy and couldn't help thinking of his friends back home. His mother. Luther and Emory. Laz and Reina. Even their crazy, old neighbor, Emmett. The thing that sickened him the most was knowing that Jurius was working for the Bloodthieves. Henna was smart but, if she couldn't piece it together, who knew what the Bloodthieves would do? And Malachus. The Lightfather only knew what the Great Lord would do when he discovered the betrayal.

Chrys looked down at the wooden floor as he walked, rubbing at his sore ribs. No give. A lodge on top of the trees and the floor felt more solid than an Alchean home. What about when a rainstorm struck? Winds must have done a number on the city.

He found his way to the lobby where a young girl sat alone. Both sides of her head were shaved and the top of her hair was pulled back into a ponytail. She was reading a book. Stones. They even had books. He thought about talking to the girl— children are often great at sharing things they shouldn't—but instead moved toward the doorway.

He imagined the sprawling treetop metropolis before the door even opened. The bright sun would be beating down over the wide-set buildings, and people would be bustling back and forth across busy wooden paths.

But the door opened before he reached for the handle.

Willow Valerian, tired and covered in dirt, nearly crashed into him as she entered.

He took a step back, bewilderment plastered across his face. "Mother?"

She was the last person he'd expected to see. The tightness in his chest loosened, and the flares of pain seemed to subside.

Her fatigue changed to joy as she threw her arms around her son. Tears ran down her cheeks. "Oh, Chrys." She squeezed him with maternal ferocity. "I knew you were alive." She spoke the words quietly, personally, as if she had been doubting their truth for some time.

Chrys held her close, then pulled back for a moment. "We're all okay, but how are you here?"

"I'm a stubborn woman. Is Iriel well? I can't imagine."

Chrys nodded. "Tired, but well."

"And Aydin?"

"Sleeping."

She exhaled. "There is so much to tell you, Chrys. But I

really must speak with the elders. Come with me. I imagine many of your questions will be the same as theirs."

Willow turned and gestured to a Zeda man standing behind her. Chrys hadn't seen him, but assumed he was a guard similar to the one that had followed them to the lodge.

She led Chrys down the hall toward the elders' council room. They passed a side table that held a bowl of Felian oranges, the sweet scent filling the air. Finally, they reached the council room, and Willow knocked. Without waiting for someone on the other side, she pushed the door open.

Inside, Elder Rosemary sat conversing with Elder Rowan and, quite surprisingly, it was Elder Rosemary that donned the frown. As the door opened, they both turned and looked. After a moment of confusion, disbelief took over.

"Gale take me. It cannot be. You're alive!" Elder Rosemary smiled wider than a feytree.

Willow walked into the room. "I could say the same about you." She smiled and hugged the older woman with a love that Chrys couldn't understand. "Less surprised about you, Rowan. You've always been as stubborn as stone. The winds couldn't take you if they tried."

Elder Rowan smiled, something Chrys had yet to see. "Second only to you, my old friend."

"I see you've met my son," Willow said, gesturing to him. "Chrysanthemum."

Elder Rosemary laughed, shook her head, and laughed again. "Of course, he is. He has your eyes. I should have known. The Father of All has a wicked sense of humor, doesn't he? I suppose the age lines up. And Chrysanthemum? A good Zeda name."

"Chrysanthemum?" he asked. Chrys' head was spinning.

His mother was acting like she was from Zedalum, but was that even possible? They were from Felia.

Willow gestured to the chairs at the table. "Everyone, please sit. I imagine we could all use a little explanation.

"Chrys, I was born in Zedalum. I was raised here and fell in love here. You were born here."

Chrys' mind reeled. He was born here? He was a Zeda? All these years believing he'd been from Felia, escaping an abusive father. Was none of that true? He could feel each beat of his heart pounding against his bruised ribs.

"Two days after you were born, before we'd given you a name, I had a vision. It was me, but it wasn't me. I told myself to take you away. That a storm was coming and the Fairenwild wasn't safe. When I told your father that I was going to take you away, he didn't believe me. No one did. He said I was being foolish and irrational, and that the pregnancy and birth had confused my mind. He had guards watch my family's house to make sure I did not leave. I waited a few days for emotions to settle and, when the opportunity arose, I took you and we left. You are not from Felia. You have Zeda blood and a Zeda name. This place is your birthright."

Chrys closed his eyes. He tried to process her words, but his mind was so exhausted that he felt like a man trying to catch the sun. "Why would you lie to me about this?"

"I always meant to tell you but, by the time you were old enough to understand, it was a life so distant from us that it would have made no difference."

Chrys' eyes were cold, a myriad of emotions stewing in their depths. "It would have made a difference to me."

Willow took in a slow breath. "You have every right to be angry. If I could go back, maybe I would do things differently. But there is more. When you disappeared from the temple, I was taken to Endin Keep for questioning. They think you are planning to overthrow Malachus or some nonsense that Jurius has planted in their minds. That's when I heard that they'd captured the priest that you'd escaped with."

"He's alive?"

"As far as I know, yes."

Elder Rowan shook her head and smiled. "Pandan that old dog."

"Pandan?" Willow choked on the word.

"You didn't know?" Elder Rosemary brought a hand to her cheek.

"I spoke with him. Surely I would have recognized him."

"You spoke with him?" Elder Rosemary and Elder Rowan both said.

Willow stared down at the table as she spoke. "It was dark. His eyes were covered, and his mouth was gagged. He'd been tortured. He only spoke to me through gestures. If I'd known…"

A fire inside of Chrys ignited, embers of truth flickering deep in his soul. Was it possible? After all the time he'd spent with Pandan, could it be? He barely uttered the words. "Is he my father?"

Before Willow could answer, Elder Rowan blurted out, "Your father's dead, boy. Pandan's your uncle."

The room warped in Chrys' vision, spinning and growing in surges. It was hard to focus on any one thing. He looked to his mother, but her eyes were vacant. Chrysanthemum? Flower boy? Stones. He should have made the connection. Every Zeda he'd met had a name derived from nature. Laurel. Alder. Rosemary. Rowan. Willow. His mother was a Zeda. *He* was a Zeda. The man who'd saved him was his uncle. The man who'd sacrificed himself was his uncle. And he was being tortured by Jurius.

"My little brother," Willow whispered. Chrys could see the pain in her eyes. She'd spoken to her own brother and hadn't recognized him.

Chrys straightened his back. "We have to save him."

The others turned to him. Elder Rowan huffed out her disapproval. "You grounders are far too hasty. It's dangerous, and Pandan knew what he was getting himself into."

"He sacrificed himself to save us! And he didn't even know who we were! We owe him our lives. We have to do something."

"Calm yourself, boy," Elder Rowan sneered. "He knew the dangers when he left. He's been in Alchea for nearly twenty-five years. You don't think he knew exactly who you were? He did what he had to do to protect his nephew and the child. Take the gift he's given you, and let him pass with honor."

He knew. Of course, he knew. The priests had records of everyone; it must have been simple for Pandan to figure it out. But why hadn't he contacted them? It didn't matter. He'd saved them. It was time to return the favor. "I refuse to rest while a member of my family is killed on my behalf."

Willow looked to Chrys and smiled, shaking her head. "You may have met your match, Rowan. Chrys, we'll figure something out, but you and I are the most wanted criminals in all of Alchea, and two of the most recognizable. Even with your current disguise," she gestured to his bruised face, "it's suicide."

Elder Rosemary nodded. "The priority is your son. We still haven't figured out what to do with him yet."

"Aydin?" Willow raised a brow. "What about Aydin? Did something happen to him in the Fairenwild?"

Elder Rowan and Elder Rosemary both looked to Chrys. They each dared the other to explain. With puckered lips, Elder Rowan nodded. "The child is an Amber threadweaver."

The moment lasted forever as the words sunk in. "I thought that was just a myth."

"We'd be better off if it was." Elder Rosemary rubbed her temple. "There are only two types of naturally occurring threadweavers, Sapphires and Emeralds. Our people know of two other types, Amber and Obsidian, but these are not naturally occurring. They are created, so far as our records say. But how, we do not know. The last known Amber threadweavers died centuries ago. No one has seen one until now."

"I have."

"Excuse me?" They all turned to Chrys.

"This is not the first Amber threadweaver I've seen." The memory replayed in his mind, tentacles of light grasping up from the ground onto his legs, pulling him toward the earth. "The leader of the Bloodthieves is a woman with eyes like the sun. She was able to somehow create threads."

Elder Rowan frowned even more profoundly. "This is very troubling. Two Amber threadweavers in a generation." She turned to Willow. "If children are being born as Amber threadweavers now, Gale take us if children are born as Obsidians. It seems you may have been right about that storm after all, Willow."

Chrys needed more answers. There was something they weren't telling him. The texts they spoke of must have more information that could help him understand. "What else do you know about Amber and Obsidian threadweavers? What do your texts say? I want to know everything."

Elder Rosemary started to speak. "A long time ago—"

"Rosemary!" Elder Rowan looked furious.

"Silence, Rowan! If there has ever been a time to discuss this, it is now." She looked fierce. Elder Rosemary had such a kind face that it was easy to dismiss her. But in that very moment, Chrys saw the true power of the woman. "Our people are the descendants of the last recorded Amber threadweavers. They used their power to protect the world by creating what we call the coreseal. They were so worried that something would happen to the seal that they built this city—sequestered from the rest of the world—and spent the rest of their lives protecting it."

The look on Willow's face was indiscernible. "How have I never heard of this? What is the coreseal? And why don't we teach these things to our people?"

"Our ancestors were clear that great danger would befall the world if anything happened to the seal. Our people are its guardians, and the best way for us to keep it safe is to keep it secret. The elders keep the secret, as do some of our most trusted advisors, and we pass along that knowledge, so it is never lost.

"So, while we may not know everything, it is clear that the Father of All has brought your Amber grandson to the home of his heritage. This is no mere coincidence, and it gives me hope to know that we have divine providence on our side."

Chrys scoffed at her words. "Divine providence? That my wife may have permanent health issues because she had to run for her life the day after giving birth? That my ribs and nose are broken? That an innocent man was killed in the temple by my uncle who is almost certainly being tortured by a traitor? That my mother is a wanted criminal? You have a skewed view of reality if you think the situation we're in is *divine providence*."

Mmmm.

Chrys stopped himself. The last thing he needed now was the Apogee whispering in his ear. *I am in control.*

"Are you done?" Elder Rowan stared blankly, unimpressed. "Of all of the priests, you got *him*. When you were about to die, a pack of ravenous chromawolves fought off your attackers and, when you were next, a Zeda girl far from where she ought to be that was bonded to that very chromawolf saved you. Without *divine providence*, the whirlwinds surrounding you would have had you dead ten times over."

Chrys was tired and frustrated, but she was right. Maybe it wasn't *divine providence*, but it was certainly a series of fortunate coincidences. As his blood cooled, he saw the rationality of it. "You're right, of course. I apologize for my temper."

Both Elder Rosemary and Elder Rowan raised their brows.

Rosemary turned to Willow. "Well that was unexpected. An apology? It seems you have raised him well. Courage is the core, but humility is the foundation."

Willow smiled. "Elder Sage used to say that."

"She did." Elder Rosemary tilted her head, smiling. "More importantly, we should discuss this business with Pandan. You said he is still alive? Tell us everything."

Together, Chrys and Willow explained it all. Chrys started with the discovery that Jurius had been working for the Amber threadweaver, then skipped to the birth. He related the happenings at the temple, of the escape and subsequent flight to the Fairenwild. While Chrys told them of Pandan's heroic stand against the oncoming horsemen, Willow teared up. Chrys' voice shook as he explained the vicious battle in the forest that ended with the arrival of the chromawolves. He told them how they would have eaten him and his family if not for Laurel. Willow took over from there and explained Pandan's imprisonment, her interrogation by High General Henna, and how she conned her way into talking with the prisoner. It was hard for her to talk about it, knowing now that she'd stood mere feet away from her estranged brother and could have done something to rescue him. Finally, Willow told of her escape from the keep and journey back to the Fairenwild.

"This Jurius," Elder Rowan grumbled, falling back into her chair. "He is not a good man?"

Chrys shook his head. "I thought he was, but he's working with the Bloodthieves now. What I don't understand is why the Amber woman is working in the shadows. She has Jurius in her pocket, and he's one of the most influential men in Alchea, right hand to the Great Lord. She could kill Malachus and take the throne, and there's nothing anyone could do about it."

"What makes you think she could kill the Great Lord so easily? She couldn't kill you. Are you greater than he?" Past the façade of amiability, Chrys caught another glimpse of Elder Rosemary's cunning mind.

"Divine providence?" he said with a smirk.

The elders did not look amused.

Chrys knew he had to tell them the truth. If for no other reason so that they could help him find it. "I was only able to escape her because of a stranger's gift. An obsidian blade."

Elder Rosemary raised a brow. "An obsidian blade?"

"Yes. And as unbelievable as it may sound, the blade can sever threads."

The sound of wood creaking echoed from the hallway outside the door.

LAUREL'S HEART QUICKENED. She pulled away from the door-way, the floor creaking under foot. The whole conversation was unreal. And just when she thought it could not get any more unbelievable, she found out that the blade she'd picked up in the forest could "sever threads". What did that even mean? Part of her felt like she should get rid of it, as if its power would somehow contaminate her. But she wasn't that stupid.

She crouched down and peeked through the crack in the doorway. They were still sitting and talking. Footsteps came from down the hallway around the corner. She pulled back from the door and leaned against the wall like she belonged. An older woman smiled at her and nodded as she passed. Laurel recognized her from her time spent as messenger for Elder Rowan. As soon as she passed, Laurel shoved her ear up against the crack in the doorway to continue listening.

"That's not possible," said the muddled voice of Elder Rowan. "Physical objects do not interact with threadlight."

"This one can."

"You said you dropped it near the eastern edge of the Fairenwild? We need to send scouts down to the site to find the blade immediately. If you are telling the truth, it could be an invaluable tool in the oncoming storm. Let's pray that we find it before someone else."

"Agreed," said Rowan. The legs of her chair scraped against the wooden floor. "I'll go gather a group straightaway."

Laurel was just about to run down the hallway when Rowan's footsteps stopped, and she spoke again. "Chrys. Where, again, did you say you obtained this blade?"

"The doctor that helped my wife when she was sick. I wish I knew more. It happened so fast and my mind was occupied by other things. Trust me, I wish I could tell you more."

"Divine providence, indeed," Elder Rosemary muttered.

The slow, elderly footsteps started back up and Laurel raced down the hallway, slipping around the corner just in time to avoid the Elder's view. Her heart was pounding, but not from the effort. She was definitely *not* supposed to have heard any of that conversation. And to think, she'd almost knocked when she'd arrived.

Her whole life she had been told that the grounders were heathens and should be avoided. The reality was that the hermetic Zeda culture had nothing to do with the grounders and everything to do with some ancient oath to protect the coreseal. What even was that? The reason the elders didn't tell anyone was probably because they knew no one would believe it. How many hundreds of years had they spent isolated from the rest of the world protecting an old tradition?

Laurel found the veins in her arms glowing faintly. The pulsing threadlight was mesmerizing, like waves flowing back and forth in a bowl. The Zeda people needed to know the truth. They *deserved* to know the truth. Part of her wanted to run out and scream it for everyone to hear—so that they all knew the elders had been lying—but she needed proof. Maybe then they could finally open their world to the grounders.

She ran outside, the light breeze tossing her blonde hair. Every bone in her body wanted to take out the blade and figure out how to make it work. Her hand shook with the desire, but she fought it. First, she needed to get to a quiet place.

She used threadpoles to travel quickly to the entrance platform. She slipped down the stairs, winking at a young guard, and leapt off. She descended fast and landed hard against the wide surface of the wonderstone.

She ignored the enticements and jumped down onto the dirt, surrounded by dozens of roses. The brilliant white threadroses slowly closed their petals as Laurel stopped threadweaving.

Laurel headed toward the base of a nearby feytree. She pulled the black blade out of her pocket and held it up toward a group of photospores. The shaft shimmered in the pulsing light. As she opened herself to threadlight once again, her veins pulsed and the nearby white roses opened their petals once more.

She smiled and focused on the thread that ran from the center of the photospore bulb down to the earth. Slowly, delicately, she slid the obsidian blade through the thread. As soon as it passed through, the thread popped out of existence and the photospore shifted upward.

Gale take me.

She grabbed the reed and broke it in two. The bulb, still pulsing with luminescent light, floated up into the air. It rose higher and higher, up into the vaulted darkness of the canopy. She watched in awe until...

Pop. A thin thread of light reappeared, connecting the photospore to the ground. Gravity took hold once again and it fell back down to the forest floor.

Amazing.

She gathered a dozen photospore bulbs, pulling them from their reeds, and laid them in a small pile. Opening her eyes to threadlight, she focused on the corethread for each of the spores. One by one she let the knife slide through their thread, each time a silent *pop* as the thread burst out of existence. Grinning from ear to ear, she watched as each photospore rose up into the dark canopy. Floating balls of luminescence spread out above her like stars under a coniferous sky.

Then they fell. It felt surreal watching as each of the photospores descended to the ground. She looked at her own corethread, a brilliant strand of pulsing light beneath her, and had a wonderful idea. A terribly wonderful idea.

What would happen if she cut her own corethread?

With a newfound hunger, she brought the blade down and carefully brought it toward her corethread. Thoughts of flight took off in her mind before she'd even severed it. Without gravity to pull her down, she would be able to soar into the sky. A bird in flight, walking the winds.

As she pressed the blade up against her corethread, her hand shook wildly and the blade seemed to blur in the air. Her corethread fought back like a magnet resisting its match, refusing to let it pass through. She tried harder, but her hand continued to vibrate back and forth. The muscles in her arm strained against the force. Furious, she hacked into the open air over and over again trying to sever her corethread. It felt like she was trying to chop down a tree with a spoon.

She started to tear up. Not for any good reason, but she did.

Her eyes closed and her arms sprawled out to either side of her as she dropped to the ground. Another failure. One more opportunity dangling overhead as she leapt and failed to snatch it from the tree.

She took a deep breath and let the sweet nectar running through her veins feed her emptiness. With threadlight, she would never be alone.

CHAPTER 22

ALVERAX HAD A GREAT IDEA.

He walked away from Jayla's house, numb inside and out, and yet, despite the pain, he felt thrill. The thrill of freedom. The thrill of power. The thrill of purpose. He'd not only been given a second chance, he'd been given something more. And he was going to use it to get a little payback.

The dank shed behind his grandfather's house was a perfect hideout. He could spend the night there and no one would know he was alive. Even with the door closed, moonlight broke through slits in the wooden doorway, lighting the inside. Because the city was only exposed to the sky at its southern and western borders, some areas of the city were pitched in shadow throughout the night; however, his grandfather's house was far enough south that the moon's glow bathed it in dim light. Massive fire-lit beacons spread throughout the city providing light and warmth throughout the night.

There was so much to learn about what he could do. His

abilities seemed to be different than what he'd heard about threadweaving growing up. Threadweavers should only be able to *push* or *pull* on a thread, and that surge would affect whatever item was on the other end. It was balance. So why was he able to make the thread vanish altogether?

And why the hell was it called *threadweaving*? Push. Pull. Break. No one was actually *weaving* anything. But, then again, do strawberries look like straw? Does one really rest in the restroom? The world is full of poorly named things.

He sat down on an old pile of blankets and tried to open himself to threadlight. The world stayed dark. He flexed his whole body and squeezed with all the power he had inside himself. The world stayed dark. He cursed the Heralds under his breath. He'd done it once; it should be easy to do again.

He closed his eyes and thought about how he had felt just before it happened in Jayla's house. His mind's eye filled with bright light as if he were staring up into the sun and, as he opened them again, dozens of threads of pure light burst into his vision. There were fewer than there had been at Jayla's house, but even still the quantity was overwhelming. His mind raced trying to take in each thread.

He shut his eyes and willed away the threadlight. When he opened his eyes, the shed was dark again. It was unnerving when he realized that the pulsing threads did not actually illuminate the real world at all. It wasn't dark *again*; it had always been dark. The physical world and threadlight overlaid on top of each other. Seen by the same eyes but disconnected. It didn't matter that the threads represented connections between real objects with real mass, their glow stayed separate from the real world.

The only way this was going to work was if he didn't get

overwhelmed every time. He closed his eyes and let threadlight flood his vision once more. If the threads weren't pulsating, maybe he could focus. With the subtle movement of hundreds of strands of magic throbbing all around him, it felt impossible.

He stared at the thread that connected him to a shovel in the corner of the shed. As his mind fixed on the shovel, all of the other threads that had been bombarding his vision faded away. Only the thread between him and the shovel remained.

That will be useful.

He squeezed his fist as he stared intently at the thread, as if to break it physically. Nothing happened. He squeezed harder. His body shook with the exertion. The thread vibrated for a moment and then returned to its previous state.

"Break!" he yelled before he could stop himself.

The thread did not comply.

He quieted himself. Making noise while hiding was...not ideal. As his mind calmed, he looked again at the thread and instinctively touched it with his mind. His veins turned black as threadlight pulsed through his body. The force he exerted on the thread burst it asunder, a small mist of light puffing out as it disappeared entirely.

His body felt warm while looking at threadlight, but his chest burned hot when he *broke* a thread. It was like drinking hot tea; the heat flowed to the ends of his fingertips. He experimented, *breaking* thread after thread of various tools and knick-knacks, finding it harder to *break* the threads of objects at a distance. Same with objects in shadows. His ability to see an object affected his ability to *break* it. That lined up with what he knew; if you cover a threadweaver's eyes they can't threadweave.

As he experimented, he found that threads had no breaking point. No specific amount of pressure that would cause it to *break.* Any amount of pressure broke it. Soft. Hard. The words felt strange in his mind, because the action wasn't physical. Either way it was true. If he focused, he could vary the pressure that he applied to the thread, and that dictated the length of time a thread disappeared. If he broke it gently, it was gone for a few moments, but if he let threadlight flare inside of him as he broke it, it might be gone for a few minutes.

He stopped filtering out the myriad threads and stood in awe at the beauty of it. Beautiful lines of light sprouted forth from him as if he were the sun itself. Below him, he saw the thick thread that bound him to the core of the world. It was how Sapphires could launch themselves into the air and how Emeralds could become immovable. For Alverax, it was what had made him float. The corethread was much thicker than the rest. Different somehow. Something about it drew him to it. Urging him to threadweave. He reached his hand inside, as if he could touch it, and swore that he could feel a warmth emanating from within.

When he pulled his hand out, he learned the final lesson.

Threadweaving too much made you sick.

After hours of *breaking* threads, he'd hit some kind of tipping point. He vomited every last bit of fluid from his body, and dry-heaved for another half hour after that. The motion tore open a bit of the scar on his chest, and he bled all over his shirt.

Exhaustion finally took him and he passed out in the corner of the shed, lying in a bed of blood and vomit.

When he awoke, his grandfather was standing over him, a shadowed vignette of relief and disappointment. The shed smelled horrid. Alverax couldn't imagine what his grandfather thought of him in that moment.

"This must be real." The old man loomed over him. "If I were imagining you were still alive, this is not how I would have pictured it. When I heard noises out back last night, I thought it was that pesky pilliwick again. Core-spawned creatures. Never expected to find my dead grandson covered in vomit. Well, let's get you cleaned up and we can talk after."

He lifted Alverax and hauled him to the house and into the bathroom. The clothes were unsalvageable, so they were tossed out. His grandfather drew him a salty bath and left him with a few towels and some soap to scrape off the blood and debris.

Alverax had never understood how his grandfather, the most selfless man he'd ever known, had raised his father, the most selfish man ever to walk the desert. He saw himself somewhere in between. Alverax was decent, skewing toward good. At the very least, he was a better man than his father had been.

After his body was clean, Alverax left the bath and put on some new clothes. His room hadn't changed. Then again, he hadn't been dead for long. It would be weird if his grandfather had removed everything. He found some clean clothes and got dressed. If there was a way to avoid talking about what had happened, he was going to take it. The last thing he needed right now was to explain how he'd died and been resurrected as a new breed of threadweaver.

He left the bathroom and his grandfather was sitting cross-legged on a plush rug in the living room. An unavoidable location. *Well-played grandfather.* "Thanks for the help this morning. Didn't mean to scare you."

His grandfather looked deep into his eyes. "I know I'm old, and you think I couldn't possibly understand, but you *can* trust me. I won't make you—Heralds know I'm not one to force a man against his will—but you won't find a more willing ear than mine."

If he thought that meant Alverax was going to tell him everything, he was wrong. This was just the out he was looking for. "I'm just not ready to talk about it yet. I need a little time to process. Tomorrow. I'll tell you everything tomorrow." He glanced outside and noticed the sun was already starting to set. Heralds. He'd slept most of the day. If it wasn't tonight, he'd have to wait another week. "I'm going to take a walk, maybe a swim in the geysers. Tomorrow."

The old man nodded. "Be careful. I'd prefer not to mourn your death twice."

Alverax didn't wait for any more conversation. Back in his room he opened the hidden hole in the corner under his rug and pulled out a bag of shines. He'd need some money to initiate his plan. Tying it onto his waist, he grabbed some food and went outside into the darkening desert city.

As he walked through sandy roads, the sun passed down below the western horizon. The southern edge of the city was a miles-long steep cliff face overlooking the Altapecean Sea, called Mercy's Bluff. Because the cliff curved around the western edge, the sunset lasted until the light fell below the sea itself.

Towering, stone buildings cast long shadows over the eastern half of the city where the Three Darlings were found. Owned by Jelium, the multi-part complex was home to the vilest citizens of Cynosure, and that was saying something. The three sections were called the Veil, the Nest, and the Pit. The most famous section was the Pit. During the day they raced camels and sandhogs, but at night they raced necrolytes. The stakes were high and the danger was undeniable.

That was his destination.

There were two paths to get to the racetrack. The first was a straight shot through well-lit roads where he was likely to be recognized. The other was through the Nest. He'd only gone there once; his friend had convinced him to go try a pinch of lytemare. It had given him hallucinations for two days and he'd vowed *never again*. The Nest was where people went to lay mindlessly in smoke-filled rooms with strangers and poor friends.

He took off down the second path with a hood pulled up over his face, darkening his already dark skin. His coarse black hair was cut short with a small strip down the center grown out longer than the rest. He'd inherited his father's infectious smile —perfect for a conman—but he hid it behind patchy facial hair.

After a time, he arrived at the entrance to the Nest. A pair of able-bodied giants stood guard at the archway. They stood staring down at Alverax and his average height. Part of him wanted to flaunt his new abilities to show them that he was more than what he seemed, but when they nodded him through without question, he changed his tune. What was he going to do? Make them float?

Inside the Nest was a huge stretch of sandy path flanked on both sides by stalls of various concoctions. Some were more popular during the day, general herbs and roots that were helpful for healing. At night, the lines shifted to the back. He could see at least four large lines farther down and a few smaller, with some stragglers vending at the "more savory" shops.

He kept his hood cinched tight and walked forward as he passed the first of the major lines. The next two lines were harder drugs: necrotol and lytemare. They were both harvested from live necrolytes and had major hallucinatory effects while providing certain levels of serenity. As hard as he tried not to remember his experience, passing the lytemare vendor made him shiver. He had no interest in the other three, but the last line, smaller than the others, was something he'd always wanted to try but never had the funds. It was also the most controversial.

Transfusers.

In Cynosure, threadweavers were not only rich because of what they could do. They were rich because of what they could provide. Blood. Threadweavers were paid richly for donated blood. If an achromat drank it, it allowed that person to have a taste of threadlight. As amazing as the feeling was supposed to be, Alverax was sure it was nothing compared to the real thing. He walked past a few eager, rich kids and remembered the tears streaming down his face the first time he'd seen threadlight.

"It's ridiculous how expensive it is," one said.

A well-dressed woman tending the stall replied to the young man. "While other solutions can make you imagine things, at the end of the day they are merely imaginings. Threadlight is real. Transfusers open your eyes to the *reality* that is all around you. Seeing it will change you. It will change how you see the world. A change of perspective is priceless, my boy."

Alverax scoffed as he pushed his way to the end of the Nest's long walkway. *I wonder how much they'd pay for* my *blood.* He felt like a god walking among children. No one here knew that he was a threadweaver. No one knew the strange power coursing through his veins. Part of him wanted them to know, but he knew it was good to be underestimated.

He slipped out the other end of the Nest and walked through a wide corridor leading to the back side of the Pit. Thousands of people were packed into the outdoor stadium, chanting the names of their favorite racers and mumbling prayers under their breath for a lucrative win. Alverax pushed passed a gang of Alirian men, and a circle of friends that must have smoked a tub of sailweed by the look on their faces.

There were three kinds of people in Cynosure. First were the *lifers*, those born and raised in the desert city. Their numbers were growing each year. Second were the *believers*. Somehow, they'd learned about the city—likely from the recruiters that were sent out across the continent—and they'd traveled far to join the anti-state. The last were the *defectors*. Exiled, or run out, or outcast, they didn't have anywhere else to go. Cynosure let everyone in but fewer back out. Looking at the Alirian gang, Alverax guessed they were of the latter.

"Hey, pretty boy." A sparsely dressed girl approached, her dark skin a perfect match to his own. "Looking for some company tonight?"

Alverax ignored her but bumped into a giantess of a woman as he walked. She looked down at him, her muscles rippling as she glared. His feeling of godhood shriveled faster than his manhood. He kept his head down and hoped she wasn't going to pummel him down. When he peeked up, she smiled...lasciviously.

That terrified him more.

He slinked away as fast as he could. It's good to know your strengths, and Alverax knew that strength was not one of his. He steered clear of the Masked Guard moving toward him, and edged closer to one of the money changers, a stick-thin man, pale as a full moon. He was collecting bets on the next race and yelling out the odds for each of the necrolytes and their jockey. This was exactly what Alverax needed to know. He had a plan after all.

"Odds for the next race go as follows. White Thorn/Jani/16-1." He provided the name of each of the six necrolytes, their rider, and the odds that they would win. They'd use these numbers to pay out winners after the race was over. "Sandstalk-er/Antonin/16-1. Shadow's Eve/Feather/12-1. Calibra/Brandon-ian/8-1. Xanaphia/Althea/6-1. And last, the crowd favorite, Spectacle/Sir Kenneth Wheeler/2-1."

Alverax had heard of Ken, the pompous, bald-headed stump who changed his honorifics so frequently it was hard to keep up. What he hadn't expected was how much of a favorite the man was to win. There are some people born with such pomposity that an axe would chip trying to break them.

Heralds save me. He was even wearing Felian lightshades at night.

Alverax could see all of the racers below on the dirt track, saddling up on their creatures. The necrolytes were the least docile creatures in the desert—perhaps the world—which is what made the races so exciting. The hard plates that lined their giant, snake-like body worked perfectly as a saddle. The riders used special gloves and grabbed tightly onto the ribbing of the black spikes on their back. Their mouths were harnessed shut, and the ribbed tusks that wrapped down from ear to chin were partially blunted in an attempt to provide at least a small measure of safety. If a rider fell off, and wasn't impaled in the process, he would most likely asphyxiate while a necrolyte wrapped itself tightly around him.

Every rider that crossed the finish line became a legend. As far as prestige went, it didn't matter who won. As far as the vast pile of shines went, it was winner take all.

There was one important rule that gave hope to many a young man: no threadweavers. Anyone could ride, so long as they were a registered achromat. That had been Alverax's first idea, but he realized it was a terrible one. Riders had to be wickedly strong, and he...was not. He'd be dead in seconds. Plus, the last thing he needed was more people looking at him.

If they noticed the black tint to his veins, or how truly dark his irises had become, he'd be strapped down to another table.

Alverax glanced around the Pit. It was built like a grand stadium but dug below the surface. Flat rings of sandstone descended gradually down the outsides, stairs leading from level to level, all the way to the bottom. In the center of the Pit was the track, a huge weaving maze of sandy pathways and hills decorated with the bones of failed racers. Or so they claimed. Smooth lines marked the path where the necrolytes moved, their weight compressing deep into the sand.

Screams rang out into the night air. Angry fans losing shines. Happy fans winning some. Drunken thugs in drunken fights. And every other baggy-eyed sinner shouting at their neighbor just to be heard. The commotion and overwhelming nature of it all reminded him, in a small way, of the first time he'd seen threadlight.

As the thought drifted away, he saw a throne perched down near the track surrounded by dozens of women. A small barricade was erected around the area setting it apart from the rest of the chaos. The throne overflowed with clothing, jewelry, and stomach.

Jelium. The unofficial Lord of Cynosure burst into a fit of hideous laughter, his jowls rocked like tidal waves beating against the shore. His wives lazed about him, contempt shadowed by riches, sisters bonded together by a cruelly dealt hand. Each of them was an immaculate beauty. Old, young, dark, light, but each thin as reeds—a sick juxtaposition to their husband. Gelatinous Jelium. His graying hair was slicked back and his teeth were slicked forward in an unfortunate overbite. Nothing about the man oozed supremacy...except his eyes.

Jelium was one of two and, though Cynosure had no true ruler, the two of them owned it all. Jelium Kirikai and Alabella

Rune. Amber threadweavers. Even from the distance, Alverax could picture the pale yellow that radiated from Jelium's irises. There were countless rumors about their power. Some said that they could control others, make them do whatever they wanted.

Alverax had heard another theory, and he'd soon find out the truth.

~Necrolyte~

CHAPTER 23

"RIDERS READY!"

Alverax watched as a short man with a deep, booming voice called out for the race to begin. Each of the six riders leapt atop their caged necrolytes, settled into their saddles, and gripped tightly onto the ribbed spikes. Watching them mount the creatures gave Alverax anxiety, and an odd respect for them. They may be insane for doing it, but the fact that they didn't all die in the process was impressive.

He watched Sir Kenneth Wheeler leap onto his necrolyte, Spectacle. It reared its head back and forth against the steel bars on either side, but they held firm. Spectacle was the largest of the pseudo-domesticated necrolytes. His tan scales, covered by charcoal plates all along its back, wrapped around to the length of a mid-size boat. Its head, flanked by huge downward cresting tusks, was topped with additional scales and spikes. Its mouth, mostly harnessed shut, contained six rows of sharp teeth, though only the upper two canines were venomous.

A horn blew, followed by a man yelling, "GATES READY!"

Well-armored helpers scrambled toward the gates containing the necrolytes, fumbling over large mechanical bars. Each of them raised a hand to signal their ready state.

"THREE." The riders settled into their makeshift saddles and clutched savagely onto the spikes.

"TWO." The crowd counted along.

"ONE." Latches lifted from the gates.

"GO!"

All six necrolytes burst forward out of their cages and onto the sandy track. Riders dug spiked boot heels into the creatures to steer them—a horribly imprecise method. The beginning was a straight shot until the first curve. The monstrous reptiles slithered down the track with terrifying speed, predators unchained.

As they rounded the first curve, one of the riders ripped free of his saddle and soared out onto the track. He'd dug his heels in too hard and couldn't handle the torque of the turn. He scrambled about in danger of being trampled.

Alverax shook the distractions out of his mind. This was important. He relaxed himself and let threadlight bathe his vision. He focused his attention on Jelium's rider. In threadlight, Alverax could see dozens of threads coming off him in different directions, including the thick corethread below him, but he was looking for something different. There. Small tendrils of light latched themselves to Sir Kenneth Wheeler as he rounded the next bend, binding him to the saddle.

Ha!

He was right! The old crustacean *was* cheating. The rider could take sharper turns and bigger risks with less fear of falling, because Jelium was binding him to his mount. *Heralds, but it is clever.* And only a threadweaver, focused intently on the rider, would ever know. And even then, who in their right mind would say anything? Never slap a happy hog.

Did he fix every race? That might be too obvious. But maybe the pudgy sandhog didn't care. Alverax didn't see Jelium as the kind of man to feign innocence if it'd cost him a shine. No, he was the kind of man who would build a racetrack, make it perfectly acceptable for the owner to place bets on races, and wield the power to fix each one. And then do it with a smile on his fat face.

This also meant that he'd been correct. Jelium's ability was the compliment to his own. Alverax could break threads, and Jelium could make them. No wonder nobody could kill him. If he could bind a rider to a saddle, he could bind any attacker as well. Unfortunately, that seemed way more useful than his own ability.

An enormous bonfire lit the winding racetrack and the necrolytes as they continued along the switchbacks. They raced up over a large hill and one of the riders was almost bucked off, but he stayed attached by the knife in his boot. One necrolyte lashed out at another, nearly throwing both riders from the force of the impact. The crowd cheered for more.

The necrolytes rounded the final bend, five of the six still battling it out for the victory, with Sir Kenneth slightly leading the pack. Sandstalker, a necrolyte with a fiery red tint to its scales, lunged forward with its tusks. Spectacle slapped its long tail at the enemy's eyes and launched its rider from his seat, sending him flying toward Jelium's subdivision. If he kept going, he would crash right into him. Alverax smiled. Mid-flight, the rider's arc stopped, and he dropped straight down to the ground like he'd fallen from the sky, as if all horizontal momentum had been stripped away.

In threadlight, Alverax saw it for what it was. Dozens of

threads of light, like hungry eels, reached up and latched onto the rider's body. As he hit the ground, he clutched his leg, screaming in pain, bone jutting out from his shin. Medics rushed toward him as the other riders finished the race.

Four out of the six had finished, a fairly standard outcome. Sir Kenneth Wheeler took the victory. Alverax watched as the money changers handed a bag of shines to Jelium.

Supposedly, when Jelium had first arrived in Cynosure, he was thin and handsome and happy. In an attempt to propagate his gift, he'd taken one hundred wives and had even more children. None of them had Amber eyes. Oddly enough, none of them were threadweavers at all. Over the years, he'd created an empire and lost his soul. Alverax had plenty of reasons to hate him, not the least of which was that he'd ordered Alverax's death for dating Jayla. As if he truly cared about daughter sixty-three.

Minutes passed and Alverax continued watching. Money changers took new bets. Drunkards swung heavy fists. Young fools smoked sailweed trying to impress their friends. And Jelium's Masked Guard patrolled the stadium. Alverax watched them carefully.

The Masked Guard were Jelium's elite. Each of them was a threadweaver. In fact, almost every single threadweaver in Cynosure was a Masked Guard. Alverax watched to see if there was a pattern to their patrolling, but it seemed random. Best to avoid them if possible. The last thing he needed was a Masked Guard questioning his black irises.

The horn blew once more. Alverax pulled his hood forward, obscured his face, and moved down closer to the track. He needed a good line of sight if this was going to work. Unfortunately, he had no idea which rider Jelium had bet on for this race.

A bellowing shout rang out as the announcer called out that the gates were ready, and then initiated the countdown. A rough group of dark-skinned Felians—that looked like they could be Alverax's cousins—stood next to him, each of them shouting out the countdown. He moved closer to them, trying to blend in.

The race began.

Six new riders burst forth out of the gates, necrolytes thrashing back and forth as they slithered down the sandy racetrack. He looked at the riders. Alverax opened his vision to threadlight and examined each of the riders before finding Jelium's threads. They surrounded a thick tree of a man who had taken an early lead. The spindly threads of pulsing light latched onto him, fastening him securely to his mount.

Alverax waited for the final switchback. As all six creatures rounded the turn, he ran his experiment. All he needed to know was if he could break a thread at this distance. He squeezed gently against the smallest thread and gasped as every single one of Jelium's threads burst apart in an explosion of threadlight. The sudden shift in gravity surprised the rider, and he was thrown off his necrolyte as they finished rounding the corner. Panicking, Alverax grabbed onto the man's corethread and squeezed right at the pinnacle of his ascent, hoping to save him from the same fall as the earlier rider. His corethread burst asunder and he started to float in the air, like a wayward bubble.

Heralds save me.

The necrolyte thrashed out at the other necrolytes around it, gauging a tusk deep into the body of its nearest neighbor. A beastly howl rang out from under its harnessed mouth and it reared back, tossing its rider off into the sand. The two necrolytes fought fiercely, dashing in and out of each other's striking distance. Their tusks tied together, and they came crashing to the ground. The tusks of the larger necrolyte rammed down through the plated scales of the other and its body went limp.

The crowd exploded in applause, but Alverax stood still as death.

What had happened? He was sure he'd only broken the one thread. Not the whole lot! He looked around, terrified that the Masked Guard would find him. Jelium was standing and yelling at people as he raised his hand and stilled the last, raging necrolytes. Two guards near him nodded and surveilled the stadium.

Gasps and curses surrounded him as fans watched the man floating in the air above the track. Alverax needed to get out. One of the Masked Guard moved in his direction. He turned and walked as fast as he could up the stairs toward the exit. It was a struggle to push past the gawking crowds. Rough men cursed him as he bumped his way through. After crashing into a fully tattooed Kulaian, apologizing, and melting away, he made it to the top of the stairway.

A masked guard stood staring at him. Alverax looked into the man's green eyes. The guard looked back. "What in the—"

Alverax shoved a thin girl into the guard and took off. He rushed through the overcrowded street, crashing into dozens of people, until a short, angry man grabbed his arm.

"Watch it, pal!" When the man saw Alverax's eyes, he cursed and let go, backing away. "I didn't mean nothing!"

Alverax looked over his shoulder, but the Masked Guard was nowhere to be seen. He ran, continuing toward the exit leading to the Nest. He could see the tunnel going in and out of view as he dodged around people.

Two masked guards dropped down from above, eyes

burning blue in the bright moonlight. They were cutting off his path to the Nest. He turned in a full circle, looking for a way out. The crowd stared at him, curious why the Masked Guard was so interested.

"On your knees. Hands behind your back." They moved forward. "Jelium would like to speak with you."

His hands shook as they moved toward him. He couldn't go back to Jelium. There was no way he'd be as lucky a second time. He looked to the guards and *broke* their corethreads. His veins burned hot as fire. He needed water. He needed to jump off Mercy's Bluff and into the ocean to cool his skin. Instead, he watched as the guards both took their next step, launching themselves in a slow ascent up into the air with puzzled looks on their face.

Just then, he was tackled from behind by a third guard. He didn't fight back; he was terrible at it. Instead, he simply complied.

The whole thing had been a terrible idea. Every time he had a chance to make something of his life, he ruined it. Maybe he was more of his father's son than he wanted to admit.

He dropped to his knees and put his hands behind his back. The guard tied a thin rope around his hands and placed a blindfold over his eyes.

Tears built up in his eyes. He was so stupid. He'd been given a gift and the first thing he did with it was to cheat a king. He should have run. The desert was only so big. If he'd run north, he would have made it to Alchea eventually. He could have started a new life. Become something more than the thief's son. Instead, he was going to die...for the second time in a week.

The guard lifted Alverax's hands high behind his back as they pushed him forward. He tripped on a rock and they beat him for it. He could hear everyone whispering as he passed, mocking him under the dull roar of the crowd. He must look so pathetic. Some poor sod. A nobody.

After a few minutes of walking, they finally stopped. With his eyes blindfolded, he had to rely on his other senses. There was no breeze, so they were likely indoors. It was quiet, which meant they were far enough away from the Pit for the noise to fade. But the most intense sensation of all was the smell. He recognized it but couldn't quite figure out what it was. Horrid, surely, but there was something familiar about it.

A door opened, and heavy footsteps passed through. Dread washed over him. He had flashbacks to the week before, but this time he was actually guilty. The man didn't speak, and even though he knew he shouldn't, a small part of him started to hope.

"I don't surprise easily."

Oh, Heralds, why?

Jelium's voice was gravelly, as if he were gurgling a pinch of saltwater while he spoke. "Yet here I stand...quite so."

Alverax knew he shouldn't, but he did. "I'm surprised you can stand at all without help." He cringed, cursing his tongue, preparing for a brutal response, but it never came.

Jelium ignored the jibe. "You know, people with not only the will but the ability to survive can be quite useful. I think you could be useful to me but, knowing your lineage, I've a feeling you would be much more trouble than you were worth. We have much to discuss, and it would be more efficient if I didn't have to extract the answers from you manually. So, do behave, and we can have a pleasant rest of the evening."

Did Jelium already know? Maybe he had a suspicion but needed to confirm. And what would Jelium do if he found out that Alverax was a threadweaver now? Run experiments on him? He already had scars from the last one. That's when he realized what the smell was. It smelled like the pit of bones he'd awoken in. The smell was death.

He'd been so focused on what he could do now that he was a threadweaver that he hadn't thought to ask how. They did this to him. Whatever they'd done on that operating table, it was what had given him these abilities. How was that even possible? Could you *make* a threadweaver?

Jelium ripped off the blindfold. "Let's have a look, shall we?" Alverax kept his eyes on the ground in front of him. "Oh, don't be shy, little thief."

The insult cut deep. Jelium knew well who Alverax's father was. He'd executed the man. And he would always see Alverax as the thief's son. He looked up defiantly, black eyes meeting a pallid yellow. He tried to lunge forward but was held down by an unseen power. "I told you before, I am NOT a thief."

"Oh, you are." Jelium smiled, tilting his head as he stared at the black irises and thin black veins pulsing in Alverax's eyes. "But you are also much, much more now."

Jelium sat down in an oversized chair in the corner of the room, smiling to himself. The rest of the room was empty. A large door with no handle to the left of Jelium's chair. A slight breeze wafting down from the open roof. Flickering torchlight barely peeking over the high walls. Just the two of them.

"I suppose the right thing to do would be to hand you over to the lady," he said with a rhetorical tone. "But, then again, you would be a powerful tool to hold onto for myself. It would infuriate her if she ever found out. You are her proof. But plans change.

"The greatest irony of it is that my most worthless daughter has unintentionally delivered me a most priceless treasure."

Alverax lunged forward, a primal defensive rage burning in his soul. He shouldn't care for Jayla after what she'd done to him, but the deepest wound doesn't cause love to fade any faster. He had barely moved before Jelium's veins lit up with Amber threadlight. A dozen tendrils of light crawled out of the earth, latching onto Alverax like vipers.

"I will break you personally. And I will enjoy every last moment of it. By the end, you will be mine, mind and body. Everyone breaks, little thief."

Everyone breaks. It made it sound like he wasn't already broken, but he was. He didn't deny that. Alverax was broken. Perhaps in time—much like threads—the broken parts of him would heal. But not if he was dead.

The thought gave him an idea. Threadlight burned inside of Alverax, his veins glowing with black effervescence, and he grasped onto the unnatural threads holding him down. He poured every ounce of hate, every scrap of pain, every fragment of his soul into the threads. They burst apart into millions of incandescent specks of threadlight. At the same time, his corethread exploded in a brilliant spray of light and the weight of the world lifted from him.

Jelium gasped in his chair, as if he could feel the breaking threads. He pounded on the door. "Open the damn door! Now!"

Alverax took a step forward, rising up just the slightest off the ground. Jelium had no power over him. As the door opened, Alverax smiled. "Goodbye, little beef."

He leapt off the ground, launching into the air with no gravity to stop him. A bird with no need of wings. The wind flowed over his body, cooling the burning in his veins. Slowly, but surely, he continued to rise. Then, looking down at the cityscape below him, he realized his mistake.

He had no way to land.

~ Taractus ~

CHAPTER 24

IT WAS AN ODD FEELING, weightlessness. Floating. Wafting in the wind. With how bad the situation stunk, Alverax was trying hard not to apply the obvious metaphor.

He'd drifted far away from the Pit but could still see the little room in the distance. He couldn't see Jelium down there, which surprised him considering the girth. A cloud passed high over the city's southern quarter. The view was captivating. He'd once climbed to Lover's Lookout with a "friend", but his current view from the sky made the other seem like a guest room in a palace.

The desert city sprawled out beneath him. To the northeast, he could see Jelium's palace with a complex of apartments for all of his children. He could see Alabella's more humble home beside it. The city center was a ghost town, filled with empty tents and quiet streets that would fill to the brim in the morning.

And, Heralds, the horizon. He'd grown so accustomed to the view looking out over the Altapecean Sea that he'd forgotten how magnificent it was. Mercy's Bluff at the southern edge of the city was an abrupt drop-off, a cliff that plunged hundreds of feet down into the sea. Down below was a collection of ships that floated in the ocean surf. Cynosure itself was miles wide and partially covered by a sandstone mountain arcing overhead like a half-completed ceiling. It's what caused darkness to constantly cover the northern quarter.

After the wind drag had stopped his initial horizontal momentum, he floated helplessly in the air, a light breeze carrying him along. He knew it would happen any moment. When he broke threads, it was temporary. But what if it wasn't this time? What if he was stuck up in the air forever? He'd already floated longer than he'd expected to. Either way, he was probably going to die. The thought was oddly reassuring. He'd already died once. What was one more time?

Then it happened. His corethread reappeared, popping back into existence, becoming brighter and thicker over the course of a few moments. The world pulled him, and he fell. Slow at first, but he knew it would accelerate until he was falling at terminal speed. An image of himself splattered over a sandy walkway flashed in his mind. He panicked. He did the only thing he *could* do. He grabbed onto his corethread. His veins filled with dark threadlight, and he *broke* it. It shattered apart into a thousand particles of threadlight and faded away.

He was still falling, but gravity no longer pulled. As he descended, he realized that the friction of the air itself was slowing him down. He'd felt a host of new feelings over the last day, but a freefall that slowed as he descended had to be the strangest. He was going to live! The Blightwoods *were* hard to kill after all.

"WOOO!" He screamed out into the open air, pumping his fists out over his head. Unfortunately, it threw him off balance, and he began to rotate. Despite being alone, he was horribly embarrassed. Hours ago, he'd felt a god, and now, he was a floppy, floating sky fish.

As if on cue, his corethread reappeared. The sudden jerk of gravity pulled him down. He crashed into a tent in the city center, rolling head over heels until he was flat on his back in a large box that smelled like stale wolfberry. He picked himself up and hopped down out of the box. His first steps felt odd, like he'd stepped off a ship onto dry land. His mind matched his dizzy feet.

It was dark in the empty market. Feeling brilliant, he opened his mind to threadlight to better navigate the world, but quickly remembered that his own vision was tied to his ability to see threads. The world stayed dark, only a few dim threads appearing. As he let it fade, he had to place a hand on a large tent pole to keep himself from falling. Not all of the dizziness had come from flying. The veins running through his arms and neck were warm to the touch.

Not again.

He vomited.

A stranger passed by on the other side of the market and Alverax remembered that the Masked Guard would be looking for him. He needed to be discreet, and, Heralds, he needed to warn his grandfather. Then, he needed to get out of town. For good.

His feet guided him home, his mind and body still dealing with the overuse of threadweaving. His grandfather's house had candles lit inside, but it was too late for him to still be awake. Alverax's heart beat faster. What if they were already there? Would they hurt him? He was old. They wouldn't. Would they?

He ran forward and almost knocked the door off its hinges as he burst into the small house. His grandfather startled awake, sitting cross-legged on the floor in the living room, eyes filled with exhaustion and worry.

"You're safe," his grandfather said.

Alverax smiled something fierce. "Me? I was worried about you, old man."

"You've never been a good liar, Al. It was obvious you were going out to do something reckless, and I was worried you'd come back deader than you were last night."

"I'm fine," Alverax said, the nausea still a dull pecking in his stomach, "but I have to leave. For good this time."

His grandfather nodded, unsurprised by the revelation. "You do what you have to do, son. Your father used to go on trips. He always came back. Just promise me you won't be gone for too long."

Alverax's heart broke. He knew what his grandfather was implying, and the thought of his grandfather passing seemed so distant. He'd always been the rock Alverax came back to when things got rough. What would he do when the man actually was gone? But if Alverax left, what was the difference? Everyone in Cynosure may as well be dead. He wouldn't see them again either way.

"I...I'll try. Jelium is looking for me, and it won't be a happy ending if he finds me." He moved toward the hallway leading back to his room. "They'll come here. It would be safer for you to hide out for a while as well."

His grandfather laughed. "I'm too old to play games. Let 'em come. Us Blightwoods don't die easy. You take care of yourself. You're a better man than your father. Wherever you end up, act like it. You're the only good thing he ever did."

He disappeared into his room before the tears came. If anyone should get credit for any semblance of goodness

Alverax had, it was his grandfather. He was just too humble to admit it.

Alverax packed a bag of clothes while he thought about his grandfather's words. It felt strange knowing that whatever he didn't pack, he would never see again. In general, he wasn't a sentimental person, but extreme times call for extreme feelings. He still wasn't sure how he was going to get out of Cynosure; they weren't keen on letting people freely leave. But he could fly now, sort of. He was sure he could figure out something.

He returned to the living room and gave his grandfather a hug before walking to the door.

The old man sat nodding his head and smiling. "I should have done it myself a long time ago. The world is so much more than the sludge of taractus turds in this core-rotten city. Go, and don't look back. Be better. I'll be just fine."

It wasn't the right time to laugh, but he let out the whisper of one. He was going to miss the old man. "Thanks for everything."

Alverax walked away from the small sandstone home he'd lived in his whole life, but he'd died this week, so it felt fitting. As he walked in darkness toward the northern exit, he thought about what he might do when he got out. Alchea felt like the obvious choice. It was the closest metropolitan city. There were smaller farming towns on the way, but if he was getting out of this place, he wanted to see more than farmland. In all honesty, he had no idea how far Alchea was from the desert, or even how far it was to get out of the desert. Was it true that there were wild necrolytes? And sandhogs? If they came at him, he could just float away. The thought put a smile on his face. He needed to invest in a really good pillow he could use for soft landings.

Being able to *glide*—he'd finally settled on the word for it—

was going to be awfully convenient. As long as he didn't do it too much. The nausea was real.

As he approached the exit, he was surprised to find it populated with all manner of caravan equipment. The few wagons he'd seen the day before had grown to dozens of partially packed wagons. People moved around, coming and going and loading travel goods and food. Two women were trying their best to wrangle a taractus. Its green, prickly skin and slow-moving stoutness made it quite difficult to subdue. A cluster of the creatures were chained up near the exit with harnesses already attached, ready to haul the wagons.

The company was completely blocking the exit. He looked up and thought about trying to glide over them, but the ceiling in this section started to recede as it formed the tunnel leading out. The passage was tall, but not tall enough for a floating man to glide through undetected.

While he watched, he saw a woman that appeared to be in charge. She had a thin reed of sailweed in her mouth and hoop earrings dangling down the side of her head. Her hair was a long, warm brown pulled back in a tight ponytail. She wore a backless shirt with thin straps that wrapped around the sides of her neck. Short sleeves revealed tattoos flanking a leather strap around her upper arm. A thin, brown silk collar curled around her thin, brown collar bones.

Right about then he decided that he had a new plan.

He gathered his belongings and walked forward confidently, putting on an air of authority. He kept his head high while he passed two workers that looked at him curiously. He pursed his lips and ignored them as he approached the woman.

"Pardon, my lady. Are you not the one in charge here?" He tried speaking like one of the rich idiots in Jelium's household.

She nodded, looking him up and down, and cocked her

head as she looked into his eyes. She opened her mouth to respond, but he beat her to it.

"Good. Good." One thing he noticed from the rich was that they spoke over each other constantly. "Alexander Grant, at your service. Lady Alabella has just asked me to bring a package to Alchea. It is very important I do so in a timely manner and without incident. You know how she is. Quite particular and unforgiving of failure. Now, I assume by the hullabaloo that you're leading this team up north. I'll be needing to tag along until we exit the desert. From there, I can continue the journey on my own. Any questions?"

It was audacious and presumptuous, two factors that made a great lie. But the girl didn't even respond; she simply stood still staring at him.

"Are you done?" She raised a brow and smiled something devious. "That was cute and, to be honest, you're cute too...for a dead man."

A shiver ran up his spine. Not good. Definitely not good. This was a terrible plan. He needed to get out. His eyes wandered toward the exit. Maybe if he ran, he could get past the guards on the other end. In an ideal world, Jelium wouldn't know about his departure but, in an ideal world, he wouldn't have been recognized by the first person he approached.

He flinched as she slapped his shoulder. "Relax, Al. Alvie? Ew. Axe? That's not bad. Name's Farah, daughter forty-four. Jayla and I are close. I've heard stories," she winked, "including the one about how our father had you murdered."

He still had no idea how to respond, so he stood there with stiff hands down at his sides, fiddling precariously with the strings on his bag.

"Shyer than I'd imagined."

He puffed out a laugh and scratched the back of his head. "Guess I'm just not used to being called out so thoroughly."

"For what it's worth, it was well-executed. Pompous, presumptuous, and peckish. The three P's of the privileged." She offered him a puff of her sailweed but he declined. She shrugged and took another drag herself, letting the smoke out in one long breath. "Problem is that I recognized your face from Jayla's drawings. That and Alabella is in Alchea so there's no way she could have 'just asked'."

"Heralds save me," he whispered under his breath. "I'll take that sailweed now."

Her laugh caught him off guard. It was loud and obnoxious —ill-paired to the rest of her. She passed him the sailweed, and he took in a deep breath of it. He hadn't smoked in a while, but he handled it well.

"So, father must really hate you."

He looked at her and nodded as he handed the sailweed back. "More than stairs."

"How dare you!" she said with a look of impish shock on her face. "Don't you think he has enough on his plate as it is?"

Alverax snorted louder than he ever had in his life. The workers all stopped and looked at him while he composed himself. "You are a terrible daughter. But that," he smiled, "was well-executed."

She winked. "We leave in an hour. One of our workers went home sick, so you can take his place. Any enemy of my father is a friend of mine." She stretched out a hand. "Welcome aboard, Sam."

She had a strong grip for a thin woman. "Sam?"

"All personnel leaving Cynosure are approved ahead of time, and Sam is the guy who got sick. Pretend to be him, and the guards won't look twice. I'll let the crew know."

"Sam it is!"

"Sam was a worker." She leaned down and grabbed a large bag and tossed it to him. It was much heavier than he'd expected. He stumbled as he caught it. "What? This can't be totally out of the malice of my heart. There's not much to load but food on this end, but we'll have some heavy lifting for you at the pickup. After that, if you want to disappear, or head to Alchea with the others, choice is yours. I'll tell the guards you died."

"Thank you," he said. He moved to put the bag away, but then stopped and turned back around. "Hey, forty-four."

She smiled. "Yeah, corpse?"

"Where do I put the bag?"

CHAPTER 25

Long before the sun rose, the caravan was prepared and ready to embark on its journey northward. Each taractus was hooked up to a wagon with a metal harness wrapped around its neck and a driver that held long ropes for guiding its movement. The creatures moved as though they were walking through sludge, each step carefully placed on the sandy rocks. Somehow, they were still able to provide a smooth ride for those in the wagons.

Alverax was paired with a man who was either a mute or incredibly rude. Together, they rode in silence for hours, staring blankly into the desert through iron bars. He could appreciate the desert more now that he was clothed and sheltered, even if it felt like he was in a portable prison cell. Looking out over the sandy ocean reminded him of nights he'd spent staring out over the Altapecean Sea, legs dangling from Mercy's Bluff. That was where he'd had his first kiss.

Even though he knew he shouldn't, he missed Jayla. Could he blame her? She'd thought he was dead. *Ugh, but why Truf-*

fles? Cored by a mushroom. More than likely, he'd taken advantage of the emotionally unbalanced depressive state that his death had caused. If Alverax should hate anyone, it was the traitorous toadstool. The human fungus. The philandering spore-bearer. Not Jayla. He'd come back for her someday.

The wagons began heating up and the Mute started mumbling under his breath. Even in the shady comforts of the wagons, there was no respite. Alverax was sure he was going to die of heat stroke. The constant, all-encompassing warmth felt like swimming in a sea of fire. He decided that he would have rather died from the Masked Guard.

Somehow, in spite of the audible groans, he survived the day. The sun set over the caravan as they made camp. There were only a dozen people in the group, each moving about silently as they settled down near a large fire. Now that the world had cooled off, Alverax decided that the journey wasn't so horrible after all. In fact, the temperature was nearly perfect.

Farah approached from the center of the caravan, her large hoop earrings gleaming in the light of the campfire. She brought him a bowl of the soup they'd made for supper. "How you holding up, corpse?"

"Only half dead," he said. "The heat nearly finished me off."

"You're lucky you have dark skin. Check out Kase over there."

An older woman with broad shoulders sat staring into the fire. The firelight made it look even worse, but Alverax could tell the woman's pale skin had turned bright red.

"Heralds. That can't be healthy."

Farah laughed. "I told her to wear a jacket, but she said it was too hot."

Just then, the Mute passed by. He was bald, but he wore a wide-brimmed hat to protect his skin from the heat.

"That guy always so talkative?" Alverax asked.

"The mechanic? Not sure I've ever heard him say more than a few words that weren't curses. Damn hard worker though. I'd take him over any two."

"I talked to him for five minutes earlier today before I realized he wasn't going to respond." Alverax took a step toward the fire. "For future reference, a warning would have been nice."

"And spoil the fun? Not a chance."

Some of Farah's movements were eerily reminiscent of Jayla. The way her lip curled when she was being sarcastic. The way her left eyebrow raised more than the right. Part of him wanted to run away, but being near her felt like home. Her carefree spirit helped him forget about everything that had happened.

"Okay, corpse. The game is called *crockpot*. Wait right there."

She jogged off and returned with a bowl and a bottle of whiskey the size of a small barrel, which she opened and emptied into the bowl. She placed a ladle inside and looked up at him. "I'm going to tell you something, and you have to decide if I'm lying. If you think I am, say 'crockpot'. If you're right, I'll drink a swig from the bowl, but if you're wrong, you will. Easy."

Alverax nodded. He'd played plenty of drinking games before, but never in a one-on-one scenario. "What if I want to drink the whisky every time?"

She leaned in close. "You might like me better with a few drinks in me."

Heralds save me.

"First one," she announced. "My mother is one of the original Hundred Brides."

Ugh. Why did it always come back to Jelium? The man was about sixty now, and he'd come to Cynosure about forty years before. He'd married the Hundred Brides all in the first year.

Looking at Farah, she could only be a few years older than Alverax, so, maybe twenty-two? Timeline was feasible. Jelium did like them young.

"True."

"Wrong!" She smiled wide while handing him a ladle-full of whisky. "Of father's original one hundred brides, eighteen have passed away and been replaced."

"He probably ate 'em," Alverax mumbled.

"Ew. That is disgusting, but not totally impossible. My mother was actually the very first replacement. Lots of rumors about what happened to the eighteen, illness, murder, suicide, you name it. At this point I wouldn't put anything past him."

Alverax nodded. "No kidding."

"Alright, drink up." She waited for him to finish the ladle. "Second truth. I was offered a seat on the Council of Heralds."

"Ha!" he laughed. She was too young to be offered a seat on the council. They were all lifers well into their fifties, selected because of their influence. Of course, by the time Alabella had arrived—ten years after Jelium—the ruling authority of the council had been forcefully diminished. It felt like a trick question. Maybe she *had* been offered a seat, but as a scribe or assistant. "Can I clarify something?"

She raised a brow. "One question."

"Was this seat on the council itself?"

"Yes," she said with quick confidence.

He looked deep into her eyes, looking for the deception, but there was none. It seemed like such an obvious lie, but if it *had* happened it would make a great truth for the game. Her dark eyes stared right back. "Heralds save me, but I think you actually *were* offered a seat."

She burst out in laughter. "You are terrible at reading

people. It's actually rather impressive how bad you are. That was supposed to be an easy one."

"That's the problem! It was *too* easy. Heralds, you're a good liar."

"I have one hundred and forty-seven siblings. What do you expect?"

He shook his head. "I can't even imagine."

She filled the ladle with whisky and handed it to Alverax. It tasted better the second time. He looked back to Farah and about choked on the last drop. The way she was looking at him. He knew that look. He'd seen it in Jayla's eyes a hundred times.

"Last one." She inched toward him, her eyes searing into his own. The heat of the bonfire was nothing compared to the burning inside him as she moved in. Her lips parted like ocean waves. "I've a taste for dark skin."

The urge to run exploded throughout his body. His heart beat fast as a flickering flame, each beat a powerful rhythm. Thud, thud. *Heralds save me.* Thud, thud. *Look at her.* Thud, thud. *Those lips.*

She moved in closer and closer until he could feel the warmth of her skin. She paused. He hesitated. His insides felt exactly the same as when he was threadweaving, like his veins were filled with the heat of the sun. He leaned forward and kissed her, his lips igniting with every powerful emotion he'd let build up inside. He was reborn for a second time.

Her hands squeezed tightly against his back, crawling up his spine, over his neck, and up into his hair. He knew it was a bad idea, but he didn't care. His own hands drifted over the curves of her ribs and along the sides of her abdomen, pulsing with each beat of her heart. He'd needed this. This raw release of careless passion. They pressed hard into each other, their shadows flickering against the caravan.

In the heat of the moment—when he certainly wasn't supposed to—Alverax thought. Was he becoming his father? Was he going to leave Cynosure, get a woman pregnant, and return home with a baby? What was he doing? *Shut up, brain.* He tried to let it go as his hands drifted lower and lower.

"Stones!" One of the other members of the caravan stumbled across them. "Sorry, sorry. Don't mind me. Just, uh, passing through. You, uh, just, uh, continue on, I guess..."

The man started to leave, but then paused and turned back to Farah. "While I, uh, have your attention. You wouldn't happen to know where the whiskey is? The others were looking for it." He scratched his head and coughed.

A mischievous grin crossed Farah's lips as she pulled away from Alverax. "I know where it is. I'll grab it and meet up with you all in a minute."

"Good, good." The man continued walking, clearing the lane between the two carts faster than a leafling running from its shadow.

Farah turned back to Alverax and smiled her devilish smile. "I know you're planning on disappearing, but at least stick around another day. I think I might have more work for you to do tomorrow."

Before Alverax had the chance to compose himself and respond, she'd already left with the whiskey. He slumped down onto the ground and laughed at himself. What had his life become? A series of insanity. Dead. Alive. Cheated on. Cheated. Chased and seduced. Somehow through it all, he'd ended up in the best possible scenario. He had a free ride out of Cynosure, and companionship.

After things settled down, Alverax thought about walking over toward the rest of the group, but he was exhausted. Instead, he climbed up into his wagon and nearly died of fright when he found the Mute awake inside staring out the wagon window. The man said nothing. It took some time, and a bit of trust, but finally Alverax drifted to sleep beside the smallest sliver of hope.

THE NEXT MORNING, the entire camp awoke with the sun. Alverax learned that they were to reach their pickup location around midday to receive a shipment from another caravan that they would bring back to Cynosure. When he asked others what the shipment was, they told him that it was mostly expensive ingredients that were hard to gather in the desert.

With that, they set back out northward toward the border of the Alchean city-state. Each taractus trudged forward unimpeded by the weight it pulled behind, and the workers lounged in the shade of the wagons while the air still remained cool. A few of the workers drank too much the night before and were moaning about the sun's reflection on the sand.

Alverax sat daydreaming about what he would do next.

One thought he had was to join up with the caravan team that they were meeting. If he worked for them, every so often he'd get to meet up with Farah. But if word got out that he was showing up at all of the pickups, Jelium would send the Masked Guard to kill him. There was no getting around it. This afternoon he'd have to say goodbye. He wanted to invite her to come with him but thought it might sound desperate.

As the morning wore on, Alverax could see the peaks of a mountain range to the east. They were less impressive in real life than they were in drawings—at least from that distance.

He trapped a small leafling he found on the side of the wagon and watched it try to escape. Its hard, rigid body left scratch marks against the wood. The leaf-shaped shell on its back looked brittle and gave Alverax the crude urge to grab hold of both ends and break it in half like a wafer. Instead, he let it go and opened himself to threadlight.

Alone in the wagon, he practiced *breaking* threads.

He drifted in and out of sleep, overheated and dehydrated, until the caravan came to a halt. He sat up, rubbed his eyes, and found himself alone. It felt nice not to have the Mute staring at him.

Muddled voices conversed outside as he stretched his arms. Farah had told him that he could trust the people in the drop-off caravan, but he wanted to stay hidden in the wagon just to be careful.

He peaked out the barred window and counted eight large wagons sprawled out over dry grassland. Some of Farah's men were unloading crates from one of the wagons, hauling them back over onto their own. Alverax thought he saw a hand reaching out from between the barred windows of the farthest wagon. Farah was in a small group talking to a woman with jet black hair slicked back behind her ears. The woman smiled and put a hand to Farah's cheek. She said something, and Farah turned and pointed toward the wagons.

Toward Alverax.

She was pointing at *his* wagon.

Heralds save me. He rushed toward the back door and tried to push it open, but it was locked. The Mute stood outside the door holding a bag of tools, staring at him with the same emotionless gaze he'd had since they had left. The wooden box Alverax sat in *felt* like a cage, because it *was* a cage.

Farah had betrayed him.

His blood boiled. Threadlight seeped into his veins and they swirled with blackness. He looked for any threads he could *break* that might help, but there was nothing. He moved forward and kicked at the lock over and over again. There was no way out.

The group Farah had been talking to was walking toward his wagon. He scuttled toward the back, angry at himself for trusting her—she was Jelium's daughter after all. The worst part was that he was so close. He could see the Alchean grass. Freedom was right there.

They reached his door and the Mute unlocked it. Farah stood next to the black-haired woman as the door swung open and Alverax got his first good look at her. He knew that face. He knew those eyes.

Alabella Rune.

She looked younger than he knew she was. Her movements, her stance, her gaze, every piece of her emanated a self-assured understanding of her place in the world. And it was nowhere near his own.

"I remember you," she said, nodding. "Subject twenty-three. Jelium's petty grudge. I watched you die."

Alverax's mind flashed back to the moment he lay chained to the operating table. She was there. This was not the first time he had been near her, and the last time had not ended well.

"Imagine my surprise when young Farah here told me what she'd caught. Do me a favor, boy. Take off your shirt."

He was going to die. It was the story of his life. Every time he found any semblance of happiness or hope, it was ripped away, leaving him even lower than he had been to start.

Farah stared at him, trying hard to hide her guilt, but he knew it was there. He pulled his shirt up over his head, for the first time realizing that the scars on his chest had completely healed. The bruising had faded to reveal a web of black veins spread out across his chest.

Alabella's lips crept upward as she eyed the scars. "Are you what I think you are?"

Heralds. He'd forgotten his only advantage. He opened his eyes to threadlight, and *broke* his corethread, preparing to launch himself into the air—it was his only chance—but as soon as he *broke* it, a barrage of threads popped into existence and latched onto him, holding him fixed to the ground.

"I'll take that as a yes," she smiled. "Let's do ourselves a favor and assume that you cannot escape. Now, again."

Before the words had left her lips, a weight unlike anything he'd ever experienced flushed over him. Dozens of threads latched onto him, each one increasing the sum. They were the same threads that Jelium had used to fasten his riders to their necrolytes, but stronger. He grabbed onto one of the threads with his mind and squeezed. The whole collection burst in an explosion of threadlight. He gasped as the pressure lifted.

Alabella turned without speaking and talked with two of her companions. After a minute of quiet deliberation, she turned around. "No one, especially Jelium, can know we have the boy." She tossed a pair of shackles to Alverax. "You, my young friend, are going to help us change the world."

CHAPTER 26

LAUREL HAD NEARLY SPENT the night camped out under a feytree but, in the end, Cara had let her stay at the chromawolf nursery for the night with the promise that she would help with the next morning's chores—Laurel knew that Cara would let her stay regardless. The year after her parents had passed away, she had spent the better part of a month living at the nursery, and often helped with chores during her visits.

Breakfast was divine. Cara's husband, Mace, had pounded out a vegetable puree to eat with some bread and fruit. Like most Zeda men, Mace was an expert with herbs and spices, and the tastes hit Laurel's tongue like a summer rain. It was the perfect meal to prepare her for a morning of hard labor.

"Okay, Elle. Let's head out. Grab that leash and meet me outside." Cara brushed a few strands of wild auburn hair out of her eyes and back into the rest of her mane. Her naturally olive skin was pale from a life in the forest, and her thin-strapped shirt showed plenty of it.

Laurel grabbed the leash and ran outside. A small chromawolf ran up beside her as she was jogging to the other side of the clearing. It jumped from side to side as it ran, taunting her. She sped up into an all-out run. The wolf sped up to meet her speed, no longer playfully moving, but intensely focused on the race. They ran all the way to the far end of the clearing where a wheelbarrow and shovel lay.

A minute later Cara caught up with them. The energetic pup still danced around happily.

"Ah, I see you met Racer!"

Laurel was still catching her breath. She wouldn't have been able to keep up with the little chromawolf if not for the thread-light she'd used to *push* herself faster. "I'm pretty sure you just made that name up."

"After decades of raising these pups, it gets hard to think up new names. One of these days, people will start giving human names to animals. Mark my words. Either that or the names will start gettin' real specific." She paused and pointed over to another chromawolf, limping as it walked. "Names like Infected-Toe-Nail, or Droopy-Right-Eye. Or He-Who-Eats-His-Friend's-Turds."

Laurel choked as she burst out in laughter. "I like him. He's got spunk. You can tell he's smart."

"Definitely has spunk. Would've been a real killer if he grew up in the wild. Chromawolves with that much energy don't know what to do with it. End up huntin' all day." Cara leaned down and gave Racer a scratch on his back, then gestured back to the den. "Get back home, Racer."

The little wolf sped off obediently with his twin tails dragging along the dirt.

"Alright, let's get this over with."

The chores took less time than Laurel remembered. An odd part of her wished they'd taken longer. By the time they were done, the chromawolves were all fed and ready for an afternoon nap. She pushed the wheelbarrow out of the gate to dump the soiled dirt and looked back with a pinch of pride.

She ran over to the pond at the edge of the camp, dipped her hands, and washed off the dirt and fur. This was exactly what she needed. A distraction from everything. Physical labor had a way of masking a bleak reality.

Cara joined her at the pond. "You've been awfully quiet this morning, even for you. Want to talk about it?"

She didn't, but she did. Cara had helped her through the death of her parents, not because of her words, but because she knew when she needed to be silent. Laurel was the closest thing Cara had to a daughter, and Cara was high on the list of the people that Laurel most cared for.

"Have you ever learned something," Laurel said, "some truth that made you want to just get up and run away?"

Cara sat down on an overturned tree stump. "Oh, yes. The truth is often infuriating, but you should never run from it."

"But what if you found out someone had been lying to you your whole life? And you would have done everything differently if you had known the truth."

"Your whole life? That's a long life for a lie. I suppose my first question would be, why? Most people wouldn't put in that much energy to something they didn't think was important. The truth is that not all truths are safe to share. Maybe they were trying to protect you."

"I don't need protection."

"I know that better than anyone. I've seen you fight a full-grown chromawolf. It's not like you to run from something. Is that what you're doing here? Trying to avoid something, or someone? We all lie, Laurel. The world would be worse if we didn't, but it's also more brittle because we do. Intent may not remove the impact, but it's important, nonetheless. You have to try to give people the benefit of the doubt. Most of us mean well."

Cara was right, of course. Laurel knew she was being unreasonable, and that was the most frustrating part. She wanted to be angry at the elders for keeping their secrets. How could she trust them if they couldn't trust her? *Try to give them the benefit of the doubt.* It's possible to understand someone even if they're wrong.

They did seem spooked by the color of Aydin's eyes. An Amber threadweaver? What did that mean? If something bad was happening, they should want to warn their people rather than keeping them in the dark.

"I don't know," Laurel said, shaking her head.

The older woman stood back up. "It's also possible that they don't care about you."

"What?"

Cara's lips curled. "If I told you that I saw the future and Bay was going to fall to his death at the edge of the Fairenwild, what would you do?"

Her brother had a blood disease. Ever since he was a kid, he'd had spells of intense vertigo and dizziness, among other things. The doctors thought he wouldn't live past his twelfth birthday, but here he was at eighteen alive and well. "He knows it's dangerous for him. He always stays close to home."

"Humor me. If I saw the future and knew this was how he would die."

Laurel didn't like the idea of losing her brother. Especially since she'd already lost her parents, and her grandfather wasn't far from riding the winds. "I don't know. I'd forbid him from going near there."

"And what if he didn't listen?"

"I'd convince him."

"By lying?"

Laurel scoffed. "No, I'd tell him the truth."

"That a crazy old woman who lives with chromawolves told you he would die there?"

A dawn of understanding rose in Laurel's mind.

"If a lie would convince him to stay away from danger, does that justify it?" Cara leaned down and pet one of the little chromawolves that had approached.

If the elders truly believed that protecting the coreseal was important, then they would do everything in their power to keep it safe. Even if that meant living in the Fairenwild, isolated from the rest of the world, with an artificial contempt for other cultures to dissuade leaving. But it had been hundreds of years. If the coreseal wasn't real, or if it wasn't actually in danger, then the whole reasoning fell through. She needed to talk to Elder Rosemary. If any of the elders were going to tell her the truth, it was her.

"I've got to go," she said, picking herself up. "Thanks for letting me stay here last night."

Cara laughed. "You know you're always welcome here. One of these days you're going to have to unload all them worries you have boiling up inside you. I'll be here when you're ready."

"I know."

Laurel started running back toward Zedalum. She should have stayed outside the elder's door and listened to more of the conversation. There were so many questions to be answered. How was she going to convince Elder Rosemary to tell her more? She'd already told the grounders, maybe she'd be more open to sharing it now.

The grounders. They owed her for saving their lives. Maybe

297

she could convince them to tell her what they'd learned. They weren't sworn to secrecy. That could work.

After summiting the entrance to Zedalum from the wonder-stone, and *drifting* through the city, Laurel made her way back to the Elder's lodge. She knew that her brother and her grand-father would be worried about her because she hadn't returned home last night, but that was the least of her worries.

Her feet carried her into the large wooden building. A group of her old friends, young women she'd grown up with, sat inside the lobby in a circle talking. They stared at her as she walked past. It wasn't until that moment that she realized how she must look after a morning of doing chores at the nursery. But it didn't matter. They had all unfriended her when she'd become a messenger for Elder Rowan—mostly out of jealousy —but she wasn't jealous of their bland lives.

Laurel walked down the hall and knocked on the grounder's door. The older woman answered, but Laurel could see both Chrys and Iriel inside staring at their child. Laurel never under-stood why people stared at babies so much.

"Can I help you?" Chrys' mother asked. Her dark hair was in wild disarray, and the fatigue on her face seemed a fitting match.

Laurel looked past her, hoping that Chrys would look up. "I need to talk to him."

His mother opened the door the rest of the way. "Chrys, it appears you have a visitor."

Both parents looked up from the baby and saw Laurel standing in the doorway. It only took a moment for Chrys to light up at the sight of her. He rose to his feet and approached her. "The one that got away."

Chrys' mother stepped aside. "The one that got away?"

"It's a long story. I don't think you've met my mother,

Willow. You two should chat sometime. I think you'd have a lot in common." Chrys stepped toward the doorway. "I would like to say that we're even, but I'm quite sure you did more for us than I did for you."

"Well, I did owe you," Laurel replied.

"You overpaid."

The way he said it made Laurel feel an odd kinship with him. He was older, and from a completely different world but, somehow, she felt like he understood her.

"Did you hear?" Chrys asked. "Pandan is alive and, apparently, he is my uncle."

Gale take me, I'm not supposed to know any of that. Laurel hesitated, then forced her eyes to enlarge as she feigned surprise. "No, I had not. That's unbelievable. How is that even possible? You've never been here."

A snort burst out of Willow. "Apologies! It's refreshing to be around such a terrible liar. I've been around nobility far too frequently over the last thirty years."

"What?" Laurel's cheeks grew red as an apple.

"No need to lie about it. You obviously knew about Chrys and Pandan already. Unless, you weren't supposed to know." Willow gave her a sly wink.

Laurel stood in the doorway, feeling a fool.

"Give the girl a break, mother."

The rocking chair creaked as Iriel rose to her feet. Her clean, dark hair tickled the baby's cheek as they moved toward the doorway. "Hello, Laurel."

"Hello," Laurel said. "So, what's the plan? Chrys is a Zeda. Does that mean you're going to stick around here for good? Probably as good as any place for keeping a kid safe."

Iriel turned to the others. By the look they gave each other, it was clear that they had been discussing it, and those discussions had left an uncomfortable residue. "Chrys and Willow want to go rescue Pandan."

"We can't just let him rot in prison," Chrys said. "Who knows what Jurius is doing to him?"

Iriel scowled. "You're in no condition to go. Not to mention you're the most wanted man in Alchea, one of the most recognizable, and I don't want to be a widow with a newborn."

"I know Endin Keep better than anyone. We could be in and out without anyone noticing."

"That's assuming you could even make it into Endin Keep unseen. And even if you made it into the keep, you think a man in your condition is going to make it out lugging a man in his condition?" Iriel's voice grew louder as she spoke. "Willow agrees with me."

Willow nodded. "I agree that Chrys should not go, because I'm going alone. One is less conspicuous than two, and a woman even more so."

Chrys scowled at her, upset that everyone was against him. "You're not going back alone. That's absurd."

Willow kept her composure. "What's absurd is looking like you do and thinking you can infiltrate Endin Keep. No one will question a woman and, when I arrive, I can find someone to help me carry him out."

Without noticing, Laurel had begun to threadweave. Her veins came alive with a slow simmering energy. She wanted to go with her. She wanted to be knee deep in the action. She held her tongue because she knew that she had more important matters to figure out. Still, she could imagine herself, teamed up with a grounder, infiltrating their massive fortress, rescuing one of her own. It would be dangerous. It would be challenging. It would be an adventure.

Willow folded her arms, annoyed with her stubborn son. "Do you have a better idea?"

"If you had help, it could work, but that's asking a lot from someone. You'd need to be able to trust them completely." Chrys' eyes lit up. "Luther, Laz, and Reina would do anything for me, and I'd trust them more than anyone else."

"They're already used to taking orders from a Valerian," Iriel interjected.

Willow's arms fell to her side. "I've met them before, so they would recognize me, but why would they do it? Besides loyalty, there's no reason for them to risk their necks going against the Great Lord and Jurius."

"They're probably being watched as well, and whoever is tailing them would likely recognize you." Chrys thought to himself. "There's got to be a way to contact them without arousing suspicion."

He paused, then he looked to Laurel.

No, no, no. She was here to get answers, not to get roped into their rescue mission. But...it wouldn't hurt to hear him out.

"The one that got away." He cocked his head to the side, brows raised, taunting her. "They would both recognize you."

Laurel shook her head back and forth. "No way the elders would allow it."

"Gale take the elders," Willow cursed. "They're old bags of dirt. I knew each of them when they were younger, and there's nothing special about the lot of them."

Something about Willow insulting the elders felt good, as if Laurel's own truths had been suddenly validated.

Chrys took a step toward her. "When I found you in the basement of the Bloodthieves, I didn't see a hint of fear in you. There aren't many people in the world that react that way when they're in danger. Trust me, it's my job to find them. I'm that way too. That look in your eye right now, I know that look. So, go ahead and protest as much as you want, but you and I both know that there's nothing in this world you'd rather do than run toward adventure."

Laurel's veins were on fire. With each word he spoke, she felt seen. Chrys understood her, heart and soul, and he was right. As much as she wanted answers from the elders, the truth wasn't going anywhere. The coreseal could wait. They needed her, and she needed this.

"Gale take you all, but I'm in."

Willow perked up. "It's settled then. Laurel and I will head out first thing in the morning and we should make it to Alchea by nightfall."

Chrys and Iriel looked at each other, both understanding that Iriel had won but neither letting it show on their face. Chrys turned to Willow. "Luther will be home. Laz is usually at The Black Eye tavern. He loves their milk stout. If he's not there, you can ask around. I've never actually been to Laz's place. Reina may be at The Black Eye as well, if you're lucky. Otherwise, she's living with a guy off Beryl Boulevard near the orphanage. And you already know where Pandan is."

"Yes," Willow added. "Unless they've moved him."

Laurel already felt the rush of anticipation. She was going deep into grounder territory to rescue a spy. A huge smile crossed her lips. "So how do we get in?"

Willow smiled. "Ever heard of a skysail?"

CHAPTER 27

DARK CLOUDS PASSED OVERHEAD as the sun set on the treetop metropolis. It was early in the year for rain, but not uncommon to have spouts of cloud coverage and light mists of rainfall. Laurel had spent the evening in one of the guest rooms of the elder's lodge. After the arguments last time she'd been home, she still had no desire to return and try to smooth it over. They could come to her.

She awoke early to the sound of knocking at the door. Willow Valerian stood tall outside, clean again and brimming with nobility. Her dark hair seemed longer somehow now that it was clean. Laurel grabbed the bag she'd packed the night before and followed Willow away from the lodge. The sun was still rising far to the east, which gave off a blinding glare as they followed the wooden walkway.

A guard had been posted just outside of the city to make sure Chrys and his family didn't leave. Technically they were not Chrys and his family so, with a little convincing, the guard let them pass and told them he'd deal with the consequences.

Laurel had wanted them to *drift*, but Willow was against the unnecessary use of their power. She understood the reasoning, especially for an older threadweaver, but their pace felt sluggish and lifeless compared to her normal speed. She'd been using her threadweaving a lot over the past few months, and the world was starting to feel dull without it.

She was most grateful for the quiet. Nothing but the sound of the passing wind and the occasional bird's song as they followed the long wooden path to the edge of the Fairenwild. Laurel had been worried Willow would want to talk the whole way, but the older woman appeared to have her own thoughts to digest.

When they reached the edge of the Fairenwild, they dropped down to the surface, *pushing* on their corethread to soften the landing. The Alchean countryside east of the Fairenwild flaunted varying shades of green as far as the eye could see. Far to the east, the Everstone Mountains peeked their crests over the distant horizon.

Laurel thought about what it would be like to live in Alchea. The sheer number of people made it hard to imagine. Living in a city where you knew less than one percent of the population? It would be overwhelming. In Zedalum, she was one connection away from everyone. If she didn't know someone personally, she knew someone who did. Something about the inherent anonymity excited her. She could be whoever she wanted. No one would judge her. No one would expect anything of her. She'd be free.

Willow broke the long silence without breaking pace. "Just so you know, after we've convinced the others to help, you are free to leave. The last thing we need is you getting stabbed by a stray blade."

Laurel wasn't sure how she should respond. Mothers were

supposed to be soft and gentle, but Willow was hard. Maybe motherhood was different in the grounder city, or maybe she was just focused on rescuing Pandan. It made sense; he was Willow's brother. If it were Bay in that dungeon, Laurel would do anything to get him out, no matter the consequence.

After passing a stretch of farmland, they reached the outer rim of Alchea proper. Small homes littered the barren streets. They passed by an elderly couple happily chatting as they hung wet clothing out to dry. Ominous rainclouds threatened to sabotage the process.

Laurel had never considered settling down. The world was too vast, she was too young, and her dreams were too grand to be dammed by a boy. It didn't help that she had never had someone in that way but, even if she had, she wouldn't throw away her dreams for it. She had everything she needed: ambition and threadlight.

Empty streets filled as they entered the westside markets. Inns and taverns nestled up next to barbers and clothing shops, all bustling with residents and guests. Laurel found the variety of clothing among the grounders quite strange. Some dressed like her in beige and browns, but others wore bright colors, flamboyant headwear, or dresses that seemed insufficient for the cold weather.

Laurel and Willow traveled with their hoods up. They followed Chrys' directions toward a small tavern. Willow posted up in an alley out back, and Laurel stepped inside.

The Black Eye was full of drunken men, and men who were well on their way. It was nicer inside than she'd expected, especially given the name, but, then again, she'd never been to a grounder tavern before.

She spotted them immediately. Laz's bright red hair stuck out like a bonfire in a field. The Alirian woman, Reina, sat on the far side of the table, straddling the line between drunkenness and sobriety. Three rough looking men and a pretty brunette barkeep sat at the table with them. One of the men, a scrawny man with a snarl to his lip, ranted about the whiskey having gone bad while the woman argued that it was impossible for whiskey to go bad. Laz sat back laughing as he sipped away at a mug.

She started making her way over when she overheard two drunkards at a table to her right, speaking as if they each were deaf.

"...swear it. I heard it from Gill who was posted in the temple when it happened. The General went into the altar room and slaughtered the recorder in cold blood! Then he snatched a priest and escaped out one of the back doors."

"I still can't believe someone would do something like that. Guess they called him the Apogee for a reason."

"Aye. And I heard from Jaysin that they got the priest, but the general got away. Can't 'spect they are going to make it far in there, 'specially with a baby in tow."

"Wait, he escaped from Gen'ral Furious with a baby in his arms?"

"You're an idiot. Ain't no one gonna start callin' Jurius General Furious. Aint no one else dumb enough to risk their neck when he hears you say it!"

"Shut it. Let's see what happens if Gen'ral Furious comes after me! I ain't scared a' him."

"You should be if you know what's good for ya. Old or no, he's still a weaver."

Laurel snapped her head back away from the table. She needed to focus. The first step was to get Laz and Reina to meet up with Willow outside so she could explain the situation.

She approached the table confidently and nodded to them all. "Good evening."

One of the men at the far end of the table looked Laurel up and down. He was a scrawny gentleman with a smile far less charismatic than he believed. "Well, hello. Always room at the table for a precious gem like yourself."

"Calm yourself, Roy."

Before Reina could finish, Laurel had opened herself to threadlight, grabbed hold of the thread between herself and a half-full mug of ale, and *pushed* it. The cup catapulted itself across the table, colliding with Roy's chest and soaking him with lukewarm fermentation.

He stood up, appalled. "Stones, girl. What's your problem!? Are you insane!?" Dripping with ale and embarrassment, he grabbed his things and stormed off in a rage.

"Ha!" Laz's deep, guttural voice burst out in laughter. "I like this one! Come, come. Anyone that offends Roy is friend of me. I am Laz. Please, please. Take seat."

As they sat down Laz and Reina studied her. Laurel caught them both eyeing her pockets and inspecting her lower legs. When she realized that they were looking for weapons, it made her feel respected. They knew she was dangerous and awarded her the appropriate level of scrutiny. When Laz's eye returned to her leg for a second time, she wondered if maybe he was just...ew.

"Do I know you?" Reina cocked her head to the side, bringing her hand up to her cheek as she observed Laurel. "Not many threadweavers I don't know. You do look awfully familiar."

Laurel turned to the other two men and the barkeep. "Would you three excuse us? I've a rather personal matter to discuss with these two."

The two men stood up hesitantly, eyeing Laurel as they made their way toward the other side of the tavern. The barkeep scowled, rolling her eyes as she looked down at the mess made from the spilled ale under Roy's seat. She left without a word.

"Stones." Reina's eyes lit up as reality dawned on her. "Lightfather be damned. You're her."

Laz looked to Reina. "Who? She is who?"

"From the warehouse."

Laz whipped his head back toward Laurel and his eyes grew wide. He opened his mouth to speak but nothing came out. He pursed his lips and swore. "Stones."

Laurel took a seat and raised a finger to her mouth. "Never had a chance to thank you. Reina and Laz, right? Chrys sent me. Said we could trust you. His mother is outside. We need your help."

"Chrys' mother?" Laz asked. "Ha! Is great news!"

Reina slapped his arm. "The guards are still watching. Don't act suspicious. Where is Chrys?"

Laurel wasn't sure the red-headed man was sane. There was just something about him that she didn't trust. She continued to let threadlight swim through her veins, prepared for anything. The tavern had less than a dozen people inside spread out across the large room. Laurel watched each of them.

"Chrys is safe. Willow will tell you everything."

Laz eyed the guards. "Problem is guards. Follow us everywhere."

Reina nodded and looked at Laurel. "If you can distract the guards for a minute, Laz and I can sneak out and meet you out back. I think they've had a little to drink themselves. Shouldn't be hard."

Laurel looked at the guards, both taking occasional glances their way. "Just tell me what to do."

Reina laughed. "You're a pretty girl. And with blue eyes like that, just flirt a little. Those two will eat it up."

Flirt? Threadlight ran through Laurel's veins. Theoretically, she knew what she needed to do. Realistically? It couldn't be that hard. "I can do it."

No one moved. Reina and Laz sat staring at her with a twinkle in their eye.

"Wait," Laurel paused. "Now?"

They both nodded.

Laurel rose from the table and took a breath. As she took a step toward the guards, she was grateful that they were both rather plain looking. They were also both much older than her, probably mid-twenties.

As she approached, one of the guards looked her up and down and nudged the other. She smiled and took a seat on a stool next to them. She opened her mouth to speak and realized she had no idea what to say or what to do. She froze.

"Can I help you?" the first guard asked.

"A drink maybe?" asked the other, leaning forward.

Laurel panicked and raised up two fingers.

"Two drinks? Stones, girl. With a frame like that?" He laughed and raised a hand. "Hey, Barb. Two drinks for my friend."

The other extended his hand. "And what do I call you?"

"Laur—" She responded without thinking of using an alias. She switched mid-name and used the first alternative she could think of. "C—"

She stopped. Corian was a boy's name. They'd never believe that.

After an uncomfortable pause, the first guard looked at her and raised a brow. "Lork? Like a Fork?"

"With a waist like that, I'd say she fairs better as a little spoon."

It took all of Laurel's willpower not to grab the nearest fork and stab them both. She'd distracted them long enough, right?

With the warmth of threadlight in her veins, she made a decision. Laurel stood up, grabbed her stool, and *pushed* it as hard as she could at the guards. It launched from her hands and crashed into both of their heads. They fell to the floor, and their drinks exploded into the air.

Laurel turned to the barmaid and smiled. "I'm...sorry about that."

Then she ran.

Once outside, Laurel rushed around the building into the alley. Laz and Reina were waiting for her, and she led them around the next corner.

"What was that loud noise before you came out?" Reina asked.

Laurel kept her eyes forward. "They spilled their drinks."

Around the next corner, Willow stood waiting for them. Her eyes lit up when she saw them. Laurel hadn't seen Willow smile since they'd left Zedalum, but Willow knew that if she wanted to rescue her brother, she'd need Reina and Laz on their side.

Willow embraced them both. "It is good to see you."

"We're just happy that Chrys is okay," Reina said. "We knew none of that nonsense about him rising up in rebellion was true."

"No. There's a lot we have to discuss," Willow agreed. "I'm just glad you recognized Laurel. We worried the guards would know who I was."

Laz gave a toothy grin. Laurel wasn't sure the man had ever

stopped smiling since she'd arrived. "I knew Chrys would find her! He is resourceful man."

"Actually, I found him," Laurel countered. "Half-dead and about to be eaten by my chromawolf."

"Hold on a second," Reina said, cocking her head to the side. "*Your* chromawolf?"

"Not now," Willow said. "Chrys said you could help us."

"With what?" Reina asked.

Willow leaned forward and smiled. "We need to break into Endin Keep."

~ Et'hovon ~

CHAPTER 28

THERE WAS something comforting about incarceration. Over the last few weeks, Alverax had grown accustomed to the warmth of cold steel and cold shoulders. His optimism wasn't completely unfounded. If Alabella had wanted him dead, he'd be dead. In the end, it always came back to his grandfather's prophetic words, "Us Blightwoods don't die easy."

Before they'd locked him away in his windowless cage, two people had been pulled out of Alabella's carts. Even from a distance, Alverax could tell that both were threadweavers. Bulging, colorful veins lined their neck, arms, and chest. They were deathly thin, and their skin was an unnatural, pallid color. They were loaded into one of Farah's carts.

He overheard some of Alabella's crew talking about taking the pod of taractus and heading back to Cynosure just before a man's scream cried out at the desert's border. Alverax had no idea what was happening, and he didn't want to. Finally, after some time, they left.

The journey north was uneventful. Alverax tried his best to

eavesdrop, but the noise of the horse-drawn carts was enough to dampen their voices. The horses were disturbing creatures. He'd only seen them in paintings, but their mannerisms in person were much more unnerving. Every time he glanced at one, he was certain it gave him a judgmental eye in return. He'd prefer to be pulled by a dumber creature, like a taractus. Something that didn't stare back.

They covered his window and told him to stay quiet. He wasn't interested in disobeying. By the clanking sound of horse-shoes and wheels on stone, he assumed that they had arrived in a city. He heard the occasional muffled voice as they wheeled down streets until finally the cart stopped.

A pair of men opened his door and let him out. They manhandled him through a large, thick door and into a sprawling warehouse crawling with people.

Alverax wasn't sure what he had expected, but this wasn't it. There had to be a hundred people in the warehouse lined up in rows washing, dyeing, hemming, and sewing a variety of clothing. The workers faced the northern wall on the other end of the building, and not one of them registered his entrance over the bustle of the job.

The men ushered him into a tight room in the corner where he found Alabella seated at a desk. She paid no mind as Alverax was led past her. The wall opened up into a hidden room with a staircase leading down into a dark, cavernous hole.

Heralds save me.

"Wait." Alabella looked up from her papers and squinted her eyes. "Come here. We should talk before you see what's down there. And take his shackles off. He's to be treated as one of us from now on. He's no slave."

The men released Alverax and gestured to a chair on the other side of her desk. He reached a hand behind him and

315

rubbed his back as he got a better look at the room. Three crates lined the northwest wall. An open box full of used parchment paper. A thick, black rug compressed under his feet as he took his seat. Across from him, a full-sized mirror was fixed to the west wall. He looked at himself and was shocked by what he saw. For the first time, he saw his eyes, and a shiver ran up his spine.

Alabella touched the end of a pair of Felian lightshades, lining them up with an ink bottle next to them on her desk. "I want you to tell me everything."

Alverax rubbed at the stubble on his cheek. "Can you be a little more specific?"

She leaned forward, eyes bright with excitement. "How did it happen? What did it feel like? Does it still hurt? Heralds. You're the first person to survive a ventricular mineral graft in Heralds know how long. The ramifications are immeasurable. If it is reproducible—which I believe it is—it could change everything!"

Alverax leaned back in his chair. Her excitement was unnerving.

"I—" she stopped herself. "Have you been outside of Cynosure before?"

He shook his head. "Almost made it on a ship to Felia once, but they kicked me off when they found out who my father was."

"A father should leave his son more than a tainted name. Very few know that Alabella is not my given name. I changed it many years ago. Like yours, mine was tainted, and I found myself in need of something more...stately."

He'd never considered it before—Cynosure was small enough for it not to make a real difference—but changing his name was probably a good idea.

"Alverax, I need to apologize for everything that has happened to you. Starting with Jelium, you have been the recipient of so much undeserved suffering. I want you to know that from this moment onward, I will do everything in my power to protect you. You needn't fear Jelium anymore. You are an Obsidian threadweaver, Alverax. A singularity. Not one person in this world will be able to guide you. I've been where you are. It's not an easy place to be. You and I are the same."

Never in all his years at Cynosure would he ever have imagined comparing himself to Alabella, let alone her making the comparison. And she was right. An Obsidian threadweaver? He'd never even heard of such a thing. No one would be able to guide him, teach him, warn him. And that's exactly how it must have been for Alabella—and Jelium, but to hell with him. If anyone could understand what he was going through, it was her.

"But enough of that," she continued. "Tell me. When did you realize you had become an Obsidian threadweaver? Start from the beginning."

"Well," he thought. "I woke up in the boneyard with scars all over my chest."

She smiled. "Threadlight must have sustained you. How long were you dead?"

"I don't know. Less than a day."

"Incredible."

Remembering that day gave him phantom pains in his chest. He rubbed at his ribs, knowing full well that it wasn't real. "I didn't know that I had become a threadweaver until that night. I got angry at someone, and it just happened."

"What exactly happened?" She relished every detail, nodding along as he spoke.

"Threads of colorful light popped into existence all around

me. I'd never felt anything like it. Like the entire world knew that I existed, and I was the center of it all. And the thick thread beneath me, it called to me. I reached out to it and it popped like a bubble. Then I started to float."

"Ha! Yes!" She slammed an excited fist down on the desktop. "You can break your corethread! Sarla is going to be furious. She was so certain it wasn't possible. Ah! This is thrilling. She'll want to study you thoroughly. Heralds, she'll probably want to marry you to keep you close."

Alverax twinged.

She laughed. "Don't worry. I'll keep away the chaff. And trust me, there will be many in your future. Queens will beg for you to take their hand. The first Obsidian threadweaver in centuries. Can you show me again?"

"Here?"

"Of course, you don't have to," she said. Her veins lit up, radiating a bright yellow as she opened herself to threadlight. "But what you can do is a beautiful thing. You should never be ashamed of it."

She was right. He shouldn't be ashamed. Afraid, maybe—it could easily put a target on his back—but not ashamed.

He let dark threadlight flood his veins and filtered out the noise. Below him, his corethread shown with a welcome intensity. He reached out with his mind. The thick thread burst, and the weight of the world faded away. He took a deep breath and tapped his toe to the ground. His body began to float upward.

The feeling was euphoric. Pure freedom. Not even the world could hold him. Despite a life of being constantly dragged down, he was weightless.

"Extraordinary," Alabella said, staring at him. "Absolutely extraordinary."

A short moment later his corethread reappeared. Gravity grabbed hold of him and pulled him back to the ground.

"So short," she said, disappointed.

"I can control the length of time it's gone."

"Of course. It only makes sense that yours would work similarly to ours. Sit, sit." Alabella grabbed a pen and wrote something down on a sheet of parchment paper to her right. "I could spend hours studying this with you—and maybe someday we will—but we should discuss some grim realities that may make you uncomfortable. I am not one to apologize for my actions, but some brighter futures require a darker present."

She stood and moved toward the hidden room behind her, waving for him to follow. They headed down a wooden staircase into a lamplit chamber. It was larger than Alverax would have expected, but not so large that he couldn't see the man tied up at the far end. He looked just like the two that Alverax had seen in the desert, starved, with skin the color of pale moonlight. Flickering flames fed the shadows dancing over his sunken eyes. Alverax shivered. A chill crawled up his spine.

Two large glass containers half-filled with wine lay next to strange equipment. *Heralds*. It wasn't wine. It didn't take long for Alverax to realize what was happening here. Much like the Nest in Cynosure, they were extracting threadweaver blood, but this was not a willing participant.

Alabella reached the bottom of the stairs after him. "Do you understand?"

He shook his head.

"If I were a brilliant engineer, perhaps we could have done things differently, though that too would have brought unwanted attention. We need local capital to fund our endeavors."

He turned around at the last line. "What endeavors?"

Alabella smiled at him. "If you had asked me this question yesterday, it would have been much less ambitious. But you, my sweet boy, enable so much more. I'm being presumptive, of course, on several accounts. Come with me and I'll explain."

There was something about the way she looked at him. It wasn't distaste, or cynicism. It was empathy. She understood him in a way that no one else could. He didn't know what to think. It was as if she were two separate people. The woman with unfaltering ambitions, willing to drain a man's blood for shines, and the woman that looked at him with motherly adoration. He wanted her to be the latter, but he couldn't discount the other.

She led him back up the stairs and through the office, out into the vaulted warehouse floor. The workers continued their duties at the rows of tables before them. Alabella guided him up a flight of stairs that led to a second story balcony where they could look down over the workers. He recognized the style of clothing being manufactured; Felian garments were popular in Cynosure as well.

Alabella leaned over the balcony and smiled. "Can you see it?"

He looked for whatever it was she was alluding to, but he saw nothing out of the ordinary. One of the workers leaned back and yawned, covering her mouth with a partially crippled hand. "They're tired."

She looked to Alverax and laughed. "As am I. But why are they tired?"

"I don't know. Probably because they're stuck doing an awful job."

"Exactly!" she shouted. "They're bored! And do you know why? Because the fount of madness is filled with monotony! This life...it's a collection of dreary moments one after the other in an endless cycle of fatigue, each day a proverbial tap on the forehead until at last you can't stand another touch, your mind breaks, and you become yet another mindless drone drifting along with no hope. It's miserable."

The truth of her words hit him like a rock. He'd felt the hopelessness before. The ebb and flow of time, some weeks more hopeful than others, but never quite able to cast off the cloud of despair looming overhead. The faster you ran from it, the faster the winds blew. Without respite.

"I was not always a threadweaver," her voice grew more solemn, "I was an accident, unlike you. A bout of fate changed me. When I discovered threadlight, the darkness that had taken root in my soul seemed to fade away. I felt real happiness for the first time."

Alverax knew the feeling. Every time he let threadlight pour through him, he felt it. It was as if threadlight rebuffed the darkness.

"That is what I want. I want to give away freely that which has been hoarded by chance. I want every person in this world to have the choice to be a threadweaver."

Heralds save me. She was insane...but was she? Here *he* stood. A week ago, he hadn't been a threadweaver, and now he was. What if it were possible? It *was* possible. If threadweaving were available to everyone, how would that impact the world?

"You're skeptical. I understand," she said. "I'll be the first to admit that the plan is overly ambitious. Sarla and I weren't even sure it was possible, nor did we have the means to make it a reality...until you. You were the missing piece. The key. You have the chance to change the world. To improve lives. We have the opportunity to give the world the gift of joy."

His mind was a blur. He might have tried to run if there weren't guards at the door, but he was glad that wasn't an option. This was important. This was a defining moment, for himself and for the world. This was where he could choose who to be. Not the thief's boy. No, he didn't want to take anymore. He wanted to give. What greater good could he give the world than the gift of threadlight? He wanted it to be true. He wanted to trust her, and as he looked into her Amber eyes, just for a moment, he did.

"What do you need me to do?"

CHAPTER 29

DARK CLOUDS GAVE way to a light rain, falling gently on the valleys below the Everstone Mountains. The wind roared over the peaks, and Laurel smiled. In Zedalum, high above the forest floor, the winds blew with such fury that the walls of homes would hum and shake beneath the storm. Tonight, she stood on a tall peak overlooking Endin Keep, and the winds were with her.

After the debacle at The Black Eye, they'd gone to Luther's home, sneaking past guards placed in the woods. He hadn't been hard to convince.

"Two threads; one bond," he'd said.

Laurel, Willow, and Laz had hiked for several hours up the mountainside, keeping out of sight while they moved toward their destination. The clouds and rain helped obscure their travels, but it also soaked them to the core. Fortunately, a bit of threadlight in the veins was enough to keep Laurel warm.

Now all there was to do was wait. At some point, they'd see a blinking torch in one of the tower windows. According to

Chrys, there was a window on the fifth floor that was always left unlocked in case of emergency. Reina would scale the tower exterior until she reached the window, open it, and signal for the others to come. When Willow had asked if Reina could handle it, the white-haired woman had smiled and said, *"They don't call me the Alirian Spider for nothing."*

Luther was to scout the hallways and meet them at the dungeon. Every entrance to the keep had an added guard detail, and they checked every person going in and out. Luther would be watched, but he wouldn't be denied entrance.

Laurel felt like she could trust Reina and Luther, but something about the stupid grin on Laz's face worried her, especially with how key his role was.

Standing on the high peak in the rain, she watched Laz unpack what they called a skysail. It looked like nothing more than a sprawling piece of black fabric, but as he laid out thick rods down the length, it locked the material into a large triangle shape.

Supposedly, they were going to fly into the keep...

Laurel had her obvious doubts, but Reina seemed to be the least convinced that it would work, especially with the rain—but Reina wasn't the one using it. Willow said they needed the rain to cover their travel, and that it would discourage the guards posted on the eastern wall from looking up. Laz swore that the skysail would work in the rain. Something about Sapphires and their weight.

It did little to reassure Laurel.

A light breeze angled the wind to the south, each bead tapping against Laurel's cheek as she stared toward the tower. A small shadow crawled along the stone walls. The Alirian spider, indeed. The rain must have been oppressing as Reina scaled the stone tower.

Laurel closed her eyes for a moment and let more thread-light pour through her veins. The warmth comforted her. Even in the cold rain, atop a lonely mountain, it felt like home. When she opened her eyes, the rain seemed to blur together. The tower grew further and further away. A distant memory. A forgotten purpose replaced with the rush of threadlight.

Willow slapped Laurel's shoulder. "Cut that out. I don't think I've seen your veins free of threadlight since we met. Save some for later."

Laurel pulled her arm away. Now, of all times, Willow decided to scold her like an over-dramatic mother? She just didn't like being cold in the rain. It wasn't a big deal.

"Look," Laz said, pointing to the tower. A small light blinked in the distant window. Reina had made it to her destination. "Ready?"

Laurel stared forward and nodded, feeling Willow's judgmental eyes bearing down on her from her peripheral.

Laz wrapped his thick arms around the waist of both women and took a deep breath as his eyes darted around at the falling rain. "Is fine."

Before Laurel could process the comment, he took them running toward the edge of the cliff and leapt. Wind caught the wings of the skysail and they glided upward, beads of rain pelting the top of the fabric overhead. She looked down and saw a group of keep guards far below, each of them with hoods pulled up over their heads.

It was actually working.

Just then, a gust of wind launched them up into the air. The right wing dipped low, and she heard Laz curse under his breath. The skysail started to shake as the air pressure shifted. Laz's veins flared blue. He *pushed* against the dipping wing and leaned toward the other. As the wings evened out, he turned the skysail back toward the tower window.

"Are we okay, Laz?" Willow shouted through the wind and rain.

Laz turned and smiled a toothy grin. "Is fine!"

Slowly, the skysail glided down until it reached the open window. It was in that moment that Laurel realized that they had never planned for how the journey would end. The wings snapped off with a crack as they passed through the opening. Laz, Willow, and Laurel tumbled forward, limb crossing limb, hair lodging in unimaginable locations. As they settled, Laurel found herself face-to-face with Laz. He was still smiling that stupid smile of his. She rolled off him as fast as she could.

Reina had taken a seat and was staring at them. "A short ride and a poor ending. Laz always did know how to treat a woman."

Laz laughed as he rose to his feet. "Is better to end with bang, no?"

"Father of All," Willow groaned. "It worked well enough. Laz, get this room cleaned up. Reina, lead the way and make sure we don't run into anyone unexpected. Did you get the bread?"

Reina nodded and tossed her a loaf of bread wrapped in a leather lining.

Laurel and Willow removed their cloaks, handed them to Laz, and exited the room. It was warmer inside than Laurel expected. Oil lamps lined the corridor. In Zedalum, where the moss that grew on the feytrees was even more flammable than the photospores, every open flame was a danger. Here, in a forest of stone, there was no such risk.

Reina led them down a series of pathways, at times narrowly avoiding run-ins with staff or worse. She turned and gestured to them to hide. They ducked into a doorway as three guards rounded a corner, talking about some nobleman named Tyberius that had gotten punch drunk at dinner and made a fool of himself. As they passed the doorway, one of the guards turned to look at the two women. "What have we here?"

Laurel hissed at him. It wasn't a gentle hiss. It was guttural, savage even. The guard startled back, bumping into one of the others, and walked away ashamed as his comrades laughed at his behest. He looked back once for a very short glance that she ended with a predatory stare.

Willow raised a brow. "What are you?"

Threadlight and adrenaline coiled together in Laurel's veins, pulsing a deep blue hue. She wanted to sprint through the hallways, drifting as she *pushed* against her corethread. They'd make better time, surely, but they needed to be discrete.

"You're doing it again."

Laurel frowned. "What?"

"Let go of the threadlight. It's not healthy."

"I'm fine."

Willow scowled at her. "I haven't come this far to have it all thrown away because you wasted yourself on unnecessary threadweaving. You'll get your chance to use it later. Now is not the time."

Laurel surrendered, damming the flow of threadlight. As it faded away, her muscles tightened. Her breath grew heavier, like she was trying to fit an apple down a straw. It took all of her self-control not to let threadlight course back through her veins. She walked beside Willow and wondered if she could be subtle enough that the old woman wouldn't notice if she started threadweaving again. But her arms were uncovered, so even subtle threadweaving would be noticeable.

Reina motioned for them to follow. They followed several

staircases down, moved through long hallways, and had no more close encounters with staff or guards. Finally, they came to a nondescript staircase leading down below the surface level.

Willow paused at the top of the stairs. "Reina, you stay here. If Luther doesn't show up soon, play his part. Otherwise, keep watch and make sure he's the only one coming down after us."

Laurel followed Willow down the stairs. They spiraled down, long shadows flickering from staggered sconces. What awaited them below was the biggest unknown. Willow had seen it before, but the guard detail had increased dramatically since her escape. The bottom of the staircase led to a short tunnel with a locked gate. Six guards stood at attention, drawing swords as the two women approached. Laurel hoped that Luther was a punctual man.

One of the guards stepped forward. "No one is allowed down here. Identify yourselves."

Willow pulled out a loaf of bread from the bag at her side. She curtsied and held it up for the guards to see. "My lord sent us down here to feed the prisoner, but we'd be happy if one of you wanted to do it instead."

"The prisoner already ate today."

They needed to stall.

Laurel had to think fast. "You're right, of course. Mum, we shouldn't lie. No one sent us down here. We just...we wanted to see the prisoner. My mum and I heard he had horns and red eyes. A demon priest, or some kind of corespawn. Is it true? Can we see him? Did he really kill a temple worker?"

The guard stared blankly for a few moments. "Get back upstairs. We don't have time for this nonsense. Take your lady-gossip elsewhere."

"Lady-gossip? How dare you," Willow shouted. She'd found her opening and proceeded to unleash her inner nobility. "We are esteemed ladies of this state, and I demand that we be treated with the respect we deserve."

The head guard shifted in his boots. "Apologies, my lady, but the fact remains. You cannot be down here. The prisoner is dangerous."

One of the others elbowed his friend. "Not after how Jurius left him."

Laurel didn't like the sound of that, and she couldn't imagine how it made Willow feel. The woman kept her air of dignity as she stood facing them, but Laurel saw Willow's eye twitch just the slightest.

Footsteps echoed up the pathway behind them. Willow and Laurel turned and walked backward toward the guards while facing the staircase. Luther came jaunting down the stairs three by three and panting like he'd been running for miles.

"Stop those women!" he shouted. "That is Lady Willow Valerian, wanted by the Great Lord on counts of collusion and evading arrest!"

The guards looked around at each other, unsure what to do. The head guard tossed down his weapons and lunged at Willow, who had her back turned still. He grappled and pinned her to the ground. Another guard, following his lead, did the same to Laurel. The two women cried out to let them go, but the men held them hard against the ground.

Luther walked and stood over them. "Jurius will be very pleased. Open the gate and put them in a cell until we can get word to the high general. And cover their eyes! Stones, have you never dealt with a threadweaver before?"

As if for the first time, the guards realized that the women were threadweavers. Several dropped their swords to the ground, realizing the danger any held item posed.

"You go get shackles and blindfolds," the head guard

ordered. "And you two go get the gate keys from General Henna."

"Wait." Luther held up a hand. "You don't have the keys?"

The head guard looked at him with a brow curled up. "Of course not. That would be a security hazard."

"Smart. You two get the keys from General Henna. We'll keep the prisoners here." Laurel could hear Luther's voice faltering. This was not part of the plan. They'd assumed that the guards would have the keys. If they had to wait, then Laz's timing would be off, and the escape would be ruined.

The three guards with assignments raced off and disappeared up the dark, spiral staircase. Laurel, Luther, and Willow all seemed to have the same thought at the same moment. Luther lunged forward and drove his heel hard into the chest of the guard holding Willow, then dropped and slammed his fist into the neck of the guard holding Laurel. The women jumped up, veins flaring with Sapphire threadlight and swung their fists into the heads of the men that had held them. They both fell unconscious.

The only remaining guard threw his hands up into the air in defeat, knowing full well that he couldn't fight three threadweavers on his own. "Don't, please!" He dropped to his knees with his hands still in the air.

Willow took a step toward him. "Move and you die."

Luther patted down the guards but didn't find what he was looking for. He walked over to the kneeling man, searched him, then looked into his eyes while he spoke. "Not complaining, but if the high general knew you surrendered this easily there would be hell to pay. Is there any other way into the cells without the keys?"

The man shook his head. "No, I swear it."

Luther scowled. "Get on the ground and don't move."

Willow approached the locked gate and examined the keyhole. She grabbed hold of the iron rods and shook it; loud clanking echoed throughout the dungeon. "We need the key, but we don't have time to wait for it. Any ideas?"

"Can we pick it?" Willow asked.

"The locks are too heavy," Luther said, "and we don't have anything to pick it with anyway."

Laurel walked forward and kicked as hard as she could. The gate rattled back and forth but held firm. "Let's break it down."

"The bars are solid iron," Luther sneered. "You can't just kick them down."

Her foot throbbed beneath her. What a stupid idea. Who kicks iron? Even so, something about kicking the gate had felt good. She reimagined the kick, her foot connecting hard with the lock, and the whole gate shaking back and forth.

"We're threadweavers!" she shouted. The others stared at her. "We don't need to kick them down. Willow, you and I *push* on the top bars. Luther, you *pull* on the threads of the bottom."

Willow looked to Luther. "You have a better idea?"

All three of them let threadlight course through them. Hundreds of lines of brilliant light flowed through the dungeon, but Laurel only needed one. Willow and Laurel's veins lit with brilliant blue as they *pushed* on the threads nearest to the top hinge, and Luther's veins blazed green as he *pulled* on the threads nearest to the bottom hinge. The gate groaned and creaked as the force flowing through the threads affected the physical world.

"Full force on three," Willow counted. "One. Two. Three!"

The gate twisted, metal groaning like thunder, until the hinges snapped off and the gate rotated like a wheel. The center hinge bent itself to accommodate the new position.

"Ha!" Laurel laughed. "I told you!"

"Nice work. Let's get inside, quickly now. You too," Willow said, kicking the guard's back.

Laurel, Willow, Luther, and the guard all crawled under the twisted-up gate and into the dungeon. There were no gates on the individual cells, but each had double shackles built into the walls. Each of the cells was empty, except for his.

When they reached Pandan, he didn't look much better. Open wounds festered on his arms, and bruises lined the entire left side of his face. The other cheek had something seriously wrong with it. Black, burnt skin crusted over the center. In the low light, Laurel could barely make out the lethargic movements of his chest as he breathed.

"Pan!" Willow rushed forward, checking his vitals, and removed the blindfold from his eyes. She worked quickly to release the latch of the chains. His arms dropped to the side, and he started to fall forward. She caught him and sobbed as she squeezed. "You're okay, little brother. We're going to get you home."

For a moment, Laurel imagined Bay chained up instead of Pandan. Tears formed in her eyes and her heart filled with anger and fear. She knew Pandan. He'd been kind to her. He did not deserve this.

Pandan coughed and tried to open his eyes. His brows furled in pain and the pace of his breathing increased. "Willow?"

Willow had never smiled so wide. "It's me."

"I'm so sorry."

"There is nothing to be sorry about. The elders told me everything. We're going to get you out of here."

"I," he groaned. "I had no choice. Please, forgive me."

Willow leaned forward. "Stop talking. You need to relax. It's going to be okay."

In the corner of her eye, Laurel saw Luther's chest rising and falling at an increasing rate. He had murder in his eyes and a quiver in his lip. Laurel didn't understand what was going through his mind, but she could tell he was looking at Pandan. And it didn't look good.

"You lied to me," Luther said, addressing Willow.

She turned from embracing her brother and looked at Luther, confused. "What are you talking about?"

"You lied to me," Luther growled. "You knew it was the priest, and you said nothing."

"He was a spy, not a real priest. Everything I told you was true. He is my brother, and Chrys' uncle. What does it matter?"

"It matters to me!" Luther roared. "He took my son!"

Willow stood up, her lips curling into something feral. Laurel knew the feeling. The anger. The need to protect. Laurel was Willow, and Pandan was Asher, wounded as the alpha approached. Willow said nothing; her eyes had said enough.

"Move," Luther ordered. His breathing grew sporadic. He was a predator prepared to pounce. "Someone has to pay for what happened to my son."

"It was the Rite of Revelation!" Willow spat. "It was your choice. You knew the law. You played the game, and you lost. If you think to lay the blame on my little brother, I swear on the wind that I will end you."

Every part of Luther's body shook. His jaw clenched with such fury that Laurel was sure his teeth would shatter any moment. Then, he closed his eyes. Laurel thought she saw tears forming. "Someone has to pay," he repeated.

A loud bell echoed down through the spiral staircase and into the dungeon. The Keep alarm. That meant Laz had played his part and created a distraction on the other side of the keep. If Luther was right, guards would also swarm to the Great

Lord's chambers to protect him. That should keep him occupied.

"We need to leave," Willow said. "Luther, I need you. Chrys needs you. Can we count on you?"

He nodded meekly.

"Good," she said. "Laurel, place the guard in shackles so he can't follow. Let's get out of here before the others come back."

Laurel led the cowering guard into a cell and locked him up.

Luther stood and watched as Willow attempted to lift Pandan's bloodied arm over her shoulders. Rather than waiting for him to help, Laurel stepped forward and grabbed the other arm. Together, they moved him all the way to the twisted dungeon gate where they had to lay him down and drag him underneath. The old man moaned and cried while they pulled him across the cold stone. The whole time Luther watched on in silence.

They pulled Pandan the rest of the way through and then back up onto his feet as they summited the dungeon stairway. When they reached the top, they were not alone.

Two Alirian women.

One bound.

One donning the uniform of a high general.

Gale take me.

As soon as High General Henna saw them with Pandan, she pulled a dagger out, spun it in her palm, and smiled. "Willow."

"Henna."

"We need to talk."

"Unfortunately, we have a prior engagement."

Willow exploded forward into the air, screaming as her veins blazed a bright cerulean blue. Behind her, Laurel stood carrying the full weight of Pandan. She had to *push* on her own corethread just to keep from falling under the weight.

There was no grace to Willow's movements. She was a feral animal descending on her prey, claws jabbing with no remorse. But she was no fighter. After the first exchange, it was clear that Henna held the advantage. She blocked each savage swipe with ease, sidestepping as Willow tried to tackle her and tossing the older woman down to the ground panting.

Luther snarled as he rushed forward. This time, Henna didn't wait for the attack. She charged him, prowling low to the ground, and swung forward with her blade. Luther blocked attack after attack until she landed a kick into his stomach. He stumbled back, spit on the floor, and put his hand forward as his veins lit with green threadlight.

Nothing happened.

The General took the opening and swiped out at his hand, the black blade cutting through the skin of his palm. He retreated back, clutching at his hand, then he charged forward. Laurel saw him reach his hand to *pull* the knife in Henna's hand. Again, nothing happened. The high general thrust with the knife and sliced into his left arm. Green blood turned red as it fell to the stone floor.

Luther retreated again, holding the wound on his arm.

Henna lunged forward and threw her fist, but he chopped down and spun to the side, throwing his weight into his elbow. Luther was stronger, but Henna was faster. She ducked below and sent a swift uppercut into his ribs. His torso contracted, and she kicked hard at the back of his knee, but Luther moved his leg just in time. Willow was back up and dove onto Henna's back, clawing at her face as they toppled forward.

The knife fell out of Henna's hand as they hit the ground, crashing out in front of Laurel. She laid Pandan down, then picked it up.

She paused.

Impossible.

It was identical to the knife in her pocket—the one that Chrys had dropped in the Fairenwild. The same obsidian blade. The same flat hilt. This dagger must have been forged by the same smith.

General Henna jabbed behind her with an elbow that caught Willow in the jaw. A loud crack echoed in the hallway. Luther pounced forward and mauled her across the head with a heavy fist. The high general toppled over, unconscious.

Luther ran over to Reina, removed her bindings, then went to check on Willow. She was moaning on the ground holding her jaw. He helped her up and led her back over to Pandan. For a moment, he hesitated, his jaw clenched tightly. "I'll help you carry him."

Laurel slipped the second blade in her pocket and threw Pandan's arm over her shoulder.

Struggling to walk, Willow turned to Reina. "Go check on Laz and make sure he is okay. Luther and Laurel, follow me."

Reina nodded. "Henna sent for more guards. Be careful."

They took slow, steady steps as they made their way through the long corridor. Reina sprinted off toward the adjacent hallway. The bell rang out once again, this time louder. There would be no way of getting out the front entrance, but that wasn't their plan anyway.

As they rounded the corner, Laurel looked behind her. General Henna was on her feet once again, shoulders hunched forward, her entire body heaving with each breath. She saw them, and she took a step.

Laurel quickened her pace. "We need to move faster."

CHAPTER 30

IT WAS late by the time they'd reached the edge of the Fairenwild, but Alabella said they were right on schedule. Several
hundred people traveled with them. The assembly had started
small when they'd left the warehouse, but group after group
had joined the mass by the time they'd reached the edge of
Alchea.

All around him men and women lit torches and others held
onto the broken stalks of strange, radiant plants. Slowly, they
stepped into an environment unlike anything Alverax had ever
seen. There were few species of trees that thrived in the desert,
even near the water's edge at Mercy's Bluff, and none of them
looked anything like these. The trunks were the size of homes
and the branches only sprouted at heights so far overhead that
it felt like a second sky. Even surrounded by so many others, the
daunting nature of the Fairenwild gave Alverax the chills.

Alverax studied every plant and creature that crossed him,
but nothing was as fascinating as the bulbous lights bobbing on
the ends of long reeds. They looked like something that should

exist in the ocean. Every few steps he thought he saw creatures lurking behind the trees, and more than once he thought he saw something crawling up one.

It was hard to believe that people lived here. When Lady Alabella had explained that there was a city deep in the Fairenwild, it seemed like a fantasy, but he trusted her, and so did hundreds of others. When howls echoed out in the distance, he was glad there weren't less. Better odds.

As they continued, Alverax became sure that creatures were stalking them, big enough to be seen at a distance, and smart enough to stay hidden. It wasn't that he was scared; it was more that he was filled with a horrific anxiety that urged him to curl up and die. He should have stayed at the factory, but Alabella said that she needed him there with her. It felt good to hear.

They traveled for hours before they arrived at the edge of a clearing. It wasn't the end of the Fairenwild—feytrees surrounded the clearing on all sides—but it was definitely out of the ordinary. Bright flowers and green grass glowed in the radiance of the bulbs, and in the center of the opening lay a massive stone slab. A perfect circle, so thick it reached up to a man's knee. So out of place it must have been placed by the Heralds themselves.

"It's true," Alabella said, smiling to herself. Her eyes drifted upward, past a drove of spindly insects, and into the distant treetops.

Alverax stood next to her. "What is it?"

"When you were a child, did you ever wish the Heralds would visit you?"

"I guess so."

Alabella nodded to herself. "Wishing. Hoping. They are dangerous words. If you hope for something to be true and it is not, that realization can break you. But until then, while that belief runs warm in your blood, it can drive you to do amazing things. This was my moment, Alverax. And what I hoped with all my soul to be true...is."

"Does that mean we're done walking?"

"It does."

Alverax rubbed his eyes, blinking away the fatigue. "And what's next? Where are the people?"

"Patience. We haven't sent our invitation."

Laurel staggered through the halls of Endin Keep, frustrated with their pace, but they were carrying a half-conscious man. She knew that High General Henna couldn't be far behind though, in the general's current state, she would be moving slowly as well.

They came to the end of a hallway and Willow paused, looking both ways. By the time Luther and Laurel reached her, she still had not moved.

"What is it?" Laurel asked.

Willow turned around with a serious look on her face. "Do you trust me?"

"Not particularly," Luther said.

Laurel almost smiled. She'd thought the same thing, but she was glad he'd been the one to say it. It's one thing to trust a noble mother of a high general, it's another to trust an emotional sister barely out of her battle rage.

"You don't have a choice," Willow responded. "Change of plans."

Behind them, Henna scrambled around a corner and into view. She met Laurel's eyes and, for a brief moment, Laurel thought that she might actually have a chance if they fought, given Henna's current state, but best not to test that theory.

Willow took over for Laurel and helped Luther as they fled with Pandan in tow. Laurel followed closely behind. They raced down another hallway and up a flight of stairs. Pandan's feet dragged along the staircase like a rhythmic drum beating to each step. At the top of the stairs, Laurel looked down. Henna was gaining on them. And fast. She took the stairs two by two, the dazed look in her eyes beginning to fade.

"Faster!" Laurel shouted.

A group of serving women scrambled out of the way as they plowed onto the second floor. Willow stopped at a large painted door with a sigil Laurel didn't recognize. At the same moment, High General Henna reached the top of the stairs. Close enough to strike.

"It's over!" Henna spit blood as she spoke. She screamed at the servants to leave.

Instead of responding, Willow knocked hard on the door in front of her. A man's voice called out, but she did not respond. Instead she knocked even louder.

"What game are you playing?" Henna spat.

"Stones, Willow! Is that—" Luther was cut off as the door opened.

A tall man with a scarred face and high general uniform stared back at them. "What do you—"

Willow punched him in the neck.

ALVERAX WATCHED as Alabella raised her hands toward the crowd, her pale-yellow eyes glowing in the torchlight. "History is not made by coincidence. You are not here by coincidence.

History is taken! History is seized upon by those with the gall to bear it. The Heralds have led us here, and tonight, we will take what belongs to us. We will take what belongs to every man and woman on this god-forsaken earth! Power is not meant to be hoarded. Power is the tax of a shit life. The world owes you! It owes you for the pain, for the misery, for the loneliness. For every grave. Tonight, we say to the world, that tax is overdue! Tonight, we harvest a future that has been ripe for far too long. Brothers and sisters, raise your blades! Raise your bows! Fight knowing that, with this victory, the power of the gods can be yours. Change is coming, and we are its Heralds!"

The crowd was captivated by her, each word a savory morsel to their famished souls. Alverax felt his blood rising as he listened. This was the moment she'd promised him. This was their chance. Whatever came next would change everything. He could feel it in his bones.

"There are those who would stop us," Alabella continued, face alight with passion. "They wish to withhold what is rightfully yours. They would keep you in the dark. Me? I want threadlight to pour through your veins like a river of living water."

The crowd responded to her words as if they were infallible. As if she were a Herald come to guide them. To save them. They not only respected her. They revered her. Alverax was beginning to feel the same. When Alabella spoke, it demanded reverence. It was sacred. And when she spoke, it felt as though she spoke to you. As if you were the only thing she cared about in the world. Even standing in a mob of hundreds, it felt as though she were speaking to him.

"It is the day of equality. If they wish to stand in our way while we embrace a better world for all mankind, we will pluck them like the weeds they are."

They cheered, banging swords and chanting unintelligible words into the night. Alverax felt a rush of adrenaline as he looked out over them. These people were not here for a peaceful negotiation. There was fire in their eyes just as much as it was in their hands. What exactly *was* her plan? *Pluck them like weeds?* A core-rotten feeling surfaced in the pit of his stomach.

Alabella quieted them down. "You will have your chance but, before we begin, I need every woman or man holding a torch to step forward."

A group of nearly a hundred stepped forward holding bright flames. Alverax watched as Alabella walked down their line and spoke to each of them individually, thanking them for being there, touching their cheek with a motherly hand, bewitching them with guile. He felt like he was going to vomit. These people were slaves. Willing or not, they looked to her as a deity. Each touch was a divine blessing. Each word a pronouncement of life.

She addressed the assembly one final time. "A smith lays flame to metal in order to form something new. Tonight, we lay the same transformative flames. They will sing out into the night and fill your ears with nightmares. Do not dwell on the horror! Think of the polished blade that comes out the other end of the furnace. And, if that is not enough to silence your fear, think of me. I will not lead you astray. Remember, the greatest good requires the greatest sacrifice.

"Emeralds, light the moss and branches. The rest of you, light the spores."

The mob of torchbearers walked forward and laid their torches at the base of the photospores. Each spore exploded at the first touch, spitting out fire as its bulb erupted. The burning liquid drooled along the base of the feytrees like magma, lighting the bark aflame.

A half dozen Emerald threadweavers ran up the feytrees like worker-ants, lighting patches of dry moss along the way, until they reached the branches high overhead. Soon, as the flames jumped from branch to branch, the dark roof of the Fairenwild came to light.

Alverax looked around at each of the faces in the crowd and cowered as he saw the myriad forms of evil garnishing their faces.

The flames grew brighter and brighter.

Alverax was unable to blink as he watched the majesty of the feytrees light up in a horrific blaze.

Alabella looked up into the treetops. "Now, my children, we wait."

CHRYS LOOKED out over the eastern horizon, rocking back and forth with his son in his arms, imagining Alchea beneath the Everstone Mountains. In reality, it was nothing but feytrees and storm clouds as far as the eye could see. Moonlight trickled over his son's cheeks. He was so small. So helpless. So brittle. As if to argue, a small groan emerged from Aydin's lips. Chrys bounced him gently until his eyes were closed once more.

He pulled the wool blanket tight to cover Aydin from the cold chill of the wind from the east. Dark clouds rolled toward them on the horizon. Chrys never liked the rain, but found himself smiling knowing that if rain was the worst of his worries, everything was going to be okay. They were safe.

A loud sound drifted on the wind from just outside of Zedalum. Followed by another, and another. Horns trumpeting.

Chrys' mind flashed back to the Wastelands, charging toward the enemy. The wastelanders' beady eyes were void of emotion while the rest of their face screamed out in a rage. Horns trumpeting. Charge. Horns trumpeting. Clash. Horns trumpeting. Hundreds of dead lay at his feet.

Mmmm. You remember.

Chrys rose to his feet, ignoring the voice.

A handful of Zeda people ran down the wooden paths, shouting frantic words. As they approached, their words became clearer, but they were not welcome words.

"Fire in the Fairenwild! Get to the ground!"

Fire? He'd seen no lightning and heard no thunder. Even the rainfall had yet to find its way to the Fairenwild. Chrys ran into the Elder's lodge holding Aydin tight in his arms. The news had spread throughout the lodge and it was alive with activity. He shoved his way through the hallway and back to his room. Iriel lay so deeply asleep that the growing commotion passed over her like a summer breeze.

He took her hand and rubbed it. "Iriel, wake up."

Nothing.

He shook her arm, and the jolt finally broke her out of her sleep. "Iriel, we have to go. There is a fire in the Fairenwild. Everyone has to get to the ground."

She yawned and stretched. "In the middle of the night?"

He nodded and helped her up.

By the time they left the room, most of the lodge had cleared out. The wide wooden paths outside were filled with Zeda as they all headed toward the ground. Chrys saw a few Sapphire threadweavers *pushing* and leaping between the large wooden poles to the sides of the walkway. The people were panicking, and that concerned Chrys more than anything.

Outside the lodge they ran into Elder Rosemary. She was directing a dozen young women and men toward the market.

"Elder Rosemary!"

She turned to face him. "Chrys, you need to get to the ground."

"What's going on?"

"Fires. It's not the first time, but it seems to be spreading faster than normal. I've sent people to bring tents and food for the evening. Others will use water from the cisterns and dirt from the fields to calm the flames. There should be nothing to worry about."

Chrys looked toward the walkway that led to the entrance platform. "How do the achromats get down?"

"There are many Sapphires amongst our people. They will carry the others. It takes very little effort with the help of the wonderstone, so there is no danger of threadsickness. You should take your family and go. You're a Sapphire, they should let you down without delay. I'll be there shortly. Go."

Chrys followed the crowd and headed toward the entrance platform. To the east, small fire began to rise between the trees. Flames hopped from dry branch to dry branch. Zeda people heaved buckets of dirt and water at the growing flames. If they couldn't stop it before it reached the city, perhaps the rains would.

"Wait your turn! Patience, please!" A Sapphire thread-weaver directed families to the platform where other Sapphires helped them drop to the surface. "If there are any other Sapphires willing to help, please come to the front of the line!"

"Iriel, take Aydin. I'll get you both to the ground and see if I can't help some of the others."

She nodded and reached out to take Aydin. They walked past the long line of anxious faces waiting to drop to the ground. Chrys looked at them all. Fear. Anxiety. Irritation. He could tell by the look of some children that they were excited to go to the ground, perhaps for the first time. Born and raised on the treetops.

They reached the platform and Chrys approached the man in charge. "I'm a Sapphire. Let me take my wife and son down to the surface, and I'll help others after that."

The man looked at him and Iriel suspiciously, then nodded and stretched out his hand. "I heard about you. We'll take whatever help we can get. Call me Dogwood."

"Chrys—" he paused. "Chrysanthemum."

Dogwood nodded his approval.

Chrys led Iriel down the steps to the platform. Far below, he could see the massive wonderstone. As he let threadlight wash over him, the wonderstone illuminated with supernatural light. Iriel held fast to the child, and Chrys picked her up in both arms.

"My hero," she said, batting her eyelashes and curling in her shoulder.

"More of a horse, really," he said without missing a beat.

Iriel smirked. "Jump to it stallion."

He did.

Wind rushed over them as he leapt from the platform. Other Sapphire threadweavers passed him on their way back up, narrowly avoiding a collision. Down they fell. Faster. He grabbed hold of his corethread and *pushed* against the force of gravity. They slowed and, at the last moment, he *pushed* hard. His feet hit the wonderstone with a soft thud.

"You both okay?" he asked.

Iriel looked down at Aydin who was squirming in her arms and nodded.

Chrys let her down and looked at the crowd of Zedas

standing in the field surrounding the wonderstone. What would happen if their home was consumed? He shook the thought away. The wonderstone called to him to *push*, and he did, launching himself back up toward the entrance platform.

As he looked out at the blazing fire consuming the feytrees to the east, he remembered a conversation with Malachus in the Great Lord's study. They'd spoken of life being like a flame, and what had he asked? *"Do you want to burn the world, Chrys?"*

A mere moment into his flight, he heard a child screaming. Not a whine. Not a plea of hunger, or fatigue. It was pain. Chrys looked down and saw Iriel falling to her knees. Her arms fell toward the surface of the wonderstone as if being gripped by an invisible force. She screamed for help in harmony with their newborn son, forced flat on the surface of the stone.

Chrys stopped *pushing* and let gravity take him back toward the ground. As he fell, he stopped filtering threads from his vision and looked into the bright light of the wonderstone. He saw what he hoped never to see again. Dozens of tendrils of threadlight grasped hold of Iriel and Aydin, latching onto their limbs and sucking them toward the surface of the wonderstone. Tears poured down Iriel's face as she screamed. Her body was crumpling from the force.

There was only one person who had that kind of power.

ALVERAX and the others hid behind feytrees just outside the clearing. Silently they watched a crowd of people fall from the sky and congregate in the flower-filled opening. Alabella held up a hand for them to wait a little longer, and they did. Alverax watched men run their thirsty fingers down blades. He watched women breathe like feral animals. They watched on as innocent families gathered unknowingly to be slaughtered.

Then he heard screaming. A woman lay flat against the giant stone slab, crying for help, and beside her, barely visible at the distance, was a child. The forest people turned to them, but no one moved to help. He wanted to help them, but feared what Alabella would do if he gave away their location. But he couldn't just sit there. He couldn't do *nothing*. As anger filled his soul, threadlight filled his veins, and what he saw did not comfort him.

Threadlight blazed forth from the stone slab. Tiny tendrils of threadlight wrapped themselves around the woman and child, like snakes constricting their prey. He knew it was her. Alabella was doing it, and he had to stop her.

Just then, Alabella stepped out of the shadows. "Now!"

It was too late. Alabella, like Jelium, was the worst kind of thief: the kind that stole life. Over in that clearing were women and children, families that had done nothing to deserve death. He looked at Alabella, and the motherly figure he'd seen had been replaced by a monster. Whatever part she'd wanted him to play tonight, he would refuse.

He watched the mob of warriors rush the forest people. A volley of arrows rained down toward their unarmed foes, striking many.

Alverax stepped away from Alabella. Her eyes seemed to sink deeper into her skull. Her skin had lost its grace. The light in her eyes had faded from passion to cruelty. He knew it wasn't true—she hadn't really changed—but now he could see it clearly.

And he wanted no part of it.

This could well be the night he died for good, and he would go with a clean conscience. With the child's cries ringing in his ears, he knew that there was at least one good thing he could do.

———————————

LAUREL STOOD in shock as the older man dropped to his knees, grabbing hold of his neck as he struggled to breathe. Willow smiled to herself and swung down with a hard fist toward his face, but he raised a quick hand and caught her blow. His eyes fixed to hers as he rose back to his feet.

"Big mistake," he growled.

He swung his other fist like a tornado, crushing down on Willow's face before she could block it. She dropped to the floor.

Henna approached from the top of the stairs. "Jurius, are you okay?"

That name. Laurel recognized it. The high general that was working with the Bloodthieves, who were responsible for kidnapping her. The one who had tried to kill Chrys at the edge of the Fairenwild, then tortured Pandan.

Jurius nodded.

High General Henna stepped forward slowly, eyeing Luther and Laurel. "No one else has to get hurt. It's over."

"Oh, it is most certainly not," Jurius said, reaching down toward Willow.

Luther dropped Pandan and launched himself forward to intercept. He screamed out as he crashed into Jurius. Green veins burned bright in both of their arms as they launched into a flurry of fury-filled blows.

Fists collided. Elbows struck. And knees slammed into thick muscle. Luther dropped low, *pulled* on the wall's thread, and smashed into Jurius with the strength of a storm. They crashed into the stone wall, cracking it with the force of impact.

Laurel saw it in his eyes. Luther had found a new home for his rage. Pandan had been freed, and Jurius would pay the full price. This fight wasn't for Willow, or Pandan, or Chrys; this fight was for the son he'd lost.

Jurius thrust his knee up into Luther's stomach over and over again until he finally released him. Luther struggled to catch his breath when Jurius launched a series of vicious blows, each connecting hard with Luther's face. Right. Left. Right. Left. Blood spewed out of Luther's mouth. Jurius sent a brutal uppercut into Luther's jaw, and he fell away, landing hard on his back.

Jurius laughed. His eyes searched for his next victim and stopped when they found Pandan on the floor. Willow came back to consciousness, and she watched with tears as Jurius approached her brother. Laurel stood still.

Jurius picked up Pandan and looked at Willow. "Is this what you came for? This worthless shit? Did Chrys care for him? Wants him...alive?"

"Jurius," Henna said, addressing the tone in his voice, "we need them alive."

Laurel, done standing by idly as her comrades were pummeled, *pushed* against the wall, and launched herself onto Henna's back. They toppled to the floor. Laurel used her long legs to wrap around Henna's waist then jammed the black knife against her throat. "Kill him and I kill her!"

Jurius hesitated for the slightest moment, then cocked his head to the side, amused. He spit blood and snorted with a cruel grin. "Nice try, but little girls shouldn't play grown up games."

He took his hand across Pandan's face and twisted. The

sound of shattering bones echoed throughout the hallway, and Pandan fell to the floor.

"No!" Willow screamed, her hands coming up to cover her mouth.

That did not happen.

It couldn't be.

Pandan wasn't dead.

That's not how this was supposed to go.

Tears poured down Willow's face. She wailed over the death of her little brother. What if it had been Bay? Laurel pictured her own brother, lifeless on the floor.

And it was her fault.

Laurel loosened her grip, falling into her own mind.

It was her fault.

She rolled away from Henna, rose, and made a mad dash toward Jurius. Out of the corner of her eye, she saw Willow do the same. Jurius crouched low, anticipating their arrival. Both of their veins blazed with Sapphire threadlight. Willow arrived first, but she was smart enough to wait for Laurel. Unfortunately, Jurius was not as patient.

He dashed toward Willow, his fist swinging in a wide arc. She slipped under it, but he *pulled* his arm toward the ground and his elbow crashed down at an inhuman speed directly onto her shoulder. Laurel arrived just as his elbow hit. She stabbed forward with the obsidian blade and sliced hard into his shoulder. He spun around, snarling, and reached for her hand that held the blade. She pulled it back and blood sprayed out as the blade cut into his palm.

"I don't know who you are," he said, "but you die next."

He dove at Laurel. She *pushed* her corethread to counteract the weight, but he *pulled* with even more force. In an instant, he'd pinned her arms down and smashed his head into her face. The force nearly knocked her out. Blood came drooling out of her nose as she stared into his face. The face of a Bloodthief.

Laurel spit blood in his eye and rammed her knee into his groin. He released her, instinctively wiping his eye clean, and she seized the moment. She squeezed the obsidian blade with all her strength and thrust it straight through his sternum. She'd expected more resistance, but it slid in with ease.

He gasped. Both of his hands came to the hilt of the blade as he stared down at his chest.

Gale take him.

"Jaymin," he mumbled. With his final moments, he grabbed Laurel's hand on the hilt, pulled it out of his own chest, and slowly turned it around.

He screamed and jammed it into Laurel's heart.

Threadlight exploded from Laurel. A sound, like shattering glass, echoed against the stone walls. Then, as if the world itself grieved the reality, the earth trembled beneath their feet. Walls groaned and wood splintered as decorations came crashing down onto the floor. Laurel tried to steady herself. Inside her, it felt as though her soul were slowly draining from her body.

She knew she was dying, but, at least for a moment, she'd helped.

THE WORLD SEEMED to expand and contract in odd pulses as Chrys looked down at the threadlight grappling onto his wife and son. His feet hit the stone and he ran to them, but there was nothing he could do. If he'd had the obsidian blade, he could have cut them free. But it was gone, the Zeda people had never found it.

He *pushed* on the artificial threads, his veins flaring blue, but it accomplished nothing. His family was going to die, and he was helpless. Powerless. He'd promised to protect them, and he'd failed, again. No matter how hard he tried, no matter how strong he tried to be, it would never be enough. Alone, he wasn't enough.

Mmmm. You are not alone.

Chrys shook his head. *No, I can't.*

Would you have them die for your own pride?

Stop!

Your sacrifice can save them. I can save them. Yield your soul to me.

The sound of swords and screaming lifted his gaze to the east. Hundreds of shadowy figures rushed toward Zeda families. A volley of arrows rained down through the vaulted treetops. Chrys *pushed* on as many arrows as he could, but too many fell. Zeda fell with them.

A dark fury washed over him as he stared out over the oncoming army.

From the corner of his eye, he saw a massive feytree, consumed by fire from trunk to crown, break at its midpoint. The world seemed to slow as the falling giant ripped free of its neighbors, hundreds of branches snapping off the tumultuous weave. A cacophony of sound. The entire Fairenwild seemed to mourn its fall. And as it fell, it fell toward him.

If nothing stopped it, it would smash into the wonderstone, and everyone on it.

Chrys refused to succumb.

He lifted his hands high above his head. It was audacious, impossible. He let the power of the wonderstone rush through his veins. It burned. Channeling more threadlight than he'd ever dreamed possible, he *pushed*. The massive tree groaned from the force, slowing its freefall. But still it fell. He doubled his efforts, *pushing* with every ounce of will and strength he had, his veins expanding with the pressure. A man holding the weight of a mountain. It stopped. The feytree hovered in the air above Chrys and the wonderstone. His entire body trembled beneath him.

Mmmm.

His son screamed beside him, threads still constricting his brittle bones. Zeda families cried out as swords fell on their loved ones. The unknown army laughed as they fought.

He couldn't hold the feytree any longer. He couldn't save them. He wasn't enough. He was never enough.

But then he saw her, jet black hair slicked behind her ears, amber eyes dancing in the light of the raging fires. Standing in the shadows as everything around her burned to the ground. The woman. She was responsible. Every problem. Every trouble. Every bit of pain. He looked back at his wife and son strapped to the wonderstone by a hundred threads of light. He heard their screams. He felt their suffering, and he would not let them die.

Mmmm.

"You can save them?" he spoke aloud.

Yes.

"Then I am yours."

Threadlight exploded from his body as ice poured through his veins. The commotion of the world blurred for just a moment before a dam inside him burst asunder. His neck moved without request. His lips curled into a smile even as his mind cried out in fear of what he'd done.

"Mmmm."

Chrys felt the Apogee reach out with his mind, tendrils grasping for prey until they finally latched onto the mind of a

Zeda man who'd just landed on the wonderstone. He didn't understand how, but he could feel the man's soul. Then another. And another. Three Zeda souls bound to his own in the briefest of moments. Their souls wove together in a binding tapestry of light. He could feel their threadlight, like wells of power, ready to be siphoned. It was pure power. Borrowed power.

The massive feytree blasted away, splintered wood bursting out over the battlefield. A shiver crawled up his spine, and the air around him seemed to expand. His lungs strained within his chest. He felt the three Zeda men collapse to the ground before he saw them.

The Apogee leapt off the wonderstone. Zedas scattered, terrified. Finally, after years of patient waiting, he was free. And this time he wasn't bound by the mutation.

He walked forward as the fastest of the army approached. He sidestepped the man's sword and gripped his throat. The impact sent the man's legs swinging forward as his momentum came to a sudden halt. "Such frailty," he said before snapping the man's neck and tossing him aside.

A spear came soaring toward him. He snatched it out of the air, turned and launched it forward into another man's eye.

He'd forgotten how feeble men were.

A blade came down from behind. He ducked below, spun, and delivered a blow so hard into the man's chest that his ribs bent inward below the skin.

He grabbed a blade off a dead man and strolled casually through the battlefield. It moved in his hands like a sickle sifting wheat, impaling, severing, striking down Zeda and Bloodthief alike. He never slowed. He never tired. He never stopped.

These men were playthings, not worthy of his effort, but

there was one different. An Amber threadweaver. A wonderful twist of fate.

When she saw him approach with blood smeared across his face, a dozen tendrils of light sprang out of the ground and hooked their claws into his body. But he was stronger. He screamed out like an animal, threads bursting apart. In his own mind, Chrys could hear the screams of three Zeda threadweavers.

Fear grew in the woman's eyes. This time, a hundred tendrils of light burst out from beneath him and latched onto his body. He fought them all. They were nothing to him. He could not be stopped. The agony of the Zeda men rang out in the back of his mind.

The Apogee fought the weight with all of his strength, his legs buckling beneath the pressure. He took two steps—the woman's eyes growing wider with each—before he stalled in front of her, howling like a caged animal, blood dripping from his cheeks. Her eyes blazed with yellow threadlight, her yellow-veined arms trembling with the effort.

Her eyes grew wide. "What are you?"

The earth quaked in response.

Alverax gave wide berth to the combat as he sprinted toward the woman and child. There was little he could do to stop the fighting, but there were at least two people he could save. If Alabella found out, she would kill him, but he'd already died once. It wasn't so bad.

He approached from the far side and stopped in awe as a man with threadlight coalescing around him *pushed* the entire upper half of a feytree out of the way like it were a single branch. Threadlight coiled around the man as he jumped down off the stone.

Alverax shook away the awe and stepped up onto the stone platform. A strange urge to threadweave poured over his mind. It felt like the stone was calling to him. It reminded him of sailweed cravings, an incessant need to consume.

He looked down at the woman and child, pinned to the stone by the artificial threads latched onto them, screaming in pain and fear. He focused on the threads wrapping the infant and squeezed. The threads resisted with a strength unlike anything he'd experienced before. He *squeezed* harder, screaming at them as his veins burned black.

"Break!" The threads burst apart like grain thrown into the air, including the threads wrapping the woman.

Before he could celebrate, the threads reappeared, small threads at first, but each grew larger and larger. And then he saw it. The child's eyes, wide open as it screamed, were a brilliant pale yellow.

Alverax threw his energy back at the blossoming threads and shattered them once again. The child was doing this to himself, overcome by the cravings of the stone and without the will to deny it.

He looked down at the bright threadlight of the stone. It was the source. He dropped down to his knees and placed both hands on the stone. This was it. A task only he could perform. A family only he could save. With every ounce of his soul, he grabbed onto the stone's threadlight. Its energy ripped through his body, filling him with such intense pressure he was sure his skin would burst. He screamed out in pain, but held fast, squeezing harder against the bright threadlight. The pressure continued to build inside him; the pain rose to a crescendo.

He threw every death, every betrayal, every mistake, and

every heartache into the burning threadlight. It was a trade, his life for theirs. The veins in his arms turned blacker than death. It was unbearable. His body shook. His legs convulsed beneath him.

But it wasn't just him that was shaking.

As he fought against the power of the stone, the world shook around him. Cinder and ash fell from burning treetops. Feytrees teetered back and forth, the world itself groaning against the quaking earth. He was afraid, but he'd never felt such purpose.

Thunder cracked in the sky through gaps where branches used to be. He squeezed harder. Another flame-consumed feytree toppled to the ground. His body was on fire from within, and he let it burn.

The stone beneath his feet fractured, a mountain rending in two. The threadlight bathing it burst apart in a cloud of mist.

Alverax fell forward onto his face, smiling as he lost all consciousness.

THE APOGEE FOUGHT the threads that bound him while the earth beneath shifted like ocean waves. A terrible pain surged through his mind with each quake, weakening him. He could feel the man inside him trying to escape. A futile effort. This time he was prepared.

He watched the Amber-eyed woman flee into the darkness. Her threads weakened with each passing moment. She would need to die, and whoever had made her. He turned back toward the wonderstone and saw hundreds of dead lying in the dirt. Bloodthieves and Zeda alike, equal in death. Massive, scorched branches had fallen and crushed a dozen people. Men groaned as they tried to get out from under them. A group of Zeda threadweavers walked through the chaos, ripe for the taking.

The Apogee looked further and saw Iriel seated on the edge of the wonderstone. She held the baby in her arms, crying. If the child grew, it too would be a liability. The Apogee looked on them with fondness. Too long spent in the mind of another.

Iriel's eyes lifted and caught his own.

He nodded to her—a token of respect—then turned and walked away.

All around him, men cried out for their lost.

Women wept for their fallen.

They gathered their families and hurried west.

But the Apogee traveled east.

CHAPTER 31

As Jurius hit the floor, the walls of the keep shook. Willow steadied herself on the ground and waited out the earthquake. When it finally stopped, she rushed over to Pandan and grabbed hold of him tightly. He felt heavier than he had just moments before. As much as her heart wanted to deny it, the brother she'd finally found again was gone once more.

She turned to Jurius who lay clutching his chest, gurgling up blood as the life fled from him. She grabbed the black blade laying on the ground between him and Laurel and thrust it back into his chest. Screaming, she thrust it in a second time. And a third. As if quickening his death would bring back her brother.

She wiped the blood on his shirt as she rose. It was then that she realized what she held in her hand. The blade matched the description Chrys had given. Could it be?

"You need to leave."

Willow snapped her head around at the sound, hiding the

blade as she turned. Standing straight-backed and strong was High General Henna.

"You need to leave," Henna repeated. "Before anyone else sees you. The window in Jurius' study opens to the north end of the keep. If you drop down from there you should be able to get to the wall."

Willow tilted her head. Henna had just tried to kill them. "I don't understand."

"Chrys warned me," Henna said. "The day we visited him in his home, he slipped me a piece of paper. It was hastily written, but it said *Jurius is a Bloodthief*. I had someone look into it. They came back with a lot of questions. Tonight, it was clear; Chrys was right. I should have trusted him. There will be hell to pay for his death, but you should not be the ones to pay it."

Willow turned and remembered Laurel. The young girl lay on the ground, a small pool of blood across her chest. She ran to her and checked her vitals. "She's still alive!"

Luther moved to join her. "I watched Jurius stab her in the heart. She should be dead. If we can get her to a doctor, maybe she still has a chance."

"I'll take her," Henna said, walking toward them. "If you bring her with you, you'll never make it out fast enough. Go. I'll get her to a doctor."

Willow paused, still doubting Henna's sincerity, but she had no other choice. She was right. They'd never make it out if they had to carry Laurel. She turned to her brother, dead on the floor next to Jurius, and ground her teeth. "Can you see that he gets a proper burial?"

Henna nodded. "I will try, but I cannot make that promise."

"Willow," Luther said urgently. "She's right. We need to go, now."

Willow knelt down beside her brother. "May the winds guide you," she whispered, tears swelling in her eyes. She leaned down and kissed his cheek. "And carry you gently home."

With one final nod of appreciation, Willow and Luther entered Jurius' study. It was filled with books, maps, paintings, and a single oil lamp lighting it from within. As they opened the tall window, a cold breeze brushed past the curtains. The rain continued, though it had dulled to a gentle beating. Willow jumped out of the window, *pushing* on her corethread to soften the fall. Luther ran down the wall and rolled as he reached the surface.

Neither spoke a word as they ran toward the outer keep wall.

They had failed.

CHAPTER 32

Alverax awoke from a nightmare.

Fire and quake and rain pouring down on a field of death.

He shielded his eyes from the bright sunlight beating down on him. His head pounded and his stomach felt like a ship at sea. A figure stood over him. He tried to blink away the haze. It was his father. His dead father stood over him smiling, and all Alverax could do was laugh. The nightmare wasn't over yet. All his father said as he looked at him was *"thank you."*

Tears welled up in his eyes. His father, the infamous thief of Cynosure, a cheat and a liar, had wormed his way into Alverax's dreams. But the truth was more painful, and no matter how hard he tried to deny it, Alverax missed him. His father's words, even in a dream, were water to a thirsty soul.

The pain in his stomach flared. He leaned over the side of his cot, heaving more than he vomited. Another figure rushed to his side, keeping him from falling over the edge. He coughed until his stomach settled once again. He looked back up to his father, but he was gone. In his place stood a woman. An angular face, dark hair and green eyes. Alverax panicked and his body trembled. His breathing became more and more sporadic as chills covered him from head to toe.

"Get me some lavender!" a second woman shouted. An older woman by the sound of her voice. She held him down and looked directly into his eyes. "I need you to breathe. Focus on each breath. Long and deep. Keep your eyes closed. You are having a panic attack. It will end."

When the other woman returned, the older woman began rubbing something onto Alverax's chest. It was fragrant and calming. He focused on his breathing and, over time, he relaxed. The shaking subsided. The world ceased its spinning.

He opened his eyes again and found more people standing over him. Two older women with gray hair and a woman holding a child. He recognized them but couldn't place how.

The older woman spoke again. "You need to rest, boy. I've not seen such threadsickness in years and I thought Dogwood was in a sorry state. You are lucky to be alive."

"Where am I?" He tried to sit up but groaned at the pain.

"West of the Fairenwild. The fires your people set destroyed our homes before the rain came. It is no longer safe for us there."

Alverax pictured flames slowly crawling up the enormous trees of the Fairenwild, split wood falling from the sky as the earth shook. Alabella had planned it all along. She had forced them down and slaughtered them. But why? At the very least, he was no longer by her side. Whatever purpose she'd had for him, she would need to find another way. Deep down he'd known who she was, but he'd wanted to trust her, and so he had.

"I'm so sorry," he said. "I had no idea that was going to happen."

The woman holding her child shook her head. Her eyes were red. She must have done her share of crying. "Don't you dare be sorry. You saved my son's life, and mine. Whatever the others did is not on you."

He didn't agree, but it was nice to hear. "Are they gone?"

"From what we could tell," the old woman said with a curious look in her eye, "all your people were killed."

The other elderly woman huffed. "We'd be better off if you were dead too. We know what you are."

"He saved us!" the younger woman interjected.

"At what cost!?" the scowling elderly woman shouted. "The coreseal is broken. We've failed."

"You don't think I understand the cost?" the younger woman said. "My husband is gone. My son may have permanent health issues. I saw the piles of dead with my own eyes. Counted myself among them. And I *would* be among them if not for him. The boy lives."

The old woman's scowl grew deeper. "Obviously, I'm glad you're alive, but the seal is broken, and that is a matter greater than you or I."

"The boy lives," the younger woman repeated. She was cold fire. "The Bloodthief with Amber eyes. If nothing else, he can help us stop her."

The old woman's lip curled in disgust. "Unless he can get her to help us with the seal, again, there is a more serious matter to attend. Besides, how can we trust that he's not working for her even now?"

"I'm not," Alverax said, shaking his head. "I swear it. I didn't even know what she was going to do."

"You don't need to explain yourself," the younger woman said. "If any harm comes to him, Rowan, I will hold you responsible, and you'll find that my husband isn't the only one handy with a blade."

Alverax was surprised to see the young mother slip into some kind of battle stance, even while holding a child in her left arm. He didn't know much about fighting, but he could tell when someone else did.

The scowling elderly woman walked away, grumbling under her breath. The others followed silently.

Alverax looked around and saw that he was on some kind of homemade, cloth carrier-table. There were hundreds of people around him, maybe thousands, many over by a stream where they gathered water and washed off soot and dirt. Most of the people looked happy despite their loss.

"My name is Iriel," the young mother said, extending her hand.

"Alverax."

She took a seat next to him, looking down at the newborn in her arms. "They're scared of you. People are often afraid of what they don't understand. Be patient. You'll gain their trust over time."

"Unless that old woman kills me before I have the chance."

"Don't you worry about her."

Alverax took a deep breath. "I just wish she would believe me. I really am done with Alabella. I didn't know what she was going to do."

Iriel cocked her head to the side. "Alabella? The woman with the Amber eyes? Why did she do it? What does she want?"

Alverax closed his eyes and Alabella flooded his thoughts. Why *had* she brought him to the Fairenwild? They were supposed to meet up with the people who lived there, which was only partially true. She'd also said that he was the key. But why? The only thing he could do was break threads...which he had.

Heralds save me.

"The stone's threadlight. I think she *wanted* me to break it."

CHAPTER 33

LAUREL AWOKE IN A STRANGE, stone room wearing clothing that did not belong to her. Somehow, despite being tucked beneath a layer of wool blankets, her body shivered. In a matter of moments, she became painfully aware of every ache and pain in her body, including a sharp pounding in her skull. When she tried to sit up, her chest erupted in pain. Her head slammed back down on her pillow as memories came flooding back to her.

Willow, Luther, Reina, Laz...Pandan...Jurius. She pulled her gown down and looked to the source of pain in her chest. A row of stitches lined up over her heart. The sharp pain was too much to bear, so she let threadlight pour through her veins.

Except it didn't.

She tried again, relaxing her mind despite the pain, and opened herself to threadlight. But again, no warmth flowed through her veins, no threads appeared in view, and there was no comfort from the pain. An immediate, overwhelming sense of fear gripped her from within.

She tried again.

Nothing.

And again.

Nothing but the sharp pain in her chest and a pounding in her skull.

Her entire body shivered. *No, no no.* Tears fell freely from her tired eyes. Her breathing grew frantic. Each breath was a battle unto itself.

"Help," she pled, her voice quivering. "Please, anyone."

She heard footsteps from somewhere outside the room. She wanted to look but, with every movement, it felt like Jurius was stabbing her through the heart once again. Agony. Dread. Panic. Terror. Acceptance.

Pandan.

He was dead because of her. She'd been so stupid, thinking she could stop Jurius. Instead, she'd dangled a slab of meat in front of a hungry chromawolf. If she'd stayed back—if she'd stayed home—Pandan might still be alive. Willow would never forgive her. Laurel would never forgive herself. If anyone deserved to be dead, it was her.

"Good, you are awake," someone said.

The footsteps continued until a woman stood over her with dark hair that lay slicked back behind her ears. She smiled beneath a pair of Felian lightshades.

"Are you a doctor?" Laurel asked.

The woman removed her lightshades, revealing bright yellow irises. "Of a sort."

Laurel's heart beat faster. It was her. The woman Chrys had told them about. She was what Aydin would become.

The woman placed her lightshades on a side table. "You are both the luckiest, and most unfortunate person in the world right now."

She knew about Jurius; Laurel was sure of it. She'd come to finish the job. "Please, just kill me quickly. I know why you're here."

"You do, do you? Well in that case, I suppose I should cut to the point." She reached into her pocket and pulled out a brilliant, obsidian blade. "First, I'd like to know where you got this."

Laurel lay quiet, refusing to respond.

The woman let out a deep sigh, grabbed a chair and took a seat next to the bed. "We can come back to that. You should know that you were unconscious for many days. To be honest, I wasn't sure if you were going to wake up, but, when I heard what happened, I had a feeling that we may be able to help each other. The pain you are feeling will fade. You will recover, but you will never be the same. Like I said, you are extremely lucky that his blade landed where it did. These last few days, your body has shown signs of a chemical addiction to threadlight, which, ironically, is what saved your life. You must have had a sea of threadlight coursing through your veins.

"Now, there is good news and there is bad news. The bad news is that you are no longer a threadweaver."

The woman had spoken something Laurel was too afraid to put into words. She was no longer a threadweaver. It was gone. Every last trace. Still her mind longed for it, like a lost friend that would surely return. She could feel the hunger inside her, the craving, the pure desire. All she needed was a bit of threadlight and all her pain would be gone. She'd taken it for granted, and now she wasn't sure that she could live without it.

The woman's eyes grew sad as she looked on Laurel. "It seems that you've already discovered that truth. The good news —and I want you to hear me and understand what I say next— the good news is that if you come with me, in time, I believe I can make you a threadweaver once again."

"You're a liar," Laurel spat. "I know you're here to kill me. Hurry up and get it over with."

"Oh, my dear. I have no plan to do such a thing. I believe I can make you whole again, but not because of me. Because you are unique. You were already a threadweaver. Your body accepted it once. There is so much that has been hidden from you. So many truths that the world has withheld. I swear I will never hide the truth from you. For instance, I know you are a Zeda."

Laurel's heartbeat rose, each beat a resounding drum against her chest. She thought of her grandfather, and her big brother. Tears streamed down her face. "I don't understand. What do you want from me?"

"I want to give you what you deserve, my dear, and no one deserves a life without threadlight." She glanced behind her and pulled out a vial of red liquid. She placed it on the table next to Laurel's bed. "If you'll let me, I can help you. Drink that. It will help with the recovery and the cravings."

Alone and defeated, mentally and physically, Laurel watched the woman walk away. She stared at the vial on the table. She didn't need to ask. She knew what it was. The queen of the Bloodthieves had offered her a boon, and Laurel was going to drink it.

If anyone deserved to be dead, it was her. And yet, somehow, it seemed that death refused to bring her under its wing. But a life without threadlight was no life at all.

Laurel lifted the vial and drank.

~ Ataçan ~

EPILOGUE

- DEEP in the Wastelands -

For years, the swamps near the entrance to Relek's Cave had been quiet—ever since the Builders had killed their god. The An'tara claimed that Relek was alive, that it could not die. Whether it was true or not, none of their people had seen Relek since that dark day in the mountains.

Tonight, that familiar peace was broken as footsteps echoed from deep within the cave.

Skyp poked its twin in the ribs. "Aye, Piksy, you hear that?"

"I hear it," Piksel whispered, stretching its arms. The An'tara would be furious if they discovered that Piksel had slept, but Skyp would never tell. "What do you think it is? Is it Relek?"

"I hope not."

They picked up their spears and stood in front of the entrance. The footsteps grew louder, a single set staggered in cadence. They looked at each other and backed away. They were supposed to make sure that no one went into Relek's Cave, but the An'tara never said anything about something coming out.

Finally, a shadow emerged from the mouth of the cave. The withered husk of a woman limped toward them, sunken eyes, skin gray as the cave itself with swollen veins running across every inch of her skin. She stopped when she saw them, her smile showing a mouth full of rotten gums. Despite the decrepit state of her body, her eyes were bright and alive.

As she approached, she spoke with a voice like gravel. "Where is my brother?"

The End of Book One

The story continues with STONES OF LIGHT

ACKNOWLEDGMENTS

One of the greatest parts of writing has been the wonderous outpouring of support from friends and family. They challenged me, motivated me, and helped me make this book so much better. In June of 2019, I posted to Facebook asking if anyone would be interested in being a test reader for Voice of War (at the time it was titled *Threadlight*), and more than forty people offered to help. Thanks to all of you, your support drives me.

Now to the list.

Thank you, Hillary, for not only being my editor (you've probably read chapter one at least a dozen times), but for being my pillar of support all along the way. You been listening to me talk about this world and this book for longer than any spouse should be required. Thank you for being my alpha reader with Brandon Williams and helping to transform the characters and the story into something so much better than it was.

Thank you to my discord friends, especially Antonin

Januska, Kent C. Dodds, and Jen Luker, who were my fountains of inspiration throughout the first draft.

Thank you to my beta readers: Sean McQuay, Shahrouz Tavakoli, Jonathan Blackham, Jeremy Stanley, and Kent Brewster. Your impressions and ideas (no matter how ruthless) made this book so much better than it was, and I'm forever grateful.

And thank you to Daniel Ignacio, an artist with patience and beautiful talent that helped bring the magic of the Fairenwild to life.

To the rest of you who I may have missed, thank you. I'm in awe at your support and hope that you've enjoyed this bit of fantastical tomfoolery.

ABOUT THE AUTHOR

Zack Argyle lives just outside of Seattle, WA, USA, with his wife and two children. He has a degree in Electrical Engineering and works full-time as a software engineer. He is the winner of the Indies Today Best Fantasy Award, and a finalist in Mark Lawrence's Self-Published Fantasy Blog-Off.